UNITY

Henchman Book Three

CARL STUBBLEFIELD

MOUNTAINDALE
PRESS

CONTENTS

ACKNOWLEDGMENTS

This one goes out to everyone who hasn't found their place yet. Anyone who feels different from the crowd because you have unique interests that may not resonate with the masses. Difference is good.

Find that unique ability to defeat the OP Boss Levels of life. Use that exploit to craft your dreams out of the ether. Be the hero of your own story. Or be the villain everyone fears.

CHAPTER ONE

Here I Go Again

"Pay attention, lazy boy! The others are waiting for you," Nick snapped.

Gus felt his face burn at the abrupt delivery. He shook himself, reluctantly pulling his eyes away from the calming effect of the rolling waves. As he did, his vision blurred as his headache returned with a vengeance.

He massaged his temples, trying to relieve some of the painful pressure that had become part of his daily routine. It seemed to worsen as the day progressed, and only soured his mood even more.

The constant presence of Tempest and the Crew also felt like they were violating his territory, his private space. They were cordial and well-behaved, yet it still felt like an invasion. Even Aurora had melded back into the group, and once again he was alone in the crowd.

He closed his eyes and inhaled deeply, trying to let everything go when he breathed out. He needed to bleed off some of the pressure inside and training was one of the few ways that seemed to release his tension. But even that would have to wait until after the mission.

"Nick, what's my status? Any problems from sleep deprivation yet?" His voice sounded weary and raw—he would have to watch that when speaking with the others.

"Despite the Nth trying to remove them, you are producing excess metabolites at an increasing rate."

"I'm not surprised—the headaches are getting worse," Gus sighed.

"Pain is inevitable, suffering is optional," Nick replied.

"What the hell is that supposed to mean?"

"Ponder upon it."

Gus rolled his eyes and sighed at the response. "Maybe later, Nick. I'm not in the mood for riddles right now."

Gus groaned as he stood; there was always a surge of pain when his blood got pumping. He shielded his eyes from the early morning light as he went back into his room and got dressed for the day.

Tempest had arranged this mission, so Gus could learn to work with other supers. Putting Gus in charge was another thing that added to his stress. He never considered himself a leader, but the way the manor was set up, he had to lead or drastically less FP would accumulate. It still felt unnatural and odd that anyone would follow him. Especially when it was so obvious he was out of place and didn't know what he was doing.

It had also been Tempest's idea to check the transport Methiochos had used to see if there were any stragglers that could pose a threat to any of the supers there. Since the source of the Dark Nth infection was unknown, part of their mission was to find and destroy any possible vectors for reintroducing the Dark Nth, whether by computer or zombie. Gus hadn't given them another thought after he had defeated The One, assuming they were all gone or dead. Just one more thing he had missed in his wide-eyed naivety.

So many reasons he would rather be doing something else, but he was best suited for the job, regardless. He stared at himself in the mirror, trying to compose his expression. He didn't want to come across as weak to the others and had felt like he had become better at hiding the tells. But it was fraying his nerves. He had kept to himself to avoid taking his frustration out on any of the others.

Stepping into the elevator, he hit the button and took the lift to the roof. Wordlessly taking his seat on the transport, he nodded at the others from his seat in the corner. They all linked comms and the transport took off.

———

Get a hold of yourself, dammit! Gus couldn't shake the visceral dread he felt in the dark ship, even though he should feel better and more prepared than ever. His eyes played across the interior of the transport as mapping drones illuminated everything with a sweeping wedge of pale blue light as some crawled across the walls and others whirred and floated down the far side of the room. They scanned and stitched together a virtual representation of the craft on the party's displays, glowing amber lines floating in the darkness, revealing what their scans had turned up.

Eyes flitted upwards as something banged through some ducts above them, retreating to the fore. *I thought I was done with all that zombie nonsense!* Gus rolled his shoulders, trying to loosen up against the tightness and tension that threatened to crush him.

"What was that?" someone asked on the comms.

"Probably zombies," Gus replied instinctually, forgetting the mental link they all shared. He winced as the mental communication also transmitted a slight quaver in his voice.

Gus was still getting used to the system that networked Nth used when in a party. It allowed limited communication and data transmission as long as the party stayed within range. Gus could see Nick playing a small video in the bottom right corner of some of Gus' old battles with varying types of zombies.

A chorus of groans and gasps came across the mental link.

Supers weren't scared of most things, but zombies appeared to be the one foe that they all seemed to fear. Gus felt like he had not taken them as seriously as he should have, based on the effect the creatures had on the others, who were much more experienced and battle-hardened than he was.

When silence returned, the party moved forward again. Gus led the small group, his resistance to infection being a primary factor. What it didn't take into account was that if a zombie did manage to jump out and attack him, it didn't mean it wouldn't hurt.

Gus looked to his left and sent a mental command to Jet to scout further ahead. The blade dipped in a nod of agreement and shot forward silently. Metallic clicks were the only sound as the spider-like mapping drones crawled ahead, shining their beams around, illuminating this area of the ship. It was the largest transport Gus had ever seen, and he was not looking forward to how much time it would take to clear the vessel.

A loud *thunk* brought him back to the present. Following its programming, one of the mapping drones did a deep scan of the wall in question, but by the time the drone went through the cycle, all that was revealed was an empty duct.

Gus stared at the spot now visible on his display, trying to gauge if a mantid could fit in the tight space. *Were they different sizes? Yeesh.* Some of the group had moved forward, following the drones.

"Rattle ya dags," an accented voice sounded in Gus' mind. Looking up, one of the Crew was motioning for him to hurry up and get back in the lead. Gus nodded in embarrassment and resumed point. The cheerful super gave him a friendly slap on the shoulder as he led the group to the next section of the ship.

The group exited the cargo area and filed into a line as they entered the main cabin, with seats on either side of a small aisle leading forward. Gus was grateful for the drones going ahead and revealing that there was nothing lying in wait between the seats. Windows had broken in the area and the plastisteel bits crunched noisily as boots walked across the debris moving to the pilots' cabin.

In the gloom, Gus could smell mold and saw a couple of mushrooms growing where moisture had pooled in the seats and on the ground. Volcanic rock had punctured the ship in this area, allowing the jungle outside to invade. Dry vines had wormed their way into the gash, filling it up and muting the light in the cabin. They appeared to have cut off their own light supply, killing themselves in their urge to explore.

"What is this, a class A transport? Enough seats here to fit a hundred, hundred-fifty easy," a deep voice asked on the comm.

"Its designation is actually SS," a female voice replied, "and there are two more cabins just like this, one above and another below us on different levels. Ship's name appears to be *The Banoi*. We need to find some intact ports to see if we can interface with the ship's computers and get some answers."

"You're using a remote interface, right? Don't connect directly to anything—" the deep voice warned.

"Yeah, yeah. I *have* done this before, alright?" Gus didn't recognize the super the voice belonged to, but he imagined her to be a mischievous pixie or elf from the lilting tone of her voice. He caught himself mid-musing, wondering how much got transferred along with this mental form of networking, and tried to focus on the task at hand.

The mapping droids had begun to make it to the next section of the ship and its layout was being stitched into existence on his display. It was odd to maneuver in the almost perfect dark sections of the ship with glowing amber lines and textures showing the world around him in monochromatic majesty. Some were so dark it felt like walking in space, supported by some invisible flooring.

"Finally!" pixie-voice cheered and brushed past Gus on her way to a bank of computers. Pulling out a small box about the size of a small dictionary, she fed some cables into various ports and powered on the machine. "It's downloading, ladies and gentlemen. Wait for it… and it looks like no contamination in the ship's computer systems. That's good, but also bad. We still need to locate patient zero or the vector of infection."

"Is it possible that all of them are gone, that patient zero was already killed?" Gus asked hopefully.

"Maybe. But we're a long way from anywhere. From what I'm getting from ship logs, this had to be a premeditated attack. What are you feeling, Harmony?"

A woman with a sultry voice beside Gus placed her hands on her temples and pinched her eyes shut. "I sense something ahead. It's dark…"

She suddenly went limp, another teammate barely catching her before she hit the floor. The rest of them looked toward the doorway that yawned ahead.

CHAPTER TWO

Electric Barbarella

"What happened?" Gus blurted out loud, rushing to kneel next to where Harmony had been gently lowered to the floor. His voice echoed in the room, jarring in the silence.

"That's just 'armony," a short, gruff super said dismissively, putting his hands on his hips. "She tends ta overdo it. Use her power for too long—"

Harmony sat up and shook her head to clear away the effects of her swoon.

"Sorry, guys. There's some bad juju up there." She waved toward the front of the ship with one hand and pinched the bridge of her nose with the other. "It feels like quicksand or a mini black-hole. Like it just wants to pull things in and devour them."

Gus' mouth felt uncomfortably dry as he looked where she had pointed and he licked his teeth to remove the uncomfortable feeling left in its wake. *Why am I stressing out about this?*

"If you want to fly, give up everything that holds you down," Nick offered unhelpfully, as if he was bestowing enlightened knowledge from on high.

Gus exhaled deeply and struggled to control the retorts that sprung to mind. He was still getting used to this new persona. The new Nick was terse, even rude at times with how painfully blunt he was. And the stupid axioms all the time! The interaction had not gone very well, to the point where Gus was grinding to hit level 30 just to get a change.

Still, the new Nick had given some sound leadership advice, which had helped him put some boundaries in place. From his advice, Gus made it clear when the Crew came to the manor that *he* was in charge, and that anyone who thought otherwise would not be welcome there. He just wasn't sure the leadership assistance was worth all the negatives.

The smug authoritarian tone Nick used grated on his nerves like a new papercut. Just when he forgot Nick was there, Gus would do something and the stinging rebuke would get him. He had learned not to get into arguments with this version of Nick though since he didn't have the luxury of a quantum server to provide an endless source of fortune-cookie counsel. He really missed the old Nicks. At least the flare of irritation doused the chill of fear that threatened to take hold.

Gus stood and called Jet back to him; it glided silently through the air and he clutched the polearm as the silver inlaid grip slid into his hand. It made him feel more secure, something solid and sure in the darkness.

Clenching his jaw muscles, he strode forward into the room beyond, bracing himself for an attack. Passing through the threshold, the drones had only begun to stitch together the closest side of the room to him. From what he could see, he was in the wedge-shaped bridge of the ship.

The room reminded him of a shipwreck, with the jagged edge of the unrendered prow of the ship missing in the gloom. The other supers held back, not entering the room. Gus slowly advanced as more and more of the area sprang into his display. The room was in disarray, with items strewn about from a struggle or the crash landing.

Gus peered into the gloom as the drones finished revealing the remainder of the room. They began to retreat to access other floors and continue their survey. The room was empty. No lurking zombies or another boss hiding here camped out. As the drones retreated, they planted small LEDs to give temporary light as the other supers began to tentatively move inside.

"It's clear," Gus said over the comms, standing and releasing his tight grip on Jet, allowing the polearm to fly free and explore. It chose to follow the drones, giving them support and protection as they continued their work.

Harmony peeked into the room and gingerly stepped inside.

"What's the big idea, 'armony? Ya trying to scare us all ta death?" The light revealed the voice belonged to a diminutive man who threw his arms in the air in frustration.

Gus stared at the super, whose mannerisms and speech were exactly like the irascible dwarven NPC from one of his favorite online games. Gus wasn't totally familiar with his powers, but his super name was 'The Keeper.'

"It's in here, Darik," Harmony said, voice breathy and defiant. She took three steps into the room and swept her head left to right. "There," she said, pointing under a storage rack. Everyone squinted to see what was glowing under the shelf.

Darik stepped forward, throwing his arms out to keep anyone from advancing. Coughing a bit as he lay prone, he reached into one of the numerous pouches on his belt and pulled something out. Unfolding it, he rotated some metal joints and held a small box with translucent hinges that fluoresced with blue light as the sides locked into place. The box hovered above his palm, slowly rotating like a large gem, which made him look even more like a dwarven doppelganger. Gesticulating with his left hand, there was a small pop and the box was suddenly full.

"What is it?" someone from the back asked.

"It looks like... a doll?" The Keeper said as he got to his feet, brushing off the dust as the box continued to rotate, showing all angles of its contents.

"Yeah, but look there at the mouth. That's some type of injector."

"Burn it with fire!" Harmony yelled from behind the group as they leaned forward in an attempt to get a closer look at what The Keeper had transferred to the box. Annoyed looks were cast her way at the sudden outburst.

"It's totally contained in my stasis cube," Darik snapped.

"I have got this." A tall lanky super stepped up from the back, whom Gus recognized as Grimdark, the owner of the deep voice with a Slavic accent. He moved his hand as if tracing arcane symbols and the doll ignited within the box. Waxy drops dripped to the bottom of the stasis cube and continued to burn until all that was left was a black residue on the bottom of the box.

"Ah, that's better," Harmony sighed, leaning forward. Her suit defied gravity, clinging tightly to her and Gus averted his eyes as they were drawn to the wide V of exposed skin that extended from her shoulders to her navel. Why did some supers design their uniforms like that? Gus flushed, remembering the mental connection was still on.

Harmony did another scan and brightly commented, "That's it! I don't feel any other influences around. We did it!" She clapped her hands and jumped up and down. Gus saw that his eyes weren't the only ones affected by Harmony's outfit, which made him smile and shake his head a bit. She gave him a furtive and knowing wink as he looked back at her.

Dammit.

"Alright, everyone," The Keeper announced. "Keep your eyes open, but let's finish this up and see if there's anything to salvage. Let's get this done, people!"

CHAPTER THREE

Everything Old is New Again

After the disposal of the doll, the mood lightened significantly. The crew scavenged some parts but the transport was so old that very few were useful. Food stores on the ship had spoiled, which was the bulk of what was in the main hold.

Yuki, who happened to be the computer expert and owner of the elven voice, had restored lighting and limited power to the ship, which made exploration quicker. The only other discovery was a nest of lizards living within the ducts of the ship. One area warmed up considerably near a crack in the ship from receiving sunlight for most of the day. A drone sent into an opening showed them to be the ones thrashing around randomly inside the ducts of the ship.

Gus made his way to the captain's quarters, led by some morbid curiosity about who Methiochos had been before he turned into a monster. The room finally opened to Yuki's decryption and the inside of the spartan room looked mostly unaffected by the effects of water, the encroaching jungle and almost half a century of time.

Besides a bed, dresser, and desk, the only adornment was a portrait of an old man. The man's features looked almost alien, emphasized even more by his silver jumpsuit and larger than normal eyes. His forehead was also more prominent through his gray hair, styled to make it appear like he had more body and fullness, but in reality only revealing his bare scalp amid the nimbus of wispy hair.

As Gus stared at the picture, a blue glow pulsed from behind the picture. He rubbed his eyes but the glow persisted. Checking his logs, he saw that his passive **True Sight** had activated. Stepping on the bed, he lifted the painting away, revealing an alcove with a crystal cube with each side about 4 inches long.

"Good luck with that," Yuki scoffed.

"What is it?" Gus asked, turning the object around different directions, looking at the different facets under the surface, faintly glimpsing some writing as the tiny panels inside the cube flickered from one display to the next.

"It's a Quorian cube. They're basically unhackable journals. They generate a code based on the user's DNA and require multiple manipulations of the surface to unlock and reveal the contents. I've never heard of one being opened by anyone but the user. After one person uses them, they're useless, as they can't be transferred to a new user. It's a pretty souvenir, but don't expect to get anything besides that." Yuki shrugged. "This room looks empty, and it's the last on this floor. I'm about ready to head back. Let me know when you want to go."

"I don't think there's anything else here; maybe in the ship's logs?" Gus asked.

"I'll run a cleanup program on it, see what data I can recover. It'll be a while though."

Gus nodded and turned his attention to the cube as he followed her back to the central access port. He pressed on one of the surfaces and saw it light up with a pinkish-purple highlight on one side, and another formed a yellowish-green halo around his finger as he touched the opposite side.

He played around with the cube until they piled in the small transport and returned to the manor. He stowed the curiosity away and focused on the other things listed on his itinerary for the day. *No rest for the weary.* At least they'd be leaving soon; he was anxious to get underway.

———

Later that afternoon, Gus sat in the command chair of the manor, squirming a little bit as his father put his hand on his shoulder, directing him on possible defenses for the manor. His emotional hackles were raised, and a visceral part of him resisted the direction Tempest was trying to give.

Sure, Tempest had a ton of experience managing Purple Faction's affairs, but Gus was on edge, ready for a play to try to wrest the manor from him. So far, that hadn't happened, but Gus was primed with what he would say and do when it did.

The odd thing was that, mentally, part of him knew the situation had changed. Rationally, he wanted to give him the benefit of the doubt, but his gut had other ideas. Emotionally, he couldn't control the strong feelings that boiled out, unbidden. He hoped it wasn't apparent, but severely doubted he was able to mask everything. He thought he had forgiven his father during his time in the bottomless pit trap, but it wasn't as easy in practice.

"I think that takes care of things for now." Tempest beamed. "You've really done something here, Gus." He squeezed Gus' shoulder in encouragement, but inwardly Gus cringed.

"Thanks," he said flatly. "I'm heading to train for a bit, see if I can level up before we have to head out. See ya." He slid out of the chair and escaped to the elevator.

"We could—" The rest of the sentence was cut off as the elevator doors closed, Gus seeing his father's hand outstretched and a hopeful look on his face. *Oh no. I'm not making it that easy for you. All those things I went through, and now we're best buddies? Yeah, right.*

Gus sighed and leaned against the back wall of the elevator rubbing his eyes, letting his head fall back against the wall. He had imagined that life would somehow be better if he only had powers, but the feeling in the pit of his stomach, the indescribable unease he always felt when he was overwhelmed with worry resurfaced. He thought back to how the hybrid-Nth had shown him being a leader.

His reality was so far away from that vision, and it pressed on him like a heavy weight. *Would the hybrid-Nth reject me if I don't make progress towards that ideal?* His experience with the robot showed that Nth could be forcibly removed, but for some reason, they chose to stay with him. For now, at least. *How much time would it take for them to realize I don't have what it takes and abandon me? Could I even go back to a life as a reg now that I have seen the other side?*

Before he could mentally torture himself more, the elevator opened on the training arena. Some of the Crew were there. His father had brought a group of talented prodigies that were willing to follow him as he went to investigate Aurora's distress signal, who referred to themselves collectively as 'the Crew.' In truth, Purple Faction had apparently written off his mother some time ago and didn't want to expend more resources for Tempest's pet project.

After his father's demotion, he decided it was time to go find his wife under the guise of finding the distress signal's source. The Crew had decided to accompany him, despite the fact that many of them outranked him now. They either respected him or his mother a lot to come along for an indeterminate period. All of them knew they could be called back by Purple at any time if a mission arose, and Gus could see Tempest planning furiously, trying to get as much done in as short a time as possible.

Gus' jaw tightened as his eyes flicked to the others in the room, but he could still train. With upgrades to the arena, the back wall had lifted and revealed five additional battle areas, arranged in a honeycomb pattern. Gus scanned himself and wordlessly got into position. He had been training and sparring with the other supers and had already learned a lot. But right now he needed to be alone, or at least away from other people and their demands.

He entered in the parameters for training then nodded to himself and got into a ready stance as the program began. He melted into habit, thinking about the latest turn of events.

He had locked himself from assimilating any of the abilities he had taken from the Mandrite core, knowing that implementation of that many changes simultaneously would be too much for him. All that power right there and none of it available. It was maddening. With the multitude of abilities he had already stolen from other supers though, he really couldn't complain.

Gus blocked a swing from a pillowbot and grappled the arm, taking the robot down. He sprang away as another attacked and only succeeded in hitting its partner. By the time the hit connected he was already across the arena, in a ready pose.

Truly, the manor had made improvements in leaps and bounds in the week since his father had come, and yet he felt unsettled. This did not feel like the Tempest he had come to know. His exuberant acceptance was something Gus had always craved. But to him, it felt like a large part of that acceptance was of his powers, not of Gus himself.

Plus, Gus was uncertain if he was being genuine. All of it kind of pissed him off. He was mad at himself too, for biting his tongue and allowing Tempest to help take the lead. In his mind's eye, he had planned to meet his father when he was good and ready. After he had leveled and mastered his abilities, not when he was still bumbling around trying to make sense of everything.

He landed an anger-fueled punch on one pillowbot before dancing away. The situation was idiotic but it was how he felt. He had dreamed of what he would say when the 'confrontation' with his father inevitably occurred, but he had been so caught off guard that Tempest just went along with everything before Nick berated him and guided him into setting some boundaries.

He recognized that the manor had to be secure enough to

leave, but he longed for the Crew to finally be ready to go. Some days were better than others. Since the incident, he hadn't been able to allow himself to sleep. So he had to do other things to occupy his time. His *Energy Absorption* ability allowed him to never feel physical exhaustion, but he had times when his brain started to just get a little foggy.

He had noticed himself react with a little more edginess and have a bit more of a temper than he was used to, but it was hard to distinguish what was due to sleep deprivation and what was due to having his father back in his life.

And just when he thought he was getting Zen, *bam*! Headaches hit without warning. Sometimes like a vice threatening to crush his temples, other times like a stiletto to the base of his skull. They came with no warning, and he tried his best to hide his handicap from the others. It would involve answering too many questions.

He grit his teeth and landed another punch; the pillowbot staggered back and fell with a satisfying thud. The impact was therapeutic, draining off a portion of his pent-up emotions. Fortunately, they were relentless attackers and Gus pushed himself to take out his frustrations on the poor automatons.

His mind fell into a rhythm while he attacked and defended, his body going on autopilot. He thought about the Quorian cube and what it contained.

The others had scavenged some meager supplies, and Yuki managed to secure some of Methiochos' personal logs for Gus. He wasn't sure why he decided to download and keep them, but after they were checked to be virus-free, he had them transferred to a small datapad.

Overall the training went well, and Gus felt like he wouldn't be too much of a bumbler when the mission actually started, but the real test was when they got into an actual battle.

The Crew were vague about their abilities for some reason, so he only had a general idea of their skills. It could be that he was still like a stranger to them; he barely knew their names and felt uncomfortable inserting himself into their well-established group.

Still. The reason for the secrecy was beyond him, but it was like an unspoken rule. One of those forbidden topics that everyone inherently knew were off-limits.

Gus continued fighting, dodging an attack and retaliating. If he didn't run an Adaptive Training program, he could let himself go on autopilot. It was rare that he would be caught off guard, and his responses were becoming honed. Often he didn't get any XP, but it kept him from boiling over.

He had actually broken a tooth the third day after Tempest arrived, from clenching his jaw so hard. His Nth had to make a hard shell over it while they repaired the enamel underneath. This required him to be on a soup and smoothie diet because he couldn't make his teeth fit together with the large dome over the tooth being repaired. Just another irritation. *Wasn't life supposed to be getting better as a super? When is that going to happen?*

"Happiness is not defined by any circumstance, condition, or person. You need not tie your happiness to anything. The choice to be happy is always yours to make. Make that choice and cultivate a happy spirit," Nick suggested. "Your father is not making you unhappy, you are choosing to feel so."

"So you think I am being too hard on my father?" Gus inquired as he kicked and pushed backward, doing a flip, instantly regretting asking the question.

"One must honor their parents," Nick responded curtly, with disdain.

"Honor should be earned." Gus grunted after an especially hard block.

"So only those who serve you deserve any honor?"

"No, that's not—" The distraction gave a pillowbot the time it needed to give Gus a good slap across the face. Gus clenched his fists at the shot. He spun and landed a roundhouse kick on the robot's torso. "Everyone deserves a certain level of respect. But those who abuse that trust have to prove they have changed."

"For how long? When will you finally allow yourself to forgive the offender?"

"I'm sorry I brought it up. I mistakenly thought you were on my side," Gus growled.

"I *am* on your side. These emotions and habits of blame are a weakness. You need to rid yourself of them."

Gus' eyebrows furrowed so much that he could see them as he tried to contain himself.

"I'm done with this conversation."

"You can run, but wherever you go, there you are," Nick said with infuriating calm. He had become so used to asking the previous iterations of Nick questions that it was a hard habit to break. This new one made him wonder if mainland supers had it right to suppress their Nth personalities. Gus almost charged the pillowbot in front of him like a mad bull when a twinkling chime and a message came over the manor intercom.

"Gus, please meet your party in the control room," the message repeated just like in an airport. *Finally!* It was time to go. Nothing good ever seemed to come from overthinking things. He grabbed a towel to mop up the sparse sweat that had accumulated. Barely anything and he had really been going at it. *At least some things are improving.*

The control room was full of the entire crew, Tempest, and Aurora, who all turned to look at Gus, the last to arrive.

"Excellent, we are all here!" Tempest said, clasping his hands. "We are off to find my wife, Gwen. You probably know her as 'The Alchemist.' She has been gone for over a decade and though I have kept close tabs on her, recently, my surveillance feeds went dark. We are heading now to her last known location. As Gus has fully recovered, her bargain is complete and she should be allowed to come home. I have reservations that her *generous* host will comply so easily, however, so we may have some work to do. Any questions?"

There was slight murmuring but no one asked anything.

"Okay, let's get going. We'll be using our transport for this mission, as Seneschal, our pilot, is more familiar with it, but we have retrieved the Manticorps vessel from a neighboring island. As we have been unable to unlock the hangar atop the manor, we have only been able to use it as a landing area. It's possible that there are ships within the hangar, but for now, we'll make do with what we have. Everything should be ready with our transport, and Crew members have checked it out. It is ready to go; let us head there now."

Tempest motioned towards the elevator and everyone piled in. Someone hit a strange symbol at the top of the series of buttons and the car slid upwards. Gus had thought he knew most of the manor's layout. There always seemed to be something new. It made him proud in a weird way.

The car opened and everyone spilled out. They were on the roof of the manor, and there was a large octagonal landing pad. At this height, the wind whipped by constantly. Gus slowly spun and took in the whole of the island. Walking to a guardrail, he looked out at the lush jungle, beaches, and the smoldering volcano. He couldn't have asked for a better place to be. Well, at least now that there weren't any more zombies or supers attacking, that was.

Gus turned and most of the others had already headed up the open gangway and entered the transport. He followed them in and they seated themselves in the main cabin. Two plush chairs on each side of the wide aisle were filling as everyone stowed their gear in the hold, while some secured items in storage above the seats. Aurora had saved him a seat. Gus was surprised; she had seemed distant after the others arrived.

"How are you holding up? You've seemed wrung out lately, Gus."

"Physically, I feel fine, but mentally, I'm fried. Plus with my father here, it feels like things are slipping out of my control."

"Well, I think you're doing great, given the circumstances." She looked up with concern. Gus' anger at Aurora had evaporated in the conflict with Manticorps and finding out she was still alive. Still, things had changed a bit. Neither had apologized, but they tacitly moved ahead. Hanging out or training a bit, but they hadn't talked as much. She had effortlessly slipped back into the others' company and Gus felt like an outsider, as they kept mostly to themselves.

"I didn't plan on all this responsibility. And at the same time, I get furious at the thought of someone taking it away from me, like I'm unable to handle it. I've always hated being volunteered for something by someone else, especially if I had other plans. Sometimes this feels like that, and even with all this power, people are still ordering me around."

"You've made it clear how you want things organized. Even I was surprised at how you held yourself and laid things out. It wasn't your typical Gus."

Gus recalled how most of that came from Nick's recommendations, but she didn't need to know that. Gus felt he had a tenuous leadership established as it was.

Tempest made his way back from the cockpit and addressed the group.

"Okay, we'll be in the air in just a bit. We're going to visit the base where The Alchemist was last held. Something has definitely happened there recently, so be prepared for a fight…"

"Is it weird he is calling her 'The Alchemist' and not 'Gwen,' or 'my wife'?" Gus leaned over and whispered to Aurora.

"That's how people addressed her in the faction, so maybe he's trying to keep it professional? Or how faction members knew her?" she replied, keeping her eyes ahead.

"It throws me off," Gus said, folding his arms as Tempest continued.

"…will go in first to assess the situation. They will relay that to me and then we will progress in teams. Gus, you'll be with me, Yuki, and Aurora. Team two will be led by Anastasia and team three by Grimdark. Everyone, accept the party invite and check your comms. We should be there in about two hours. Any questions?"

No one responded, so Tempest made his way back to the forward cabin. Gus tried to peek up to see if his father was helping fly the ship or just observing the pilot. *Is he a pilot, too?* Gus had to admit he didn't know. *How well do I know my own father?* He conceded he had been self-absorbed for a while with his own life now that he was out of the house.

Gus leaned forward and rubbed his face with both hands. He usually liked to sleep on planes or transports, but there wasn't anything to do. He could really use a handheld game system, or communicator to distract himself. With the constant chaos taking most of his mental RAM, he hadn't had time to be bored. He needed something to do or level, or he felt like he was wasting time.

With a resonating hum that made his back itch until it cycled to a higher frequency, the transport lifted off and turned in the air. They were finally off.

CHAPTER FOUR

Soul Man

Gus leaned back and enjoyed the sensation of takeoff. Unlike his friend Chuck, who hated flying, Gus liked the feeling. For some reason it made him feel like a super, even before he ever had any powers. It was a far cry from the actual sensation of flying with powers, but they still elicited the same swell of emotions. As he dwelt on why, he recalled that whenever he had flown in the past, it was usually either for a family vacation to some exotic place or the start of a mission with his fellow henchmen.

Something new and exciting always seemed to await them. He closed his eyes as he was pressed slightly into his seat as the transport rapidly accelerated to their cruising altitude. When he opened his eyes, Aurora was already asleep in the short time it took to take off. He had planned on continuing their conversation but she must have thought he was taking a rest and decided to do the same.

After fidgeting for a while, he got bored, so Gus popped out of his seat and dug the cube from his backpack in the overhead storage. Staring at it, he tried using some of his abilities to see if it would reveal anything about the mysterious box. *Telepathy* did nothing, but perhaps it only worked on living things. That made him wonder what **Electronic Mind** would do to the cube. His tentative probe felt like it clicked into place when he tried to understand what the cube was hiding. Whether this was due to his skill or possibly some changes in himself from absorbing Methiochos' ability, he could not say.

As he looked at the cube, he had a sudden feeling of falling forward. The side of the cube he was staring at appeared to stretch in all directions and there was a feeling of transition as he crossed the plane of the surface.

Then the world changed.

———

Looking around, Gus found himself within a labyrinth. Walls the color of circuit boards were chased with protrusions and soldered elements. Yellow pulses zigged and zagged through them. Sound seemed to be muted as when underwater, and Gus looked at his hand, which also seemed to move more slowly through whatever medium made up this place. It was the closest he had ever felt to being awake in a dream.

Gus began to wander down the halls formed by the green walls, looking upward to see them extend into a vanishing point above him. A misty white light filtered down, its source masked by the fog or clouds above. Gus tried to fly and found that he couldn't activate any abilities. Trying **Bound** met with similar results. Apparently, in this place, he could not use any abilities.

Gus began to explore, his footsteps making a hollow echoing *thonk* as he stepped ahead. The scope of the labyrinth must have been vast, because he noticed no visible change after what felt like half an hour of walking. He would need to find a way to move more quickly or he would never be able to explore this area fully.

He began to be aware of a high-pitched tone, faint at first but becoming more pronounced the longer it was there. All of a sudden Gus felt a pull backward and he was once again in his seat, the stab of a headache driving in his temples. A quick look at his MP showed it was bottomed out. **Electronic Mind** must have been draining MP the entire time he was exploring.

Accompanying the pain was the hint of a rising nausea, and it took him some time of massaging his temples with eyes closed and deep breathing before the feeling passed. He sheepishly looked over at Aurora, not wanting to throw up around her a second time. She continued to sleep, a slight smile on her face.

He wondered how long he had been inside the cube, but hadn't checked the time beforehand so he had no real frame of reference. He would need to figure that out so he could avoid bottoming out again. Nick usually would warn him once he was getting close to hitting the 5% mark, but he had no such warning while in the cube. A quick check showed that he had progressed in the skill, but was still around 20% short of getting another level in **Electronic Mind**.

He committed to check some of the logs Yuki downloaded to see if there were any hints or references that would allow him to navigate the labyrinth somehow as he waited for his MP to recharge. Stuffing the cube in the pouch behind the seat in front of him, he retrieved the tablet from the backpack. There was probably nothing there, but it was the only other lead he could think of at the moment.

He searched for Quorian and cube, but only found two small references:

6/25/2020 - I have come across an unbound Quorian cube. I have had to pay a heavy price for the item, but it was necessary to secure the help from Dr. Flak. His intellect and innovation will serve us well on the island, allowing us to reach new heights as we implement his research into inte-grating—

He fumbled the tablet, almost dropping it. The horizon rocking through the windows revealed that it wasn't just him. He blinked a couple times and realized that the transport itself was jockeying back and forth. The blast of large explosions made the transport shudder as the pilot went into evasive maneuvers. The cabin rotated as they dodged and rocked back and forth to avoid getting hit.

"The damned base defenses are still active!" Darik yelled, face plastered to the window on the other side of the transport like a little kid.

Gus almost laughed, but the transport dropped in freefall for about five seconds as a loud boom shook the ship from above. The impulse engines kicked back in and they sped forward, briefly shoving everyone into their seats until the dampeners reoriented.

Through the oval window, Gus saw them skimming across the water. He could see multiple contrails crisscrossing the air all around them, but they had difficulty targeting them at such a low altitude. A nearby explosion splashed water over the windows, momentarily blocking his view of the outside.

"Hold on!" a canned voice blurted over the intercom. The ship began to pull sharply to the right and Gus was pulled almost out of his seat as they slid. They drifted and the transport began to wobble as it skittered across the water. Something dark was quickly approaching the far side of the transport and everyone braced for a crash that never came.

A large pulse of the inertial dampeners flared and the ship stopped neatly in a cove under the base, bobbing on the water, a huge wake rolling away from them. The maneuver reminded Gus of the Blues Brothers parking in a tight spot between two cars. Water sloshed against the nearby pier and the ship settled on the water's surface, bobbing up and down as the waters settled.

A cheer went up among everyone and they began unbuckling and getting their stowed gear. This seemed like an everyday occurrence with how unflappable everyone was with the whole affair.

Gus sat wide-eyed, hands gripping the armrests for dear life.

Aurora yawned and stretched. "Are we already there?" she asked lazily, acting as if she was totally unaware that anything had happened. Maybe she was. Gus looked over to her and nodded numbly.

Seeing everyone almost ready to disembark, Gus shrugged and got up. Grimdark opened the side hatch and secured the transport to some pylons near the dock. Everyone filed out, assembling into their groups and adjusting their gear as needed. It was pretty damn impressive to see a group like this in action.

Definitely a different affair from henchmen getting ready for a raid or mission. Most of his groups more closely resembled someone waking up late for school, grabbing something quick to eat while half-dressed and running out the door, almost forgetting their books. These individuals were disciplined, organized, and knew how to support each other.

Gus scratched his head, having nothing to do, as he didn't have any real gear. Jet managed itself, floating nearby. As if in response, his hybrid-Nth armor changed configuration and formed the hex-mesh pattern, the gunmetal color spreading like a wave over his body, with thicker plates over key areas.

"Not bad," came a voice behind him. Gus turned to see one of the Crew giving him a thumbs up and a broad smile. Gus gave him a 'thank you' nod and waited for the rest of his group to form up. He kept forgetting the guy's name, but he sounded Australian.

Tempest was the last to leave and he gave some last instructions to the pilot before stepping out on the deck. He strode purposefully to Gus' group, eagerly whispering to Gus, "Are you ready?" He gave him a surreptitious thumbs-up before turning to address the group.

CHAPTER FIVE

Ones & Zeros

Tempest's abrupt whistle brought all the fiddling with equipment and murmured discussion to a stop.

"As you can see, external base defenses are engaged, so expect internal ones to be active as well. Take proper precautions and proceed to the designated nav-points. There has been no response to hails, which means they don't want us here or are not able to respond. Anastasia and Grimdark will lead the other teams, and we will rendezvous here…"

Gus heard a ding and his minimap populated with a map of the base. Green dots showed up around him and he found he could mentally rotate the map to get a top-down or a three-dimensional view of the different levels of the base. He stopped toying with the views when he saw a message icon pop up on his display. He opened the window.

You have been offered the Group Quest: **Rescue The Alchemist.**
Clear the facility and locate the super known as The Alchemist.
XP dependent on contribution.
Restrictions*: Not everyone in your group is receiving notice of this*

quest. Choosing to reveal it without Tempest's permission will result in an XP penalty and possible loss of level(s).

Before he could think too much about it, a pulsing chevron appeared on his minimap and Tempest continued.

"Report any anomalies along the way; we don't know what we're dealing with here. I'd like to keep this non-confrontational, but protect yourselves if attacked. This should just be a research facility, but it has resisted Yuki's probes, so it's obviously more than it appears. Alright? Everyone knows their rally points, let's move out." He twirled his finger and everyone separated into their groups and began entering the structure.

Tempest led Gus' group and he received a prompt to join his party. Four additional avatars populated the left side of his display, with vertical bars denoting their major pools. With less people, he could see their full names instead of only initials. Gus was relieved that he knew the other members of his party, if only briefly.

There was Yuki, who was an augment with hacking skills, and would be the scout of the group. Today, she dressed in a goth-inspired schoolgirl outfit with thigh high-boots laden with unnecessary buckles. She kept to herself, preferring the company of tech over people, and all Gus knew of her was from exploring *The Banoi* earlier.

Pulse, who specialized in light-based powers and energy blasts. Aurora, Tempest, and Gus rounded out the group of five. Pulse looked like the textbook superhero, exaggerated jawline and all. Gus had sparred with him a couple times and he was relentless, attacking constantly and never appearing to lose any stamina. It would be nice to be fighting with the guy instead of against him for a change. Despite having sparred with a few of them he still did not know how he would fit in during an actual battle.

"Gus, you're the least trained to work in groups," Tempest mentioned as if reading his mind, "so I'll ask you to hold back and guard our rear. Be careful of friendly fire on those in front of you. It may be better to hold back and let us do the heavy lifting, but feel free to take care of anything behind us, got it?"

Gus nodded and instructed Jet to help him monitor their six. Jet spun in place, and a red handkerchief tied to the blade guard flared like a girl's dress when spinning around.

Where did you get that? The spear briefly bowed towards Harmony who winked as Gus saw her and gave an enthusiastic smile. *Dang, my polearm has better social skills than me.*

Tempest led the way to a futuristic-looking bulkhead. Yuki typed on a virtual mini-keyboard fastened to the back of her forearm, then extended her typing hand to the panel. The bulkhead disappeared into the ceiling and everyone moved inside.

A smell of acrid burning mingled with roadkill puffed past them as the door opened. Gus wrinkled his nose, squinting as he waved the fumes away and followed everyone inside. It wasn't too bad—yet. After turning the corner, Tempest accessed the stairs and everyone filed up. After climbing five flights, there was a conspicuous pool of tacky blood underneath the door. Tempest held up a fist and the party stopped. Yuki came forward again and extended her hand forward close to the blood. Two telescoping projections came out of the center of her palm, gently touched the blood, then retracted. After some typing, she held the projected screen above her forearm toward Tempest for him to review.

He grimaced and nodded, then motioned for everyone to stand behind him. He then extended his hands and a gray mist covered the door, becoming more and more condensed until the door was lost in the fog-like material. With a sudden **pop** the door imploded and swung inward. The other supers moved to the sides of the doorway and looked back at Gus who stood there, looking through the doorway.

Aurora gave him a quick wide-eyed look, jerking her head to the side repeatedly. *Message received. Get in cover when clearing a door, dummy!* Gus scrambled to the side and waited for the others to enter. Pulse dashed in and surveyed the room, announcing 'clear' over the comms.

Peering inside, there wasn't a body, but there was a lot of blood. The overhead lights were dimmed as if on some energy-saving setting. Bloody handprints could be seen on the inside of the crumpled door as if someone had struggled to escape.

Gus could not recall smelling old blood, but the metallic scent triggered a visceral part of him to tense up. One by one, they filed through the door and the other supers evaluated the room and moved systematically around the perimeter. Tempest signaled and they progressed along that path, clearing any rooms along the hallway.

Despite Gus' tension, there were no surprises as they made their way through the complex. Only some areas appeared ransacked while others appeared orderly and neat. They found no other blood or any bodies, but the disagreeable smells never disappeared. They would wax and wane in intensity without rhyme or reason, which made it difficult to tell if they were getting closer to some site of carnage or not.

Eventually, they made it to their destination—a control room that reminded Gus of the Foundry with the exception that it was much larger. This room looked like it could double as an atrium with the wide spaces. There were no windows to the outside from this room, its large windows instead showed machinery below. The tiles were illuminated and small workstations were visible, abandoned like the rest of the facility.

Yuki strode to the most prominent console there and began to set up. Reaching the terminal, she extended her keyboard hand and the same two probes snaked out of her palm and inserted into it. She typed frenetically for a minute or two then grinned, blowing a bubble with her gum and popping it. She bowed to Tempest and swung her hand towards the console with an 'after you' gesture.

"You have five minutes, so be quick," she chirped, smiling.

He accessed the computer and scrolled through various menus. Opening folders, glancing at the contents, then moving on. Occasionally he would make a motion and slide a file to

Yuki who stood there, arm extended. Gus could see folder icons appearing on the projected screen as the data was transferred.

As Tempest searched the system, Gus noticed a slight buzzing and a flutter to the already dim lights. It was subtle but seemed to be affecting lights in different parts of the room. Not only that, but the disturbance seemed to be moving closer to where they were.

"Guys… does anyone else detect anything here…?" Gus slowly asked, unsure if he was overreacting.

Aurora turned her eyes away from the computer, pulling her hair from her eyes. Her eyes flared open as she screamed, "*Wraith!*"

CHAPTER SIX

Bad to Worse

What's a wraith? Not knowing what else to do, Gus put up a shield in front of him. No sooner had he done that than a demonic-looking face pushed into the bubble. A gnarled claw dented the shield slightly inward but it resisted the creature, rebounding and throwing it back. A nearby trash can dented and was launched into the dark hall beyond.

The lineup changed as other supers moved in front of Gus, encircling him. He gave them room and stepped back, then shifted the curvature of his shield to cover himself and Tempest while he searched through computer files.

"I almost have it," he shouted to the other supers.

Gus watched in fascination as the team did their work. Aurora flung out shimmering, dust-like particles and a figure was revealed as it moved through the dust, displacing the glittering specks and announcing its location. Pulse shot a beam of light at the figure, who raised its hands to shield itself.

Gus wanted to help but was worried he might interfere with what the others were doing. They seemed to have the situation well in hand. A pink glow appeared where the beam trained on the creature, and slowly spread outward. The figure came into view, but its appearance seemed… fractured somehow. Almost as if viewed through a cracked window. Sweat poured down Pulse's face as he tried to maintain the beam that was sapping his MP bar on Gus' display.

"Done!" Tempest exclaimed, turning to aid in stopping the threat. He pulled his fists back then shot them forward. Electricity crackled in front of his fists at the specter and there was an explosion of pink sparks that popped loudly as they settled to the ground.

"Dammit, wraiths! That changes things," Tempest barked. "Yuki, update everyone's minimap and let's rendezvous with everyone at medical."

She waved and the details of the minimap became much more detailed, with labels and a blue pulsing arrow showing the quickest way to reach their destination.

Tempest began speaking to the other team leads as the group began to move, warning them of the wraiths and altering their plans. They hurried through the hallways and stairs quickly arriving on the floor.

"What was that?" Gus gasped to Aurora.

"The wraith? Ohh, they're the worst. Some supers have a rare ability that allows them to gift some of their abilities to constructs. They are usually invisible and require no maintenance of MP, though they do take a lot to create. They follow usually a single command until they are destroyed or they fade away when the MP invested in them dissipates. They can't be reasoned with and depending on how much MP is used to create them, they usually require an equivalent amount of damage to be dissipated."

Gus shook his head; apparently virtual ghosts were a thing too. With powers no less. "Anything else I should know?"

"Usually supers prepare them beforehand and then use them to drain an attacker's energy, giving them an advantage as they will have recharged MP by then. So there theoretically can be a lot of them; keep your eyes open."

Gus turned and saw Pulse chewing vigorously like an angry

cow, his jaw flexing. He swallowed then threw in another blue gel. Checking the display, he could see that Pulse's avatar indeed had regained 75% of his MP and was still rising.

Gus felt oddly reassured that his investment of FP into the cafeteria wasn't just a waste of points, and that he had actually done something to help with the mission. While no one had said anything, he felt a need to prove himself. If not to them, then to himself. That he deserved to be part of the team.

Turning a corner, the smell of antiseptic in the air announced that they were near the complex's medical wing. Grimdark's team was already there, and he stood there stoically with his arms folded in front of him, a dark look on his gaunt features.

"It's not good, Tempest. Harmony has not sensed anyone left in the base. Upon our searches, that means no *bodies* either, even though there is evidence of a massacre. The barracks have multiple beds stained with blood. The walls are marked with blood splatter as well as in areas that would have had high traffic. My assessment is that this was a surprise attack, but it is difficult to tell what has happened with what we have, or if anyone escaped. I'm sorry."

"No!" Tempest shouted, shaking his head. "There has to be something. Have you heard anything from team two?"

"They're en route, but they also ran into a wraith, so are resting and recharging before moving forward."

"This is all wrong." Tempest pursed his lips, his brow furrowed in thought. "Alright. I know I've only shared this with a couple of others, but it's time you all knew. Someone or something is targeting the Factions. Not just Purple, but all of them. There has been a large increase in attacks and disappearances as of late, and I have been trying to investigate without revealing my awareness of the situation. The presence of wraiths here is just a confirmation that this is not some extremist reg group but someone with powers actively targeting supers. But what connection this has with my wife—"

A scream broke into Tempest's explanation and immediately after, BoJack rounded the corner, running at full speed and yelling in terror. The rest of team two followed with The Keeper lagging behind, due to his shorter legs. Drywall and thin metal supports spewed into the hallway right behind him as something enormous burst through the wall. The small man bellowed a litany of curses as the team ran past the others.

A being that appeared to be made of living electricity stood in the hallway and shrieked. Papers wafting down from the chaos began to burn as they touched the creature. Wraiths emerged from surrounding rooms, drawn by the noise. Team two turned and caught their breath while the others closed ranks and stood to face the threat.

Tempest curled his lip in a sneer of challenge and pulled his fists back, mists swirling about him as the rest of the team began charging attacks and getting into position.

"You know what we're dealing with, people! Let's do this!" Tempest shouted.

Then all hell broke loose.

CHAPTER SEVEN

Electric Blue

Not knowing exactly what he was dealing with, Gus marveled as everyone moved in unison to meet the threat. Harmony dropped back and Gus noticed a series of buffs show up on his display. Avatars for members of teams two and three populated the upper and right sides of his display automatically.

The electro-monster stomped forward, leaving singed and melted three-foot-wide footprints in the carpet as it moved. The creature was giant, consisting of only a torso and four appendages sprouting out of its sides. It appeared cobbled together from bits of metal and debris, held together by arcing strands of living electricity. Its legs were thick like an elephant's and shook the floor the closer it got. The crackling blue energy coursing around what made the outer skin of the beast was mesmerizing, and it was hard not to stare.

Gus briefly saw the wraiths, with their rotund bodies that resembled spiders supported by spindly legs and arms much longer than normal, both tipped with bony claws. Upon seeing the group of supers, they went from a gauzy consistency and dropped into stealth, disappearing from view. Gus blinked away afterimages the crackling countenance of the electro-monster had burned into his eyes after he managed to pull them away.

The creature lifted two of its paddle-like arms and hordes of tennis-ball sized spheres of blue energy floated out, targeting different members of the group. They moved slowly, but tracked and followed as the Crew dodged them. The lower arms elongated and began whipping unpredictably forward, each one making a loud *crack* as they snapped in front of the behemoth, discouraging any frontal attacks.

The Keeper calmly moved in front of the group and began gesturing, making a window with his hands as if he were framing a picture, then twisting and repeating the process in rapid succession. Small portals began to open up in the path of the energy spheres, gobbling them up. He continued to make more frames and it was only the shriek of the wraiths that drew Gus' attention to where the spheres were being redirected.

Multiple tiny portals dumped the spheres behind the phalanx of wraiths lurking past the electro-monster. Each one pushed through the wraiths like a hot poker through wax, illuminating them with a blue hue as they left, leaving gaping holes in their wake. The energy balls shrank and slowed as they expended energy pushing through the wraiths as they tried to continue towards their intended targets.

Hearing the shrieks, the monster extended one of the whip arms toward the wraiths and emanated a weblike substance that pulsed down the attachment and stitched the wounds together. The monster shuddered and shrank slightly at the expenditure of energy. The attack spurred the group of wraiths to spread out and scurry around, like ants from a kicked anthill. As soon as they were healed by the boss, they faded back into invisibility.

In response, Tempest spread his fingers as if he was getting ready to play the piano. Pulling a calculated amount of energy out of the air, the excess humidity transformed into a fog that revealed the wraiths in clear contrast. The extra moisture popped and cracked around the boss, and it bellowed in fury.

"Don't let it touch you!" Tempest warned, stepping back

while maintaining the fog, expanding it to the confines of wherever the wraiths tried to flee and hide.

Pulse began targeting one, and it froze and trembled while he overloaded the construct with energy. Aurora took flight and sent an ion storm into the midst of a cluster. Wraiths wailed as the energy ripped through them like a shotgun blast. The height made targeting easier and she strafed side to side, raining damage and preventing their advance past the boss.

Gus activated **Wreckognize** to see if he could get any information about the boss that would allow him to contribute.

Revenant (Electric Fulminant)

Revenants are reanimated supers who have been raised and programmed with a singular purpose. They cannot be reasoned with and have lost their humanity, acting as puppets to their creator, and retain some of their abilities from life.

HP:2460/2500
MP: 942/1200
Special skills: 1) Spawn: Conversion of biomass into wraiths.
2) Sap: Absorb MP by direct contact. When MP reaches 0, begins draining HP.
3) Sphere: Create targeting spheres that stun enemies.
Weaknesses: Unknown.

Wraith

Wraiths are constructs that attack any living thing. Their touch is paralytic and allows them to immobilize prey for consumption.
HP: 232/250
MP: 100/100
Special skills: 1) Death's Door: Can absorb energy from an ally for self-healing.
2) Last Breath: Physical contact paralyzes all bodily functions of the target. If sustained can cause massive damage and even death.
Weaknesses: Susceptible to dissolution with energy overloads.

"Hold it down while I drain it!" Grimdark yelled and braced himself as he waited for his allies.

Dark cables snaked out of the metal armbands around BoJack's forearms and he grappled the whip like arms and leg of the left side of the Revenant. The grapple spun around the twin arms, cinching them together. BoJack stomped and a metal band around his calves drove a hook into the ground. With a deft flip, he looped the cables underneath and leaned back, just in time for them to snap taut as the Revenant flailed. The surge pulled him forward like a bucking bronco but he was able to maintain his hold and dig in his heels.

Electricity coursed down the cables but was grounded by the hook as BoJack flashed a cocky smile at the Revenant. Another flip and the cables were securely anchored by the tension.

Distracted by BoJack, another super slid to the right. Anastasia placed her hands on the wall and swiped them left. The wall erupted, different materials flowing like vines and encircling the Revenant. Cement flowed like malleable clay and pooled around one of the mammoth feet, while wires and pipes slithered out and held the arms. The lithe super glanced and nodded to Grimdark, her long, shimmering white hair reflecting the electric blue energy and fanning out from the movement. More materials poured out of the gash and continued to bind the Revenant tighter.

Grimdark approached the monster and thrust his hands forward into its body and sunk them down to his wrists. Both began to bellow, a large maw opening in the torso of the monster, revealing the inside of the creature to be identical to the outside.

With his head thrown back, Grimdark's eyes glowed with the same brilliant blue hue. Phosphorescent glowing blue tears dripped out of his eyes as he struggled with the creature. Both appeared to be trying to absorb the energy of the other. Blue light blazed and dimmed and Grimdark appeared to be slowly winning the tug-of-war.

Gus' display flashed as a teammate began to lose MP and a prison icon appeared by the avatar of the super named Prime. This super was one of the more reclusive and Gus didn't even know if they were male or female, as the individual rarely spoke, and always wore a helmet and androgynous body suit.

A wraith had appeared behind Prime with its claw-like hands around their helmet, talons encircling the entire visor like some macabre game of 'Guess Who.' The materials Anastasia used to bind the Revenant at first stopped moving, then began to degrade as it slipped and pulled two of its arms free. They contracted and hit Grimdark with a huge double-backhand, flinging him into Gus' shield, where he slid to a seated position. Aurora screamed in anger and targeted the offending wraith, blowing off its head.

Gus winced at the hit. Grimdark looked groggy, shaking his head and failing at his attempts to get back on his feet. Gus looked back at the Revenant and saw that both of its arms reached for the cables as BoJack lost his grin. Splintering could be heard from around the hook as the monster redoubled its efforts to pull.

Without thinking, Gus dropped his shield and activated **Amber**. Twin gouts of material formed in front of his hands and splashed around the creature, intertwining with the wreckage and debris Anastasia had used to bind it, severely curtailing its ability to move as it had to lift everything attached to it as well as pull on the cables.

BoJack's grin returned as he nodded to Gus. Mentally calling Jet to him, Gus ran toward the Revenant, reaching up without looking as Jet flew into his grasp. Finding a gap in the amber residue, he thrust the naginata into the blue coursing electricity and activated **Vampire's Kiss**. The behemoth began to spasm as if in pain and visibly contracted.

The amber prison condensed as the Revenant shrunk and held fast to the receding figure as it began to congeal. There was a sudden loud pop, and the stench of ozone wafted through the room.

Inside of an igloo made of crispy amber reinforced with all sorts of materials lay the figure of a skinny boy. Gus guessed that he looked around fourteen years old. The room was uncomfortably quiet after the altercation, the wraiths having been dispatched by the other supers. Milky eyes stared up at the ceiling, and the boy's pallid skin had the sickly cast of a body that had been underwater for too long. Gus ignored the blue notices that popped up on his display post-battle and just stared at the dead boy.

"This changes everything," Tempest said gravely.

CHAPTER EIGHT

Going, Going, Gone

"Revenants are made, they don't just happen. And they're made by supers. Also a handy way of cleaning up so there are no bodies to examine. There's something else that unsettles me about this. Some of it is too familiar, but without my access to the Faction database, I can't be sure. I just hope there's something in the files we obtained to give us another lead." Tempest shook his head then turned and punched the wall, creating a cloud of dust as the drywall disintegrated. Harmony ran over and put an arm around him.

"We'll find her…" was all Gus could hear, the rest lost in murmurs.

Yuki motioned to BoJack and they headed into medical and started working on one of the consoles there. Gus saw them searching the medical records, but by their expressions the news wasn't good.

BoJack glanced at Tempest and pursed his lips as he began, "She was here, and not too long ago. They had her on high concentrations of sedatives and she was in a pod, similar to those used in game hospices. They could have been controlling what she viewed as reality for who knows how long."

"For fourteen years, six months, and two days most likely," was the deadpan reply. Tempest stared ahead, and Gus noticed the weariness there. *How long had his father had hopes of this being the end of his separation only to find it a dead-end?*

"If you did not hear, exactly fourteen years—" Nick began, intruding on Gus' thoughts.

Enough! Obviously, I know that. I just never thought my mother's absence affected him as it did me. Nick remained silent but Gus could sense the AI was miffed at his reply.

Gus looked closer at his father, always a bastion of strength and impassivity. He was always so unflappable and in control, but he looked on the verge of breaking. It was such a shock and out of character that it was hard for him to process. As far as Gus could remember, he never showed weakness of any sort. But now, for the first time, Gus could see how old his father had become.

"Do you have everything?" Tempest asked solemnly and Yuki nodded. Without a word he turned and began to leave. "We're done here then. Let's go."

A beefy hand clapped Gus on the back, startling him.

"Good on ya, lad. The Crew and I had some concerns about how you would do in a real situation, but you made me proud. We could have been in a spot when that beastie got free." Darik smiled broadly at Gus.

A smile stole across his face at the compliment as he watched Darik walk away, rubbing his spiky faux-hawk hair while he congratulated other team members. As everyone made their way back to the ship, many of the Crew congratulated him or gave him a thumbs up. The distance they had maintained had definitely relaxed a bit.

The ride back home was uneventful. Yuki had apparently turned off base defenses or got the system to recognize their ship because no missiles harried their departure. Occasionally Gus looked back at where Yuki and Tempest were working through the files. It must not have been good, because his father kept running his fingers through his hair then sat clutching his chin as he searched through the files they downloaded.

As they neared the manor, Tempest stood and addressed the team.

"I have some bad news. The attack on the facility was unexpected and I can find no links to who may be responsible. The only thing we did find out was that they were experimenting on individuals and a lot of that research seemed to be focused on inducing regs to become supers and developing ways to teach a skill from one super to another. They had very few successes, one being the individual we fought as a Revenant. No information exists on where these volunteers came from, or if they were even there willingly. But apparently over two hundred people were part of the research and trials. That's just what we know about the patients at the facility. Who knows how much support staff was there in addition to that? I'm afraid that's all we have." Tempest slapped the headrest of the chair he was holding and turned to sit down.

A female super, one of the two Gus had never spoken to, began speaking to Tempest. **Wreckognize** revealed her name to be Seneschal, and Gus mentally kicked himself for not using the ability earlier to learn everyone's names.

While Gus could not hear everything, he was close enough to pick up some of the arguments. While he had never learned to read lips, he saw that *True Sight* had activated and he could interpret the whispered words.

"Absolutely not! Who knows what she will ask for!" Tempest hissed.

"You said that we have no leads, what else are we to do?" Seneschal pleaded.

"She's too unpredictable. On top of that, I don't trust her. I would have gone a long time ago, but the demands she gave the last liaison that Purple Faction sent to her were laughably unreasonable. I wouldn't doubt if she's gone insane."

"You don't know that. She could be our only lead."

Tempest glared at her, face torn with emotion. "I'll consider it, but I'm not getting my hopes up. Who knows if she's even still around? The last I heard of her was five years ago," he said dismissively.

"Leave it to me. I realize this situation is difficult, but don't get mad at the team. We're all here to help you, so you need to rein it in."

Tempest nodded in assent, and his expression became stern again as he made his decision. He stood again and did his curt whistle.

"Listen up! Against my better judgment, Erika—" Tempest cleared his throat at her angry glance. "—excuse me, *Seneschal,* has convinced me we need to go see the Oracle." Groans and gasps sprang up from many of the Crew and Tempest raised his hands to quell the unrest. "I know, I know. Believe me, this is *not* something I am looking forward to doing, but I don't see any other options. If you want to stay on the ship, I understand. This is my fight and I don't want any of you beholden to her demands."

Tempest went on to discuss his intentions. Gus cocked his head and looked at his father, wondering if he really was the same man that he had known growing up. He remembered him being more authoritarian, 'my way or the highway.' Had he always been this way and his teenage angst had skewed things negatively or had his father softened in the years without Mom? Internally he wanted to keep avoiding his father but doubts crept up in Gus' mind if he was being overly harsh. A shout disrupted his thinking.

"Well, you can count on me, brother!" Darik shouted, waving a fist in solidarity. The rest of the Crew was less enthusiastic, but from the muffled conversations that began to spring up, most were planning on going with him regardless.

Dreading the answer before he even asked, he questioned Nick.

Who in the heck is the Oracle?

CHAPTER NINE

Eye in the Sky

"The Oracle is a super whose talents lie in predicting the future and accessing hidden information," Nick replied. Gus almost awaited some annoying addition but none was forthcoming.

"So some kind of fortune teller. Why the resistance from everyone?"

"The Oracle has a reputation for exacting onerous tasks and impossible challenges for the information she offers. Often it appears calculated to be at direct odds with one's morality, or related to close personal tragedy. Most refuse, and the Oracle never allows another petition if one is left undone. Once given, she will never renege."

"Woof." Gus tried to imagine what types of Herculean feats had been asked of people in the past. If supers balked at them, there were sure to be some doozies. Gus had a lot of possible things he felt he could ask, but wondered if given the chance to look at his future, what question would he want answered? How would that change everything having that knowledge? From past regrets, he knew a lot of things he wished he could go back into the past and change. Erasing missteps and lost opportunities. But what if those decisions led to even bigger problems?

Tempest spoke up again after conferring with Seneschal, interrupting Gus' thoughts. "I plan on heading straight to the Oracle now, unless anyone has any reservations. Anyone? Anyone?"

Gus had to repress the urge to shout out, "Bueller? Bueller?" or, "Voodoo Economics," knowing probably only his father would get the joke. Afraid they would be the only two, and not wanting to make things awkward now that some of the others were warming up to him, he sat there in silence.

No one had any objections, so Tempest turned and told the pilot to set in the coordinates. The transport banked sharply and began to climb.

———

As the Crew settled in for the trip, it grew quiet as some slept and others played with their displays. It reminded Gus to check his own notices.

You have contributed to the defeat of Level 12 [Revenant (Electrical Fulminant)]! 1000 XP gained!
Quest objective complete: *Clear the Facility.*
Quest Rewards based on participation: *500XP, 300FP.*
Next quest objective: *Gain information on The Alchemist's location from the Oracle.*
XP dependent on participation.
5,160 XP to level 21.

Crap. It's going to take me forever to get to level 30 with the XP all divided out among the group.

"Considering your contribution, it seems more than fair," Nick replied.

Gus pressed his eyes together and tried to go to his happy place. When that failed, he sought refuge in the Quorian cube. He grabbed it and examined a different surface. This one had a peach tint to it and he once again activated **Electronic Mind.**

A familiar sensation of falling forward occurred and he found himself within a totally different environment. The sky was burnt orange with the sunset reflecting on the clouds. Gus was in the midst of a dense jungle, but unlike the island, large planes of what looked like water shimmered like doors looking in on the jungle. The orange hues made the greens of the grass appear extra vibrant for some reason.

Gus walked forward and noticed afterimages of his hands moving. As he paid more attention, he saw that there was no breeze or movement of the plants. He touched a nearby broad leaf hanging low from one of the trees and it cut through it like an electric knife through Thanksgiving turkey. He pulled the finger close to his face, but could detect no vibration, just the ghost-like trail that took a while to catch up with his movement if he stayed still.

What the hell is going on with this cube?

Before he could explore more, he felt pulled up and out of the scene. Snapping back to reality, Aurora was shaking him.

"Sorry to interrupt your meditation or whatever you're doing, but we're here."

Checking his display, Gus saw that he still had 75% of his MP bar full but that over four hours had passed! At most, it felt like he was in the jungle for ten minutes. The ship was already descending into a clearing surrounded by forests, with the green treetops extending as far as he could see.

"As I said before, anyone who wants to stay aboard can do so—no questions asked. The Oracle is unpredictable, and I don't want anyone to get obligated to a group task they are unwilling to complete. Just being present makes you fair game for her demands, so be aware if you decide to come," Tempest warned.

Only Harmony and Yuki stayed aboard. Harmony folded her arms petulantly, muttering how there were too many psychic disturbances and it was already giving her a headache. Yuki was plucking away at her keyboard, engrossed in some project and she waved away the interruption as she typed.

Gus rolled his head, trying to loosen his stiff neck. He wondered if he was frozen in the same position when he did a cube-dive. The transport door opened and a deep earthy scent wafted into the ship.

Glad I don't have allergies, Gus mused as he breathed in the air redolent with pollen. Undertones of fungi also permeated the air. A small, barely noticeable trail left the clearing into the forest, and a light fog hung in the air. Not enough to obscure things close, but past fifty feet or so, the trees disappeared into the mist.

"Mmm, I love the smell of petrichor in the morning," BoJack said while inhaling deeply, a content look spreading across his face.

It did smell nice. Fresh and clean, full of possibilities. Tempest left the ship with his brow furrowed and a sour look on his face as he resolutely marched down the path. Everyone filed after him, conversations quiet. The ferns and plants that lined the path dampened everyone's legs as they proceeded along the path.

After a ten-minute hike, they began ascending a small hill, aspen trees lining the sides of the path. Their white bark blended with the fog and gave an ethereal look to the place. The branches that extended over the path reminded Gus of a sword arch he had seen at a wedding once, as he walked under the unique configuration of trees.

Tempest paused as they reached a plateau, as if gathering his strength, and then stepped forward. Reaching the same spot, Gus stepped onto something hard and looked at a fifty-foot circle. It looked like it was the remains of an enormous tree, but his mind rejected that there could ever have been a tree this size in existence. Its diameter dwarfed the redwoods he had seen on another family trip along the California coastline.

At the far end of the circle, a large emerald throne sat, with a skeletal female figure sat upon it, wearing a gauzy gray gown that looked eerily like spiderwebs.

As the group approached, Gus saw that the chair looked to

be carved out of an enormous oak. Thick spongy moss covered the inner surface of the tree throne, the vibrant life in contrast with the bony arms draped on the armrests.

Gus wondered if she was dead as the gaunt figure sat reclined in the chair, unmoving. A couple of the Crew shuffled uncomfortably, glancing at each other. Tempest stood there calmly, waiting for the crone to acknowledge him. Biting his lip, Gus resolved to keep quiet.

A small vibration permeated the area, incredibly subtle. Once he became aware of it, it became impossible to ignore. All of a sudden it was gone, but Gus could still feel the residual resonance. Tempest stepped forward and kneeled on one knee. As he began to speak, the woman came to life and stared at him with sunken eyes that seemed to smolder like an ash-covered coal.

"Ask your question," she intoned in a voice stronger than the frail body would indicate.

"I am searching for my wife, The Alchemist. We have no leads where she could have been taken and need your guidance." The words came out stilted as Tempest struggled to get them out.

"Dean, son of Alan, what you seek is in Hinansho, and it will lead you to your wife. Is that all? Then begone, tempestarii." She slumped back into her throne as before and the silence hung in the air.

After thirty seconds of quiet, Tempest finally deigned to stand again. Where was this task that everyone was concerned about? Tempest stared at the woman for another tense moment, but when nothing else was forthcoming, he turned to leave.

"But you..." A withered hand pointed at the crowd. Tempest looked over his shoulder, but she was not talking to him. Supers along the path of her finger pointed to themselves and stepped back as she shook her head. Gus stood there awkwardly as the old woman singled him out, cocking her head left and right as if seeing an oddity and trying to ascertain its function.

"Born of water, cleansed by flame, polished by air—and you yet have to embrace the earth and be born anew." She sang the words, slightly off-key.

Before he knew it, the woman had crossed the distance and Gus felt unsettled as cold fingers caressed his cheek. He tried his best not to pull away or show any signs of revulsion that would offend the woman. He stared at her eyes, which he had mistaken to be milky white and blind when he first saw her, but up close, they appeared to shimmer with iridescence like pearls. Though he could see no pupils, this woman obviously was observing him closely. The scent of balsam accompanied her movements and the strong scent cleared Gus sinuses. The scent hit Gus like a wave from the compressed air of her sudden approach.

"And an oneiromancer too." Her hand cupped to hold Gus' jaw, turning his head slightly to view him from all angles. With the additional contact, her dry, rough hands felt even colder, and Gus became transfixed as he stared at her eyes, frozen like a deer in the headlights as she assessed him. She gave his cheek a playful pat. "But you have closed yourself off from even dreams. You have a knack for making things difficult for yourself, boy," she chuckled wryly.

How does she know? Gus' instincts told him to get away and flee, but the Oracle was not done with him. His stomach soured and tightened. He was already having difficulty fitting in with the other supers in the Crew; what revelations would this crone give out to further ostracize him from the others?

"You. You interest me." She wagged a finger at him as she turned and walked back to her seat. "And that is not easy to do. It is hard not to grow cynical and jaded when you know the end from the beginning. But with you, there are possibilities and delightful uncertainties."

She spun and had a finger poking under Gus' chin, moving faster than anyone her age should have had the ability to do. She pivoted his head with a slight twist of her wrist, as he looked on in startled silence.

"I can tell you the answers to your questions. The ones you hold inside, even from yourself. But not without cost. Are you strong enough for the truth? Can you withstand its edge? I warn you, that by revealing this to you, you will not have rest for quite some time. There will be no neutral ground; you will have left it forever. Win or lose, you will have to fight 'til the end."

Her face got closer, invading his personal space, filling his nostrils with the mixture of balsam and now cloves as her breath mixed with the strong scent wafting around her.

Leaning uncomfortably close, she asked, "What say you?"

CHAPTER TEN

Something to Believe In

"I can handle it," Gus boldly replied. His eyes focused on the woman, and he noticed the colors play across her pearlescent eyes, much more captivating when viewed this close.

"Gus, no!" Tempest shouted, trying to move to intercept but Seneschal held him back.

"So be it." The Oracle leaned in close and whispered a name into Gus' ear, so softly that even he barely heard it. She put a finger on his lips. "Do not repeat it; he knows when he is revealed. It will be bad enough for you now. That is the start of your journey, keep pulling at that thread and all will become clear."

"What about you?" Gus' voice faltered. "Why would you put yourself at risk?"

"I am not part of his plans, and our paths do not cross, nor will they from here. So worry not your mind about me. Worry for yourself and those who accompany you. And tell no one of your *unique* abilities, it will go better for you if you do…" Her voice trailed off mysteriously. She glanced at Tempest and back at Gus, then nodded slightly.

In a blur, she was gone. Gus blinked and saw she faced Tempest, peering at him with stern eyes.

"You. I have but one request for your payment." Tempest winced in anticipation of the cost of the information. "Your son lacks keys. Keys that this one and this one hold." The crone pointed to BoJack and Prime. Keep them together until he has the keys and you can consider your debt paid." She waved dismissively at Tempest.

"And you." She pointed at Gus and sidled closer. "You come back when you have passed your trial of earth. We are not done, and I have a task for you. Yet you are not ready..." She moved back to her padded chair and dropped into it, collapsing as if her strength had suddenly left her. "I tire, go now." She turned her head to the side and shooed the Crew off the circle with an indifferent wave of her hand. In seconds, the crone was snoring obnoxiously and the group turned to leave.

Gus stood dumbstruck as everyone filed out. Tempest grabbed him by the arms and shook him out of his stupor.

"What were you thinking?! You *don't* want to be beholden to this woman," he growled, looking back in panic at the Oracle. He put a hand on Gus' back and ferried him out and down the path.

"You don't know how she works. You should always ask the cost before you agree!"

"You didn't," Gus retorted. This was the Tempest he knew was lying beneath the surface.

"I didn't have a choice! I have no other avenues for this information. This was my absolute *last* resort, and so I would pay any price. But you, Gus, what could you possibly need to know that badly?" Tempest pleaded, and Gus felt the defiance in him melt as he saw the sincerity in his father's eyes.

"All of this has been a huge change, and I'm still trying to figure a lot of things out—"

"Gus, *we* could have helped with that." He swept his arms, pointing to the rest of the Crew further down the trail. Tempest ran fingers through his hair. "I never anticipated this. We need to have a talk when we get on the ship." Before Gus could object, Tempest raised a hand to forestall his argument.

"There are a lot of things you don't know that I haven't been able to explain. I thought we would have discussed them by now, but I know you've been avoiding me. Maybe if I had done a better job at telling you, then this whole Oracle debacle wouldn't have been necessary. But who knows? Either way, there are some things that may change how you progress along your path and I know you would want to know them. You *need* to know them."

As they boarded the ship, Tempest led him to a small room in the back, away from the rest of the crew. There was a table and two chairs with seat belts that resembled suspenders, coming down over his shoulders and attaching to the waist belt. The chairs here were less plush than the ones in the main cabin.

"Sorry about the accommodations, but I think we need a little privacy for this." Tempest and Gus sat there, maintaining an uneasy silence. Tempest grimaced, struggling to find where to begin. Finally mustering the courage, Tempest began to speak.

"Gus, before you say anything, I realize I haven't been there for you like I should have been. I'm not going to make up a bunch of excuses, but I want you to know that I'm mostly to blame for the rift between us. There's a lot you don't know, and I think it's time we put it all on the table. I'm hoping you will understand a little better where I'm coming from and why I've made the choices I have. I'm reevaluating if a lot of those choices were wasted time, and I'm not enthusiastic about the answers."

"I'm listening," Gus said, folding his arms.

"When you were about seven and a half, your brother got his powers. You probably don't know how a legacy super gets powers, but basically the sponsor has to essentially give part of themselves to complete the process. It leaves the donor drained—"

"So they give up some of their Nth?"

Tempest's eyes narrowed. "How do you know about that? Never mind. No time to discuss it now. It may save me some verbal dancing, however. Yes, the donor gives up roughly half of their Nth to someone. The donating super loses a significant amount of levels; both total levels and skill levels are lost as the donor has less of their original Nth to support their abilities."

"Why don't they just fabricate some more?"

"How? You think they just grow on trees? There are only five known facilities that can produce Nth in the world, and the resources are extremely scarce. Anyway, I'm getting off track. The plan was for your mother to do the same with you when you came of age. Ideally, it is best for someone to undergo this process when they are around eighteen or so—after puberty and most major growth spurts have finished. Your brother was a little early. The rationale is that occasionally some Nth get dedicated to mere stat augmentation, which is not as useful in the long run because stats will naturally develop as a super levels up, and often as an adjunct with certain skills. More abilities mean more opportunities. Most supers have around six. I personally have eight, which is high." He paused, and took a deep breath and leaned forward.

"Really, eight is high," Gus said skeptically.

"Don't worry, being this new I'm sure you have one or two abilities tops. Don't get discouraged; it can take years to develop abilities. But let's stay focused on you. What happened next was kind of a perfect storm of bad coincidences. We were at your grandfather's house. You wouldn't know this, and I'm sure he never told you, but his super moniker was *The Extractor*. He had the ability to sap a super's stats and transfer them to other supers, usually distilled into a tonic. This may be hard to understand, but information can be condensed into actual physical matter."

"You don't say..." Gus smirked, thinking of the Mandrite crystal.

"The process actually created a tiny crystal, but he could grind this into glitter-sized flakes and the information was not compromised. Anyone drinking these elixirs could supercharge their Nth, as they were able to upgrade themselves with the concentrated specialized information." Tempest shook his head. "I'm not sure if any of this is making sense—"

"No, go on, it makes perfect sense."

"Okay, well, you managed to make it into grandpa's secret stash and, jealous of your older brother's new powers, you drank the entire lot trying to 'be like Alan.' Without Nth to process the information, your own cells and DNA tried to assimilate it and the results almost killed you. If it weren't for your mother's abilities you would have died that day.

"She managed to stabilize the effects but when one issue was treated, another would manifest. It was all she could do to keep you alive. I don't think she slept for three days and she was at the end of her stamina and we had depleted all of our stamina regen resources. In desperation, we contacted Dr. Weft.

"I won't go into the specifics right now, but a deal was struck. He could use dimensional folding to bury the affected areas until you could tolerate your own Nth, but it would be tenuous. For some reason, endorphins can prematurely trigger the effect. Dr. Weft actually emphasized that it was best if you were kept in states of stress or anger, as cortisol and adrenaline had a suppressive effect and would maintain the folds he had crafted.

"However, if you got overly excited or happy, you could relapse. For that reason, I tried to keep you away from things that could possibly set you off, and I know I came across as an asshole. I was. I felt I had to be to keep you safe and I know that was hard for you. I hated doing it but I realize I held you back and crushed a lot of dreams and aspirations. I hated Dr. Weft. I still hate him. For making me do all of this, and for the price he made me pay. I hope you can forgive me."

"Go on." Gus cleared his throat, the revelation hitting him like a physical blow.

"Yes, yes, I'm getting ahead of myself. The worst part was that the memories of what had happened right after involved your mother almost exclusively. Those had to be buried as well, and an unintended side effect was that not only were the memories of your mother trying to heal you suppressed, but almost all of your memories of her. When we saw what had happened, your brother and I had to go along with your assumption that she had died, fearing relapse from what would happen when you found out the truth."

"So that's why I can't remember anything from that time?"

"Yes. When you were ready, the work Dr. Weft did would be slowly reversed, allowing you to access the upgrades, and the information could be translated in a controlled manner by Nth working with your own cells to handle the stat upgrades. One stat that could not be hidden or folded by Dr. Weft were increases to luck.

"There are certain cells that have special affinities for certain stats. Intelligence for fatty tissues that make the brain, spinal cord, and nerves. Strength for muscles and certain hormone glands, like the adrenals. Luck is an anomaly and has no affinity, and as such is dispersed throughout the body with no apparent rhyme or reason. It is difficult to quantify as well, because it relies on so many factors.

"Do you remember when I discouraged you from running for some class election of some sort?"

"Yeah, I was super pissed," Gus said, feeling the heat rise in his face at the memory.

"You may not have known it, but my heart was in my throat when you announced that, because if you focused your attention strongly enough, you could have swept the election, getting every vote. Your luck stat is that high. It can affect and bend reality in ways that your grandfather and I are unsure of what limits it has.

"I think that is how the Oracle is able to do what she does, seeing and picking what needs to be done to funnel reality down a certain path. It's probably why she took special notice of you. But pay attention to me right now." Tempest turned and looked Gus straight in the eye. "You must be very careful about what you set your mind to do going forward. For better or worse, you are going to have a big role in the future of mankind, and I'm not exaggerating."

"No pressure, right?" Gus joked, trying to disperse some of the tension.

"Exactly, no pressure," Tempest said, laughing. "I just wanted you to know because it's going to be a heavy burden."

"There is always responsibility, regardless of whether there is great power or not." Gus murmured, remembering his grandpa's advice.

Tempest nodded in agreement and they sat there in silence for a while, Tempest not wanting to interrupt his thoughts as he processed all that had been said.

"What are you thinking right now, Gus?"

"Tell me about the watch." Gus held up his arm. "There's a lot of weird stuff going on and—"

Tempest held up his arms. "Right, right. How could I forget? Dr. Weft gave that to us as a way to ease you into your stats as you level. It controls the unfolding until you can manage the increases to your stats, he told us usually around benchmark levels." Tempest coughed and cleared his throat. "Your mother gave it to you right before she had to leave."

"Why did she leave at all?"

"That was Dr. Weft's deal. Until you recovered, she would have to work for him, no questions asked." Gus's eyes widened in horror as his father continued, as if in a trance. "There was nothing I could do. She was determined that she would pay any price to get you better, and she implored me to stay strong. It never occurred to me that with her gone, where would we get the legacy Nth to give to you?"

"Hindsight is always twenty-twenty. I would probably have missed that too."

"Dr. Weft went through the conditions of his 'treatment' for you. Your mother left with him when you had stabilized, but before you awoke. I was so much less without her there. I was angry at the situation, and felt trapped by the circumstances and the only release was to bury myself in work. You remind me so much of her, Gus, whether you know it or not. I thought this was going to be resolved by now, but we only had the barest sliver of hope. So that's the broad strokes." His father exhaled deeply. "It feels good to finally tell you after so long." His face relaxed as he sagged back in his chair, but his expression remained grim.

"I think it's time to go get Mom," Gus declared and looked at Tempest.

"Are you still sure you don't mind me tagging along? I know I've been trying to put myself back in your life and you may not be ready. I get why you would be angry at me. If you need time—"

"No, I'd like that, Dad," Gus interrupted. "What do we have to do next?"

"Hinansho." Tempest sighed dejectedly, his shoulders slumping.

"What's that?"

"You know what an augment is, right?"

"You mean like a Minmax?"

"No, I mean like a reg that has altered themselves to give them abilities or appearances that are beyond normal humans; they can be cybernetic or genetic."

"Alright, I've heard of them, but never really seen one."

"That's because they aren't allowed in Faction-controlled territories. Which is a lot of the civilized world. Anyway, because of this, they created their own city: *Shibogu no Hinansho*. Supers are obviously not welcome there, so we'll have to figure out a way to get in." He massaged his temples as he thought.

"I know of a slicer that could get us the access codes, but we'd need another ship. No way they'd allow this type of transport there, it's almost exclusive to Faction use and would never make it past the screens."

"What about the Manticorps ship?" Gus suggested and a bit of hope sparked in Tempest's eyes.

"Okay, okay, that should work. Now we just need to get those codes."

"Maybe I'm missing something, but she was super vague about what we should look for when we get there. Unless you have some ideas?"

"No, that's how she works. I think it limits the possibilities if she gives too much precise information. We just have to go there and see how things develop and follow our gut. If we do what we intuitively would do otherwise, we have the greatest chance of things working out. I know it's not very reassuring, but she does have a perfect track record as far as I know."

"You would know better than me, I suppose," Gus said.

"Okay, I'll tell Erika what the plan is. We need to rest up and get that ship, we may need to make some modifica—"

Red lights flashed and an alarm sounded, obnoxiously loud.

"What now?" Tempest asked through gritted teeth.

That was the last thing Gus saw before he heard a loud metallic shriek like nails on a chalkboard, so deafening that he covered his ears and closed his eyes. There was a blast of air and sudden decompression and Gus was falling again. When he opened his eyes, he saw the other half of the transport flying away as he tumbled to Earth, still secured in his seatbelt. His father was nowhere to be seen.

CHAPTER ELEVEN

Catch Me I'm Falling

Aurora had settled in for a nap again as soon as she boarded the transport. With the new ability **Tinker, Tailor, Soldier, Spy** that Gus had given her, she acquired a new tab on her display. When activated, she could open a window and design objects virtually with a fairly low MP cost. She found that by experimenting with simple designs, she gained new tabs that she could access, and then subtabs within those as she designed various creations.

At first, she had focused on apparel, which then developed the tabs for clothing and armor underneath it. Initially, she just played with the interface, but the more she designed things, the more intuitive things became. The epiphanies and discoveries became more frequent the longer she worked on a project.

So many ideas were springing to mind that she jumped from one thing to another in a very stream-of-consciousness way, without any real direction or goal. It was incredibly fun, and almost like a game to get the proper configuration and to tweak the aspects of her designs. When she had produced a viable product, a name and stat table would appear. She could save that design at that point and then work on modifying aspects to improve stats or improve how it looked.

She had already designed some cute outfits and some shoes that she would love to try on. When she wondered what she would do with all of these designs, inspiration on different materials and how to manipulate and shape them was revealed to her.

The system prompted her multiple times if she would like to sync with an established workshop to produce either the raw building blocks or even finished products depending on her own or the workshop's level. She would have to see if Gus could unlock a workshop in the manor to facilitate the production of the things she would need. It seemed like an offshoot of the Foundry, and probably wouldn't cost a lot of FP. She would get around to making things that weren't just cute but functional. Eventually.

A big surprise was that when she fell asleep, her ability created a vivid dream state where she felt she was actually *in* her virtual workshop. Playing with designs was much more direct and she could mold materials with a combination of thoughts and gestures. Instinctively, she knew how to enlarge, compress, remove, and edit her designs. Then walk around them, or simply have them rotate themselves to view an aspect of the model. She found herself trying to grab naps and looked forward to sleep just so she could tinker more easily with her designs.

Not to mention the XP! Even if she was unsatisfied with something, when she got to the point the interface allowed her to save a design, she received a generous boost to XP, so she made it a habit to save everything and then simply save future adjustments with a version number, which also gave XP once it was significantly improved. In the short time she had the skill, she had already leveled it to seven and added an overall level and a half of XP from that skill alone.

After seeing the Oracle and hearing that they would be heading to Hinansho, she started trying to design cloaks and stealth devices that could conceal one's identity. She had barely begun when she was forcefully woken, and ejected from her workshop. She had not been able to complete the design she was working on and as a result her progress was lost. She angrily looked around for the source of the disturbance to see a drone zip by her window.

Pressing her face to the plastisteel window to get a better look outside, she could see there were over twenty of the small craft, pummeling the transport with different colored beams of energy.

The transport groaned then the fuselage tore. In an instant, Aurora removed her seatbelt and was flying to match the trajectory of the ship. The engines managed to maintain some stability in the front half of the ship, however the back half began to tumble down and was lost amid the clouds, swallowed almost immediately.

Wind whipped everywhere and she had to squint as she used the chairs to anchor herself as the ship began to shimmy and lose altitude. She saw Jet sawing through Darik's belt and then allowing him to get astride like he was a witch. She saw the little man wince as he tried to maintain himself stably on the polearm, clinging on for dear life. Whatever ability Jet had to move was severely compromised with the added weight of the super, but they disappeared out the torn roof of the transport as Jet began to slow their descent. Darik's curses were lost as the transport fell away from them.

Aurora found Yuki, whose eyes were bulging out of her head. She knew Yuki needed to be ferried, as she had no flight skills of her own. Aurora held her as she fumbled one-handed with the release. Her tray table was down and she tried to stabilize her laptop as it jumped around with her other hand. At last she got the belt loose and she grabbed the laptop close to her, hugging it tightly. Aurora grabbed her under the arms and began to lift. As the ship continued to fall away, she saw Pulse burning through Grimdark's seatbelt and then the transport pulled away, engines still propelling the craft forward.

Aurora arched her back and pulled, trying to balance her MP usage to slow their descent while still maintaining enough to stay aloft. She alternated with flying and free-fall until they got closer to the ground to minimize their acceleration and then gave it all she had. The skill leveled off about a hundred feet above the ground, giving just enough of a boost to slow them from a 'certain injury' to a 'this is going to hurt' level of speed.

They hit and rolled, and a large -56 flashed in red along the side of her display. Fortunately, she had managed to steer towards a gently sloped meadow amid the trees. Yuki held on to her computer, tucked in the fetal position as she bled off momentum and rolled down the hill. Despite the landing zone being softer than usual, Aurora hit her shoulder hard on a rock before she came to a stop and pain shot down her arm. Another -118 flashed, along with an *Incapacitated* debuff to her left arm.

She finally rolled to a stop and shook as the pain intensified with her arm akimbo, straining the already wounded area. The impact drove the air out of her lungs and she gasped desperately until she could pull in some ragged breaths as she stared up at the overcast skies.

Miraculously, Yuki was unscathed and ran to her side after ensuring her laptop was intact and seeing that Aurora was hurt. As gently as she could, Yuki pulled Aurora's arm down next to her body, wincing as Aurora gasped in pain. After panting briefly, Aurora visibly settled.

As the adrenaline burned away, she felt fatigue set over her like a lead blanket. She closed her eyes and tried to manage her pain using a focusing technique they had been taught at the academy. An out-of-place high-pitched whirring caused her to snap her eyes open. Three drones approached out of the sky, flying directly towards the women.

Yuki forward rolled and deftly picked up her laptop. She began typing, staring at the drones approaching ever closer. Aurora tensed as she saw the beam guns underneath the drones begin to cycle up as they charged. In unison, a red light burned to life and they fired.

CHAPTER TWELVE

Cruel to be Kind

Aurora flinched as the superheated rock near her exploded, pelting her with debris and kicking up a plume of dirt. The tang of singed hair and dust filled the air. Just as she was about to cough, a hand slid over her mouth. Blinking away the grit she saw Yuki there with her finger over her lips. Turning back to her screen she continued typing, occasionally wiping dust away from the screen. The whirring of the drones dropped in intensity. A slight breeze began to clear the haze around them.

Yuki sent a party invite and Aurora accepted. It was customary to drop all party links when a mission was over so people could relax on the trip back to base. Unfortunately, that meant they were on their own until they found the rest of the Crew.

"Okay, we should be in the clear now," Yuki replied, the edge evident in her voice. "I altered their targeting and have changed their checksum algorithms to show mission completion and targets eradicated. We should follow them to see who is behind all this."

Yuki turned to her laptop and three tracking dots appeared on Aurora's minimap.

She whimpered as she sat up and the weight of her arm stressed her dislocated shoulder.

"There's no way we're going to keep up with them," Aurora gasped as the drones sped off into the distance.

"Don't worry about that. I've installed a file that should ping us when they get to anywhere there is a free connection. We're tuned in on their frequency, and I've set them to track even when we get out of direct transmission range. I just love the connectivity the satellite matrix allows." She looked up at the ever-darkening clouds. "Those could be a problem though. I'm only at 37% battery life on the laptop. I can use solar to recharge but with this much cover, it'll be harder to get a satellite link as well as recharge my laptop. Without it, it's going to be a *lot* harder to get back to civilization. First, we have to see who attacked us and why.

"Who even knows where we are? And they only brought drones to a super fight? Seems more like a delaying tactic rather than an attack. We should be on our guard for what comes next."

Aurora had to agree. A glance at her display showed that it was a little past 5 PM, and that it would soon be dark and cold. Snow capped the tops of the mountain ranges nearby and the sun was almost slipping behind one of the large mountains. A stab of pain drove out any attempts to plan for the future.

Aurora got to her feet, brushing off the dust as much as possible. Her shoulder was clearly dislocated, and Yuki's eyes followed hers as she assessed the damage.

"Let me know when you're ready," Yuki acknowledged, shaking her arms to loosen up before getting herself in a balanced stance for the gruesome task ahead. The academy was good at getting you trained to expect the unexpected. Especially with challenges that fell outside your power's skill set.

"Can you pull some of those gels out of my pocket? The red ones, they're on that side."

"How many?"

"Two. No, three. Take any if you need some for yourself."

Aurora winced as she had to hold her wrist and support her arm, the mere weight of it caused stabbing pain all around her shoulder socket. "It feels like... hot icepicks are jammed in there," she grunted through clenched teeth. She instinctively clutched her arm closer to her

"Here." Yuki held out the gels and Aurora opened her mouth for Yuki to put them inside. She bit the corner of one and slowly sucked out some of the gel. Her breathing slowed as it eased the edge of the pain.

Aurora knelt down so the shorter woman could get into position. Finally, she released the protective tension on her arm, allowing Yuki to put firm hands on her inner bicep and outer forearm. With a grim look, Aurora nodded to Yuki.

Aurora had to fight back the scream that wanted to rip through her, but she had to keep the gels in place. Her nostrils flared like an angry bull as she tried to breathe through the pain. Yuki exerted an ever-increasing pressure on her arm, and Aurora was glad she wasn't standing as the torment intensified, or she would have buckled and fell as the intense pain caused her whole body to tremble.

With a *pop*, the joint reseated and there was another burst of pain. Aurora bit down on the gels in agony as the intense pain finally began to diminish. Yuki eased her to the ground as she went boneless, her rigid muscles draining away their tension and with the release she slumped down.

She continued to hear unsettling gurgling and cracking noises and saw her suit ripple as the damage was repaired from the inside, distending the skin and suit as they worked. After her breathing had returned to normal and the easing of the pain-induced vertigo, she wiped away some tears that had combined with the flour-like dust covering her.

Yuki helped her to her feet and she slowly began to move the arm again, testing its range of motion, massaging her upper arm and shoulder as she rotated and twisted. In a couple minutes, the pain was replaced with a mild itch as the Nth began the next phase of repairing the muscles and damaged tissue now that the bone was reset.

Finally feeling a bit better, she took in more of her surroundings. They were fortunate to have found a small clearing with a tiny creek running through it. Due to its slow movement, the water was green with algae and other swampy-looking materials, and didn't look appealing to drink.

The area was encircled by tall conifers, and a mountain range encircled them. Since she had fallen asleep to design, she had no estimate for how far the transport had gone or where they possibly could be. A chill wind blew past and she hugged herself and massaged her upper arms to generate a little heat while she took in the situation.

Before she could ask, Yuki slid something from her display and Aurora's minimap updated. They were somewhere in Colorado, their exact location unclear, but a large yellow circle on the minimap displayed their most probable position.

"Let's get a shelter built, then maybe I can cobble something together so we don't lose any juice for this laptop."

Wondering if her crafting skill would work, she activated **Tinker, Tailor, Soldier, Spy**. Under the Soldier tab she found simple plans for forts and barriers to withstand infantry advances. A cave would be ideal, or at least a rocky wall to reflect some heat and give a little less area to guard from the elements and predators.

A subskill under the Soldier tab was called **Quarter-master**. Curious, she activated this skill and a ring pinged out to about twenty feet before rebounding to her and disappearing. A few branches were highlighted, as well as some components and kindling for a campfire. That would save time hunting for things, but they still needed a place to make it through the night.

Sliding the display over to Yuki, she could then see the highlighted objects. She looked at a downed log here that had the name:

Downed Timber (Small)
Component in small shelter, crude-tier weapons, and basic frameworks.
More blueprints available from experimentation or increasing skill level.
Breakdown for following components:
Firewood
Kindling
Ash
Sap

"If you want to gather some stuff for a fire, I'll try to find someplace I can build a shelter."

Yuki threw a thumbs up and tore into a piece of gum she had, chewing aggressively as she gathered pine cones and small twigs.

Aurora walked up the meadow and found an area where some trees were growing in a small alcove. The area below was clear, but large branches reached up over the area, giving it extensive cover above. Enough so that it would protect them from the rain.

"I think I found it; bring what you've gathered over here and we'll set up," Aurora urged on the mental link.

Yuki came kicking some larger pine cones with arms already loaded with smaller versions that occasionally shifted and abandoned ship, leaving a trail of them as she tried to balance the ungainly kindling.

Aurora had already started gathering branches, fallen leaves and dead grass to make mattresses for them. With the raw elements highlighted, she quickly found what she needed. By concentrating her **Ion Storm** into a beam, she was able to adjust the heavier parts that would make the frame of the mattresses so there was less to drag.

"I'm seeing the value of sleeves on uniforms now," Yuki griped as she saw the scratches on her arms where the pine cones had dug in and pinched or scraped.

The two returned to their tasks and when Aurora had

finished, she got the design up to the point where she could save it.

Save template? (Y/N)
250 XP gained for crafting Leaf Mattress 1.0
Tier: Rudimentary

Aurora hit yes and looked at what she had wrought. They looked like tiny pigsties filled with leaves and grass. They were only about a foot and a half tall, but they should be high enough to keep them from getting wet or rolling down the hill.

Yuki hadn't been a slouch while she was making their beds. A fire pit had been dug and lined with smooth, wide rocks. A square log-cabin with thin branches leaning against it was in the center of the pit, and dry pine needles peeked through the tiny spaces left in the construction.

Smiling her way, Aurora thanked Yuki and pulsed a small burst of energy into the center of the pine needles, controlling the flow so that it didn't collapse the wood. The tree above should offer enough protection from rain. They didn't have any tarps or waterproof materials that could serve as a tent, but the idea stirred Yuki to action.

Yuki knelt and removed a large belt and buckle from her outfit. Flipping it over, she unzipped a long zipper that extended from one side to another, revealing two folded rolls inside. These she unfurled above and below the plane of the belt, and two flaps consisting of multiple zippers were aligned in series on the material, each having at least ten zippers about two feet wide.

Opening the fourth zipper on the top flap, Yuki stretched the mouth wide and retrieved a small penlight from the open hole. Holding it in place with her teeth, she aimed the small beam inside, and reached in and pawed around the compartment.

Aurora peeked over and saw that it was very organized, but everything was packed in super tight.

Yuki found what she was looking for and set down the light and leaned into the zipper. After a brief tug-of-war, she came back with a handful of silver squares in cellophane pouches. She closed the zipper and grinned like the cat that got the cream.

"They're space blankets! Have you ever used them?" Yuki huffed in exasperation.

"I've heard of them, but why would you have them?"

"Computers are delicate things; you've got to protect them from the extremes, both hot and cold. These things can be a lifesaver in the right situations. And we just happened to find one of those."

They unpackaged the blankets which seemed to have a -5 debuff on stealth with the noisy way they crackled and murmured as the crinkly material rustled against itself as the women bundled up by the fire. They were smaller squares, only about four feet on a side, but Yuki had pulled out six packages. They were able to mummify themselves adequately just before the ambient temperature plummeted noticeably when the sun dropped below the mountains.

Yuki turned back to the zippers and came back with some instant ramen cups and two large bottles of water. She also had some contraption that looked like an oil filter that she added water to and set next to the fire, dropping in some twigs and pulling a tiny hot coal to add to the center of the cylinder of the strange contraption. When the fire was going, Yuki pulled out a narrow teakettle and set it atop the tiny stove. Finally, she set out a line of wood to keep it going. Aurora gave a curious glance.

"It's a BioLite Campstove. It generates electricity. The narrow kettle heats the water a lot more quickly as all the water is above the flame." She cocked her head and put her arms on her hips. "What? Why are you looking at me like that?"

"You're much more… prepared than I ever thought you would be, like an Asian Mary Poppins."

"You can blame my mom for that. She always overpacked, and it must have carried over. Still, these are the best for holding all my gear. I have everything I could possibly need right at my fingertips."

They stared at the fire as it slowly cracked and popped, occasionally adding in another piece of wood. Yuki plugged a USB into the BioLite and the laptop, being careful to keep it as far away from the flames as possible without tugging on the small cord and tipping the tiny campstove.

When the water was hot enough, they made their ramen and ate quietly, both trying to process the day and what tomorrow would look like. The warm broth helped thaw the chill that Aurora didn't even know was settling upon her as she wound down from the excitement of the day.

Aurora looked at Yuki, and realized that she really didn't know her that well. Casual acquaintances that could recognize each other, but she knew nothing of Yuki's upbringing, how she got her powers or why she had come on this of all missions.

"So what's your story, Yuki? We usually don't see a lot of hackers in the field; they like their lairs, takeout, and fountain Mt. Dew. What brings you out here in the middle of nowhere?"

Her eyes pinched in suspicion. She stared a good minute at Aurora, as if assessing her intentions then relaxed. "Might as well tell someone."

CHAPTER THIRTEEN

Break My Stride

"How do you see me?" Yuki asked, lips pressed into a tight line.

"You're part of the team—"

"No no no!" She violently extended her raised palm, stopping Aurora from continuing. Yuki closed her eyes and inhaled deeply. "Before this mission, how did I fit into the Faction?" She spoke slowly, each word having a slight edge as she carefully enunciated them.

"Well, I knew you worked with computers…"

Yuki opened her eyes and gestured in a circular 'go-on' motion.

Aurora struggled to add anything more, and succeeded only in stuttering and stammering.

"…and that was about it, wasn't it?" Yuki finished as if this was a foregone conclusion. She turned to look at the fire, using it as a focus as she continued. "I could see what was going to happen if I kept doing what everyone wanted me to do. I would be the IT girl, always fielding inane questions and getting the computers to work again. You probably wouldn't understand since you've been in the field so often. But this was my chance to show what I could do. I didn't really know Tempest's wife like most of the Crew who volunteered, but I had to do it. I'm not going to let myself get funneled into that job. I feel like I have so much more in store for me. I'm not going to settle for that. It's not why I joined a Faction and went through all that training." She turned and looked Aurora in the eyes, and the flames of the campfire were reflected in barely restrained tears.

"My strengths are almost all mental. I probably should have gone Green Faction, but that would be the same as working for a corporate thinktank. Using my abilities to datamine and make money for someone else. All under the guise of helping the Faction.

"My father is watching me like a hawk, waiting for me to fail. His pride was bruised that I did not agree to work for the family business. Seeing my powers as just another asset that he could leverage to surpass the frenemies he works so hard to impress. While they work just as hard to show some ridiculous superiority through their own business successes. My brothers all fell into line, and rebellious little Yuki is destined to bring shame to the family playing with supers."

"Yikes. That sounds like a direct quote." Aurora winced in distaste.

"It is," Yuki spat, "the kind said intentionally loud enough to be heard by the intended target, complete with the accompanying mock embarrassment. I'm not saying that I have everything figured out, but I know I want more than the limited things others have planned for me. I'm almost to the point that I enjoy their shocked and offended looks." She shifted on the rock she was using for a seat and wrapped the space blanket around her tighter, gripping it with clenched fists before going on.

"Well, it's probably more accurate to say that I'm getting numb to their disdain." She turned back to the fire, coughing and clearing her throat. "I think I need to prove to myself that I can make it in the field. But so far I think I'm doing pretty damn good."

Aurora turned and looked at the fire as well. "You've been doing awesome so far. And thanks."

"For what?"

"For sharing that. I have been so driven to progress that I haven't really worked that hard at creating any relationships within the Faction. Either that, or I've been promoted into departments where I haven't known anyone. I guess after a while I just focused on the job at hand. I doubt many people know about my past either."

"So tell me," Yuki remarked simply.

And so Aurora did. It was easier to tell the story while looking at the fire. Relating her past as if it had happened to someone else. It *felt* like it had happened to a different person. Yuki didn't interrupt, and encouraged her with occasional acknowledgements. Soon she had summarized her time with Purple Faction, and how she had ended up on the station, and how proud she felt to have progressed to the command of such a prestigious position.

Then she related the attack on the space station and her time in Manticorps' dungeon. She decided to edit out discovering her Nth and when going on to discuss the events that happened on the island, giving a truncated version of what had happened there. She had no real reason to do so, but she felt that if Gus wanted to fill in the gaps about everything then she would let him do that. Aurora could tell by her occasional glances at Yuki that she could tell there was more to the story, but Yuki didn't press.

A loud rustling sound distracted her as she was nearing the end of her story where the Crew arrived on the island. She stopped and looked over at Yuki, who was unfurling and opening a zipper on her belt. Yuki reached inside and came out with a handful of oblong packages.

"Sorry, my stomach is starting to grumble. What sounds good to you? Let's see… I've got: birthday cake, red velvet, peanut butter fudge, chocolate chip." She held up the packages to the firelight to read the writing on the covers.

"Let me try the red velvet."

Yuki tossed the package over to Aurora and she unwrapped

the meal bar. The difference between the protein bars at the manor was evident as she bit into the flavored wafer that was as good as any candy bar. She hadn't realized she was hungry until she started eating and Yuki threw another bar over, seeing Aurora scarf the first one as quickly as she did.

While the cafeteria had done a good job at making meals, desserts weren't really an offering, and sometimes she just had a craving for something decadent. The second bar turned out to be peanut butter and Aurora took more time to savor the chocolate coated treat. She closed her eyes and exhaled deeply.

"Yuki, you are a lifesaver." Aurora sighed.

"I love these things. The owner of the company is a super who has specialized in molecular gastronomy and I don't know how he gets these to taste so good with what's in them and how good they are supposed to be for you. Better living through superpowers." Yuki licked her fingers, removing some of the white cream-cheese frosting from the cake bar.

"What else you got in there?" Aurora scooted over closer to Yuki and they checked out what else was in the stash. From there, the conversation drifted into less intense subjects and the two laughed and bonded under the bright starlight far into the night.

CHAPTER FOURTEEN

Connection

Sitting in the small room, BoJack had to admit he was impressed. Unlike most airline lavatories, the ones on the transports were of a decent size, most likely to accommodate larger supers. The ample sink space and large mirror could be an influence of female supers as well. Plus a little privacy was nice after being around people for weeks.

He liked the brief solitude a bathroom break offered. He'd have to look into a suit redesign as well. He didn't know what was more of a hassle, the suit getting untucked and exposing his midriff to attack or when he had to take care of business and practically undress to answer the call of nature.

The transport rocked violently with some turbulence, and he bounced in the air off the toilet. He hit with a loud *_clack_* as the rim was slammed down when he fell back upon it. His face contorted in revulsion at the sensations that he had felt with the brief bounce.

"Should have done that courtesy flush," he muttered regretfully.

Then the room dipped and he was free falling.

After healing, BoJack's second most evolved ability was the

manipulation of light into solid constructs. He usually fashioned them into different thin appendages and had worked his way up to controlling six independent constructs. Forming a sheet next to his exposed posterior he pushed away the offensive material and sealed the barrier sheet like cling wrap over the toilet, tying off the construct so he could focus on the next task at hand. He struggled to wiggle back into his suit which was more difficult than one might expect while free-falling. Once his arms were in, a construct arm zipped him up and he burst out of the lavatory.

"Definitely redesigning this damn thing!" he shouted.

The wind whipped furiously and the tail of the transport was dipping. BoJack extended more cable-like arms to grab the seats and climb towards the breach as the section of the ship became nearly vertical. When he was four rows from the top, he saw Gus finally wrestle free of his seatbelt and dive out. BoJack kept an eye on him as he propelled himself up and out. He leaned forward, arms at his side like a bullet and was gone.

BoJack scrambled to get out and follow as he modified two of his constructs to wing-suit shapes on either side of his body. The constructs caught the wind and slowly he pulled away from the falling wreckage. He could hover by using his cables as propellers, but he couldn't propel himself like other fliers. He wanted to be as far away from the transport as possible in case something decided to explode.

If only he could have reached Gus first, he could have attached a cable to him like he was water skiing. BoJack threw out a party invite to Gus, hoping that he wasn't out of range.

"Act faster next time," he berated himself. His cheeks began to burn as the air rushing past began to chill him. He extended a construct to cover his exposed skin, as well as protect his eyes. Immediately, without the distraction of the air blasting against him, he could see the snow and trees rapidly approaching below him. He adjusted his posture, trying to slow his fall. When he noticed no slowing, he pushed the edges of his construct out further, hoping to create more drag before he was among the trees. He was managing to stay around twenty feet above the treetops, following the downslope of the mountain below. Suddenly, the forest dropped away and he was over a deep ravine. He breathed a sigh of relief until he saw another wall of trees ahead of him on the opposing rise.

He leaned hard to one side, trying to turn parallel to the ravine, but he was approaching too fast. He closed his eyes and braced for impact. He barreled into something and found himself spinning in another direction. Expecting a sudden stop and intense pain, he opened his eyes and saw Gus circling around trying to catch up to him. His trajectory was altered and he was spinning upwards, tumbling like a fly ball. Instinctively, he extended four short propeller cables to stabilize himself. They slowed his spin but were insufficient to stop him from corkscrewing toward the tree line again.

Another jolt and he stopped spinning. Gus held him a bit awkwardly, like he was trying to give him the Heimlich. BoJack vanished the propeller cables that whipped close to Gus' face and they leveled out. The trees below fell away, revealing a large lake nestled between two steep rises.

Their descent slowed and with a clumsy landing they both slipped and slid on the round rocks that lined the shore of the lake, but managed to keep their feet under them. Staggering to a stop, they both remained bent over, arms on their thighs as they caught their breath.

"Thanks, mate," BoJack said over the mental comm.

Gus nodded and gave a weak salute. When they had both caught their breath, Gus motioned for BoJack to follow.

"I saw a large section of the transport go down over here," Gus motioned towards one particular rise. "There's no smoke and I didn't hear it crash so someone must've helped it land without damage." Gus began to fly again as the dense under-growth surrounding the lake became a thick mass.

BoJack extended multiple cable arms and used them to climb up to the treetops and held himself aloft as the cables snaked out and found purchase points. Gus was impressed at the super's skills, appearing like a scuttling spider as the cables bounced him along, swaying to maneuver around trees. Occasionally, one cable would break the branch underneath it and he would dip a bit, but there was enough support from the other extensions that he never seemed in danger of falling.

"Who do you think attacked us? And why?" Gus asked over the mental link to break up the monotony of travel.

"Can't rightly say. Bloody rude of whatever egg decided to attack us though, especially when I was indisposed." When Gus looked over with confusion on his face, BoJack quickly went on, "Never mind about that. So tell me about yourself, Gus. We haven't really had a chance to get acquainted, but I think you did right by the team when fighting those wraiths. I think all of us were wondering how you would handle yourself."

Gus was unsure of what to say or where to begin. He really had no framework for what was normal among supers in general and what was kept close to the vest. The words of the Oracle about not discussing his unique abilities. Which ones were unique? They all seemed a bit strange and new and, from what he had gathered from Aurora, there seemed to be no cohesive theme to his powers as it seemed like most supers had.

"You okay, mate?"

"Sorry, just trying to figure out where to start. I didn't get my abilities until a little over a month ago. It's kind of been a whirlwind and I'm still figuring things out."

"No worries, cuz. Why don't we do this: I ask a question and then you ask one and we go back and forth to pass the time. I'm sure you have a lot of questions; I know I did when my powers first arrived. Go ahead, ask me anything."

Gus exhaled and he felt his tension drop a couple of notches. He felt awkward opening up to someone who was almost a stranger, but BoJack's encouraging smile soothed his usual need for privacy. *Oh, why not?*

"Well, lately I've been feeling kind of overwhelmed," Gus began, surprised as the words spilled out. "I don't really know what's normal when supers interact. I mean, I got along fine when it was just me and Aurora, but I kinda feel like an outsider when everyone is in a big group. I don't know where I fit in, and don't really know how to break the ice, so I've been staying to myself."

"That's not really a question, but I can see you're having a mare about this." Seeing Gus' confusion he amended, "I see you're having a tough time with fitting in, which is understandable. Let me tell you our side of the situation and then I get to ask my question of you.

"All of the Crew went to the Academy years ago, and we've all been on countless teams and missions. Some of them I know better than others, but we have a feel for everyone's abilities and personalities. It's considered kind of impolite to be too nosy about someone's powers, but working with people in training and on missions, you get a feel for how they work and how you can support each other.

"Not having any idea of how you fight or what abilities you possess has made you a bit of a mystery. Up until that last fight, we didn't really know what to expect when things got serious. Some trainees fold early on and never make it out of the Academy, so we never have to deal with that in the day to day. I think we all breathed a collective sigh of relief with how you managed yourself.

"Some supers are too reckless and others are too timid. You need the right blend of balls and brains to support the team. I'll bet you made your dad proud with how you held yourself and weren't afraid to jump in and help. That says heaps in my book."

"Well, thanks, that's actually encouraging to hear. I think I'm still a bit starstruck being around you guys. You seem to have it all down."

"Don't put any supers up on pedestals, cuz. We're all just people. Don't ever let yourself forget that." BoJack's naturally ebullient, friendly voice turned serious and severe. "I'm serious about that. It's kind of in the super handbook to project this aura of control and authority, and for the most part everyone believes it. But just so *you* know, a lot of us are faking it until we make it."

Gus nodded in surprise as BoJack continued, "So what has been the biggest change since you got your powers, Gus?"

Gus blew out a breath. He knew the answer but was hesitant to say it, but figured, *what the hell.*

"I think I'm still trying to find out what I want to do with my powers and how life is going to be different. I won't lie, I was on cruise control for a long time as a reg and now I'm having all these ethical dilemmas and trying to figure out what to focus on and improve. Lately I've been kind of stagnating compared to how I was progressing earlier and it's a bit frustrating."

"What have you been doing? I'll try to help you out—don't worry, I'm counting that as my second question, so you get to ask two."

"Fair enough. First, I was fighting zombie Dark Nth left on the island and I was gaining skills left and right. Then I was…" Gus almost talked about leeching powers, but quickly revised it to, "…fighting supers to keep the manor. But now that has slowed down and there's not as much XP to be had."

"That's to be expected. My abilities improved a lot in those early years. Now I have to innovate and apply my current abilities in inventive ways if I want to gain any XP at all. So if I get this right, you've just been fighting and training skills? What about crafting?"

"I've done a little bit making shelters on the island and even making clothes. That's about it. Unless you count **Ether Weaving**."

Gus kept flying forward and when the silence dragged on, he looked back to see BoJack standing agape, having stopped crawling across the trees.

"What?" Gus asked, flying back.

"You're serious? You have an *ability* named **Ether Weaving**?"

"Yeah. What's the big deal? I thought most abilities use it to some degree or another for their powers."

BoJack looked down at the swaying tree tops below, as if studying something there.

"Tell me already," Gus said, worry starting to edge into his voice.

"Are you really telling me you have no idea?"

"Does that count as question three?"

CHAPTER FIFTEEN

Dream Weaver

BoJack shielded his eyes as he looked at the sun.

"Let's head down and set up a camp. This may take a while and I don't want to be distracted."

They descended through a narrow gap caused by a fallen tree, breaking the dense canopy of trees. BoJack reminded Gus of a lineman working on an electrical pole with how his cables slid down the trunk to the tree.

The scent of pine grew thicker as they settled to the forest floor, dense with fallen needles. It was also much darker with the branches overhead blocking out the waning light, making it seem later than it was.

"Okay, long story short, Gus, is that I think we both could really benefit from working together. Are you familiar with mentors as it relates to supers?" BoJack's eyes were wide with excitement and his eyes darted around as if trying to plan and assess multiple things at once.

"Nope, sorry."

"That's what I figured. No matter. I'm going to assume you don't know anything about history as it relates to supers, but let me know if I go over some things that are redundant. There's a lot to cover and fortunately I can show you some things that will help with making our camp so we can kill two birds with one stone. To get through this, you may have to save some of your questions until the camp is set up, just so we don't get bogged down. Do you know how to take notes on your display?" He was speaking frantically and it was difficult to understand him as he rushed to get information out.

"Go to the gear icon in the upper right and access settings. Got it? Now scroll down to storage, then under that tab should be notes. Try asking a mental question once that's open."

What should I ask?

The text filled in the blank page, and Gus nodded at the utility of the new feature.

"You can do a lot with that section of your display, but since you haven't been trained at all, there's probably a lot other supers take for granted that are a mystery to you. That section can also take pictures and video if you need it for future review. I almost always have mine running during an active mission so I can review it and see my performance. The Faction can actually stitch the team's experience together and you can see how you performed through another's eyes. It's a bit trippy, but also very helpful for feedback.

"Getting back on track. I'm surprised you have **Ether Weaving**, as that's rare to have as a simple ability. While many powers manipulate ether in varied ways, they only manipulate it in a limited fashion. It frames how they access and express their will when they activate a skill."

"So that's a good thing, I'm taking it?"

"Oh, more than you know. I have a skill called **Ether Design**. **Ether Weaving** is one of the subskills that I picked up fairly early after I developed powers, and is just one way to interact and manipulate this material. That's a big part of how I use my ability. I've never known anyone who can do what I do in the same manner. I want to see how you access your ability and what it looks like to me, then give you some feedback. Next,

I'll create something and I'll show you how to change your approach to do the same."

"So just try to make what you make with ether?"

"Yes. If we work together, I get XP for training you and you get XP from learning new skills. I don't have any direct experience being a mentor, but I've heard that the quantum computer is very generous with XP allotments."

"You know about the quantum computer? What about Nth? I didn't think they trained supers about that."

BoJack threw his hands out to stop the barrage of questions. "Put those in notes for now, we'll get to them. They're important and part of the history lesson that you need to hear in a bit. For now, would you show me how you use that ability?"

"Alright, just a second." Gus noted his questions, surprised at how many popped into existence in the minimized window. He then looked upward trying to recall what to make. He settled on a simple basket and wove the ether threads, tying them off and securing the construct midair.

BoJack cocked his head as he examined the basket as it swung lazily there. A single cable extended and poked and prodded at the basket.

"Not bad for a newbie. And did you say you haven't developed any crafting skills?"

"No. I've heard that's another way to get a decent amount of XP besides battling or leveling skills."

"Yes, yes, it is…" BoJack said distractedly, squinting his eyes at the bands of ether that made the approximately gallon-sized basket. "Gus, what energy do you use to fuel the construct?"

A dumbfounded expression swept over Gus' face. "What energy do I use? I'm not sure what you mean by that."

BoJack turned back to the basket and grabbed one of the strands with two cable constructs. He looked at Gus apologetically. "May I break this?"

Gus shrugged okay, and BoJack pulled apart the section of basket. It began to thin and then held as the cables trembled a bit when it stopped stretching. There was a tiny *snap* that sounded like getting shocked with static and the weave fizzled out of the cables holding it, burning like a fuse as the construct unraveled and disappeared. BoJack sped to observe it from different angles before it was totally consumed.

"Fascinating," he drawled in amazement, then stood scratching his head staring at the blank space where the basket had been.

"Okay. That was different. Kind of changes things a bit, but we'll work with that."

He shook his head to clear it and then turned to Gus. "Alright, I need to shift gears for a bit here. Gus, can you see this?" BoJack outstretched a palm in front of him and then put his other hand above it, like he was seasoning his lower palm with salt. He then drew it upward and a six-inch shard formed over his palm, floating in the air. BoJack pinched it to taper the upper point of the shard but did not touch his fingers. When he drew them away, Gus could see that the top of the shard was open. He could also see that what he was observing was visible by its outline on his display, but not visible to the naked eye.

"You can see that on your display, right?" BoJack continued as he saw Gus nod. "It's a plain construct of ether. The only thing sustaining it is the faintest whisper of energy from MP. Now I'm going to infuse it, so watch."

BoJack looked upward to the small breach in the trees above and a thin fiber of light began to extend down, ending in the empty shard. Immediately next to the thin filament, everything became as dark as pitch, the intensity of the darkness lessening the further away from the strand.

Gus looked up as it disappeared above, catching an occasional glint as the thread appeared to literally catch and suck in the light. An increasing glow caused Gus to shift his gaze to the shard, which was slowly brightening with a shimmering soft white glow. Beads of golden light dripped off the end of the thread and pooled in the shard. The intensity increased to the point where Gus couldn't look directly at it anymore, and squinted his eyes as he watched BoJack motion with his upper hand and seal off the shard. He handed the tiny crystalline construct to Gus.

Turning it around in his hands, he expected it to be warm like a light bulb, but the shard felt like a simple piece of glass. Looking at it end on end, he could see that it was a perfect hexagon shape in cross section. He handed it back to BoJack.

"Now we have light for the night. You probably couldn't see it before, but this ether construct is selectively permeable. The interior looks like a mirror so the photons are maintained inside. Only at a certain angle will they be able to pass out, but enough photons are packed in there that we can have light and this will last until the morning. This is called infusing a construct. Your basket appeared to be infused only with MP. I can detect no other type of energy associated with it. An interesting application, but unfortunately it is pretty inefficient. I can create a construct like that for one or two MP. I'm not sure how much you used but I'm sure it's way higher than you actually need."

"You want me to make another one and check?"

"Maybe later. Do you have any powers that use something that you recognize as a form of energy? Whether it's heat, electricity, magnetism, anything as long as it's something that affects matter in the conventional sense. Try not to find anything that is powered directly from internal energy, but one that uses ambient or external sources to power it."

Gus pored over all of his abilities and only three seemed to be relevant. **Krackle**, whose description only mentioned "energy" but not what specific type. Then there were **Shake** and **Shatter**, which used vibration or kinetic energy.

"Got one? Now it's your turn. What did you decide on?"

"Vibration?" Gus said, fearing he would be wrong or misunderstanding the concept.

"Excellent! We'll need a heat source and that will do well. It will not be as long-lasting as other types, but it'll give you practice on creating more. Depending on the type of energy you are trying to infuse, that will dictate what form your construct needs to have. You need something that will perpetuate and preserve the energy as much as possible, but still allow some to escape somehow. It's best to pick something you need, such as this crystal giving light or your vibration providing heat. Mind you, it doesn't have to be heat, you can use the energy to turn a turbine that creates other effects but let's keep it basic for now." BoJack tapped his lip with a finger as he thought.

"We'll need a fire for the night, how about that?" Gus asked.

"I like how you're thinking, but let's make sure you understand some things first. One of the things you need to think about is how to collect and change energy into a usable form, while at the same time streamlining the transition so it's efficient. That may sound easy, but often it's the hardest part of this type of crafting.

"Ether in and of itself is an inert form of matter. It requires some other form of energy to help it maintain its form. In one sense, that makes it incredibly versatile as you can use many types of energy to achieve the same ends. The drawback is that if that energy is not maintained, a construct will quickly fall to pieces."

BoJack was becoming more animated the more he explained. "Am I losing you yet?" he asked, peering at Gus from under bushy eyebrows.

"What about tying something off? I have made some things and it helps them stabilize if I tie them off."

"Yes, yes. Exactly. It's probably easiest to think of like a balloon. You can inflate a balloon with air, but if you don't manage a way to retain that energy, it will rapidly escape. Unlike a balloon, however, a collapsing construct can be very, very bad. Not always, but it should be avoided. Think of a fireman's hose that is fully engaged but unmanned. It can whip around and cause damage or injury if not controlled. Now imagine the hose is filled with gasoline and is on fire. That's probably a closer approximation."

"Whoa." Gus looked upward, imagining the sight while BoJack continued animatedly.

"But yes, if a construct is formed correctly, it can retain the energy inside and use that to maintain its form. The more ideal the container, the less energy is drained away to maintain the construct and it has more permanence. With vibration, there are a lot of ways to generate energy and heat. How familiar are you with how that ability functions at a fundamental level?"

Gus screwed up his face. "Not... very? Sorry."

"Okay, that isn't great, honestly. Vibrational energy can be propagated from waves, like a sound wave hitting a tuning fork. It would help to know exactly how you generate the energy to know how best to capture and maximize the energy."

"Why don't we just test it?" Gus offered.

"I guess just give it a try on this piece of wood and see what happens, then we'll try it on something with more internal energy."

"Internal energy?"

"Hmm. It's complicated, but some materials have more ability to absorb and transfer energy. Just like some metals can be affected by magnets but many cannot due to their molecular structure. For now just try the ability on both, and I will observe." He handed Gus a broken twig about the thickness of a finger.

Gus activated the ability and found that the dry piece of wood shook, more aggressively at the end opposite of where he was holding, until it snapped in two. BoJack took a ring of keys out of his pocket, removing one and handing it over to Gus. He activated **Vibrate** on the key and at first felt a numbness envelop his thumb and forefinger where he grasped it. Despite the loss of sensation, he noticed immediately when the key began to heat up and he dropped it, shaking his hand wildly.

BoJack watched Gus like a hawk and knelt down to look at the key where it lay in the dirt. He poked at it until it cooled and then inspected the edge. Once he ascertained that the key wasn't permanently damaged, he fished out the ring and slid it back in place.

"So it appears you are manipulating ether in and around a material to move in different directions. Just think of a wet sponge in a microwave. Your ability is like microwaves, causing the water in the sponge to rotate, which in turn causes the whole thing to gain kinetic energy and heat up. This will be ideal for you, because while this generates heat, it typically dissipates fairly quickly.

"Now you just need to make your construct. You can make a simple box and put water in it and vibrate that or play around and develop something new. I'll leave you in charge of that so we have heat, but make sure you clear a spot and keep things under control. We don't want anything exploding or burning the forest down. Start *small*. If we need to, we can start a campfire, but this will give you something to begin with that won't blow up in your face. I'm going to show you how to sculpt a box out of ether, then you see if you can copy me."

Using his fingers, BoJack touched his fingertips together then spread his hands outward. A thin film like a soap bubble began to form. It reminded Gus of how he had to exert a pressure to create the interior of the dimensional bag. As he reached a certain size, he changed direction and the corners of a box formed, as if he were stretching plastic wrap around an invisible container.

He maneuvered gently again, forming the upper corners, then he stretched the film over itself and around the opposite corners on the top of the forming box. Slowly pinching his fingers, he sealed off the construct and plucked it out of the air where it hovered, handing it to Gus.

It appeared the same glasslike substance the shard was made from and he gingerly picked it up, fearing even slight pressure would shatter the sides.

"You don't need to be that careful with it, it's fairly durable. Go ahead, try to squeeze it."

Gus pushed in with a finger on one side of the box, expecting it to implode and possibly cut his finger, but he only saw the smushed imprint of his fingerprint through the transparent box. Gripping it more solidly, he tried to push in with both thumbs and the box resisted any type of flexure or deformation.

"Ether constructs are like that. They have a high resistance to elastic deformation because they actually store that as a form of energy instead of breaking. It actually gets stronger the more stress placed on it, until the whole construct fails cohesively. But it takes a lot to get there. I was able to break your basket weave because it relied on MP too heavily to keep it intact. Once you refine your constructs, it will become intuitive which containers best hold different forms of energy."

"I still don't know what energy you're using to do that."

"Don't worry about any of that for now though. Just use MP to manipulate the ether into a box, we'll use the energy to sustain it. I think you can modify your weave to do this same thing, just try to make a band that is wide enough to copy what I have done, and mentally manipulate it into the shape you want. I'll be working on our shelters while you do that. If I finish before you can manage a decent heat source, we'll call it good and just make a campfire. Sound good, mate?"

Gus nodded and turned his attention to trying to form a box from ether.

"Ah, ah, ahhh," BoJack said, wagging a finger as Gus started stretching his hands apart as he had seen BoJack do. "You're infusing it with MP already. You want to manipulate ether without filling the box at all. It takes a bit more finesse. Think of pulling it rather than pushing it."

Gus shook his head and focused on the space in front of him. Instead of his typical method of blowing a bubble he tried imagining tiny fish hooks grabbing a section of ether. On his display a blob of ether resolved into a tiny sheet as he delicately pulled the corners outward. The hooks were glowing in his display and he could tell that his MP was funneling into them, but it was at a much lower rate than his usual MP drain. As Gus tried to form the corners, the film popped and dissolved.

"Um, yeah. Corners are hard. I should have mentioned

that. At first keep them rounded; it's easier to maintain force along a curve than at a sharp point."

Gus tried again and was able to make a box that resembled a square bar of soap. As he brought the top of the construct over itself, it blended, forming a single layer. Ever so slightly moving his fingers closer, he slowly disengaged the hooks and the shape wobbled but stayed.

"Quick, grab it," BoJack urged. Gus grabbed the construct and turned it around in his hands. "It looks like you have the basics, ah. That's nice. I just got a ping!"

At the same moment, Gus also got a notice on his display.

CHAPTER SIXTEEN

Gimme Shelter

Far away from the camps of supers, the final remaining eight drones clustered together. The more there were, the better their processing power. They ran through scenarios, attempting to find the optimal plan to achieve their programmed goal. That goal was to destroy those who had gained the master's attention.

Unable to tap into local area networks, they became severely limited in this remote location, away from the typical transmitters that allowed them to piggyback off their signals. Their targets turned out to be supers, who had managed to destroy a majority of their number as they defended themselves after the drones attacked. Unfortunately, this variable had not been presented and resulted in more losses than expected.

Among these supers, a statistically improbable number could fly and thus avoided death, despite the loss of their ship. The trajectories of the survivors were calculated and options evaluated. Due to the limited number of drones, remaining tactics and options were evaluated and the drones sped away in different directions as they reached a consensus.

Gus felt a surge of hope when the message surged onto his display.

Skill gained: Ether Crafting (Level 1)
Ether Crafting: *You now have the ability to shape ether into various vessels to contain energy. This ability unlocks the ability to **learn** elemental forces, but you have not currently gained control of any of these affinities, merely the opportunity to learn of them. Experiment with constructs to discover insights.*
Affinities learned: 0/12
Affinities mastered: 0/12
1000 XP awarded.
4,160 XP to level 21.

"Check this out!" BoJack said with delight, sliding a message over to Gus' display.

Skill gained: Didact (Level 1)
Didact: *You have unlocked the mentorship skill tree. As a result, you gain a percentage of XP based on how effectively you train your protege. Current: (Tier I) of XP increases to skills related to your training.*
Note: This applies for one month after you have completed your final training session or when protege stops gaining XP advancement in skills, whichever comes first. Continue to cultivate their growth to maintain Didact bonuses.
Current skills training: Ether Crafting
1000 XP awarded.
26,895 XP to level 62.

"That's pretty sweet," Gus congratulated BoJack.

BoJack tapped his temple with a finger. "At higher levels you have to work smarter, as well as working harder. Training positions are coveted in the Academy for this reason." His face sobered, excitement stilling as he turned to look Gus in the eye. "Thank you for trusting me. I'll do my best to train you well. It's rare for the skill to unlock in general, so now that it has, you've opened a new path of progression for me."

"No problem," Gus shrugged, trying not to make a big deal out of the chance for him to learn; he was probably getting more out of the deal than BoJack ever would. Finally, he could start progressing again. He had been training but felt like he had hit a plateau, and the XP gain was much less than he had become accustomed to when allocated based on contribution when fighting in a group.

While it was good to learn that type of teamwork, it slowed down any kind of progression. At last, he had a bit more control over his own growth, with new avenues to explore. This could be his very own personalized academy crash course. As he distractedly thought of the possibilities, he could see that BoJack was looking at him expectantly. *Did he say something and I missed it?* Gus tried to diffuse the intensity of the moment, blurting out the first thing that came to mind.

"Dang, XP requirements really go up as you level. 62, huh? How is your Nth interface after the sixth change—" *Stop babbling!*

Gus snapped his mouth shut, realizing he may have committed a series of faux pas asking about strengths or levels.

Seeing his distress, BoJack's face softened again. "Relax, I was going to explain some of the unsaid stigmas we supers have. Why don't you keep working on your ether constructs? Don't try filling them yet, but focus on making as many as you can. Without infusion they will dissipate, but don't worry about that. Finish one and start working on another. Unfortunately, this is mainly a trial and error process that takes a lot of practice before you will get ideas on how to optimize the constructs. I'll explain while we work. You have caught on much more quickly than I expected. That gives us time to discuss some other things that you need to know."

BoJack extended two cables in front of him which merged and formed a blade similar to a bulldozer. He trudged forward and cleared a swath of the forest floor. Gus turned his attention back to forming constructs as BoJack began.

"I suppose the best way to start explaining is to see if you know anything of the Rockland conflict?"

"Doesn't sound familiar," Gus replied, shaking his head.

"I'm not surprised. A lot of effort was put into erasing that bit of our history. I get a feeling you know what an Nth is?"

"Yes, I call mine Nick."

"You're referring to the interface. But I guess that's what I mean as well. They're what allow us to access our abilities. From what I know of you, Gus, you're new to powers and Nth assistance, correct?"

Gus began stretching the ether again, fighting against his reflex to manipulate with anything but the faintest of MP assistance as possible. "Yeah, but I thought that was kind of not common knowledge, Nth and all."

"I could tell you had an idea about Nth. You responded with recognition when it was mentioned, instead of the blank looks that us veterans usually see.

"I'm afraid that's all tied together. There's been a shift in how supers are trained now. In short, the Rockland conflict was a failed coup of a coalition of younger supers, augments, and hybrids. To prevent further uprisings, the system for training supers was modified in an attempt to control and manage the strength new supers could reach.

"At its core, it was to maintain the power base of the old guard—I personally think it will come back to haunt us as we are creating a weaker, less effective group of supers. Hobbling the next generation to avoid dissent is cowardly and unbefitting what we should be standing for as supers. Inflexibility is what ultimately led to the conflict and 'winning' and the resultant fallout only compounded the problem."

BoJack threw out cables from tree to tree above the cleared space, anchoring them. He then created wide bands of material, rolling it out from his outstretched arms. The area became visibly darker and colder as the ambient energy and light were sucked out of the area like a sponge. After securing the sides of his ether tent construct, the area appeared to brighten, but not to the level it was before. It reminded Gus of a time-lapse video from early dusk to twilight.

The sudden chill motivated him to focus again on his constructs, realizing they may need more heat than expected with all the crafting BoJack was doing. He returned his attention to making containers as BoJack continued.

"Communication with Nth personality constructs was discouraged and it was found that, as a result, the new generation of supers could still improve their skills and level them without interaction with an interface. However, their overall levels stayed the same and they couldn't apply any stat increases their Nth unlocked. New supers did not have access to the exact quantified data that a display offers at all.

"Somehow, they adapted to get a general sense of where their HP or MP was. Fortunately, they could see HP bars above enemies, which is essential in battle, so things settled out and have been the same ever since. The Factions shared their findings and it became pretty universal. Know this though, Gus..."

Gus peered over his shoulder as BoJack stopped talking.

"The veterans are counseled never to speak of this. I could get reprimanded or even demoted for sharing what I have. I have always disagreed with it, but I'm not ignorant of the shift that's been happening in our Faction in the last couple of years. We need to make some big changes. This has created more of a rift than it is preventing, and it becomes more pronounced the longer it is maintained. You can't tell anyone of this, Gus. Not yet. Hopefully things will work themselves out, but I'm not confident in the direction we've been heading."

"It's in the vault," Gus replied and BoJack nodded, turning back to his task. From there they finished their preparations without too much new discussion. Gus was caught up in thought, both with crafting and checking his XP gains, and BoJack had fallen into a somber mood as he went inside the ether tent and was working out of sight.

When he had finished, he poked his head out and motioned Gus to come inside.

"Bring those ether vessels as well."

Gus scooped up as many as he could carry, surprised that he had made so many while they talked. He expected them to clink together as he gathered them, but they did not respond like the glass containers they resembled. Dropping a couple of them on the way, Gus elbowed into the flaps of the tent and saw that BoJack had made bunks, two chairs, and a small table at the far end of the tent.

He set the ether vessels down on one of the cots and BoJack grabbed some, motioning for Gus to watch. BoJack created a simple piston that seemed to compress the air inside. He set it aside and the piston kept working with barely perceptible clicks. He picked up a couple more and repeated the process, then let Gus finish the rest.

At first it was difficult to maintain the simple machine parts, but after referring to the others that BoJack had made and altering his approach, he was able to duplicate his first piston. His next one was a failure so he picked up the initial container BoJack had infused and was surprised to see it was very warm, bordering on hot. Setting it down quickly, he put his hand over it and felt a mild heat radiate from the small container.

"You'll have to recharge them after a while but they usually keep going for about four hours, depending on how much MP you channel in there," BoJack answered Gus' unasked question when he saw Gus trying to puzzle out his next construct. "Don't be afraid to put a lot in there, the ether can handle it, and then you won't have to wake up in the middle of the night to recharge them."

Gus spent the rest of the time charging mini heaters and when he looked over, BoJack was already asleep. The walls of the tent held out the night and the insides quickly became a comfortable temperature and Gus rubbed his eyes, deciding to settle down for the night.

Regardless of when he had made them, the pistons all fired

their soft clicks at the same time and the sound relaxed him. Gus had to shake himself and slapped his cheeks a couple times as the increasing warmth was making him drowsy.

Can't sleep! That was close.

Gus murmured mentally then turned and grabbed out the Quorian cube. Spinning it, he found another surface to evaluate. *Purple? Why not? I need something to occupy my time.*

CHAPTER SEVENTEEN

Hot in Herre

Aurora awoke, her coughing pulling her out of sleep. Orange light flickered off the low hanging clouds and the smell of the campfire was overwhelming. Rubbing her stinging eyes, she blinked and saw that it wasn't their campfire at all, but a thick haze hanging in the air.

Realization struck her as she reached over and shook Yuki.

"Fire!" she yelled as Yuki moaned, curling tighter in a ball, wrapping her blanket more tightly around her.

"Yuki, get up!" The super lifted her head pleadingly, eyes still closed. Tasting the air and licking her teeth she grimaced in disgust.

"What the...?"

Aurora cast the crinkly blanket aside and hauled Yuki up to her feet.

"Hey, get away. I'm so tired..." Aurora helped Yuki walk away from the orange glow as fast as she could, urging her to move faster as she stumbled like a marionette with only Aurora to prop her up.

Despite Aurora's best efforts, Yuki's lumbering foot caught a rock amid the pine needles and she fell onto her face. The impact was enough to shake her more fully conscious and her drowsiness turned to anger as she turned and glared at Aurora. For the first time she saw the hellish light reflected above and Yuki scrambled to her feet and began to run in earnest.

"Let's go, Aurora, stop goofing around!" she yelled as she tore off. Aurora rolled her eyes and followed after. There was enough illumination from the reflected light that they could see in front of them, their shadows stretching in front of them as they ran away from the conflagration. Yuki pulled up a collar that looked like a turtleneck and covered her mouth and nose and continued running. Aurora masked her face and created a small bubble of ionized air over the back of her hand.

The tang of ozone wasn't the best of smells, but it beat smoke inhalation. The sterile air had an almost bitter taste to it as she gasped as she ran. Aurora saw the back of her hand visibly darken as particulates in the air were drawn to it. The women ran downhill, half sliding, half running to outpace the flames. The clouds above began to flicker ever brighter as the fire increased in intensity. A hot wind began to flow past them as the superheated air rushed by, as if to goad them into faster flight.

Ahead of them the trees thinned then disappeared. Yuki skidded to a stop on the rocky surface, seeing that there was a sheer drop off, looking back in panic.

"Just go!" Aurora shouted but Yuki desperately shook her head no. Changing direction, Aurora tackled her in a bear hug and, using her momentum, propelled them both off the rocky edge. Her shoulder flared its displeasure at being used before it had totally healed. It had recovered enough she had forgotten about it, but the impact woke it with a vengeance.

Aurora winced as Yuki screamed directly in her ear as they fell downward. Struggling to keep her eyes open she began to fly as well as she could, but they were still dropping precipitously. Her shoulder hurt the longer she held Yuki and the distraction drew away her focus as they plunged downwards into the darkness until they hit the bottom.

———

Less than a mile away, Gus settled in and activated **Electronic Mind** and stared at the purple surface of the cube. He felt the pull inside, although there was more resistance as he entered this go around. Not much, but it felt like pushing through gelatin. Once he had squirmed through the rubbery barrier, he found himself floating. Trying to determine if it felt more like being underwater or floating in space, he ultimately decided it was somewhere in the middle.

There had been mandatory zero-g training on Graviton's station, so the sensation was not altogether unfamiliar. Unlike reality, he found he could propel himself along with thought. Checking his MP, he found that he had not activated flight or any other ability, but he had more influence in this plane of the Quorian than he had in the others he had visited.

Turning to take in the surroundings, he noticed a series of floating islands off to his left. Giant amethyst crystals glowed and pulsated on the undersides of these islands, and Gus could resolve a paved pathway on their flattened tops. He drifted toward the nearest one and found that as he got closer something akin to a magnetic attraction pulled him securely to the surface of the island. Taking a couple steps, he felt as if he were walking normally, none of the sucking feeling of walking through a muddy bog that the magnetic boots often had while on the orbital station.

Besides the path, there was not much on this island, so he followed it until he reached the far edge. Kicking a rock off, it tumbled forward into space, following the trajectory of his kick. Looking down, he could see only billowy lavender clouds, moving imperceptibly. If he peered for a while, he could see brief bursts of what he supposed was lightning, intensifying the deepness of purple for a moment before fading back to normal. There was no thunder that he could detect.

In fact, he did not notice any sound at all. He clapped his hands and noted no noise was produced. He could breathe normally though. An attempt at talking let him feel the vibrations in his throat but as the sound reached his lips it was quickly absorbed by the air around his mouth. He tried a scream to similar effect, leaving him more aware of his blood pumping more notably from the strain of his prolonged scream.

Looking ahead, he saw the next island ahead and above him slightly, so he backed up a bit and took a running jump. He soared upward as if assisted, the effect much like using the **Bound** ability. He actually overshot the edge but like before was able to change his trajectory and drift down to the next rock.

This island was bigger, having exotic plants populating the sides of the path. As far as he could tell they all looked various shades of purple extending to an almost black on the leaves and stalks. He silently moved ahead and traversed a dozen more islands before he saw a castle looming on a massive island.

Upon reaching it, he saw that it was in severe disrepair, with large sections missing from the walls and ramparts. The broken sections were much higher than the ground, and as Gus attempted to jump up to gain entrance to the castle, he found that he was back to normal in terms of movement. He could not drift or fly either. Looking back at the previous island, the gulf between him seemed much too wide to pass if his change in mobility stayed the same.

Moving to one of the large sections of wall, he sat on one that reminded him of the "S" shape in Tetris. Instead of supporting his weight, the massive piece of stone tipped over like a movie prop, tumbling him onto the ground.

Gus leaned forward to touch the stone and found that without even contacting it he could move and position it. He extended his palms in front of him and lifted the large stone easily in the air. Twisting his right wrist the piece rotated clockwise and counterclockwise. Pushing his left palm forward or back rotated the shape away and towards him. Once again, this took no MP and he showed no active abilities on his display.

Setting the rock down, he put his hands on his hips and looked up at the castle ramparts. Picking up other pieces of debris and manipulating them, his inner gamer began to see some distinct patterns with the broken sections on the ground.

Gus found his original piece, which was one of the smaller ones, and manipulated it up into the broken rampart. After positioning it, he 'set' the piece and it clicked in place just like a Lego block, locking in position without the need for mortar. Nodding to himself, he set to work trying to fix the broken walls.

It turned out placing small pieces first was a mistake, as there was no place for the larger pieces. It quickly became obvious that there were enough stones in the rubble pieces to entirely rebuild the section of the rampart and no remaining openings, so Gus put himself to the task of fitting everything together. The pieces snapped apart just as easily when he had to remove them, but he could only manipulate one at a time.

Once he flipped a piece and inverted it, he could see how its unique configuration would slide into the right side of the breach. After that, the other large piece could only fit one way and this drastically cut down on the area he needed to fill. As he slid the last piece in place, the edges of the bricks flared and the rampart was whole again, becoming indistinguishable from the remaining intact sections of the castle.

Gus found that he could no longer remove the individual pieces either. A large portcullis stood to the right of the section he had just repaired. After a minute of nothing happening, he went up to the bars and peered in, but could see only darkness as he held onto the cold steel bars. There was nothing to manipulate here, no handles or levers, so Gus began walking around the castle walls.

As he turned the corner around a cylindrical tower, he saw another section of broken rampart. Thick vines had grown around the blocks in this area and Gus had to pull on certain vines and untie them from knot-like growths to free the blocks before he could set to repositioning them in the wall.

Instead of rectangular blocks, these pieces were hexagonal and took much longer to manipulate and get in a correct orientation. Instead of putting them up on the wall, Gus climbed onto a tree thick with vines and used the vantage point to flip and turn the blocks until he finally managed to get them to fit together.

An advantage to this approach was that as two blocks connected in a correct way, a purple light would flash and the pieces would connect. As before, it became much easier once a couple of pieces were in place, and after much trial and error, Gus had the entire section back in place.

There were four more broken walls, each with increasingly difficult challenges. There were smaller sections which increased the time it took to figure out how to place everything. Tougher knots encircled pieces and some were partially buried in the ground. Then there were extra pieces that did not belong in the wall that increased the time it took to single out what belonged and what did not.

Finally, when he had the last piece in place there was a tension in the air, then a popping sensation. Gus rattled his jaw left and right and he could hear again. A rasping noise could be heard in the distance like stone sliding across stone, peppered with the tinkling rattle of chains.

Gus jogged back to the front of the castle and saw that the portcullis was raised, and torches had sprung to life along the corridor leading inside. He walked an unnaturally long time before finally seeing daylight glowing at the end of the corridor. There was no way the walls could be that thick, but it was probably due to some way the cube functioned. Gus wondered if this was a simulation, another dimension, or what he was actually experiencing as he came closer to the end of the tunnel. Loose dirt and an arena could be seen ahead as if he was entering a coliseum.

The realization made him tense up and he slowed down and warily exited the tunnel. No one attacked, but a large blue window opened up in the center of the large arena. A pleasant female voice cooed, "Welcome back, Dr. Flak."

Gus read the screen.

Directory (Amethyst)
- *Sapphire: Hybrid Research (Mammalian)*
- *Ruby: Transdimensional Effects*
- *Citrine: Hybrid Research (Insectoid)*
- *Emerald: Augments and Enhancements/Blueprints*
- *Diamond: Mandrite Crystal Research*

As he gazed at the different options, a portal would open under the display and the dominant color would populate the inside of the portal. The edges looked like a liquid form of neon that appeared to flow around the borders of the portal. Gus sensed that it would not be a good idea to touch it, but his curiosity did make him wonder what *would* happen if something did graze the edge.

Gus recognized the circuit board walls visible in the augments and enhancements selection, as well as the jungle tinged with orange. He was about to step through when he smelled a pungent smell. At first, he thought it was coming from the portal, but as he deselected any of the choices from the directory, the smell persisted, becoming more pronounced. Something was burning. He could see no smoke but began to cough. It became so persistent that he exited the cube.

When reality had snapped back into place, he was shocked at what he saw. Through the milky opaque walls of the tent, he saw flames on every side.

They were somehow in the middle of a huge fire.

CHAPTER EIGHTEEN

Die in a Fire

Gus began to panic as the air became more difficult to breathe. Somehow, BoJack lay there still sleeping, mouth agape. Gus shook him violently and he blinked to life.

"Whass goin' on?" he asked dreamily.

"We're on fire! It's all around us!" He spun back and forth, looking at the orange and yellows flickering just outside.

BoJack yawned, unmoved by the news. He tapped Gus on the shoulder. "Calm down. It'll be okay. I'm interested to see what you think we should do though. How would you handle this? What are the challenges, and what should be done?"

"Can we do this later?" Gus asked impatiently.

"No, this is perfect."

"How are you so calm?!"

BoJack scrubbed his face with a hand as he stood and fixed Gus with a stern look. "I'm calm because I know myself and what I'm about. You want experience. This is how you get experience. I could have you show me your abilities and what would be the best to do in this situation to quickly resolve everything. But you have to train yourself to think. I know with the few abilities you have, it may be difficult to think out of the box, but you have to get used to stretching yourself. If you want XP, you're not going to get it staying in your comfort zones. The greatest gains lie just outside of what's familiar, tried, and tested."

"But the fire…" The words died on his lips as he saw BoJack stand there unflappable, arms serenely folded, awaiting Gus' assessment. "Okay. It doesn't seem hot in here, even though the flames look right outside. And it's fairly smoky, but nothing like it should be in the center of a forest fire, so why is that?"

BoJack nodded encouragingly and Gus continued.

"So is the ether acting kind of like a heat sink, somehow? That's why it isn't hotter?"

"Good job. Unlike other materials, ether has never been infused to failure. It has a yet undetermined upper limit for energy absorption. That's why we usually use it as a container for different types of energy, because there are at least five phases that we know of as more energy is pumped into ether itself."

Gus looked nervously as the oranges became brighter, crinkling his nose at the permeating smoke. "Should we…?"

"I guess the term 'infusion' is a misnomer, because we are not really putting the energy into the ether itself, but inside of a shaped compartment of ether," BoJack continued, as if he didn't sense Gus' distress. "And no… we shouldn't. Don't let yourself get into the habit of relying on your powers instead of your brain, Gus. Think it through as if the fire weren't there. Compartmentalize."

Gus coughed on the smoke as he took a deep breath to relax. *He mentioned containers, is that some sort of hint?*

"You remember how easily you broke my basket weave earlier? Why didn't it just resist your efforts to tear it? If ether absorbs energy, wouldn't it resist your efforts to stretch it?"

"Because ether has no will. It can be manipulated by some people and even though you created it, I also can manipulate ether and was able to affect it. If I had tried to light a fire or use a laser to cut through it, that would be a different matter. Does that make sense?"

"Ehh, sort of," Gus said, wobbling his hand palm down.

"I don't understand it all either. Just that our Nth allow us to interact with this stuff we call ether based on our intentions with enough consistency to produce reliable effects. Depending on how well it is crafted, it has extreme durability. Look at our tent. I'm sure your perception stat is above ten?"

"Of course."

"Good, then you have some form of an *Identify* skill. I'm not sure what yours is called—they're all over the map name-wise—but it lets you get information from the environment, translating Nth passive scans into data you can use."

*That must be **Wreckognize** for me,* Gus thought.

"Have you used that skill for any type of problem solving?"

Gus squinted one eye. "Like how?"

"Scan the environment. Everything. And really look. What are your problems right now that you need to solve? Hold that need in your mind as you scan and look for what catches your attention."

Gus activated **Wreckognize** and slowly looked at the inside of the tent. He expected to see a leak by the entrance of the tent, but his scan showed the sides were sealed. He looked closer at the flaps that made the doors. *If they're sealed, why is it getting smoky?*

Gus just stared at the doors, trying to understand what was happening and, like a small focusing of a camera lens, he intuitively knew a tiny bit more about the walls of the tent. The effect was strange, because they weren't blurry to start out with, but the resolution was more vivid. Maybe a better description would be he upgraded to a televid with more resolution.

Whatever had happened, he could see that the tent had some properties of a permeable membrane. It was letting oxygen in and carbon dioxide out. As the oxygen concentration was used up, it tipped the balance, allowing a slight bit of contamination to pass through in an attempt to increase the amount of oxygen inside the tent.

"Huh," Gus murmured with the realization.

"I know that look. What have you got?"

"I just saw how the tent lets oxygen in and carbon dioxide out. And I think I know why it's smelling like smoke in here."

"It also lets out methane too, mate. Didn't know if you were a gassy sleeper or not, but definitely something to think about in close quarters." He winked at Gus. "Keep going."

"So, if we wanted to get more oxygen in here, maybe we could extend a periscope up above the flames to access some clean air?"

"Where do you think all this hot, smoky air is going?"

Gus frowned. "Yeah, probably straight up."

"Don't get discouraged. This is exactly the process you need to get used to doing on the regular. Then get quick at making these kinds of assessments and acting. If this were a real crisis, I would grab the reins but, as it is, we're safe and you get a good field exam out of the bargain."

"I guess I could make one laterally, but I don't know which direction the fire is coming from." Gus looked over at BoJack expecting some form of hint, but all he received was a raised eyebrow.

"Okay. Maybe that's the wrong problem to be solving. Besides air, I need to do something about the flames. If ether is such a good heat sink, maybe I can use it to absorb or contain some of the energy."

Gus thought he could use his **Energy Absorption** ability and just drain the energy from the fire, but didn't know if he would *learn* anything from that. Plus it was probably best to keep the full range of his abilities as close to the vest as possible.

Turning to BoJack, he asked, "How do you infuse something?"

"It depends on the type of energy. You have to think of what's happening at a molecular level and make it easier for the energy to go where you want it than where it already is."

Gus bit the inside of his cheek. He had always taken wood or paper burning as something simple to understand. But knowing something would burn was a far cry from knowing what was happening to it as it burned or why it burned when other things didn't. He scrambled to think of what he had learned back when he was in school. *Wasn't it something to do with energy being released as bonds break?* He honestly didn't really know.

"Why do you not just check?" Nick asked, somehow infusing a disappointed sigh into the words.

"Check? How?" Gus asked, but Nick had gone silent again. An idea popped into his mind that he almost immediately dismissed but then thought better of it. *Worth a shot, I guess.*

Gus knelt on one knee by the door flaps and placed his hand where the flaps and the floor of the tent met. Initially, he thought they were on bare ground, but with **Wreckognize** engaged he noticed there was a floor, it was just transparent in relation to the opaque walls. He hadn't even noticed they weren't tracking dirt around inside the tent until he made the realization.

He closed his eyes and focused on extending an ether construct to the outside, connecting it to the inside of the tent. He extended it outward, finding it difficult not to use MP to force the shaping. He could sense the container growing at a measured rate, a perfect two-by-two inch plank extending outward. Meeting some resistance, Gus turned his focus for **Wreckognize** onto his construct.

After a slightly nauseating disorientation, Gus had another point of view. He could see a strange panoramic view of everything around the construct he had made, giving the world a strange fish-eye effect. It was blindingly bright at first, but reflexively he lowered the intensity to a manageable level. Flames danced around the construct, with areas near the corners becoming blurry, the sharp edge not giving a good resolution of things in the 3 o'clock and 10 o'clock positions.

Focusing on the construct, Gus shifted the construct from a square to an oval shape, resembling a snake. This took away the blurry areas and he perceived that the end of his construct had struck against a tree trunk, halting its progress. Altering the trajectory of the construct he began to curve around.

The flood of movement and visual information gave him an instant case of what he could describe best as 'car sickness.' Sizzling drops of sap and burning debris fell amid the flames, landing in front and onto Gus' construct. Only by dialing down the visual input to a bare minimum could he have enough information to bypass the tree and continue out in a fairly obstacle free path.

After pushing the construct about fifty feet away, he began to notice a strain on his ability to keep it intact. Breathing deeply, he kept visual input to a minimum and turned his focus to his surroundings, imagining himself as if he were the construct. As he stayed there, he became more attuned to the little snake-like tube of ether. Melding with it.

He could feel the energy from burning pine needles and sap around him, quickly dispersing as it touched his skin. His attention turned to the energy touching him. Everything grew as his attention focused on a smaller and smaller area. A pine needle became as large as an aircraft carrier and he could see a combination of gasses released then being consumed as the needle burned.

Scale magnified over and over and particles sped away like bullets and hit his skin of ether. Bullets which grew to the size of beach balls then beyond. As the huge particles hit the ether, they came to an abrupt stop that reminded Gus of a pool ball hitting another and stopping as the force was transferred.

In comparison, the ether particles were tiny as sand, shifting slightly with the impact but quickly returning to their original configuration after a brief flutter. Gus watched in fascination as the incoming projectiles suddenly stopped after hitting the ether, reminiscent of a spaceship dropping out of hyperspace from some of his favorite movies.

How do I use this, though...?

The thought echoed in his mind as he pulled away from the

construct, becoming a little light-headed as he retreated to a normal perspective. After things settled, he had an idea that might kill two birds with one stone. He didn't know the exact design, but he pushed the intention of what he wanted down the length of the construct. A pump that would convert the kinetic energy of the heated particles to pump oxygen into the ether snake he had made.

With satisfaction, he felt the microscopic pumps form like gooseflesh all along the length of the construct. As the pumps began to do their work, they robbed the fire of an oxidant and the fire guttered and died in a swath around the ether. Gus pushed out in different directions, this time using the energy of heat to fuel the creation and snake after snake unfurled like New Year's Eve party favors.

With the insurgence of clean air, the smoky smell dissipated and the light playing immediately outside the tent dimmed more and more. Gus kept pushing, and while the areas near their tent became inert, the flames continued to sustain and allow the ether constructs to extend further and further away from the tent.

An indeterminate time later, Gus found that he could reach no more. Using **Wreckognize** again he saw that around his network of ether constructs remained blackened char and ash. He let his constructs drop and blinked back to himself. At some point he had fallen back on his butt, his hands in front of him, palms up.

A slow clap sounded over his shoulder and Gus turned to see BoJack beaming at him. He wiped at a tickle on his chin and saw that a thin trickle of drool had slipped out somewhere along the line. He hurriedly wiped it away before BoJack could see.

"I did not expect *that...*"

"Did I do something wrong?"

"Oh no, mate. I thought you'd give it a go and then I'd have to show you something to mimic. You were quite in the zone there for a bit. How are you feeling?"

"Better now, kind of like I just took a good nap, actually. I feel oddly comfortable and relaxed. Is that typical?"

"Hmm, not that I know of mate, but that's choice. Good on you for figuring that out. I knew you could do it. I'd check your logs. Probably some good news there, if my guess is right."

Some of the accumulated strain from not sleeping had significantly dissipated somehow through crafting and focus with the ether constructs. He basked in the feeling for a moment akin to a mental massage. When he opened his logs, he found BoJack was not wrong.

CHAPTER NINETEEN

You Don't Know Jack

You have leveled up the skill: **Ether Crafting** *to level 2!*
100 XP awarded.
200 FP awarded.
You have leveled up the skill: **Ether Crafting** *to level 3!*
150 XP awarded.
300 FP awarded.
You have leveled up the skill: **Ether Crafting** *to level 4!*
200 XP awarded.
400 FP awarded.
3,710 XP to level 21.

"Is that it?" Gus mumbled aloud. "I thought there would be more levels or XP." Gus thought he saw BoJack wince a bit, but it could have been his eyes playing tricks on him. It was dark again in the confines of the tent without the open flames raging.

"What did you level up to?" BoJack asked.

"Only four in **Ether Crafting**."

BoJack grabbed Gus by the shoulders, turning him to look directly at him. "That's actually amazingly good. I can see we need to work on perspective with you. It's just strange that you have no frame of reference so you can't tell what is a great gain versus normal progress versus a plateau. Listen to this, Gus: don't let yourself get discouraged. At level five, you may be able to unlock a healing sub-skill of **Ether Crafting** and can start cross-leveling, which gives you double the XP for the same effort." He let go of Gus and sat back on his cot, leaning back and crossing his legs.

"Healing *and* crafting? What's that all about?" Gus questioned.

"It's a little complicated. Let me see if I can explain. Most of the other supers don't know this, but my wife and I were doctors before I ever became a super. It's how I discovered my powers, and I got mine late in life, relatively. How old do you think I am, Gus?"

Gus assessed the man. "I'd say late twenties, early thirties."

"Try seventy-three years old."

"Seriously?"

"Yeah, mate. Seriously. I started out as a healer and evolved to other specialties, but that's what I am at my core. It does have some fringe benefits."

"Okay, you've got my attention," Gus said as he followed BoJack's lead and sat on his cot.

"I got my powers in the early Nineties, when powers were fairly new to the world. At the time, I was still working at an internship while my wife was working full time at the same hospital. This was before supers were in control of most of the world's governments, and it was a different time.

"To handle the stress of my workload, I had taken to meditation and a lot of visualization. Whenever I did my rounds, I would try to visualize what processes were suboptimal and what needed to happen to make my patients healthy again. Somewhere along the line, patients under my care started having an unusually high recovery rate."

Gus leaned forward, listening intently—he loved origin stories.

"After a while people began to notice and accompanied me

on rounds, but no one noticed that I was doing anything that was out of the ordinary or special. Hell, I didn't know what I was doing either. Things were going well for a while, then we had a series of challenges all at once. I won't go into it, but it was an incredibly hard time for me and my wife. And it only got worse from there. Ultimately, the issues took over our whole lives and I left my internship and stopped practicing medicine altogether."

Gus sat up straight. "Were you indentured? I heard medical school was so expensive most people agreed to be conscripted to cover the cost."

"No, fortunately. But I was rolling in seas of debt. On top of that, I was in a really dark place for a long time, I had lost so much. I was never suicidal, but it was so difficult to find any reason to go on. For a while I just existed, taking no enjoyment from anything, yet refusing to give up for some reason." BoJack sat there for a while, lost in thought, despair etched on his face. Gus wanted to know what had happened but felt embarrassed to pry. With a deep sigh, BoJack continued.

"I was fortunate that I got another chance. I had really let myself go, and I sold everything my wife and I had owned. I now deeply regret losing all those things that I just gave away when I was in my funk. I long for just a single memento that she just had to have to turn our apartment into a home. She really got into the whole nesting thing. It was never really important to me at the time, but she made that space ours. When she was gone, I just let it go. Maybe they were just painful reminders, tokens that proclaimed that she was gone. Either way, I wish I had kept at least one."

The way he worded that sounded like she had died... Gus realized.

"We lived in a lower rent area of town that was close to the hospital, so we wouldn't need transportation. Student loans came due, and since I was not working, I was sliding down a slippery slope, avoiding the inevitable crash and loss of the little I had. Were it not for one of my neighbors, I'm sure I would have ended up homeless and probably would have died on the street a short time later.

"An immigrant family that lived next door knew my wife well, and me as an acquaintance. They respected my wife, the doctor, and I could tell the mother wished her daughter could reach similar success in this land of opportunity. Well, one evening I heard a frantic pounding on my door.

"I had fallen asleep on the couch and probably hadn't showered in a couple of days. I had gained forty pounds and the apartment was a mess. Like college-days level of neglect. Food cartons and discarded clothing were everywhere. Had the knocking not been so insistent, I probably would have stayed on the couch and slept there the rest of the night. Have you ever felt like that, Gus?" He turned his cold blue eyes on Gus. They appeared to glow with feral intensity.

"I've been down, but in comparison, nothing as extreme as that."

"Anyways, somehow I did manage to mosey over to the door and found the neighbor there, holding her daughter in her arms. There was blood everywhere, and I recognized the frantic, desperate eyes of a parent whose child may not make it. She pleaded with me to do something in her broken English, and I motioned her inside.

"Kicking away garbage and debris, I ran to grab a clean blanket from a laundry basket. Fortunately, I had done some laundry the week before—even if I hadn't put it away. The girl must have been around six or seven years old, and looked like a broken baby bird as her mother gently set her down. I distinctly remember hearing a voice in my head saying: 'Now is your time.' I shook it off and assessed her injuries.

"Apparently, she had fallen off of something, but I couldn't make out if it was the fire escape or some playground equipment. When I touched the girl, though, something was definitely different." BoJack broke his gaze with Gus, eyes growing distant.

"Unlike my time at the hospital, I felt like I could see what was wrong with her. Her femur was broken in multiple places, one very close to the growth plate. With her age, I knew that if things healed incorrectly, one leg would be much shorter than the other, affecting her for life. Like riding a bike, my mind fell into visualizing the system working perfectly.

"I didn't realize it then, but I was creating an ether structure to position and stabilize the broken shards of bone, gently guiding them to where they needed to be. Small probes of ether pulled apart the surrounding tissues under her skin so they wouldn't be damaged by the movement of the sharp pieces of bone.

"I made patches from ether on her torn femoral artery and others that were leaking precious life blood out of her poor little body. When I say I did this, I only realize what I had done, now, in reflection. At the time, I just acted, pouring my whole self into making her healthy, imagining what I wanted to happen.

"I didn't care about myself but maybe I could help this one, who had her whole life ahead of her. Looking back, I must have pushed out all of my MP, using whatever I could to give her a chance at a normal life. In my mind, I saw little green specks that somehow I knew to be health. My health. I urged them to move from me to her. And they did! Not all of them, but a large portion. I kept going, and only stopped when I felt something like a blackjack hit the back of my head and I passed out."

"Someone attacked you while you were helping that girl?" Gus blurted in disgust.

"No, I had bottomed out my MP, along with transferring almost all of my residual energy from my own cells, and the backlash feedback was brutal. I think I was out for a day and a half. Luckily, the little girl made it. The family took care of me until I woke up, even cleaned my apartment to my deep embarrassment.

"When I saw the bags of trash, I realized how much I'd been living like an animal. That flipped a switch in me, and after that my Nth spoke to me more and more. So long story short, that's how I came to realize that manipulating ether and making it guide the body to heal overlaps into support classes."

They sat there in silence, contemplating the story. BoJack rapt in memory and Gus still trying to sort out his thoughts. With the new information, ideas began to bombard him that BoJack could probably easily answer.

"Not to change the subject, but what's your Nth like?" Gus wondered if the more experienced super had some experience with a NIC that just didn't mesh.

"My Nth? He's great. Even when he changes every ten levels or so."

"Yeah, how do you deal with that? Have you ever had a personality you didn't get along with?"

"I guess at first, but it's all worked out in the end. I don't know how the quantum server does its analysis, but, as far as I can tell, it streamlines your progress so you can level the fastest possible. I don't know if it tries to put you in difficult situations, but it definitely knows how to stretch your limits."

"Is that what makes quests and determines the Nth interface and all that? That never really was clear."

"Quests? I guess it amounts to the same. Mine are 'objectives.' From my understanding, the quantum server dictates what actions unlock access to information that your Nth can utilize. Apparently during REM sleep, the Nth take advantage and sync with the quantum server while the mind is otherwise occupied."

Crap, is that going to hold me back because I'll get less frequent quest prompts?

"I've heard of it also happening from deep meditation when theta brain waves are really prominent. Those mimic REM sleep, but I don't think there's a complete sync unless you actually sleep," BoJack said almost as an afterthought.

The information hit Gus like a slap to the face. Was that the answer to his whole sleep deprivation issues?

"Does **Ether Crafting** use theta waves at all? Is that maybe why I felt rested after I was in deep with that construct?"

"Maybe, I've never thought about it. You just kind of do it after a while and the individual steps become a little hazy. It's definitely possible," BoJack conceded, yawning. "Sorry, but since all's good here, I'm going to get some more shuteye. I'm still pretty beat. Tomorrow we'll see if we can make it out of the wops, and find the others." He rolled over on his cot and was quickly asleep.

The wops? Gus almost asked about the slang, but didn't want to disturb the other super. He lay down on his cot, but his mind was on fire. He had a clarity he hadn't felt in a while from his deep dive in **Ether Construct**. The constant low-grade headache he had come to live with had disappeared, and he just felt better. More hopeful.

Even his awkward relationship with Nick lately seemed less daunting. As he looked up at the tent above, he thought about possibilities. Despite multiple series of poor, often desperate choices, he had a new way to progress and level again.

A tiny pang of guilt hit him as he thought about BoJack's story with the little girl. Would he make the world a better place? So far, he had to admit: not so much. Yet.

He cast his mind to those damn pirates and wondered if he should have handled that any differently. At least he had helped the family, so there was that. But considering his abilities, he should really be able to make some changes for the better if he got his act together. And what would happen after they found his mother and the Crew went back to Purple Faction? What then?

Maybe I'm getting ahead of myself.

Instead of trying to compare himself to sometime in the future when he finally had everything mastered, he pulled his mind back to the next tasks at hand. Practice crafting, get to level 30, find his mother. Focus on that for the next little bit. He could tell his mental habits wanted him to escalate and ask harder questions, about what his future would be like, what would be the fallout from his next poor choices, but letting those go for a moment, he allowed his mind to think about what he wanted if everything went perfectly.

Maybe like BoJack, he could visualize his life in perfect order and he would be just a skosh closer to making that his reality. The tension that threatened to build subsided and Gus sat there thinking, for the first time in a while allowing his mind to enjoy itself for a change.

He imagined a much better version of himself, with things all falling into place. He imagined his family back together again, without the tension and dysfunction. Whether it did any good or not, Gus felt better than he had as the light outside the tent began to filter through the opaque material.

Gus stood up and opened the seal on the tent, stepping outside. His senses were assaulted by the smell of burning and smoke that still lingered in the air, filtered so effectively by the tent and his ether constructs that he had not thought about how much they had been keeping away.

Greasy ash coated his boots in just a few steps, tiny plumes of ash puffing into the air with each step. Gus marveled that the tent stood there behind him, stained but untouched by the destruction around it. The early morning light filtered in through the jagged spires of burned wood. He activated **Advanced Flight** and flew up above the area, surprised to see the expanse of the devastation. The swath of forest that was burned was much larger than expected, but that was not what caught his eye as he looked over the scene.

CHAPTER TWENTY

Night Swim

Yuki hit with a mind-jarring slam. The air was knocked out of her, bursting on impact resulting in a spew of bubbles. A split second after, the shock of cold hit her. She spasmodically gasped for breath, but she could pull nothing in. This, however, was fortunate since she was underwater. Faster than she thought possible, the icy water swallowed her, draining away feeling in her hands and feet as they succumbed to numbness in seconds. Panic was quickly muffled by a dark fog of obscurity as everything went dark.

Above the lake, Aurora managed to slow her descent and hover as Yuki fell from her grasp, barely stopping before crashing into the lake herself. Yuki sank below the surface quickly and Aurora thrust her hands under the water where she saw her friend disappear. Rather than trying to dive into the inky black water, she stretched the extent of her power to the limit. She focused on forcing it as deep as she could to avoid hitting Yuki in the process.

The waters began to roil and bubble as ions shifted and tiny bubbles began to rise and pop. Encouraged, she forced more

MP deep into the water, trying to widen the base of the area she was affecting, hoping that it was below where Yuki was. She had never attempted this before; she had thought about it, but never got to test the idea. In her mind, it felt right so she doubled down and pushed more power into the water. The flow of energy managed to counteract the icy chill of the water and it began to churn as more and more bubbles flooded the surface. At long last, a limp figure bobbed to the surface, face down.

Aurora grabbed the back of her outfit and flipped Yuki onto her back, skimming along the surface as she flew to the shore. The sodden woman looked up weakly, gasping like a fish. She reached up with a trembling hand, and Aurora gripped it with both hands, pulling her totally out of the lake.

Surprised by how cold Yuki was, she tried to wipe off as much water as possible from Yuki's outfit and waved hands over her. Activating a controlled burst of **Ion Storm,** she carefully evaporated the water clinging to the trembling super, hoping that the heated water would warm her up a bit.

Yuki's gasps became stronger and she pulled in rough breaths, sucking in the air as much as her body would allow. When Aurora had finished drying the water, they held each other, shaking from cold and the fading effects of adrenaline.

"T-t-that s-sucked," Yuki said flatly when she had regained enough of her faculties to talk.

Aurora burst out with a laugh, eyes wet with tears that had not fallen, grateful that she was alright.

"Yes, it did," she said, hugging Yuki tightly.

Yuki looked above at the flickering clouds.

"It looks like we're safe. I don't think the fire will spread down here. What did you do? The last thing I remember was tons of bubbles that lifted me out of the water."

"I didn't know it would work. It was just basic electrolysis. I separated hydrogen and oxygen in the water with a little ionization and I grabbed you as soon as I could."

"Maybe I'm kidding myself that I can be out in the field."

Yuki flopped onto her back, squashing the plants lining the bank of the lake. Aurora joined her and they both looked up at the combination of smoke and clouds drifting above.

"I'm totally unprepared for anything out of my wheelhouse. If there's tech, I'm golden. Out here, I'm just as good as a reg."

"So develop some new skills. Or have Gus give you one…"

Yuki rolled over onto her side and stared at Aurora intently.

"What do you mean?"

"Never mind! Not my place to say." She covered her mouth with her hands.

"Ah, no. You're not getting off that easy. Spill it, sister. What do you know about our fearless leader's son? Besides that he's got the angsty superhero act down pat."

"Really, you should ask him. But don't tell anyone else, please?"

"I've never heard of anyone giving away powers. Is it like a legacy super? I didn't think that worked if a person already had abilities." Yuki waggled a forefinger as she tried to puzzle out the ramifications.

Aurora shrugged, but this didn't deter Yuki from rapidly talking to herself.

"But maybe it's an ability of his. The only thing is the implication I could choose what ability I wanted…" Yuki peered at Aurora, eyebrow arching comically as she continued her mock interrogation.

When Aurora only bit her lower lip in reply, Yuki went on. "I'll figure it out. Don't worry about that. What would I choose though?" She tapped her lip as she thought. "Something that would go along with my prime abilities. Maybe an electrical attack? No—it can't only be offensive. I would need something I could adapt and use like you did with the electrolysis thing. But what?"

Aurora rubbed her eyes as the other super mused.

Yuki got to her feet, and brushed herself off. She began to talk to herself in lower and lower tones until Aurora couldn't make out the mutterings as she paced up and down the side of the lake, lost in thought.

Aurora rubbed her eyes again. *I'm sorry, Gus,* she said to herself. She knew Yuki would not be letting this go. As the yellow pinpoints of light subsided from pressing on her eyelids, she jolted suddenly in surprise.

CHAPTER TWENTY-ONE

Together Again

"Well, it looks like the transport is shot. What's left of it," Tempest said, lifting a torn piece of plating with his foot and letting it fall to the dust.

"It's not the only one," Darik added testily, constantly trying to adjust his pants but never seeming to get comfortable.

"Don't be a little witch about it," Harmony teased.

Darik turned on Jet with his fists on his hips.

"Are ye happy? See what you've done? Would have been better to fall to my death than bear the barbs this lot will heap upon me 'til the end of time."

Jet wobbled and drew a small face on the dirt with X's for eyes. Then an oblong oval, followed by a frowny face.

"What is that? Emoji? What's the middle one?" someone asked from the back.

"I think it's an eggplant, if I had to guess…" Harmony piped in.

"Enough of this!" Darik bellowed, using his foot to wipe away the characters, stirring up a cloud of dirt in his fervor. The remaining Crew laughed at his discomfiture, secretly glad that they had all survived relatively unscathed.

"Darik, can you make a portal back to the manor?"

"No. Don't you think I would 'ave done that already if I could? I don't have a good enough idea about the manor's location to travel from here to there. I need to know both endpoints clearly and distinctly. I'm not remotely close at the manor and that should tell you how much less this point is in the middle of nowhere. Even if I did, I could only bring one person through at a time, then it'd bottom me out, and we'd have to wait at least four hours before we could bring another person through."

"What about a smaller jump to a portal, then we could gate back to the manor?"

Darik puckered his lips and bobbed his head back and forth.

"Now that may be do-able. Though what I could create is less a portal than a skipping jump. I'd need a direction though, and I think we're far enough from civilization that we lack the necessary landmarks. I only have a limited amount of MP for jumps and they would need to be precise with a group this large, if we all wanted to make it there without waiting forever for recharges."

"Are the comms functional? Can we send out a signal?"

"Unfortunately no, captain," Grimdark drawled in his thick Romanian accent. "We lost engines and batteries when we hit trees. It was good fortune that we skip to this inlet, but ship is useless now."

"I should have expected as much," Tempest sighed. "Alright, everyone link in team chat. Pulse, how are you doing?"

"I've got some pretty good burns from those damn drones, but I'm fine. Wish BoJack was here to fix this up though."

"You and me both. Anyone else hurt severely?" There were some light complaints but overall the Crew was only roughed up a little. "Pulse, can you send a beacon periodically to notify the others where we are?" Tempest asked.

"You're not worried about any remaining drones?" Anastasia piped in.

"I look forward to them coming," Tempest growled.

"Maybe we can get some answers. What are your thoughts? Who attacked us and why?"

"I doubt that they knew we were supers, or their tactics would have been different," Anastasia replied, pulling a strand of hair behind one ear.

"The Oracle warned that this might happen," Darik added.

"So a remote viewing ability? No one comes to mind with that as a major skill set. Anyone know anything related?" Tempest asked, looking around the group. When no one offered anything new, he soldiered on. "So what we do know is that this awareness does not seem to know who is inquiring, but it does seem to know where or they couldn't have found us so quickly. Those drones were some of the latest models from what I could tell, so we are looking at someone well-established and well-funded. The fact that they tried to kill us just for knowing about them also is telling. It indicated to me a weakness. A need to remain unknown to be able to do what they want uncontested."

"So does whoever sent them know they failed?" Harmony piped in from the back.

"I'm not totally sure. Yuki would know; it all depends on how connected the drones are to the network. But if we are having communication issues, I would assume those drones are as well. And that's good for us."

"You don't think they can tap into the satellites and connect?"

"After seeing the firepower those drones carried, I would doubt that they would have much room for the processors needed to manage targeting, full communication, and that offensive capability. My guess is that they were dispatched here and someone will be following them to retrieve them after they have completed their mission."

"So how much time do you think we have, Tempest?" Harmony said, hugging herself and shuddering in the increasingly cold twilight.

"We were much higher when the drones made contact, so I would estimate eight hours to travel to where the drones found our ship. They probably communicated then, and had contact with the satellite network there, or piggybacked off of our ship's signals. After we went down, my guess is that they did not plan to end up in an area this remote. On top of that, Pulse destroyed a fair number of those drones, which would weaken their collective signal strength. Anyone arriving to check out the aftermath would need to ping the drones to find out where they ended up. What I don't know is if they could detect that we were able to retaliate and destroy some drones. If they do, that would change what type of welcoming party we can expect."

"It looks like only Gus, Aurora, BoJack, and Yuki are unaccounted for, so we have to find them or make it easy for them to find us and get to civilization. We may need to leave a couple of people behind if we don't manage to find them, then send someone back," Anastasia recommended.

"I don't like teams smaller than four, so I hope they're together."

———

Across the lake, Aurora saw the glint of metal in the moonlight.

"Yuki, look."

"What are you talking about?" Yuki squinted at where Aurora was looking but no recognition passed across her features.

"You think that's the rest of the Crew?" she asked, voice full of uncertainty.

"Look at the trees, you can see where it came down," Aurora said, pointing.

"How are you seeing anything out there? It's so dark." Yuki continued to look but couldn't see anything, try as she might.

Is it because she hasn't put as many points into perception as I have? I probably should tell her about Nth and how to access her levels...

"Well, I trust you can see it even if I don't. I'm sorry I can't fly. It would probably be easier to just swim across, but I am *not* going in that water again. It's like ice cold. Why don't you fly over there, and you can get a couple of people to bring me back?"

Aurora nodded. "You'll be okay?"

"Hold on, before you go, let me try linking comms... Okay, I sent an invite but no one has accepted it yet. Not totally sure anyone has received it though. You think they're sleeping?"

"Someone would be on watch, regardless. Let me try to get their attention." Aurora braced herself and fired **Dazzle** and **Ion Storm** simultaneously. The shimmering effects reflected off the glassy still lake and the trees along the banks flickered with reflected light. Two quick red beams shot up from the area of wreckage in response.

"That's Pulse." Aurora smiled. "Glad we found some of them."

"I hope that's everyone, I'm ready to get out of here."

"Me too."

CHAPTER TWENTY-TWO

Your Friend Will

As Gus flew above the smoky remains of the fire, he was impressed with the level of destruction around their camp. His eyes panned around until there was a bright wink of light. Focusing, he used his perception zoom and saw that the glint came from the transport! Tiny figures moved around the broken section of the ship and one portion of bent back metal had reflected the light like a mirror. Surveying the area all around, his mini-map filled in with additional information and he put a marker on the ship's location. He descended and took care not to stir up too much ash with his landing.

Popping his head into the tent, he yelled at BoJack to wake up. The older super didn't move until Gus told him what he had found. That got him moving. The older super sprang to his feet and in a matter of minutes, he had unraveled all of his constructs and the only thing remaining was a relatively untouched rectangle of smooth dirt, out of place in contrast to the black scarred ground.

BoJack didn't trust the charcoal spikes that remained of the trees, so he just propelled himself above the ground on his cables as Gus took to the air. Soon they had passed the area of fire damage and BoJack hoisted himself above the treetops again.

"Which way?" BoJack deferred to Gus.

"This way," Gus pointed as he shared the nav-point on his display and began to fly.

"Let's go."

They traveled for a bit in relative silence, with only the crunch of cables attaching and the swoosh as the trees bent back and forth as BoJack moved.

"Gus, can I ask you a personal question?" BoJack asked through the mental link, surprising him.

"Sure, I suppose," he replied.

"What do you have against your father? The whole Crew can see how you keep him at arm's length, and you always get incredibly tense around him. From my experience, Tempest has always gone above and beyond to help the other supers in Purple Faction. I doubt you would get this many people following him on a personal mission if he wasn't doing something right."

"Maybe he just treats supers better than regs," Gus shot back, a bit too quickly.

"Mmmm, I don't think so. There are definitely those in Purple Faction that are exactly that way, but your father doesn't give out that vibe. So what's going on?"

"It's complicated." Gus didn't like where this conversation was heading, so he flew a little bit more quickly.

"Does it have to be? I know from personal experience that I have a tendency to make things a lot harder than they need to be, or exaggerate the size and scope of the rift between myself and others. I've wasted a lot of time being stubborn and prideful, telling myself the other person has to change. This may just be me talking—I don't want to put my experience onto you—but it just seems… familiar."

They traveled in silence for a while as Gus mulled the situation over. The silence became ponderous and Gus had to fill the void, even if it meant sharing something he'd rather have kept to himself.

"There's probably a little of that going on, if I'm being honest." Gus turned around and hovered as BoJack crawled towards him. "There's just so much to sort out, and I feel like I'm trying to drink out of a fire-hose at full blast. It's over-whelming, and I feel totally inexperienced and inadequate.

"Then Tempest shows up and all those things just get bumped up a notch. Except now he seems like a totally different person, all accepting and friendly. A part of me feels like he's only accepting my powers, and only now am I important to him. That makes me both angry and suspicious. I don't know what his true motives are, where his loyalties lie, and I'm afraid of losing control and losing everything I've worked for, like the past." The words flowed out, having been pent up and pushed down for too long.

BoJack came closer. "I get it. I think every super goes through something similar. Maybe not with a manor involved, but trying to find your place, especially when you're around other people who are amazingly talented. It can be a bit daunt-ing. Not to mention transitioning from how people saw you from before, to the new, improved you."

"That's for damn sure," he said, a little relieved that BoJack could relate to some of what he was feeling.

"And it's even worse if you're trying to lift that whole load on your own. I know you don't really know any of us on the Crew, and maybe don't trust all of us yet. But your father is on your side whether you believe it or not. And we are on his side, which makes us on your side as well. I think you would do well to let some others in and allow them to get to know you. I don't think that I would have gotten to know you as much as I have if all this hadn't happened." BoJack gestured, mimicking the crash and fire. "Am I wrong?" He peered at Gus, making eye contact before Gus could stare elsewhere.

"No," Gus said, looking away as his face flushed.

"You know Wheaton's law?"

Gus chuckled a bit. "Yeah."

"Well, take it to heart then. You're not a moody teenager anymore; you're a super, so you have to up your game. Got it?" BoJack's tone was encouraging, hopeful, and didn't immediately throw up Gus' deflector shields and make him defensive.

"I'll make more of an effort. It's hard though; some things are like a reflex. I feel awkward and inadequate around you guys and how you all get along and know how to work with each other. I don't feel like I belong—like I'm some phony trying to fit in."

"Everyone gets that at first. Okay? You're normal. You're hyper-aware of your own flaws and failures, and all you can see is everyone and the ease with which they do things, right? You've been doing this super thing for how long, a couple months?"

Gus nodded as he did some mental calculation. "Yeah, about two months."

"So two months, teaching yourself, fighting monsters that scare any super out there, and coming out of it all intact. That doesn't make you feel good? Then defeating a whole horde of other supers and keeping the island. Aurora still won't tell us exactly how you managed to pull that off, says it's your story to tell. So I don't know what the big mystery is, but have you ever considered that some of the Crew may be as intimidated by you as you are by them?"

"Whatever."

"And then how the Oracle singled you out like that? Do you think that's normal? Supers are afraid of her, and what she can see and what she will ask in payment for that information. I have never heard of her taking an interest in anyone before either, so that's another mystery. I don't know what's in your future, but I want you to be ready to meet whatever it is. It may be more important than anything supers have done in a while, if you're affecting that many events and powerful individuals."

"Dang. No pressure, right?"

"I hate to break it to you, mate, but if you got into the super business for a life of ease, you picked the wrong profession. It's hard, thankless work if you don't find your inner motivations."

Which I still need to figure out, Gus thought.

"Okay, I don't mean to pry. But can I give you some advice?" BoJack asked.

"Sure."

"First, don't be so hard on yourself. You're doing fine, probably better than a bunch of us did when we were at the same stage in our development. Second, like I said, give your father and the Crew an honest chance. Put yourself out there, and just trust that you'll be okay whatever happens. Your dad is trying, but no one can keep that up forever if there's constant resistance. If you want to know his motives, ask him. It doesn't sound like you've been that close the last couple of years."

"No, we haven't," Gus replied matter-of-factly.

"But things change. People change."

"Do they though? It seems like most people generally make the same mistakes over and over."

"True. Some do. But Gus, you have Nth. I don't know what your whole path has been like, but I know one thing for sure. You are not the same person you were before those Nth entered your life. Sure—they change a part of your physiology and help you quantify your progress, but a large portion of that is based on your choices, Gus. Do you know what happens to supers who don't grow?"

"Don't they stagnate and lose their powers?"

"Exactly. So if you know that, why would you cling to anything that holds you back? These Nth don't just give us super abilities, they help you improve *any* skill in life if it becomes an area of focus. Just because most don't use them to improve the other aspects of life doesn't mean that they can't.

"Listen. My personal baggage kept me from progressing and developing when I was in your position. As a super but also as a person. You can have amazing powers and abilities yet still be someone no one wants to be around. That was me for a long while. And how can you help anyone if you're in a pity party of one? I'll tell you. You won't. Family's not around forever, and you will feel it when they're gone, trust me. You've already lost your mom, don't choose to lose your dad."

Damn it, he's right. Gus nodded in agreement. "Okay, I'll do it."

"And the same goes for the Crew. Lower the walls and don't wait for everyone to come to you. Sometimes to show you're approachable, you have to extend the first olive branch."

"I can do that too."

"Gus, you're probably somewhere in the 20s in levels, am I right?"

"Well, yeah."

"You're in the sweet spot for massive gains. For some reason, the requirements to level up and the ease of improving skills is magnified from about level 25 to 50. I squandered that and wasted my time. You can skate by and things will slowly level you out of this zone, even though it takes a lot more time doing it that way.

"But if you focus, you can really flesh out some of your abilities and make them your own. That's what frustrates me about this new way we train supers. They have no Nth assistance, so they are losing massive guidance and probably wasting time making errors that would be so easily avoided with a mentor. You're fortunate you know about yours. You asked me about my relationship with my Nth, how is yours?"

Gus' heart fell another dip, just like he'd been on a roller-coaster or in transport turbulence.

"Not so good lately," he admitted.

"That's the last thing—and I promise I'll leave off the lectures, although it's kind of the same thing. I don't know how the quantum server assesses us, but that personality is just what you need right now to progress the most. Its main directive is to help you evolve in every way. You may not understand it or even like it. But take advantage of your Nth. Make a game out of finding what exact flaw that personality can help you overcome.

"I can tell you this: life has a funny way of giving you more chances of learning important lessons if you kick the opportunity down the road. Knowing what I know now, I wish I would have learned what I should and moved on rather than face the same challenge over and over, but ultimately the choice is up to you if you want to do the same."

"Were you like a psychiatrist or something before you were a super?" Gus joked.

"I'm a healer at my core. Sometimes the body is only a small part of what makes a person ill. We would think someone taking poison on a regular basis would be an idiot, but we do it all the time with poisonous thoughts and habits. I sense that in you. I'll admit I've done the same, and I know how it's held me back. Don't let it do the same to you.

"I don't know why you're at odds with your father, but he probably was doing the best he could with the resources he had. I shudder to think if everyone judged me on my behavior on my worst days. We always tend to do that, don't we? Judge others on their behavior and ourselves on our intentions. Don't make that same mistake. You have more, so be more." BoJack pointed a cable arm at the lake that had yawned into view beyond the trees. Gus lifted his pensive eyes and saw the lake for himself, his mood brightening.

"We're almost there!"

Gus had been so lost in contemplation that he hadn't realized how far they had been traveling. BoJack lowered himself to the water's edge and made a boat out of a few planes of ether. Two cables extended underwater, making an outboard motor and rudder and they were off across the water.

CHAPTER TWENTY-THREE

Get Back

As Gus sped along the surface of the water, he could see the Crew on the other side of the lake. One must have seen him because they all turned and started to wave. It was a relief to see as many there as he did, probably everyone had made it, he counted and found eleven others. All present and accounted for.

His heart began to fill with excitement at meeting everyone again, and the chance to really get to know them this time around. He still felt awkward as hell, but he was just going to push through it.

The Crew started to cheer as they got close and then BoJack executed a deft maneuver where he let his momentum carry him as he slowly dissolved the sides of his ether boat, fading to a semblance of a surfboard, until he was skidding to the shore on just his heels. The effect was expertly executed; it had to be something he had practiced before. He stepped effortlessly onto the bank and was met by high fives and shoulder claps.

He landed and grinned as he watched his new friend's warm welcome. Gus was almost knocked over as he was grabbed suddenly from behind. He stiffened from the unexpected assault.

"We were so worried about you guys! I'm so glad you are alright!" a perky voice chirped in his ear, the heat and proximity sending a slight tingle down his spine. He recognized the voice as Harmony's at about the same time she jumped on his back in a tight bear hug. He instinctively grabbed her legs as she wrapped them around him, squeezing him tight. The silky feeling of the fishnets along her supple legs caused him to flush at the closeness.

The scent of some fruity perfume wafted to Gus' nose as she rested her head on his shoulder, her blonde ringlets bouncing as she squeezed even tighter. Gus stiffened some more, albeit in a different way than before, as he realized what was pressing against his back with the embrace.

At that moment, he realized another big disadvantage of the spandex-like suits but fortunately with a little hybrid-Nth assistance, things were sorted and mischief was managed. Gus gulped and thanked his luck stat that he was facing mostly toward the lake during the encounter.

Releasing her softly, she slid to the ground gracefully. *She was so light!* Without thinking anything amiss, she loped over and gave BoJack a big hug as well.

Taking a deep breath and shuddering, Gus looked to the side and saw Aurora watching him with interest. He nodded in acknowledgement and she shook her head with a wry smile, turning back to organizing a pack she had salvaged from the transport.

The rest of the Crew heartily welcomed Gus, with Darik using both his hands to shake with Gus. This time Gus leaned into the reunion, hugging back with as much gusto as he received, happy to be back with everyone once again. Even Jet did a flourish, welcoming Gus back to the group.

He turned and there was a brief pause as his father had his outstretched hand. Instead of going for the stilted handshake, Gus pulled his father close, clapping him on the back as they embraced.

As he pulled away, Tempest cleared his throat and nodded

to his son. "Good to see you again." He looked deep into Gus' eyes and held on to his shoulder, as if he didn't want the contact to end. At last he turned to Yuki.

"Yuki, have you worked out exactly where we are? We've been discussing our plan to get out of here, but all of it hinges on knowing our exact location."

"Yes, sure. I mean, sir." She slid her belt off and unzipped a panel, sliding her laptop out. She screwed up her mouth as she tried to orient herself in different directions to get a signal. Then typed a bit, moving and talking to herself. "Um, can I get a little boost here, Seneschal?"

The woman nodded, moving to stand beside Yuki. Putting a hand on her shoulder, a tiny sparkle could be seen twinkling around her hand at the point of contact. She reached her other hand skyward, a thin white stream extending from her index finger, disappearing into the dense clouds above.

"Oh yeah, thank you, girlfriend!" Yuki cheered, shoulders bobbing as she typed, as if she was dancing to some music only she could hear. Her jaws moved in time as she chewed some gum, a wide grin spreading on her face. With a flourish, she hit a final key and information flooded everyone's displays. Exact longitude and latitude, as well as extensive maps overlaid the Crew's mini-maps.

"Everyone ready?" Darik asked.

Gus looked at the others with confusion.

"Just follow our lead, sport," Yuki said, popping a fresh piece of gum in her mouth.

Darik whistled and winked at Yuki. He then clapped and rubbed his hands together, breathing in and out quickly as if hyperventilating for a deep-water dive. He then extended one hand in front of him, rotating it in circles, his back hand wobbling by his ear as if he were trying to help himself hear something faint. Air hissed as he slowly exhaled and waved his hands, minute beads of sweat peppering his forehead. As the extended hand widened its arc, Gus could see that he somehow was stabilizing a portal with the back hand as if balancing a spinning dish.

Through teeth grit in concentration, he growled, "I think that's big enough, lasses, go for it. I dunna know how long I can hold it!"

Aurora and Harmony dove through the spinning disk and Darik fell backward onto his butt, puffing out the last of his stored air as they disappeared from view.

He laid back on the sparse grass and weeds panting. "I'm tapped. Whoo! That took more out of me than I expected."

"Now what?" Gus asked no one in particular.

"Now... we wait," Tempest said, sitting next to Darik on the ground. "Since we have some time, why don't you fill us in on your adventures?"

So BoJack began, asking Gus his opinion on the details. For the first time, he felt like he was part of the team as they laughed and discussed BoJack's predicament when the transport was initially attacked. However, BoJack didn't talk about his mentoring of Gus at all, so he kept that detail to himself.

Less than an hour later, the girls showed up with a large van-like transport. It was much smaller than their ship but everyone managed to pack inside. They stowed anything worth salvaging in the back and Aurora took off.

"We're in luck. We found a portal super close, so we can head back to the manor," Harmony squealed in her peppy voice.

"Rory is going to be pissed about the transport though."

"That wasn't our fault. Not really..." Tempest began.

"Doesn't matter. Those ships are like his children, he's super protective of them regardless," Aurora admitted.

"Well, a problem for another time then." He then turned to Gus. "I'm glad you made it out, that will make all of this much easier than if we had to travel all the way back to the island. You have the portal codes?"

"I do, I think?" Gus replied, not certain at all.

Nick came to his rescue. "The portal codes are keyed to me

and therefore you. Just get us to a station, and I can initiate a one-way jump and ensure the coordinates are erased after we all are through."

"Okay, I just checked and we're good as long as we find a station, apparently," Gus announced to the group.

"Easy-peasy, lemon-squeezy," Harmony sang. "There's a station right by where we rented this beast."

The trip was only about twenty minutes, but even with the fan at full blast, the press of bodies made the short trip less than desirable. The "just-been-camping" smell that had permeated Gus' outfit became extremely apparent in the confined space. He had barely even noticed the extent of the fire's effect while outside.

Finally, they arrived and everyone spilled out, perhaps a bit too enthusiastically. Strictly speaking, they had filled the van beyond capacity and at least a third were wearing no safety restraints as they made the trip. A cold wind greeted them and Harmony strode forth purposefully, waving everyone to follow as she clutched her arms in front of her. As Gus was about to leave, he heard Aurora sigh audibly.

"You want me to stay and help you return the rental?"

"No, they'll need you at the station for setting up the portal. But thanks for thinking of me." She cast an irritated glare at the others.

"If you're sure…"

"I'm fine—go. We're all tired. The sooner we get back, the better." Aurora waved him on as she grabbed her things to go, fishing some paperwork out of the glove compartment.

Gus jogged to catch up with the others and the group made their way to an unmarked, plain building that looked like a small storage area for grounds-keeping supplies. Seneschal waved her wrist in front of a small key-card panel and the door opened with a *hiss*.

Beyond was an escalator that led underground. As the group filed in, the warm air inside quickly dispersed the chill they were feeling. Stepping off the escalator, Gus took in the station with a little awe. There was no one else here and their steps and voices echoed on the slate tiles in the large domed room. A huge circular ring stood free standing at the center of the room, with the inner edge of the ring flush with the floor as if it had been cemented there.

"You're up!" Darik said, clapping Gus on the back.

Gus stepped forward tentatively as Nick showed some coordinates and codes on his display. There was an eldritch glow that skated along the inner surface of the ring as it began to power up. When it had circled around to touch itself, there was an audible pop and Gus felt his ears click at the sudden change in pressure. He worked his jaw and tugged his earlobe to relieve the feeling.

Without any more fanfare, the others began to move into the portal. Gus stood there in wonder, walking to the other side where he could see a slight haze, but the Crew was not visible at all from this vantage. He peeked back and forth, unnerved by the strange effect.

"First time using a portal?" someone asked and Gus was brought back to the moment.

Looking up, he saw Harmony there, a little closer than his usual bubble of comfort dictated.

"You always remember your first time." She winked and sauntered through the portal.

Gus stood there shell-shocked while the other supers eagerly entered the portal. All except for Grimdark. He seemed to be psyching himself up, as if he were going to jump into a cold pool to do morning laps. With balled fists, he marched through, leaving Gus there by himself. Then he waited there for Aurora to arrive, since he didn't know if he had to be on this side of the portal to keep it active or not. Five minutes later, she jogged down the escalator.

"Thanks for waiting, Gus. I appreciate it," she said warmly as she went through the event horizon. Gus stepped through, longing for his own bed.

CHAPTER TWENTY-FOUR

I Got No Time

Gus shivered as he stepped through the portal. There was a slight resistance and he felt a brief pins-and-needles sensation spread over his face and envelop his body as he pushed through the plane of the portal. After enough pressure, he slipped through the gateway and the sensation passed before becoming painful, leaving him feeling itchy all over. The trip was instantaneous and Gus observed he wasn't the only one fidgeting and scratching. Gus had to squint at the change in light from the dark subway-like confines of the station to near-blinding brightness.

"I hate portals!" Grimdark muttered as Gus stepped through the shimmering doorway. He was fidgeting with the belts and buckles on his outfit, making sure everything was as it should be.

"I like the tinglies it gives me in the stomach, myself," Darik said, laughing at Grimdark's discomfort, since he was usually so stoic and unflappable.

The portal room had white tile and a large circular window opening directly onto the beach from a different angle than Gus was accustomed to seeing. He walked to the edge of the room and soaked in the sun, enjoying being warm for the first time in a while. The briny scent of the ocean wafted in and Gus sighed. Harmony apparently had the same idea as him, and she had opened a door and was marching determinedly onto the sand.

"Good, everyone's back. Why don't we unwind for a bit and meet for a post mission debriefing and plan what's next? Sound good?" Tempest asked.

There were mutters of general assent and the Crew began to disperse.

Gus filed onto the elevator and made it to his room.

———

Sighing as he looked at the plush bed, Gus slipped out of his dingy suit. As he did, he saw the hybrid-Nth peel away from the outer surface of it. They hovered like a cloud of gnats and then reattached to his bare skin. After settling, they shimmered and became translucent, mimicking his skin tone. Areas where there was ground in dirt began to slough off like water on a newly waxed transport.

He went and stood in front of the mirror and wondered if his Nth could manage the banalities of personal hygiene. As if in response, he felt a tickle and a thin layer of gunk fell away from his skin, clipped fingernails, along with his ungroomed facial hair fluttering to the bathroom tile. Clumps of his unkempt hair also slid off his shoulders like hot butter on a skillet.

He stepped away from the disgusting pile around him and a small orb the size of a tangerine rolled out of a tiny recess as a tile slid open. Like on the beach, the little ball rolled over the 'sheddings,' spiraling inward until it had sucked up everything and retreated back into the wall.

Flipping weird!

Gus changed into the other suit, noticing the process reverse as he pulled on the jumpsuit. It wasn't as relaxing as a shower, but nice to know he wouldn't get funky if he was on a long mission.

He opened the large glass window and stepped out onto the balcony. Sitting down, he turned to face the sun and closed his eyes. Even through his eyelids, he could feel its brightness. He searched for the feeling again, when he had crafted and formed ether constructs in the forest. He tried attuneing himself to the ether around him.

"Do you want my assistance?" Nick asked.

By his tone, Gus could tell he expected to be shut down abruptly.

"Have I really been *that* irritable and rude?"

"Yes. A full vessel can carry no water. You have been dismissive and prideful. Utterly unteachable," Nick replied in a huff.

For some reason, the rebuke didn't immediately make Gus get defensive. Reflecting, he had been out of sorts and grouchy for no good reason. Maybe it was the headaches.

"I'm sorry for how I've acted, but I think I'm feeling more centered now. Even though the headache is building again, I think it was really affecting my mood. What do you have for me?"

"If I am to teach you, I expect you to listen and apply the exercises I give to you. Without bargaining, without negotiation. Are you able to agree to that?"

"But, why—"

"And without doubt and questioning. Normally, we are not able to discuss what changes in this phase of levels, but since BoJack has already given you this information, it is not giving you an unfair advantage to suggest it anymore. He is correct though; to optimize your growth, you should capitalize on certain behaviors and skill growth right now, and if done recklessly you can lose any benefits and stifle future growth. In assessing your current path, you have not had a level of focus necessary to streamline your development. I wish to help you with this. But it will be grueling and painful. In the end, you will be much more capable, and is this not what you want? Better control and personal power?"

Gus had to close his mouth that had dropped open. Is that what he wanted? Needed right now? He tried to find something that he wanted more, but he did feel like if he could get a better handle on his abilities and his emotions, then he could be much more like the ideal self that he had always envisioned himself to be.

"Yeah. I mean yes… I'm putty in your hands. What should I be doing?"

There was a pause, as if Nick was assessing his sincerity, but he must have passed muster because he continued with a softer tone. "Are you familiar with a Zen koan?"

"Vaguely."

"It is often an unanswerable question. I want you to expand your vision and this is one way established among humans that is most attuned to what you need to accomplish. Instead of me simply giving one to you, I want you to think of your own unanswerable question and I will evaluate its suitability for the task. You may begin."

Gus twitched a little bit at the unexpected task.

"Umm, can you give me a little help, maybe?"

Nick had gone mute so Gus sighed and let his mind wander. *What even is an unanswerable question? What's the meaning of life? What's the best thing I could be doing right now?*

"What about those?"

"Keep trying."

"Can you give me some examples?"

"I can. But I will not. Examples often direct you along certain paths and this is your personal journey. Look inside and find what *your* question should be. This is the way."

"Alright," Gus said, exhaling again, trying not to get frustrated. He let go of any worry or expectation with each exhalation. He imagined blowing out stress with every breath. Then just letting go and following where his mind wandered.

At first, he was monitoring closely, looking for any inkling of inspiration, but this attention seemed to be inhibiting anything from developing. For a while he simply sat, feeling the light on his closed eyes and face, the occasional caress of a cool ocean breeze, the screech of a bird looking for food. His increased attention to his non-verbal senses seemed like it was a distraction, so he gently steered it back to the question of "What?" *What the hell am I doing?*

He laughed a little and returned to his breath.

What.

Unbidden, he recalled the experience where he was making constructs and he had seen the ether interacting up close.

What.

His mind tried to make sense of exactly the reason for this memory, and what he was to learn, but as he tried to wrestle the answer, he could feel himself pulling away and things becoming less focused. Relaxing, he surrendered to the experience. Trying just to be an observer. Floating on the river, letting it take him where it wanted to go.

The memory crystallized again and he saw the interaction of normal matter hitting the ether and how it reacted. There was nothing really new here, as far as he could tell. But he just watched. It became almost soothing, seeing the molecules bombard the ether and how they just kept absorbing the stresses put upon them.

At the corner of his vision, Gus thought he saw a flicker. When he moved his mental focus, he could see nothing as he looked more fully at the expanse of small black particles. Looking directly at it instead of the borders, he couldn't tell if it looked more like an ocean made up of marbles or desert dunes of black sand. Occasionally the mass would undulate like a wave, other times they seemed totally static.

Flicker.

There it was again. But gone as he looked directly at where he thought he had seen something.

What.

Exactly. What is doing that? What am I supposed to get from this?

The out of focus sensation returned so Gus calmed himself yet again, surprised at how hard it was to just let go and observe. It took longer this time, but things slowly came back into focus.

Flicker.

Instead of trying to find out what was causing it, Gus just stared ahead. As if it were a skittish creature, the flicker began to appear more at the periphery of his awareness more frequently the less he tried to get an exact look at it.

What.

The flicker began to become more prevalent, although the intensity dropped as Gus began to notice its presence more and more until it transitioned from a random flicker to a low glow present all around except where he was looking.

Suddenly everything became unfocused and Gus felt a backward pull similar to when he was done using the Quorian cube.

"Gus, Gus! Are. You. Reading. Me?" a voice asked impatiently on his comm.

Disoriented, he couldn't tell who was talking to him. He blinked his eyes open and staggered back into the room, closing the balcony's sliding glass door behind him.

"Who is this?" Gus asked, still feeling a bit groggy.

"It's your father. We've been trying to get a hold of you for a while. Did you forget we're having a quick post-mission debriefing? Everyone's waiting for you. Head back to the conference room, and hurry."

"Already?"

"It's been four hours since we got back, Gus. We need to plan what's next."

"Okay, sure."

That can't be right. Can it? Four hours?

———

Gus followed his display to the new conference room that had been recently unlocked by Basileus and company during their brief reign at the manor. Entering the room, there was a large table in the middle and screens along the walls. Tempest sat at the head of the table and motioned for Gus to take the foot on the other side.

"Okay, from what the Oracle told me, we have to get into Hinansho city. How are we going to do it?" Tempest started.

"They can detect supers, so don't forget we have to get by that," Yuki said.

"We can use the old Manticorps transport, it shouldn't stand out," Grimdark added.

"That's good, what else?" Tempest encouraged.

"What about Leto? He's gotten us in before. For relatively cheap too, we just need to get him memory modules for his network," Darik suggested.

"He's still working on that thing?" Seneschal asked in surprise. "How many years has it been?"

"Decades, at least," Darik replied. "And he never leaves his little lab. You sure his stuff is current enough to get us in?"

"He's a hermit, but he's connected," Tempest said. "But that brings up a point—What can we expect to find there? Anyone else been to Hinansho before?"

Prime nodded slightly and Grimdark raised his arm, as if he were answering a question in class.

"I wouldn't trust seeing Kenway with less than four people," Grimdark warned.

"Agreed. I would prefer at least six, but we'll have to see what Leto can get for us. Yuki, I assume you can make contact with him and make him an offer? Start with the standard and see what he counters with," Tempest said.

"On it." Yuki began typing furiously.

"Where do we get memory modules? Does the manor have any?" Aurora asked.

"If it did, they'd be pretty old, and there have been massive changes in data storage capacity since the manor was made. I have some contacts that can get us what we need," Seneschal offered.

"So assuming Leto can get us the codes to get in, what about cloaking so we're not detected as supers?" Darik asked, putting his hands on his hips.

"Leto has access to that, but he is outsourcing it to someone. He'll do it but he'll charge us a premium and we won't be able to get a lot of cloaks either," Yuki added, blowing a large bubble and popping it with a *crack*.

"I can outfit the ship so anyone inside would be able to avoid the sensors," Grimdark volunteered.

"Good, anyone able to help Grimdark with the ship?"

Yuki raised a hand quickly without looking away from her screen and resumed typing.

"I might as well volunteer too. Everyone needs me to crawl around dusty innards of ships to connect things. I'll pitch in too." Darik held the back of his neck and leaned his head backward, anticipating the cramped spaces in his future.

"I can help with the scramblers and configuring everything," Aurora added.

"So we've got our transport, and Leto has the rest of what we need. Anything else we need before we go?" Tempest asked, leaning on the table and assessing his team proudly.

Aurora raised a hand a bit tentatively.

"I've been working on some new suit designs, if anyone is interested. I was going to head to the Foundry to see if I could perfect some prototypes. We need to unlock Fabrication, if it's okay with Gus, but then we can manufacture designs I have been working on."

"I'd be interested to see what you've come up with." Tempest nodded to Aurora. "What do you think, Gus?"

"Yeah, that sounds good, allocate the points. We're still good on FP, aren't we?"

"Uh, boss…" Yuki interrupted. "We got a problem. Leto says he's finished his network and doesn't need any memory cores. Says he doesn't need money either." Yuki winced as she read the demands.

"So what now?" Tempest rubbed his eyes then slid up to massage his temples. "There's nothing that he wants?"

Yuki typed some more then settled back in her chair.

"There is, but I don't think you're going to like it…"

CHAPTER TWENTY-FIVE

Bad Times

"Lay it on me," Tempest groaned dejectedly.

"Well, don't kill the messenger... but Leto says that he doesn't need anything from anyone anymore." Yuki held her breath expecting Tempest to explode at yet another obstacle.

Instead he just hung his head and asked, "And?"

"...and that includes credits or memory modules. He does say that you can run an errand for him and that he'll get us what we need."

"That sounds ominous," Grimdark stated in his deadpan voice.

"It gets better. He says he already has two interested parties en route to do this task and he doesn't care who does it, but he's only paying the first to get there."

"Where is it? We may not have time for long detours."

"The good news is that it's in Hinansho, so two birds with one stone."

"If he gets us into Hinansho and gives us cloaks then that's all we need, right?" Tempest figured, voice sounding more optimistic.

"Yes and no. If we fail, he says he'll turn us in for a bounty for being in Hinansho without authorization and disable our shrouds so we'll be stuck inside—"

"That little snake!" an incensed Aurora shouted. "After all we've done for that little creep."

"How much of a lead time do we have?" Tempest asked Yuki.

"Only a couple of hours…"

"Dammit! No rest for the weary, I suppose. Can you track our competition?"

"I can but as soon as I connect, they can track us as well… Is it worth it?"

"Yes, no use in rushing over there if there's no chance of success."

"On it. Okay, two other identical pings to the data package we need to deliver, and one's from the mainland, one from the Communist Conglomerate, but they're far enough away to not be a factor. We should be able to arrive with a sliver ahead of the mainland team if we leave in, like… ten minutes."

"You heard her, let's get that transport ready! You three will have to make your changes and outfit the ship on the trip there. Grab everything you'll need—no, grab *more* than you need, just in case, but make it fast!" Tempest barked at Grimdark, Yuki, and Darik, and the rest of the Crew took off.

"Is this how it always is?" Gus asked BoJack in a stage whisper.

"Pretty much par for the course. Usually it's like running down the street naked at ninety miles an hour with your hair on fire," he replied with a grin.

"Yeah, I'm kind of getting that," Gus said wryly as he ran to grab his things.

"I assume you can pilot the ship?" Tempest pointed to Seneschal, who nodded curtly and headed purposefully to the lifts.

Was she the pilot all along? Gus wondered as he jogged back to his room. His pack was still there, leaning against the wall, so he just grabbed it and headed out and hit the button for the lift.

When it came, Grimdark and Pulse were already aboard. The car rose, heading to the roof. Gus assumed a forward-facing stance, observing proper elevator etiquette: he stayed absolutely silent, preserving the awkward silence that must prevail when riding in elevators with acquaintances.

As the doors opened, they all were hit with a big blast of exhaust as a transport landed on the tarmac. This ship was much less sleek than the previous Faction transport, and looked to be cobbled together of scavenged parts from at least three different models of vehicles.

As it rotated into position, it made a pitiful moan reminiscent of the TARDIS before setting down with a heavy *thunk* like a weary beast of burden.

"Perfect." Grimdark clapped his hands with approval, showing a hint of a curved lip, which was the closest thing to a smile Gus had ever seen the super achieve. Pulse shook his head and jogged under the ship, disappearing into a thick cloud of exhaust and steam-like emissions.

No one really could have done a better job of arranging a mismatched conglomeration of parts and wear to simulate a broken-down transport if they had tried. Manticorps must have been down on their luck indeed, if this was the best they had to send over to take the manor.

"Do you think it's safe?" Gus asked, slack-jawed.

"Maybe. Maybe not. But perfect," Grimdark said, shrugging. He clapped a hand on Gus' shoulder and they walked to the ship like they were old pals.

Grimdark carried him along to the underside of the transport as a gangway lowered with a rumbling hum of hydraulics, spilling a miasma of exhaust and steam as the ship ticked and rattled as it cooled down.

Up close, the preponderance of duct tape and jury-rigged improvements were painfully evident. Grimdark patted the scored dark paneling under the ship, eliciting a hollow noise as he *thunked* away. Gus looked sideways as a small plate came loose and began swinging back and forth from Grimdark's love pat.

"This is made to last. Reminds me of home." The rest of what Grimdark was saying was lost as he stomped up the gangplank and disappeared inside.

Gus tried in vain to reclose the loose plate, finally giving up and letting it swing free. The elevator slid open again and two mounds of cables shuffled out. He rushed to help, relieving a large toolbox that was heavy and unwieldy, even with his increased strength. The three hobbled up the gangway, the rest of the Crew joining them, picking up components that had dropped on their trip.

Darik muttered angrily as he put his hands in the small of his back and stretched. After an audible *pop*, he reached into a satchel and threw a magnetized net over the cables, holding the gear secure as Seneschal fired up the repulsors.

"Looks like we're all here. Hang on, ladies and gentlemen," Seneschal said over the comms and the ship shimmied and shook as it slowly pulled away from the manor.

CHAPTER TWENTY-SIX

Bullet with Butterfly Wings

Gus, Darik, and Yuki held on as the transport lumbered into the air and banked to their new heading. Darik pushed a button on the side of the toolbox with a kick. A low hum, audible over the transport's engines, could be heard. The toolbox that was slowly sliding away stopped abruptly and fixed in position as its base magnetized.

After quickly reaching their cruising altitude and leveling out, Darik grabbed an armful of materials and motioned for Gus to follow him. He disengaged the magnet and carried the toolbox over to a small panel on the side of the wall. Opening it revealed a small passage with a myriad of colored wires in a tiny room beyond.

This must be where Aurora hid, Gus noted as he saw the brownish gray dust disturbed on the floor of the small passage and a hand-print along one wall. He never would have considered himself claustrophobic, but the area inside was *tight.* The thought of getting turned around and stuck inside unsettled him. Yuki pushed past, dragging cables and a Ziplock bag with various chips and wires within.

"Are you in the control room, Grimdark?"

"Yes."

She curled into position inside and began connecting wires like an old-time phone operator. Gus wondered how she was going to get out as the tiny cords crisscrossed back and forth in the tiny space. She disappeared from view, moving upward. Every once in a while, her hand could be seen as she grabbed a cord and pulled it upwards out of sight as Darik held the line and fed it to her, keeping it from pulling or getting tangled on anything.

"Gus, go grab BoJack, I'm going to need him for this next bit," Darik asked over his shoulder.

When they arrived, Darik instructed BoJack to hold various cables and connectors in place as they were positioned against the walls and attached to various ports and others were directed to the other floors. BoJack made staple-like fasteners of ether which allowed the cables to remain up and out of the way. Yuki poked her head out of an opening in the room above and BoJack extended the ends of the cords up to her.

"Gus, while many supers can manipulate ether with their powers, shaping it into permanent constructs is a lot more rare. Maybe one in four can create something that will last longer than a day. If you do make something like this," he gestured to the staples, "you have to make sure that you'll be around to take them down. Due to the nature of ether, they are very hard to destroy outright when done properly, and it could cause problems if no one can undo what you have done." BoJack instructed as they headed out of the cargo area up a small stairway to the commons room above.

Gus bit the inside of his cheek, wondering if he had permanently tied up those pirates what felt like a lifetime ago.

"So... hypothetically, if I did something like this," Gus made some of the ether ties form around his own hands, "just how durable are these?"

BoJack stepped out of the stairwell and looked at Gus' restraints.

"Yeah, these are like what you've done before. They're not

infused, or that is to say they're only infused with your MP. I'd give it two, maybe three weeks then it would dissolve on its own."

Gus was simultaneously relieved and worried at the news. On one hand, he hadn't shackled people for life, but on the other, what if the trip took that man and his family more than a couple of weeks? Did they get free and overpower the family again? *Why didn't I get a name or contact so I could follow up with them? I probably could have even used* **Wreckognize** *and they wouldn't even have to know—*

"Gu~u~u~s…" BoJack said. "Why are you asking about restraints? Aren't all the other supers in the manor's brig?"

Before he could answer, Darik elbowed between the two and started directing where the connections and cables should be placed and the conversation shifted to the task at hand. Gus took the opportunity to keep the conversation elsewhere.

"So are we making some type of shield?" Gus asked, looking at the ceiling and the odd pattern of wires and cables.

"Do you know what a Faraday cage is?" BoJack replied, going on when Gus shook his head. "Well, it's based on that principle. We have to mask the energy signatures of our Nth as there are scanners and sensors that can detect them. For obvious reasons, they do not want supers there that are uninvited, although there are a lot of citizens of Hinansho that have Nth."

"Really?"

"Yes, those newer supers who fought against the status quo were blacklisted and the Factions actively suppressed any attempts for them to find work, not only with Factions themselves but in industries they had a strong influence upon—basically everything legitimate. Places like Hinansho are a sanctuary, and they are accepted there. They do have to keep their markers on, but that's not a big deal for most people."

"Markers?"

"It kind of looks like a neon blue face-paint. Goes under the left eye. Plus anyone who uses an interface or display can read your stats and abilities. However, those who take the mark are free to live there as they please."

"So why don't we just do that? Seems simpler to use what they already are doing."

"Well, for starters, it's irreversible. Anyone can see your powers, their level and requirements, and your full complement of stats. Makes things a lot easier to exploit if there's a weakness. Besides that, the marker is a tattoo filled with human-made nanobots. Also permanent. You've heard of the Scarlet Letter? That tattoo is lovingly referred to as the curse of the 'Azure Bonds.'"

"So what's the Scarlet Letter? Was it some super's logo, something on their suit?"

BoJack shook his head in mock disgust. "What do they teach you kids in school anymore? Sheesh. Look it up on your display when you have the time."

A twinkling chime sounded over the comms.

"Weather's been good and we've made excellent time. I had my doubts with how this ship looks, but it's been kitted out perfectly. We should be in Hinansho in less than an hour. How are we doing on cloaking preparations? Do I need to modify our speed to give you more time?" Seneschal asked in her polished Queen's English.

"No, lass, we're finishing up. An hour will be plenty," Darik replied as he wrestled more cords out of a pile and lined them up. Less than twenty minutes later, they were done and Yuki crawled out of the access port fanning herself.

"Whoo, it gets hot in there... and dusty." She attempted to brush off the gray lint that had accumulated on her stockings and arms as she crawled around inside. "They need to spring for a vacbot drone. I'm totally going to need a shower and we haven't been out for even two hours," Yuki said dismally.

Aurora stepped away from a panel she was working on and raised her hands. They began to crackle and snap like a bug zapper and some of the bigger pieces of dust and lint leapt off of Yuki to a space in front of Aurora's palms. Yuki took advantage and fluffed her hair and brushed herself off.

"Thank you, Miss Lint!" Yuki said, giving Aurora a brief hug after they had removed anything not too ground in. Aurora let the waste fall into a nearby bin as she disengaged the static and went back to her project.

Gus took in the wide room that reminded him of a dive bar. There was a countertop and bar along one side, with the drinks strapped in securely. Chairs lined the walls with four-point harnesses. Tables were bolted to the floor, and they could be spun to raise or lower their height.

Pictures and memorabilia littered the walls, and Gus recognized some of the supers who came to take the manor in some of the pics. Apparently not all of the people working for Manticorps were mercs. He had let them slip out of his mind after the Crew showed up. Would he just leave them there indefinitely? Would someone come looking for them? Problems for another day.

"Gus, lad, could you throw that switch?" Darik had climbed up to an interface hub and was checking a small display there.

Gus looked around and saw a console. He pointed at different toggles and switches until he got the thumbs up. The cables lit up like Christmas lights.

"We're in business, boys!" Darik cheered, dropping down to the floor. "How're our power levels, Yuki?"

She gave a thumbs up and kept typing on her laptop, periodically unjacking and moving to another cluster of electronics.

"We are linked," Grimdark responded over the ship's comms.

"That was a right bit of fun." Darik clapped his hands and rubbed them together. "And I think I've earned myself a reward." He made his way behind the bar and took stock of the bottles, ooh-ing and aah-ing with pleasure as he saw what was available.

Aurora also finished whatever she was working on and waved Gus over.

"If you've never seen Hinansho, I'd check it out as we approach. It's pretty impressive."

"You've been there?" Gus said, raising an eyebrow.

"Of course not. The Academy has a whole rotation where they show you the sanctuary cities. Then warns you that if some rebellious young super wants to go exploring—you are on your own. No one from the Faction will come rescue you. Then they show what happened to the four or five students who did just that."

"Pretty bad?"

"You would think gruesome, but that wasn't what made it disturbing. From what the intelligence shows, they're still there. Being tortured or experimented on, who knows what. Those who were directly involved in the Rockland conflict have long memories, and I'll just say their ethics are a bit more flexible than most people."

"And we're waltzing in with a jury-rigged cloaking device and some dated shrouds. Awesome. Good times."

"We should be fine. But listen and follow orders implicitly. It's no joke if one of us is detained for *any* reason."

"No problems here, I don't mind if I just stay aboard. I don't even know what the plan is."

"We're meeting Leto's courier outside of Hinansho and delivering this encrypted data cube to a group inside. We then collect their payment and return it to the same courier. He'll have the shrouds and codes we need to get in. Problem is this group moves their headquarters around a lot. I guess among hybrids there are a lot of attempts at demonstrating who is the alpha and attempting to climb up their caste system. It's complicated and I don't know much about it, but step one is finding out where they even are."

"Then all we have to do is beat the other teams trying to do the same job, avoiding detection the entire time, and trusting that Leto won't just turn us in anyways at any point along the way."

"Yep. Pretty standard," Aurora quipped. "Oh look—you can see it from here." She pointed out one window.

They were flying above the clouds, and despite the height there was a large, dark cylinder in front of them. Upon closer inspection it looked like a dark storm, grayish-black clouds roiling around and around.

"That's wild. How does it stay there like that?" Gus squinted and used his perception boosts to zoom in and see the spectacle with more clarity.

"Some type of containment field. Keeps out deep scans and prying eyes from any satellites and such. Trade off is that it's perpetually night and always rainy. Or at least damp."

"Small price to pay for freedom, I guess."

"Hinansho is the biggest of the sanctuary cities; there are thirteen around the world. Hinansho isn't only big, it's tall. To take advantage of the field, they grew upwards, buildings upon buildings. They were lucky they had tons of engineers among the augments. The higher up you are, the better things are there."

"What's on the lower levels?"

"You don't want to know." Aurora hugged herself, feeling a sudden chill.

CHAPTER TWENTY-SEVEN

The Devil You Know

"What was this place called before it was transformed? Correia?" Darik asked no one in particular as he joined the group staring out the window.

"Something like that. It's been so long and who knows what really happened there. The fact that the existence of sanctuary cities is not taught in schools should tell you something," Harmony said bitterly. "If you all don't mind, I'd rather stay on the ship while we're there. This place gives me the creeps."

The ship banked to the left and the column veered away. Everyone had to grab something to hold on to while they dropped into the clouds and their speed slowed.

"Sorry for that," Seneschal apologized over the comm, "just got the rendezvous coordinates. Good news, we'll be the first team to arrive. ETA fifteen minutes. No need to strap in, we're making the transfer while airborne and then heading to Hinan-sho. Remote city scans are about fifty miles from here, so we should be fine. Darik and Yuki will have to integrate everything, but it's plug and play. Should only take a couple of minutes if everything is set up. Seneschal out."

There was an irregular shuddering as the ship slowed, pulses and halting jerks as they stopped in the air. Through the window, Gus could only see the haze of inter-cloud 'fog.'

Tempest came out of the pilot's cabin and nodded to Yuki. She grabbed her laptop and followed Tempest as they went down the gangway. Gus could feel the vibration of the cargo hatch opening on the back of the ship.

Less than five minutes later the same vibration occurred as Yuki came up the stairs. She handed Darik a handful of modules and disappeared into a panel, contorting with more agility than Gus had ever seen her exhibit.

"I'm reading everything connected up here. You need to make any more adjustments before we head for Hinansho?" Yuki called out from the panel.

"Nah, we're good to go here, lassie," Darik countered. "We're ready when you are!"

"Brace yourselves, this is going to be a bit annoying," Seneschal warned. A shriek like a banshee knocked the supers who weren't seated to their knees. Slowly the high-pitched tone slowed and everyone recovered as it faded into a pulse that diminished in intensity until it became white noise in the background.

Gus thought it wasn't even an audible sound, but something that their Nth could perceive by signal overlay. Once they regained their composure, the ship began moving again, turning and exiting the clouds and they set course to intersect the large column.

With the rattle of chains, the cargo elevator opened, revealing Tempest sitting on a crate. As everyone approached, he opened it and addressed the Crew.

"Looks like we only have four shrouds for this mission, and while they are newer than the ones I have used before, they are still about two generations behind the latest models. Whether that means anything or not remains to be seen. The scanners may be able to easily see through this type of shroud, depending on how sophisticated they are themselves. I'm confident that Darik and Yuki got the cage working, so I'll have Seneschal keep the transport as inconspicuous as possible."

"If she's piloting, how will she fly the ship from inside the cage?" Gus asked.

"She won't. She's not a super, she's an augment. She'll show up unregistered, but that means the same as 'tourist' to the locals. Shouldn't raise too many red flags unless we attract unwanted attention. I'm sure this old bucket has an autopilot feature though, in case we need her. Just like before—I'll only take volunteers, so none of you have to do this. The shrouds have to be configured, so let me know who's willing and we'll choose our team."

Gus would have liked to visit, but recognized that he would probably be the least helpful choice. He was ignorant of what was 'normal' and expected of the typical resident of Hinansho and imagined he would stick out no matter how hard he tried.

Kind of weird, since I was super good at not being noticed before I had powers.

"What do you mean it won't work on me?" Darik shouted, interrupting Gus' thoughts.

"These must have been used previously and customized for other supers whose powers aren't compatible with yours."

"Well, this could be a problem, doncha think?" Darik gruffed, folding his arms and frowning at Tempest.

The other supers who were willing to try the shrouds found that only Tempest, Aurora and Grimdark were compatible. And that was after two had to switch, a particular shroud being specialized so Grimdark alone could wear it.

Prime hesitantly stepped forward.

"My suit has a stealth mode that would shield me too. I could come and go in Hinansho and no one would know the difference." The voice was modulated through the helmet, filtering out even slight emotional cues.

"Every little bit will help; it gives us more options."

"I don't want to go, if you don't need me, just to be clear."

"I'll keep it in mind. If you're uncomfortable, I won't ask you to do anything, don't feel obligated."

Prime nodded and retreated to a corner to be alone.

"Well that looks like all of us. Still a suit left. Are you in or out, Gus? If not, we'll just have to do this with three," Tempest asked.

Gus accepted the suit, sliding the shroud over his shoulders and fastening it near his collarbones. Once in place, someone made some adjustments from behind and a green light pulsed on the fasteners in the front.

"Looks like you're in if you want, Gus. What do you say?" Aurora asked, something in her voice sounded almost pleading.

It'd be a chance to try to 'connect' as BoJack suggested... Gus thought before finally saying, "Okay, I'm in."

"If I'm not going to throw things off, I'd like to check it out." Yuki said, lifting her laptop, displaying it like a model in a game show. Tempest nodded in approval then returned to the cockpit to speak with Seneschal.

"Everybody get in the cage. We're about to enter in five..." Seneschal warned over the comm soon after Tempest had spoken with her.

Gus found a seat by a window and buckled in. They were now so close to the barrier that the interior lighting of the common room became distinct as the light from outside disappeared. Tempest was the last to buckle in and the ship penetrated the barrier.

Rain began to pelt the windows, moving like a screen swipe as they passed through the field. Bright lights guided traffic down large tunnels. If this didn't work, their ship would be boxed in and easily captured. Slowly, they worked their way forward in the queue until they hovered by the checkpoint. After what seemed like an extra long wait, they were waved through.

On the other side of the tunnel, bright lights strobed and flickered off the mists. Large buildings materialized out of the mist, hidden until the holo-ads came to life, detecting the motion of their ship. A beautiful woman brought a hand to her face as she pursed her lips indicating 'shh.' The image panned back, revealing more women, all exotic and beckoning them to visit the 'Kitty Club.'

"Look at this place," Pulse said in wonder, face plastered to the window. Dark and brooding, it looked like Gotham and Blade Runner's version of Los Angeles had an ugly baby. Neon signs in kanji and holograms illuminated the foggy, overcast city. Hovercars and the bike-like craft similar to the ones Gus had nicknamed 'jet-skies' raced through the gloom, somehow avoiding accidents in the tumultuous traffic.

"Kind of makes you wonder what we could do if there weren't so many restrictions by the Factions, eh?" Darik grumbled.

"No—it does not! This is what happens when people run amok. You know what goes on down there—" Harmony objected, eyes wide and pointing downward.

"You can't believe all those urban legends," he sighed, waving a hand in dismissal, "that's just stuff for horror holos."

"Those people are willing to do anything. Illegal cybernetics to try some twisted attempt to be like a super. Wet-ware shops that will perform all sorts of dangerous surgeries and trans-plants, no questions asked. It's chaos, and people somewhere down the chain are getting hurt. Don't even get me started on those abominations they call neo-furries!"

"Neo-furries?" Gus whispered to Aurora unfamiliar with the term.

"People who insert animal DNA into themselves to grow wings, talons, scales, or some other trait. Not very compatible with human physiology, but those people are tenacious, and some of the wet docs love experimentation. Apparently there's more work for them than they can handle."

Gus shivered at the thought. He had wanted to be popular and noticed when he was a teenager, but never even dared coloring his hair a wild shade, let alone getting a tattoo or piercing for fear of how his father would react. He was still mad at himself that he had been so cowed. Still, those people were only affecting themselves, so what was the harm? Harmony seemed to act like they were being exploited.

Darik put up his arms placatingly. "All I'm saying is that there's probably a happy middle ground somewhere in there. Sure, we maintain order with Purple Faction, but it stifles innovation. People are afraid to step out of line, and that only lasts so long."

"You should have joined Orange. They love augments and tinkering with DNA," Grimdark said archly.

"Aw, shuddup. Things have been stagnant, and you know it. People are getting restless, and we've had to step in to manage more civil disturbances the last five years than in the previous ten. Eventually rebellion springs when people are oppressed."

The ship slipped down into the fog, following the pre-programmed course given by Seneschal.

"I don't like this. Leto was never that trustworthy, and I trust him even less now that he has what he wants and doesn't need to keep us happy for future trades," Yuki murmured.

Tempest grimaced, hearing his own fears verbalized.

"I think we all feel that way. Let's work quickly and be on our way."

CHAPTER TWENTY-EIGHT

Private Eyes

"How are we going to find our contact?" Harmony asked.

"Why don't we do as one of the locals?" Yuki suggested as she did a quick search and held up her laptop so the Crew could see. A spartan web-page showed the contact information for the nearest private investigator, who went simply by 'Shamus.'

"Not very impressive, is it?" Anastasia asked, scrunching her nose.

"I kind of like it. Not too flashy, maybe he's no-nonsense, get to the point. Usually if you have to brag, you're compensating for something." Darik leaned in close to read the text. "Says he specializes in surveillance, background, and missing persons. Over twenty-five years' experience. Could be just what we are looking for."

"I agree. If he's good at finding people who don't necessarily want to be found, that will save us a lot of time and legwork. Can you set up the appointment, Yuki?" Tempest asked then gathered Aurora, Grimdark, Prime, and Gus over to him. She threw him a big thumbs up and got typing.

"We probably don't need all of us to go in here, but I would like someone to keep watch outside while I meet with him. We need to be discreet."

Grimdark raised a hand solemnly and folded his arms in front of him.

"Thank you. Prime, how are you feeling? We won't absolutely need you; did you want to stay onboard?" A quiet nod in response and preparations were done.

Aurora showed them the supply closet she had used earlier and they all put on coveralls that hid their conspicuous suits. While the shrouds would hide their Nth signature, they were unreliable as far as visually changing one's appearance. Best to have the greatest margin of protection.

"Let's double check everyone's shrouds and get ready to go," Yuki said while still typing, eyes never leaving her screen.

Yuki scanned and analyzed everything, and determined that it was all functioning as it should, calibrating the shroud to their new outfits. Seneschal notified them that they were at Shamus Investigations as they set down on a landing plate that served this district.

They walked down to the cargo bay, and Gus noticed the jet-sky vehicles stored in recesses. Closed chutes yawned underneath them, hinting they could be used for rapid deployment. His hand traced one as they waited for the gangway to drop.

They exited onto a paved lot wet with condensation. Contrails of fog spun in little vortexes as different vehicles zipped by in this more remote area. The area was fairly foggy, and Gus inhaled the moist air. A stairwell led down off the lot and snaked around the sides of buildings.

After a couple turns, they arrived at a humble office, with a simple LED sign proclaiming Shamus Investigations. Nodding to Grimdark, the team entered the small office while Grimdark stood watch on the landing.

Tempest brushed some water off of his shoulder as he stepped inside the tiny waiting room. A hologram of an attractive woman with coiffed hair meticulously stacked atop her head materialized in front of them.

"Good evening, I am Eliza. Mr. Shamus will be with you shortly, please wait here."

After a brief pause, the metal door separating the small entryway from the rest of the office slid into the ceiling and the group entered. Gus slid a bit, barely catching himself from falling on the smooth floor. Something dark stained the tiles, streaking away from where he stood.

Was that blood? Or motor oil? Maybe even something I stepped in on the way over here?

"You okay?" Aurora asked as Gus recovered from his awkward 'Twister' pose. Gus nodded as Eliza reappeared and gestured to a door on the far side of the room. As they walked in, a chime rang and Shamus turned around in a large chair. Gus started as he saw the heavily augmented man who at the moment was missing his left arm down from the elbow. The investigator's expression darkened when he saw the group.

"You gotta be kidding me. No way. I should report you right now," Shamus growled, his dark expression replaced with one of outright hostility.

"What are you talking about—" Tempest began to protest.

"You three are supers—clear as day. If you didn't get the memo, you are *not welcome* here in Hinansho. I've already had enough trouble today, and I don't need any more drama. This," he waved a dismissive hand at them, "looks like a whole ball of drama I don't want any part of." The augment twisted, ready to spin his chair around and terminate the conversation.

"We can make it worth your while," Tempest countered.

"How does he know?" Gus whispered to Aurora.

"We can make it worth your while," the older super said again, stepping forward boldly, encouraged that his offer had obviously caught the man's attention.

"Unless you can get me a new arm, I'm afraid I'm not interested." A smug smile settled over the man's face as he leaned forward, challenging Tempest to meet his offer.

"Done. Now if we can discuss the details—"

"Hold on. I'm not talking about just any arm. I'm talking

about a Serif 800-XT with full sync and specs." With this revelation, he leaned back his chair. He tried to fold his arms in defiance but missing one made the gesture look odd as he fumbled
a bit until he finally settled his lone arm on the chair's armrest.

"Like I said, done."

"And I want it integrated before I start." His voice adopted
an even colder tone as he dropped the ultimatum.

"Now I believe we are being more than reasonable, Mr.
Shamus. We will get you fitted, but I will keep the spec key until
the job is done. Contrary to what you think, I know the value of
that hardware, and how likely you are to have anyone as willing
to provide it to you for such a simple request as we have."

"I'll be the judge of just how simple your task is," the investigator spat. Gus could tell his father had overcome the man's
main objections and it was now a matter of ironing out the
details.

"What time frame are we talking about here for this 'simple'
little task of yours, super?"

"As soon as humanly possible," Tempest stated and Gus
winced. *Inhuman* was the equivalent of a racial slur to those with
augments, and his turn of phrase could easily be interpreted as
offensive.

"That is to say, speed is of the essence. We are on a contract
and competing against others to deliver something as soon as
possible. Your discretion and promptness will be appreciated.
Let me contact my people, and find out how soon we can get
what you need." Tempest gathered Gus and Aurora close as he
opened a comm to the ship as Shamus turned to a console on
his desk.

"Yuki, tell me you can get a Serif 800-XT," Tempest whispered urgently.

"Here? I'm sure they have them. These guys know their
encryption though, so it's not like security in the Factions. These
guys have taken cybersecurity to a whole new level."

"Work your magic, I trust you."

Gus peeked back at the mechanical man who waved with

his remaining hand, a broad smile on his face that was disconcerting. After Tempest had finished speaking with Yuki, they all turned to face Shamus again.

"So why don't you tell me what you have in mind? I still haven't totally committed to whatever fiasco you guys have cooked up. First of all, how did you even find me?"

"To be brutally honest, you were the closest private investigator when we did the search."

At first, he seemed pleased, then suddenly angry. *Was this guy the best for the job? Seems a touch unstable...* Gus thought.

"We need to find someone, specifically the headquarters for the Aslan clan. We need to find them quickly and without them knowing we're looking. Can you handle that?"

"And I suspect you want me to break in and retrieve something, I'm assuming?"

"No, just the location. We can handle the rest," Tempest urged, trying to make the job seem as simple as possible.

Shamus leaned forward and stared, squinting his eyes as if probing their souls.

"You know what could happen to me if the clans got wind that I was spilling their secrets, don't you?"

Aurora's jaw muscles twitched as she tried to restrain herself.

"We are counting on your discretion. Both for us and for yourself. If this is out of your skill set, let us know and we will be on our way," Aurora spat, turning to go.

"I didn't say that." He held up his remaining hand as Aurora sighed and turned back to look at him. "I just want you to know what it is you're really asking me to do."

"We do. And compared to what *you're* asking, I believe it's a more than equitable exchange, wouldn't you agree?" Aurora pressed.

He laughed and nodded. "Okay, you got a deal. I'll need some time though. Meet me in two hours and give me your contact," he conceded. Tempest slid his info to the investigator.

"We'll be in touch," he said, and lost interest in them, turning to the console on his desk and typing.

The group looked at each other and took this to mean that the interview was over. They filed out and Tempest jumped on the comm again and began working some of the details out with Yuki.

"That went better than expected?" Aurora asked, her voice tentative.

"It could have been worse. He didn't balk at the ask though, which was good. I think he can deliver, which will save us time. Like us, the others will have to find the clan headquarters before they can deal, so this should maintain our lead," Tempest said, pushing outside of the office and into the rain.

A siren barked to life, accompanied with flashing blue and red lights. The group froze in panic as bright headlights targeted them. The vehicle approached, siren getting louder as they braced for the worst. Frozen in place, the enforcer or whatever the equivalent was in Hinansho turned and sped off down another alley. The siren wail waned as it drifted in the distance.

"Hells to the bells, that sucked!" Gus gasped.

They had an uneasy laugh as they made their way back to the ship.

CHAPTER TWENTY-NINE

Ghetto Blastah

"Are you sure you can hack in? These are big players and you don't know this system," Tempest asked Yuki.

Yuki inwardly groaned.

Why is everyone always underestimating me? Have I ever failed to deliver when it comes to this? He said he trusted me, was that just lip service? She shook off the irritation and replied simply, "I'll be fine, trust me."

Tempest looked skeptical, but nodded anyways.

"I've calculated the ideal time for the mission and based on traffic patterns and shift cycling, there will be the least activity in the area around Serif in one hour and seven minutes. That's when we should make our attempt," Yuki advised, touching her forehead then her wrist so everyone would sync their displays.

"I'll form the distraction and we will get Yuki, Gus, and Aurora inside," Tempest said. "You two will need to steal something of value and then flee with me, drawing the sentries away. Yuki, how are you going to get past internal security?"

"Serif is fully automated at the location we will be hitting. The entire operation is automated. Only robots making augment parts; there are no human workers or even supervisors there. Access ports exist in case systems need to be updated, however. At the very least, there will be pressure plates, thermal detection, cameras, and motion detectors. Sentries all can fly and will have multiple armaments. You will need to take them seriously—they're deadly." Yuki eyed Gus and Aurora.

"As for me, I'll need to find some way of overcoming those security challenges in a little over an hour, so no pressure, right?"

Prime stepped forward, approaching the small group.

"Sorry to insert myself in the conversation, but I think I can help with Yuki's part of the plan."

Yuki's face visibly calmed as her eyes widened with hope.

"She could borrow one of my stealth suits. It might be a little big on you, but it should work out perfectly. Active camouflage technology and wall-walking. Completely thermally shielded with wave-dampening technology."

"Um, yes please!" Yuki exulted. "Do you guys need me for anything else?" When no one had anything else to offer, Yuki followed the demure Prime. The spartan quarters showed no real decorations or pictures, just a closet full of four suits.

"Try this one," Prime pulled out a suit at the far end of the closet. "It's the smallest one I have."

Yuki grabbed it and, uncertain about undressing in front of Prime, slipped into the small bathroom by the cabin.

No one knows if Prime's a dude or not, so better to not make it weird. The pants were extremely stretchy but felt like they were made of a breathable vinyl or leather. As she put on the upper portion of the suit, there was a jacket-like portion embedded with all sorts of electronics on the internal surface, totally hidden by the hard armor on the exterior.

She was only able to get it partially on, so had to have Prime help her attach and adjust everything. Once it was all in place, Yuki did some deep stretches and practiced some kicks. The material was extremely supple, and remained silent as it stretched with her various movements.

"This is how you turn on the stealth functions." Prime

showed her a set of ridges along the right side of the chest-plate. As Yuki depressed them, a quick-button populated her display with each of the features. Active camouflage, wave dampener, gravimetrics.

"Aw, yeah! How does this work?" Yuki asked, activating gravimetrics. Her feet felt suddenly heavier, as if mired in mud, and she had to exert herself to lift her legs.

"You can refine that to a degree. You still need to have a base support to manage your body weight. Try it out here." Prime grabbed the mattress of her small bed and slid it onto the ground.

Tentatively, Yuki gingerly stepped onto the wall; the mired suction feeling grabbed the wall. She had a couple of false starts, as her brain refused to lift her supporting leg off of the floor.

"You've just got to commit. Trust me, you won't need the mattress, but it helps your brain let go for the first couple of times," Prime encouraged.

Yuki stepped and flung her arms out to catch herself if she fell, but there she was, hanging on the wall. The suit was stiff from a tiny bit above her knee, reminding her of snowboarding.

"Now straighten up," Prime directed, and as Yuki stood horizontally on the wall, the suit somehow compensated, supporting her and reducing how gravity pulled her upper torso to the ground. Blood didn't appear to be affected, so hanging upside down would be trickier.

"I wish I had more time to get used to this. It definitely has a learning curve."

"You also have to be careful what you step on. Most walls are sheet-rock, which will not support you; you'll rip a chunk out and still be attached to that piece as you fall to the ground. For the same reason, avoid ceilings. Here, let me toggle this…" Prime reached to the helmet and tapped the side, moving fingers as if sliding bars up and down on the cheek of the mirrored helmet.

"That should do it. Okay, I'm going to let you borrow the

helmet too, but it's the only one I have. Since I like my anonymity, I'm going to hand it to you outside the door and stay in my cabin until you get back. I'm *trusting* you, Yuki. If you lose this helmet, I do not have another. Got it?"

Yuki nodded gravely, vowing to herself to be careful.

"Practice a little bit. The suit learns your mannerisms and movements the longer you use it. I'd practice until you have to go."

Yuki walked around, noticing how she had to swing her weight side to side as she took a step. The suit almost felt like it was pulling up on her "ceiling side" and solidifying on the "floor side" as one leg disengaged from the wall. She felt like Frankenstein as she clumsily tried to move around, but Prime was right, she never fell. As Yuki stepped to the floor again, there was a brief moment of vertigo as her world reset to normal and she deactivated the gravimetrics.

"That is trippy!" Yuki said, eyes wide as she laughed.

"You kind of get to love it," Prime admitted, laughing a bit as well. "Don't go messing with any settings—I calibrated it so it's as close to autopilot as I can make it. Let me know when you're ready and I'll hand the helmet out to you."

Checking her internal display, they only had thirty-eight minutes left.

"Now or never, I guess. Thanks again."

Prime nodded as Yuki slipped out the door, holding it almost closed. A hiss sounded and then there was a slight tap on her fingers. Prime passed the helmet out, and Yuki heard Prime's actual voice for the first time, instead of the digital filter everyone associated with the super.

"Sorry, it's probably a mess. I never take it off unless I'm alone. You may want to clean it before putting it on," a soft voice replied. Prime was female. Unequivocally. Yuki stood there processing the revelation as the door clicked closed.

———

The group of supers slid down the chutes, bouncing as their transports engaged and began hovering. The jet-skies were really called "Psiycles," since they hovered utilizing some technology that used psi-waves to somehow interact with gravity and weak attraction and repulsion forces to stay aloft. Gus preferred the term "jet-sky" more.

Yuki held onto Tempest, riding double as the three psiycles bobbed as they slid out of the transport, which sped off to await them at the rendezvous point.

Tempest raised one fist upward as they all slowed their bikes, a deep fog forming and becoming ever denser. Pulling in moisture, Tempest thickened the cloud that masked their approach as Yuki readied herself.

They pulled up to the landing and she activated **Hack** as Tempest maintained the psiycle hovering by the login panel. Since the process was totally automated, she spoofed a delivery request and probed for the appropriate protocol markers while searching for upcoming manifests and deliveries that the facility was expecting.

Yuki pried away the layers of digital defenses until the loading door slid open and they floated inside. A quick search of the factory database indicated some valuable processors and actuators were getting critically low. Stealing these would elicit the highest retaliatory response. She sent the info for the storage location of these items to Gus and Aurora. She wanted those sentries riled.

Gus and Aurora sped off, and Tempest let Yuki get into position before he retreated to await her extraction. A tense couple of minutes later, all hell broke loose.

It was on!

CHAPTER THIRTY

Hack 1/Charlie X

Aurora and Gus flew past Yuki, who waited just outside the loading dock. They were traveling faster than she had ever seen psycles fly. Sentries of all sizes and configurations followed them like a huge robotic hive had been disturbed, splitting in two and weaving out of sight as it followed the two as they fled in different directions.

Yuki activated all the stealth features of the suit and entered the factory. The facility was extremely basic in its layout. She had to make it to the core, which was, as expected, in the very center of the plant. The brain and heart of the building all in one. As such, all corridors throughout the facility led to it.

Passing the now-empty outer layers, the passageways became crowded as she entered the manufacturing portion of the factory. A couple of times she had to backtrack and get out of the way as large components that took the entire corridor were moved from one section to another, not allowing even an inch clearance on the sides.

The dampening field muffled her movements and it felt unnatural. As the activity picked up around her, the hyper-awareness of silence faded as materials clanked and settled as robot loaders of different sizes and shapes interacted with materials.

Passing deeper into the building, the inner walls, floor, and ceiling were an opaque plastisteel illuminated from within. She continued until she arrived at the mainframe control room. Seeing that it was only a Medusa class G made her smile a bit. At least five years old, her skills should be adequate for this.

Not supernally difficult, but she had no history with Serif or their AIs. That had never stopped her before. She still was a master tester for her father's firm on the rare occasions she visited home. The programmers were always trying to stump her with difficult AIs in all types of environments.

Automated bots and even the smaller AIs had trouble with extensive lateral thinking, so they were ineffective at hacking bigger institutions. Without the capacity and versatility of one of the prohibitively expensive networks her father offered, they weren't resilient enough to battle an AI that could adapt and modify attacks against it. It was the primary reason her father's company had skyrocketed to the forefront of digital security.

Yuki wasn't just a hacker though, and not just an augment either. She was a super.

Yuki steeled herself for the infiltration. Her hands trembled slightly in anticipation, more excitement than fear. She had been fighting AIs that were prototypes for all the major corporations before she was in her teens.

Never losing a possible advantage, her father had noted her gift with computers early on and capitalized on it. As one of the world's leading developers of software and artificial intelligence, he leveraged her prowess to catapult his company CyberDynamics to the forefront of AI development, specializing in security.

She had enjoyed it more than any game. When she was "in," she felt like all her barriers were sloughed off digitally. At first, her father would take time as they reviewed her battle technique, analyzing her methods and tactics to defeat the system. It was the first, and unfortunately only, time they bonded.

It was more than disappointing when the interactions waned and eventually she began reporting to Ludwig, whose all-business attitude made the task feel more like a deposition. Cold, clinical probing and questioning, all the while looking down his piggy nose through those ridiculously small glasses perched on the very tip. It was as if they were designed so that he could look down on others to make them functional.

Despite all that, when she was inside—she was free. The irritating things of her life didn't apply when she was "in." She could live out her favorite anime and manga. She had always been adept at coding, and the transition of this into AI battling was intuitive for her on a level that seemed to be difficult for others. No matter which prodigies her father managed to gather to the company, they never pushed the system to the limits like she did.

Even now, she ported in remotely and fought the latest creations her father's company created. She would have done it even if she didn't get paid, but she didn't stop them from sending the embarrassing amounts of money anyway. It was a poor substitute for a real relationship with her father, but somehow it felt like sticking it to him by making him pay. For her, it was never about the money, though. Part of her wondered if it was a way that her father maintained his feeling of superiority and control over her. That if she was an employee, he would always have the upper hand.

She shook her head that he felt the need to do that to his own daughter. Still, if the illusion of control made him feel better, she would gladly take the money in case she ever needed it. That was the trick, letting others think they had the upper hand while retaining it all along. Whether she was "in" or "out," it was all the same.

The maddening thing was, no one would ever see her like this. When immersion hacking, she felt almost like a demigod. No matter the foe, she knew how to pinpoint and determine its digital weaknesses. She had fashioned her gear with a meticulous perfectionism that pushed her to be on the bleeding edge of ultimate protection and amplification of her abilities. She would make some tweak or refinement to push the stats of her gear to make them even that much more formidable. Without the massive monitoring system at CyberDynamics headquarters, there was no other way others could watch her do what she did so well.

It was why she didn't go into Green Faction—she would be just another cog in the wheel there. Not to mention her father's heavy influence on their inner workings thanks to the reliance on the technology his company produced. He would forever be pulling strings if she had gone Green Faction.

In Purple she was unique, but they didn't really know how to use her. She couldn't prove herself in the same ways and so her assignments were unfulfilling and so far below her abilities she had questioned her choice more than once.

Before she could get too frustrated, the interface faded from orange to green as she overcame the inner defenses. And that was just to log in!

And just like that, she had bypassed the outer security firewall and could jack in directly. She rubbed her fingertips together, activating the implanted receptor pads embedded under her skin. Softly, she caressed the import jack and engaged the Charlie X protocol which would sync her access with the computer.

Unseen to the human eye, tiny Nth bridged the gap and made the connection. With a virtual *thock*, Yuki knew that the system had opened like the door of a huge keep, yawning wide before her. A thrill of anticipation shot down her spine. She loved this feeling.

Yuki activated her **Slice** ability and dove into the system. The Nth transmitted her consciousness into the machine, facilitating the conversion of her core personality into the environment of the system.

With a *twang*, she materialized and fell to crash onto the

surface of a large building. She braced herself and executed a perfect three-point landing, absorbing the shock as bits of concrete shattered and flew away from the landing zone. Cracks spidered away from her in concentric circles but the rooftop held.

Getting to her feet, she heard the tumultuous roar of ocean waves crashing all around. The spray and mist were thrown up as water rammed against the building, becoming tinged orange in the evening sun before falling. This appeared to be some metropolis, swallowed up in some post-apocalyptic tsunami so only the highest buildings remained, skewed at different angles like a ramshackle cemetery.

A tight pressure on her right shoulder reminded her of the presence of her familiar Argus. Argus had always been there from the early days of her coding, and manifested as a rudimentary interface. Just a bobbing light like a will o' the wisp. Over time he had evolved until he resembled a miniature Transformer or Gundam.

His personality had also evolved the bit's level, where he could only respond yes or no, to giving vague impressions akin to 'this might be worth considering.' Further evolutions improved his ability to communicate directly and give advice, warning against impending attacks and parsing the wild attacks and abilities she imagined into code, shaping her intentions into virtual reality.

As she looked over the edge, she saw the remnants of a large city, with skyscrapers the only remaining structures visible in the churning, swirling waters. Some tilted at odd angles and some had tipped, only being supported by other larger buildings. In this environment, it appeared like the ocean had risen about five-hundred feet, leaving only the tops of a ruined civilization behind.

A glowing yellow light caught the corner of her eye as something disappeared deeper under the waves. Yuki scanned the area, evaluating this arena and its immense size in comparison to others she had fought upon in the past, and readied her abilities.

Mist hit Yuki in a plume as something large burst forth from the surface of the white frothy waves. Bits of a metallic framework glinted in the sun as water poured out of sections of the creature that had been damaged.

A massive jaw opened, the weathered and worn steel screeching with a deafening shriek as the creature articulated and parts of its framework scraped against each other. Intact sections were coated with sharp, jagged sections of coral, giving the appearance of fins along the back of the appendages that separated from the body of the monster, fanning out like a hydra, and undulating in unison. Creatures scuttled along the surface like ants.

Through open sections of the outer surface, bright yellow shone through, the creature somehow holding in its molten blood despite the breach.

Yuki activated her **Data-mine** ability and squinted at the small creatures. As she expected, they were not simple sea-life living inside the coral, they were active minions that were part of this AI boss's defenses.

Deathapods
HP: 250/250
MP: 100/100
Active Attacks:
Buzz Saw *(Passive): Slashing damage (variable), must be initiated by* **Kraken.**
Swarm *(10MP/activation): Stop prey by attaching securely while alive to cover and overwhelm target. Reduces Dexterity .5/deathapod. (Effect stacks.)*

With a whip of two tentacles, some of the creatures spun towards Yuki.

She activated **Overclock** and her perception of time slowed the environment around her, the crablike creatures resembling buzz-saws as they tucked their appendages inward and the sharp barbs on their shells spun like saw-teeth as they flew towards her with alarming volume and in different directions.

She leaped into the air and jumped on the nearest creature like a stepping stone. Their carapaces were slightly rounded but Yuki was able to jump from one to another. She flipped and twisted to avoid the barrage of spinning deathapods, one of the tails of her modified qipao being neatly sliced away as she arched her back to vault over the incoming mobs. The slice of fabric evaporated in a flash of pixels, leaving the revealing outfit a little draftier than before.

She pirouetted and leaned back, kicking incoming crabomi-nations, directing them back at the tentacles. They sped off in real-time and sunk deep with meaty *thunks* as their barbs dug deep into the metal, sometimes tearing through and sailing into the waves beyond. Occasionally one would explode in a burst of pixels as she scored a critical hit with the sharp heel of her boots. They would be utterly impractical in the real world, but here, she could look good *and* kick some ass.

While she flowed and moved, Argus pummeled incoming deathapods with beam weapons, slicing neatly through those outliers that were approaching on erratic vectors, making the way clear for his master.

There was a brief respite and Yuki pressed forward. She sped ahead, running horizontally along the floating deathapods, pushing off and sailing through the air.

Holding her hand out to the side, she activated **Zanbato BFS**, which materialized an obnoxiously large sword with a triangular hooked tip. She crashed into the creature, where she plunged the zanbato into the end of the tentacle, her momentum pushing the blade deep into the surface. Coral exploded from the impact, spraying bits away, revealing the rusted metal beneath.

Holding her arms back, she ran down the length of the tentacle, dragging the zanbato as it carved a deep furrow along the length of the flailing appendage. Gobbets of molten metal flew as the sword burned through it like butter, hissing angrily as they hit the wet surface of the tentacle.

The depth of the zanbato served to anchor her as the creature swung the arm back and forth, trying to flick her off. Streams of the molten blood shot out of the gash, cooling and hardening into metallic shapes with swoops and curves.

I am an artist of death! Yuki thought with mirth as she wreaked havoc on the beast.

In reply, the Kraken dove suddenly, the crash of water hitting Yuki like a wall. The blast of water cooled the molten metal spurting out and locked her zanbato in place, a large glob of steel anchoring it in place despite her attempts to pull it free. Pain exploded in her ears as the water pressure increased, feeling like two icepicks.

She screamed **NEGA TYPHOON!** Bubbles streamed from the corners of her mouth as the ability activated. Water repulsed away from her, forming a barrier a foot away. Yuki spat and coughed up salty water, flicking her wet hair out of her face with a quick neck whip.

Downward the Kraken dove, and the darkness quickly swallowed her, the only illumination was the yellow ports where the creature's blood illuminated the murk. Gritting her teeth, Yuki began to yank the zanbato back and forth, attempting to free the blade. Metal began to crumble next to the blade and glowing yellow material dribbled from the breach. With *Nega Typhoon* keeping the water away, the metal could not cool and the blade was soon free.

Yuki didn't know where this AI was taking her, but she didn't want to find out. She plunged the zanbato back into the tentacle and ran around its circumference in a spiral pattern, circling towards the main body. Light flared then was quickly doused as the leaking blood supercooled as her protective bubble retreated from the molten material.

The tentacle frayed as it was systematically spiralized. The damaged tentacle ripped free and gouts of metal flooded out, forming glowing red cloud-like shapes as the blood cooled and fell away. The Kraken continued its frenetic dive faster than the metal could be pulled down through the water.

Yuki almost lost her grip when the Kraken rammed into something at full speed. One shoulder was definitely wrenched and she took 87 HP of damage, but she managed to stay clinging to the zanbato. The creature then wormed along the rocky underwater floor, twisting in an attempt to scrape her off.

She crouched down and held on tight, plunging the zanbato a little deeper and lowering her center of gravity. The sudden changes in direction lifted her off the back of the creature more than once, while she clung desperately to her weapon. ***Data-mine*** revealed that this tactic was slicing off chunks of the AI's sizable HP pool. Her efforts had taken off about a third of the total but her options felt very limited as she hung on for dear life.

That was the problem challenging a virtual god to a battle in their universe. They controlled the where and the physics of the fight. The problem with gods was that they often underestimated everyone but themselves. And usually this was enough, due to the huge power discrepancy.

Yuki clenched her fists around the zanbato, letting fury build up inside her core.

Don't you ever *underestimate me!*

CHAPTER THIRTY-ONE

Holding in the World

Yuki blazed with anger and let out the compressed rage that she had been taught to hold deep down inside, funneling that energy into her attack.

"*Data Kicking Inferno!*" she yelled, and poured all the energy straight into the breach by her sword which had slightly sealed as she had stopped moving. The gout of energy lit up the surrounding structures and illuminated the craggy rock wall in the trench they were scuttling through. The area of impact began to implode and crumble inward like a sinkhole. As Yuki's zanbato was freed, the force of the attack propelled her away from the Kraken.

Upwards she soared, propelled like a rocket through the water. The heat of the beam created a plume of steam and released dissolved gasses which hid the combatants from view. Yuki kept feeding her fury into the attack. She hadn't tapped into this energy for a while and she had much more available than she was expecting, a wicked grin spreading across her face.

She shot out of the water just as the power started to ebb, and her momentum propelled her high enough that she made an easy landing atop one of the tilted towers. The euphoria that attack generated was beyond most things she had ever experienced, and part of why she loved battling AIs. Her body thrummed with the residual resonance. Releasing that toxic yet powerful energy caused a refractory relaxation that was second to none. The subconscious wrestling of the fury beast could ease. For a while, at least.

The release also served to purge her system. The mental sludge that accumulated over time, like the gunk in drainage pipes, was blasted away, resulting in a temporary increase in her mental stats: perception, intelligence, and charisma. She smirked, remembering how she had thought charisma was a useless stat to boost in a battle, until she felt a surge of confidence and security in the scope of her abilities that allowed her to push past the fear of fighting an impossible foe. The boosts would only last a short time; she needed to use them to their best advantage.

Her mind focused, she peered at the bubbling water below. Steam and large air pockets burst the surface in a stream. A telltale furrow and large wake followed the Kraken as it sped back to engage her again. **Data-mine** revealed that despite her ultimate attack, the creature was still at 40% max health, which equated to over 200,000 HP still remaining! She needed to get this creature out of the water and fight on her terms or she would run out of juice. Plus, the longer this took while "in," the more time was passing on the "out," and the chances for detection went exponentially higher.

She wasn't sure what had happened to her body while she was slicing, but countless warnings had been given that if she died during an AI battle, she would become a ghost in the machine. Unable to merge her consciousness back with her body.

This was part of what irked Yuki. No one she cared about seemed to know the real risks of what she did—and how amazing it was she pulled it off, time and time again. Maybe she made it look easy. They only saw what they thought was a simple hack or breach of a firewall and they moved on. This was a constant struggle, but one that made her feel truly alive. She just wished someone could understand.

Yuki backed up the sloping roof of the skyscraper, trying to draw the creature out. She had frenzied it, and its tentacles snaked out, rabidly searching for purchase and pulling the lumbering mass of its body out of the water. Without the water to support it, the creature looked unwieldy as it pulled itself onto the rooftop, caving in concrete with its bulk. Instead of stopping it, this created more footholds and purchase points, slamming metal tentacles into the building like pitons as it grasped its way toward Yuki.

Checking her own MP and health, she was still doing alright, having taken little damage, but her ultimate had dropped her MP down dangerously low. She would only have one trick left in her arsenal and she needed to make it count, as she could only use it once per slice. It only took 1 MP to activate, but it was her most powerful skill.

She looked through her choices as she kept her attention rapt on the morbidly fascinating progress of the Kraken as it scrabbled and clawed its way out of the water. Such a thing shouldn't exist. Couldn't exist in reality, an unsightly agglomeration of bits of Lovecraftian horror. The site of her ultimate attack had left a large bulbous mass where the molten blood had cooled, resembling a gargantuan tumor. The irregular mass slowed its progress, giving Yuki the time she needed to consider her options.

Her back hit the other side of the rooftop, a railing preventing her from tumbling over the other side. She was as high as she could go on this particular tower. Nothing else was close enough to reach, and she knew she would lose if she tried to reach another building and allow the Kraken to return to its element.

The utter size of the monster was surprising; it kept pulling more of its bulk from the water like a magician's endless handkerchief. The slug-like body tapering only slightly as its body disappeared into the waves as it squelched and surged towards her. Over two hundred feet and who knew how much was hidden.

Yuki was swiping between her options and suddenly returned to one she passed in haste as she quickly searched. Yes. That one.

One of the unique advantages of fighting AIs, that was Yuki's alone as far as she knew, was her super ability of **Summon**. It allowed her to gather an AI to her bestiary and call them forth in future battles once she had defeated them. She quickly scanned the profile of the summon in question:

Jade 'Banefire' Phoenix
Acquired: Jaybird Industries, 3/24/2037.
Emerald Ever-flame: This summon fires a plume of emerald flame that lasts five minutes. During this time, the flames are unquenchable, dealing fire elemental damage to the target. Upon using this ability, summon will subsume into the target and is unavailable for other forms of damage.

Not the best at straight up melee, but consistent, unblockable damage on an elemental weakness. It was the right choice. Yuki started the gestures that triggered the summon for the Jade Phoenix, and a conduit of light melted through the evening clouds. The ever-present winds that constantly whipped in every direction stilled and sonorous tones, as if from a heavenly choir, whispered then increased in pitch and intensity as an almond shaped mass descended along the green light like a tractor beam.

When it was a hundred feet overhead, the phoenix unfurled the wings tucked tightly around it and the singing reached a crescendo, air shimmering around the viridian flames that the creature's wings appeared to be made from. It let forth a triumphant screech, and the Kraken paused in its climb at the appearance of this unexpected foe.

Wasting no time, Yuki ordered it to use its sole ability and like a dam bursting loose, it surged forward. Simultaneously, the dulcet tones disappeared and the wind reappeared with even greater intensity, as if enraged it was forced to subside, albeit briefly. The phoenix dove at the Kraken and a gout of emerald flame basted the surface of the AI.

Coral cracked and exploded as it was super-heated and sublimated away, along with the metal skin beneath, which split and tore like an overcooked sausage. The phoenix plunged into the opening, and never stopped spewing green flames as it burrowed inside the creature, tearing the outer metallic flesh like paper as it pushed its way inside.

Yuki dropped to her knees and covered her ears from the shrieks. They were so intense that she felt her legs becoming numb as the entire rooftop vibrated with the sustained noise. Prying her eyes open, she saw the remaining HP of the creature slowly trickle downward, speeding up as she saw the phoenix do its grim task. The outer surface plumped and tore as the phoenix burrowed.

The Kraken writhed all the more, tentacles flailing and pelting the rooftop with deathapods. Fortunately, no errant tentacle or mob hit Yuki; she couldn't have dodged if she tried as incapacitating as the death wails were. The Kraken made a last-ditch attempt to push itself back into the water, but its massive girth was too much to move with this much out of the water, and it could not control itself in a coordinated way due to the internal attack.

HP began to drop more precipitously and the intensity of the shriek diminished to the point where she could move again. She got to her feet, knees still trembling, and stared at the Kraken as it shuddered and the last dribbles of life evaporated.

Congratulations, you have defeated the **Kraken!**
AI added to Summon bestiary.
35,000 XP awarded.
You have reached level 38.
You have reached level 39.
You have reached level 40.
Root access allowed. Do you wish to exit? (Y/N)

Yuki closed her eyes and let the cold wind wash over her. It couldn't touch her with the leveling euphoria. When the feeling eventually waned, she let out a contented sigh and exited the simulation.

After a brief moment of disorientation as she re-sleeved, Yuki accessed the system and recalled the sentries. She wiped the logs of an incursion and faked invoices to account for the materials that Gus and Aurora had taken. There was a possibility they had lost some or all of the materials in their flight and it would be best to leave no trail.

She searched and found the appropriate prosthetic that Shamus had requested, then her smile widened as she saw a next-gen prototype in the same series already being produced and stockpiled for release in Q1 of next year. Checking the stats, she whistled at the improvements Serif had accomplished in less than a year.

Shamus thought he would be getting what he had lost; well, Christmas would come early this year. Hell, she'd send him both. Never hurt to have a backup. She filed the invoice for immediate delivery. Then she ordered the bots to make dupes to replace the ones Shamus was receiving.

That done, she added herself to the registry. She walked calmly down the halls, the way gravity intended. In minutes, the sentinels returned, zipping past her and finding their charging kiosks and awaiting future activation.

Seeing some kiosks remained empty, she made and masked orders to build replacements to restore the original numbers. Confident she had left the facility so that it would appear nothing had happened, she sat at the loading dock and signaled Tempest to pick her up.

CHAPTER THIRTY-TWO

Bicycle Race

Gus and Aurora proceeded to the racks where supplies were kept in large open drawers. Occasionally a transport droid would fly to a bin, and in one deft motion retract the drawer, vacuum out a number of pieces, then replace the drawer and speed off to parts unknown.

Anticipation got his heart pumping as he readied himself to send the building's security crashing upon him. As Gus pulled open his drawer, the lights illuminating the plastisteel walls went from a bright white to a deep red. Alarms buzzed and panels opened, spilling out sentinels.

Aurora ripped open her drawer as soon as she saw Gus make his move. She scooped out a big swath of components, twisted her bag shut, and dumped it into the compartment behind her seat, and was gone on her psiycle.

Gus shook his head, gathering his own bagful, securing it and taking off, sentries much closer due to his dawdling. He ducked down as energy beams flew past his head, some hitting him in the back, but his hybrid-Nth armor absorbed the shots. The odd sensation tingled as his adaptive armor crawled across his body, forming a thicker protective layer on his exposed back and head.

The beams still smarted when they managed to hit close enough together to be totally absorbed or deflected, but there was no real damage or loss of HP. Fortunately, Gus could follow Aurora, which made navigating out of the facility easier than expected amid the distractions of the beams flying all around him. He had to keep accelerating as she was not waiting for him. The psiycle whined as he twisted the accelerator to max, pulling away ever so slightly from the pursuing mob.

Cool air hit him as he blasted out of the loading bay and his lead began to be chewed away as he had to slow and navigate around the buildings as the sky-way twisted and turned around the larger structures. Aurora was nowhere to be found, and after a couple of turns he saw the majority of the sentinels were following him like predators on the savanna, focusing on weaker prey.

There was luckily not as much traffic this time of day, but he still had to do a fair amount of dodging, being unfamiliar with the sky-ways and layout of the city. This also served to slow him down and the distinct hum that the sentinels made raised the hair on the back of his neck as they came ever closer.

As they got within a couple meters, one of the sentinels had a burst of speed, as if to ram the psiycle. It stopped short, but in reaction, Gus' psiycle lurched forward, ripping his hands off of the handlebars and he barely caught them again, losing another chunk of lead. Now he was surrounded by around a dozen sentinels of varying sizes.

Within the swarm, he was jostled side to side as the different attacks caused the anti-collision system of the psiycle to ricochet back and forth among the pests. His mouth ran dry as a particularly effective feint almost shook him loose off the psiycle, and he barely hung onto the handlebars like some trick motocross rider doing a Nac-Nac. Twisting with all his strength, he managed to pull himself back onto the seat, redirecting the bike as he got control again. Gus bounced and lifted off the seat unless he gripped the seat tightly with his thighs and buried his toes in a small recess by his feet.

Playing it safe is going to kill me!

"Nick! Can I turn off the anti-collision? It's going to throw me soon," Gus thought in a panic.

Before Nick could respond, the jostling stopped. Just in time too, Gus pushed down on the handles, dropping the psiycle and narrowly avoiding colliding with an off-ramp sign hovering in the sky-way. Three of the sentinels could not course-correct in time and slammed into the sign, being damaged enough that they dropped into the awaiting mists below.

Assessing that they could not cause him to be shaken loose, they adapted and began taking pot shots at his arms while one of the larger ones tried to obscure his vision and fly in front of him, blocking his line of sight. This sentinel had an uncanny ability to predict where he would try to move and maintained its dizzying motions, threatening to hit his face as it twisted and spun less than an inch from his face. The beams hitting his arms were partially blocked as they tried to ablate his suit and skin off of his forearms and the hybrid-Nth reconfigured to strengthen shielding in this area.

Despite the adjustment, he started taking damage, with attacks coming from too many directions to avoid. Just in time, too, as the remaining sentinels increased the intensity and quantity of beams playing across his body. Thinner layers of protected areas were created as the hybrid-Nth moved to compensate were insufficient to block the assault, and Gus was peppered with new needles of discomfort. Struggling to maintain his speed and bearing in the sky-way, Gus passed a large building and saw a new cluster of sentinels bearing down on him from the left. He tried to swing the psiycle in the opposite direction, braking and trying to drift but they were approaching too quickly.

Gus winced, preparing for the impact when he felt a wave of heat wash over him. The sensation quickly passed, and he cracked his eyes open to see Aurora dropping her psiycle down, having barely cleared jumping over him into the path of the oncoming fliers. The sentinels hit the angled base of her psiycle and ricocheted into the walls as their momentum was diverted by the ramp-like base.

She threw a look over her shoulder, winked, and sped off. A searing pain hit his forearm as he watched her go, and his eyes snapped back to his pursuers, firing neon orange beams at him with abandon. The scent of burned hair wafted into his nostrils as he punched the accelerator and took off down another alley.

"Aurora, thanks for the assist. Let's do that again and whittle down their numbers."

"Not likely they'd fall for it. They're very adaptable and learn from their mistakes. I have an idea though. Go to these nav-points," she advised and clicked off the comm after a brief yelp.

"Aurora! Are you okay?" he asked but received just static.

Just trust her, he thought as purple chevrons appeared ahead of him in the air directing him to the nav-point. With a definite direction to go, Gus found he began to gain ground again, getting more used to the psiycle's physics and how to refine his movements to cut corners and turn at the last moment to cause some of his pursuers to zip past and have to reroute.

When he gained a certain lead, the orange beams thankfully stopped. Whether they lost enough power to be effective or the bots were programmed to avoid collateral damage was unknown. It was a welcome change, either way. A green diamond outline was visible on his display through the buildings as his intended destination. A distance meter above it rapidly sped down as he juked and jockeyed around the buildings. Yuki had picked an excellent time; he barely saw another vehicle in the air that would have made navigating this route reckless or even impossible.

Another turn took him on a straight path to his destination. He poured on the speed and passed through the diamond destination marker, it disappearing as he zipped through.

Now what? Gus thought as he looked over his shoulder.

Through a narrow breach between two buildings that should have been too small to fit through, Aurora appeared in a flash, a small tether on the back of her psiycle. Attached to it was one of the mobile floating billboards that patrolled the city, this one peddling some alcoholic beverage with a scantily clad hybrid woman being carried on a litter by muscular men, hoisting her over their ripped shoulders. More than half of the sentinels crashed into the sign, causing the image to flicker and go dark. There were explosions and lights flickered behind the billboard.

Gus fist-pumped until he saw the stragglers fly above and below the sign and he pulsed the accelerator and took off again. Making a blind turn, he found himself in a dead-end alley, with a mesh walkway above him and a landing zone below. A large loading door stood locked at the end of the alley. He traveled to the end and saw the doors were thick and there were traces of rust from a lack of use. No one was opening these doors anytime soon.

He turned to face the sentinels, hoping he could speed past them, but by the time he had turned around, they had organized themselves in a big grid. Beams shot out their sides and formed a large net as they connected with their neighbors, quenching any hope that he could just zip through and blast past the weakest area. As he watched in horror, their forward beam weapons began to glow, ready for imminent firing. He tried to move in the limited space, but he couldn't get enough speed or distance to effectively dodge and he saw the guns tracking his meager attempts to avoid their targeting.

He was sorely tempted to use his shield, but feared that would reveal unregistered supers in the area and make the rest of the mission impossible for the others. Gus had decided he would try to blast through, upending his psiycle and using the base of the bike to smash through. His stomach knotted up, knowing deep down that they probably would just cut through it. The sentinels passed a metal landing on one of the buildings and as expected, melted through it effortlessly, the shorn metal tumbling down and clattering on the landing strip twenty feet below, ends still glowing where they had been cut.

An odd tranquility washed over Gus as he looked at the approaching sentinels. This looked like it was the end. It was a fun ride, especially working with the Crew. He had started to feel like he belonged out here with these 'real supers,' and he wouldn't betray them just to protect himself.

While they approached, he set the command controls to default to Aurora when he died. If he couldn't use the manor, it shouldn't go to waste. Tightening his jaw, he stared at the sentinels as they loomed ever closer, not even bothering to use their beam weapons anymore. They knew they had him dead to rights. Gus knew it too.

Bring it on... he thought as he glared at the relentless robots bearing down on him as he revved the psiycle.

CHAPTER THIRTY-THREE

Ahjussi Swag

Shamus fidgeted at his desk. Part of him wanted the supers to fail, old memories and old grievances hard to forgive. His more pragmatic side had wrestled his ego down and held out hope that they could deliver. It would save so much time to have his arm returned to him again. Just getting back to what he was used to feeling, the void in his capabilities erased.

He had only felt like he had turned the corner six months ago, and things were finally coming together. Years of pushing the flywheel, not seeing any movement or rewards. Then this. He looked at the input prong at the base of his missing arm, twisting it and staring at the tiny blue lights pulsing all along the plate at its base, studded with inputs.

He mentally flexed his missing arm into a fist, gritting his teeth. He pulled up the picture from his internal feed and froze it on his display. A tattoo on the inner wrist of one of his attackers. He knew he had seen it before, and could have easily pulled up and compared it to his history if they hadn't taken his stacks. Without those organic memory storage devices, he had lost an enormous amount of his hard-earned abilities.

You don't know what you've got until it's gone.

The memory he sought hovered at the back of his mind like an irritating cough. Ever-present but nothing would calm its incessant tickle. He had seen this tattoo somewhere before, but where?

It was the only thread he had for solving Scarlett's case. That's not why he wanted to find out though. He would figure out who was behind this and they would have a reckoning. There were some unsaid rules in Hinansho, and poachers and scavengers were among the lowest of the low. This was supposed to be a sanctuary, and those who attacked their own deserved no quarter here.

A tone sounded and Eliza materialized, breaking his reverie.

"You have a delivery."

"From who? I'm not expecting anything—"

"It is from Serif Industries. I believe you *were* expecting something…"

Shamus sprang to his feet and scrambled out the door. He slammed the button to open the inner waiting room and there it was. A large box with the black and gold Serif logo. Grasping the handle on the side, he pulled the package inside and closed off the entryway, locking it.

He quickly grabbed a knife from his workbench and sliced the seal with reverence. He pulled apart the flaps, removing contoured foam revealing two large cases that could have held electric guitars. Long and rectangular, the cases gave no hint of what lay inside to an outside observer.

Shamus eyed the cases suspiciously.

Two? What's going on with this?

He removed the slightly wider case and unbuckled the four catches on the sides.

With a hiss, it opened. The distinct smell of polyfoam and machine oil wafted into the air. Shamus took it in like a bouquet of fine wine. His eyes started when they saw the contents. He initiated a full run-down scan and his processors digitally analyzed the arm that lay inside. It was unlike anything he had ever seen, and his display spooled out the analysis, forming a three-dimensional image floating above the arm, some sections disassembling and reassembling to show internal features and configurations.

Looking at the breakdowns, he had to refocus a couple of times to make certain he was reading the specs correctly. Advanced kinematics, predictive algorithms directly embedded, and dynamic nano interface capability, among other features, each more stunning than the next. He could find no serial number or product name, but it was obviously a Serif design. He had thought he had the top of the line before the incident, but this was a whole new level of sophistication and design.

He lifted the arm reverently from its polyfoam housing, staring at the limb with awe as he admired its heft. It felt solid, but lighter than the 800 models, almost half of the weight. A data window expanded as he focused on it, showing a reinforced nanotride housing protecting the intricate machinery within.

Another window enlarged, illustrating the arm's own self-repairing mechanism via an internal nanobot reservoir. That was new. It would save him so much time tinkering and working when something was damaged.

With awe, he clicked the arm in place and felt the brief discomfort as the calibration and synchronization process started. Tiny fibers snaked out and connected with the baseplate, directly wired to nerves unused since his arm was taken and his brain perceived a variety of sensations as the arm went through its protocol, most of them intense and unpleasurable.

When the arm had finally synced, he felt a wave of pleasure as the refractory endorphin hit sank in, mollifying the intensity of sensation, allowing him to better tolerate the procedure. His tension eased as the endorphins smoothed out the transition.

He flexed, opening and closing his fist in front of him, admiring the pure artistry that had gone into this magnificent piece of tech.

Those supers have really outdone themselves. I guess I am giving them that little bonus...

As if on cue, the pleasant wind chime tone indicating someone was at the door sounded. Shamus closed the case, slid the package under a nearby table and sat down at his desk, attempting to be busy and preoccupied.

Eliza appeared and confirmed that it was indeed the supers, so he allowed her to open the door, and tried to appear as nonchalant as possible. The three came in, the younger man looking disheveled, his hair whipped at crazy angles, as if he had just come out of a bar fight. Shamus noted that the girl and older man kept their usual poise and calm demeanor.

"I see you received our gifts," Tempest said cordially, nodding towards the new arm.

"Indeed. And I have found the information you were needing as well. Here are the schedules you wanted. They're only accurate for the first couple of pages, usually because of changes in the deliveries and arrival times. I'd recommend acting as soon as you can. That's in restricted hybrid territory, and I'm in no shape to travel there as I am. Your best bet is to go to one of the delivery points and follow the courier to their destination," Shamus said in a smooth, even tone. This was business, and he didn't want to show these supers any advantage with the magnitude of their gift. Chances were they didn't know what they had done.

"That's it?" Aurora spat. "You're not even going to take us there?"

Tempest raised his hand to calm her. "It's okay, Aurora, we can take it from here. The nav-points are all in here, I assume?"

Shamus nodded to Tempest. "Of course, I'm a professional. I usually *would* take you there, but certain circumstances have occurred recently that, well, let's just say I'm not at my best."

Tempest nodded knowingly and scooped up the folder, gesturing to his companions that it was time to go.

"Oh, one more thing. You'll want to use this." Shamus tossed a small USB device to Gus before he could turn and leave.

"What is it?"

"It lets you hide your position and access to the local network using a spoofing protocol. We don't use the satellite network you outsiders are so fond of, on account of all the storms." He twirled a finger overhead as he leaned back in his chair, feet up on the desk. "Our system is cobbled together, but it gives us a similar level of connectivity, although to communicate with the outside world, you need to visit a kiosk."

The group looked confused, so Shamus elaborated.

"When you piggyback unprotected on a local network, they can see and hear everything you're doing. You need to scramble that kak, especially if you want to keep your conversations private. You've been jumping from network to network to communicate—not the best idea in Hinansho."

The wind-blown super thanked him and Shamus just tipped his hat.

After they were gone, Shamus had Eliza lock the doors again and once again began to stare lovingly at the new arm.

I'm back.

A glint formed in his eye as he mapped out his plan to get back what had been taken from him.

CHAPTER THIRTY-FOUR

In My Foreign

As the three supers entered the dilapidated transport ship, Yuki bounced up with a big grin on her face.

"Good news. To better blend in, I GTA'd you a vehicle, *and* one advantage is that it is shielded so no one can peek inside. That means I can be your wheel-man!"

"When you say you—" Tempest asked archly, before he was cut off.

"Don't worry, boss, I guess I exaggerated a bit. It was all aboveboard. We're renting it, but under an alias, and we're using one of the Faction's scrubbed accounts. No worries."

Tempest just raised a skeptical eyebrow and she stared right back, mouth screwed up in a mix of a pout and a snarl. When she didn't back down, Tempest dropped his stern expression.

"Okay, I believe you. Given your talents, I'm impressed you had the restraint to do things by the book this time. The last thing we need to do is call any undue attention upon us. So what did you get?"

Yuki checked her display and smiled a Cheshire grin.

"Should be delivered by autopilot any second now," she said, strutting to the window and grinning.

"Whatcha think?" She bumped one hip out and presented the window like she was a game-show hostess.

Gus peered through a window and saw a sleek ebony vehicle that was all sharp lines and angles. It looked as if it had been carved out of an immense shard of obsidian. It bobbed in the air, having reached its delivery coordinates, menacing like a feral animal as it awaited activation.

"So where are we going next?" Yuki asked.

"We need to track someone to the Aslan clan's current headquarters, and we do that by following a courier," Gus said distractedly as he gazed out the window.

"This is perfect, then. It also has external stealth features, as well as internal. It's diplomatic grade, so it can take some damage and become practically invisible if needed. Primarily, it's for escape when attacked, but it could easily follow someone undetected, especially if they aren't wise to us. What are we waiting for? Let's go!" Yuki cheered and slid open the gangway.

"Can we all fit in that?" Gus asked skeptically as they approached.

"Just watch…" Yuki said over her shoulder and her right hand danced over her holo-keypad on her left forearm.

The vehicle began to move, sections sliding across each other, rasping like sharpening knives.

Somehow it managed to maintain a menacing appearance, but now it was more the size of a minivan instead of a sports car.

"After you." Yuki gestured in a mock bow as Tempest, Gus, Aurora, Prime, and Grimdark piled inside. Closing the door behind them, she slid into the pointed cone that formed the front of the vehicle.

"If you wouldn't mind sliding me those coordinates, gov'nuh," Yuki asked in a cheesy British accent. Tempest made a sliding motion, and a series of nav-points showed up on the console in front of Yuki. She selected one and the vehicle sprang to life, silent as a jungle cat.

Gus was sitting next to Prime, and they were becoming more agitated as they approached the nav-point.

"Everything okay?" At first, he thought Prime must have not heard him.

Well, I do have a bad habit of mumbling.

He tried again, "Prime, are you okay?"

Gus saw his reflection in the mirrored helmet as the super looked his way.

"Hinansho is full of bad memories for me…" Prime said in a flat electronic tone. They turned to look out the window. "… but you don't need to worry about me."

Despite the filtered and modified voice, he could sense the melancholy behind the words. He knew the Oracle said that Prime had a key for him, but how would he ever be able to learn what it was if Prime remained so aloof? And finding out exactly what it was would just add to the challenge. Perhaps this mission would give him some hints.

"Let's rock!" Yuki exulted and hit the accelerator without warning. Gus' head slammed into his seat and he pressed into Prime and Grimdark as they took turns at breakneck speed. Yuki was obviously familiar with navigating sky-ways and weaved effortlessly through the burgeoning traffic. More quickly than expected, they arrived near the pickup location. Yuki found a nearby vantage point and backed their vehicle to be less conspicuous. There was a shudder as it anchored itself to the brick building behind them and the engine powered down. The lights dimmed and Yuki activated the stealth feature. There was a shimmer as the outer hull mimicked the wall upon which it rested, aided by the shadows and wisps of mist.

"Now we wait. I've always wanted to do a stakeout," Yuki said excitedly.

"You won't after this one," Aurora countered, knowing full well how boring they could be. Especially without snacks or a reasonable diversion that didn't distract too much.

"According to the schedule, we shouldn't have to wait long,"

Tempest reminded them. "Less than half an hour if they're on time."

"Perhaps we should remain quiet, to be less detectable when they arrive," Grimdark added ominously.

"Don't worry about that. This baby is sonically shielded too, so no one can listen in on us. Nothing but the best for my Crew!"

"What kind of vehicle is this, Yuki? I've never seen anything like it," Gus asked.

"They're not common in the United Commonwealth, and they're super expensive to own. This is a Seek 2000 in Ebony. I fell in love with it as soon as I found it was available. Apparently, no one wants to rent them because the price is too prohibitive. Purple Faction has deep pockets, and I know how to invoice so we won't get any flak from the higher ups. We need an edge. But it would be best if the leadership did not know we were ever here in Hinansho." She looked over her shoulder at Tempest for confirmation and he nodded.

"It's worth it," Tempest said simply. Then a prolonged period of silence followed as everyone stared at the loading dock across the sky-way, lost in their thoughts.

A soft buzz came from Prime after a couple of minutes. Turning to look, Gus saw Prime's helmet leaning against the window—was that a snore? Waving a hand in front of their helmet and gently asking if they were awake, he got no response.

If there was one thing that made Gus antsy, it was waiting around for an indeterminate time for something to happen. Especially when it was someone coming to pick him up 'around' a certain time, and he didn't have any time to get started on something only to have to leave at the drop of a hat. Gus appeared to be the only one disturbed by the quiet, and his mind looked for any distraction.

Maybe if I use **Telepathy** *on Prime, I can find at least some common ground,* Gus thought. A few more minutes of silence convinced him to try to level the skill a tiny bit more.

He activated **_Telepathy_** and stared at Prime, wondering if their helmet and suit would shield them from his attempts. It was slightly more difficult, and he had to concentrate more, but he found his sight resolving into new surroundings. His sight was blurry and sounds were muffled for a brief time until everything came into focus.

Prime was talking with someone on holo-chat, a young girl, around ten years of age.

———

"Daddy says we have to keep it short," the girl said sheepishly.

"You forget what he says. I barely get to see you as it is!" Gus felt himself saying. He felt his fists tighten and his heart rate spike; it was an odd feeling experiencing the anger but being detached at the same time.

"Okay, Mommy."

"So how is school? Anyone giving you a hard time?"

"No. I don't think they know I'm a hybrid. Daddy tells me to keep that a secret and it will be easier for me."

"Honey, you have nothing to be ashamed of, but I understand. Kids can be cruel, especially with things they don't understand. I got bullied a bit when I was in a mixed school. There are a lot of people with some pretty stubborn prejudices because of things their parents taught them. I don't like it, but I don't disagree with your father on this. But you will have to be prepared for what happens if or when people find out. You will have to be strong, got it? You have it in you, I know it."

The girl nodded demurely, still unsure of herself.

"Promise me," Gus insisted.

"Okay, I will," she finally agreed. "It's just hard sometimes."

"I know it is, baby. But you have to be strong. I don't want you to ever forget how wonderful you are. You don't need to be afraid of anyone, or let them push you around. Got it?"

"Yes." The reply was a little less timid. She looked away as there was muffled talking.

"Daddy says I have to get off now."

"It hasn't even been five minutes!" Gus felt his throat tighten and his eyes water. "Harlan, Harlan! Come on, why do you have to be this way? You've won. Why can't you let me have this one thing?"

A handsome face appeared in the vid-feed, eyes cold and hard. "I'm sorry, but we have to go, she has an event—"

"Maddy, do you? When does it start?" Gus felt himself turning and addressing the girl who looked sheepishly up at her father, afraid to answer.

"It doesn't matter, Sanura. And how dare you try to go around me and interrogate our daughter?! You should be grateful I'm gracious enough to allow you any contact. You always have to test me." His voice raised sharply in retaliation.

"I'm sorry, Harlan, but there has to be more time. I get so little with her already…"

His stern features were mollified somewhat. He liked her to be submissive. He liked getting his way. She would do whatever it took, Maddy was her only lifeline.

"It can't be helped. Perhaps we'll have some time later, but this is a very busy week, and month. I'll have Eldon contact you when there's another time."

The holo-vid shut off abruptly, disconnected without even a goodbye. Hot tears finally began to fall as sobs racked Gus' throat.

"Baby, I'm so sorry," Gus muttered amidst gasps of breath.

———

"What is this? Sleeping with your eyes open?" Grimdark grunted, elbowing him in the side once again. "Snap out of it," he brusquely said to Gus and Prime, who silently turned and nodded.

Gus wheezed, whether from the none-too-gentle prodding or choking back emotions he had absorbed from Prime was hard to tell. He had felt every emotion as if it were his own.

"They're making the exchange," Grimdark pointed at the loading dock, a small crate being loaded in the back of a sleek torpedo-like skimmer. After a clipboard was passed to the driver and back, the skimmer took off as Yuki began to start up the Seek 2000.

"I hope you have your seatbelts on!" Yuki warned and Gus slammed against the seat as the ship took off in pursuit.

CHAPTER THIRTY-FIVE

In My Cult

A pulsing light caught Gus' attention on the bottom of his display and he opened his logs to find his voyeurism had gained him a level in *Telepathy* and some XP and FP. He had to dismiss the window before reading the particulars, as reading with the reckless driving was making him carsick.

As Yuki swerved and maneuvered through the alleys off and on the sky-way, the group was pressed side to side against each other as the inertial compensators failed to keep up with the constant shifting of forces. Yuki was somehow aware of the courier she was tailing at all times, breaking off and then returning to her pursuit, briefly crossing paths later. Traffic had increased with an early surge of commuters, which made blending in all the easier.

The realization that Prime was female pressed on Gus' mind as the vehicle made an abrupt turn and he was pushed into her. The revelation struck him again and he pondered what he had seen. Instead of finding a point of commonality, he had found something painful and private that would not help relate in any way. It only made him feel weird and uncomfortable with how he should react and more uncertainty on how to interact normally with Prime.

He fought the tension that made him stiffen when the car shifted him towards Prime, as if she would detect the change in his posture and know what he had done. It was difficult to know what he should be doing to improve and level up, but he felt unsettled with using his powers in this way.

He was horrible at breaking the ice and was so uneasy with new groups, especially those who didn't share his own interests, that he was surprised "awkward pause" wasn't a skill he had leveled up to a mastery level. Social interaction was easier one on one, but in bigger groups he tended to fade into the background, content to watch and observe, trying to find his place.

There was an abrupt jolt as the vehicle suddenly stopped. Below them, the courier could be seen landing in an alcove and delivering a package to a nondescript weathered door. A small window opened, reminding Gus of a speakeasy, and after a brief interaction a package was slid into an opening in the base of the door. The courier hustled back to the alcove and took off.

"This is the place," Yuki announced.

"Good luck getting in there," Grimdark said without emotion.

"Leave that to me. Let's get this over with," Prime said, obviously agitated but resigned to see this through.

Yuki nudged the transport gently down to the same alcove the courier had recently occupied and powered down the vehicle.

"I'll be ready to go at a moment's notice, but give me a heads up when you can so I can have everything ready to go," Yuki suggested.

"Hopefully, this won't require a speedy escape, but noted," Tempest said. "Everyone ready to go into the lion's den?"

———

The tiny rusty panel slid back, revealing large, wide-set eyes.

"Who are you? Whaddya want?" a deep voice demanded, eyes flitting to the different members of the party.

"We have a delivery—"

"Don't recognize ya, you're not one of the authorized couriers—so see ya, bye-bye," the gruff voice barked, punctuated by a slam of the tiny panel.

Tempest stared at the closed door, unsure of how to proceed.

Prime let loose a large sigh and stepped to the front. She knocked on the door again, insistently. An irritated grumble followed by a deep growl resonated on the other side of the door.

"We request an audience," Prime insisted, removing something from a pocket on her jacket.

The irritated voice slammed the panel open again, eyes reappearing, more bloodshot and enraged. A tirade of curses and threats began to spill forth as Prime calmly held her palm to the window. And Gus briefly saw the eyes morph from rage to fear before Prime's hand obscured his view.

"I'm sorry, mistress, please forgive me," a demure reply murmured, thick with embarrassment. Prime replaced whatever she had in her hand as multiple locks and clicks sounded and the door swung inward ponderously. The Crew followed Prime as she strutted through the doorway as if she owned the place, her demeanor changing to one of haughty bearing.

As they passed the doorway, Gus saw the doorman standing sheepishly behind the door. A stocky creature nearly as wide as he was tall stood there, obviously exhibiting signs of being a human-rhino hybrid. His tough, rubbery gray skin and a prominent set of dual horns were bowed, avoiding eye contact with Prime as she passed.

A willowy hybrid in an almond-colored tunic motioned for them to follow, but Prime paid her no heed. She walked purposefully forward and through a shimmering curtain that twinkled like a waterfall of colored beads of light as the guide hurried to catch up.

Stepping through, Gus had to blink away the glare as the dingy environment was replaced with a pristine formal throne room. The scent of cinnamon and citrus hung thick in the air, almost, but not quite, masking the feral scent of animal musk that was heavy in the room. The Crew goggled at the unexpected sight of something so regal hidden among the dinginess of the exterior.

A court of advisors and individuals stood conferring with each other, while others stood at attention, awaiting orders from their betters. Walking down a carpeted pathway towards a raised dais, they passed all forms of hybrids, also in the tawny sleeveless robes. Different textures and colors on the exposed arms hinted at the cowled figures' unique hybrid nature. No simple human skin was evident in this inner sanctum.

It was amazing to see how much could be done with blending DNA, and Gus had never seen a hybrid in real life, and here was an entire menagerie. Intelligent eyes peered at him from the shadows of their hoods, evaluating him and the others as they followed Prime closer to stand in front of the dais.

"I request an audience in appeal to the accords," Prime said resolutely, almost defiantly, at the two hooded figures sitting on dual thrones near the center of the circular room.

"What do you know of the accords, outsider?" A large robed figure stepped forward defensively, baring large fangs. His black fur glistened and a large paw clutched a jeweled staff, claws extending without subtlety.

The vizier pulled on his whiskers, exaggerating his already contemptuous sneer.

Prime began to repeat her request, "I know my rights—"

The large panther-man slashed down with his paw. "Silence! You are owed nothing! We are not regs to be intimidated by your oppressive Factions. You have no authority here!" He bared his fangs and a low guttural growl resonated in his throat.

One of the enthroned figures raised a placating hand.

"Calm yourself, LaVarn. If I am correct, the prodigal has returned at last," a sultry female voice purred, lightly sniffing the air as she turned to the visitors. "Approach and show yourselves."

Undaunted, Prime reached to the helmet and released some fasteners that kept it connected to the jumpsuit. There was an audible hiss, and gloved hands removed it. Aurora gasped and an uncomfortable quiet settled over the other supers at what they saw.

CHAPTER THIRTY-SIX

In My Life

Gus' jaw dropped when he saw under the helmet for the first time.

"Nekomimi…" the vizier whispered in astonishment.

Prime brushed down the damp fur, sweaty from being under the helmet, into a semblance of order. She turned and faced the other supers, eyes set.

Gus thought he saw a brief glint of withheld tears, but it could have been the light.

"My parents were both beastkin and the procedures were done before I even had a choice." She turned to Tempest. "I'm sorry I never told you, but Purple Faction had been the only place where I have truly felt like myself. I know some have prejudices against my kind, and I understand if this changes things between us. I hid this aspect of myself precisely for that reason. Just know this: I did not choose this. It was put upon me, and I have learned how to deal with it the best I can."

She turned and faced the vizier again, becoming resolute, pleading tone gone from her voice.

"I make this request again, as a beastkin and not as a super. And the council will hear about this breach of the accords. I.

Seek. Audience." She punctuated her words with a staccato rhythm, biting off each one.

Gus looked back and forth between the thin cat woman cowing the larger steward, trying to absorb the change in dynamic. He looked to the rest of the Crew and saw similar expressions of uncertainty and confusion.

The vizier stammered, looking back to the figures seated behind him, mouth working but no sound coming forth. With a lazy paw, the female figure dismissed him, and he disappeared behind a curtain.

Prime hung her head, but her hands clenched into fists and released.

"I'm not sure what prejudices you've been talking about, but I'm totally okay with you," Gus leaned forward and whispered to Prime, trying to show some form of support. The royals left them standing there, drawing out the silence.

"I told you she would return," the queen finally said, satisfaction thick in her mellifluous voice. "I grant you audience, my little cub."

Gus cast his eyes around and was surprised to see even Grimdark's mouth agape at the news. What was the big deal?

"Before you get your hopes up, I am not here to claim the throne. I am merely here to deliver something to fulfill a commitment."

A loud roar emanated from the king, and he raised a massive paw. The denizens of the court fled through multiple portals, leaving the supers alone with the royals and a cadre of surly guards carrying large halberds.

Prime took a step forward and the guards sprang to life, forming a bristly barrier that prevented any further approach. She reached into her jacket and the guards reacted further, some rearing back as they readied to launch their weapons. Raising one hand in surrender, she slowly extracted the remaining hand and placed a small data cube on the ground, then deftly stepped back, keeping her arms raised in a placating gesture.

One of the closest guards approached and pushed the drive with the tip of his weapon. When nothing exploded, he dared to grab the drive and grimaced while he turned to a curtained door and let loose a shrill whistle.

A simian hybrid entered, pushing up circular glasses that had difficulty balancing on his short, sloped nose. He nervously kept pulling down on a pinstripe vest that constantly crept up as he shuffled toward the guard and took the drive. Drawing a small device from a pocket, he plugged the data cube in and typed on a virtual keyboard similar to Yuki's. The layout was different, for the altered position of the ape's digits, but he was adept at typing and turned to the throne and nodded before bowing and retreating from the room.

The larger figure on the right throne removed his hood, revealing a luxurious mane. Piercing eyes full of malice fixed directly on Prime as he stood, crossing his muscular arms in front of him.

"You have had your audience, now you may leave, since you have no intention of fulfilling your duties."

"I do have a request since, of the residents of Hinansho, you are among the most well informed."

"Dear daughter. That is poor form," the queen purred, also removing her hood but staying seated. Gus stared at the stunning woman who was a blend of either a cheetah or jaguar. She crossed long legs and leaned forward on one crossed knee, cupping her exquisite chin with a furry, but human-shaped hand. "The information you just delivered has already been paid for previously; you were just the courier. You have no right to make any other demands. If you are unwilling to aid the clan, then we really have nothing to talk about. You can see yourself out."

"So that's it? I've never asked you for help before, despite all that I've been through. Despite all you put me through—"

"Hold your tongue!" the lion shouted, commanding respect. "You have never appreciated all we have sacrificed to give you the opportunities you have. All we have had to go through to reach our station, only to have you throw it all away."

"I never had a choice in the matter. You made all those decisions for me, and I am the one who had to live with the consequences, not you."

"You know nothing of suffering. You were so young when those procedures were done, you don't even remember them, do you? I remember the pain of having my bones broken and reshaped to this form. Muscles ripped away and re-positioned. I know of that pain and it almost broke me mentally. Why would I allow you to go through that? Children take to the procedures much more easily."

"Why am I even arguing with you? You still have no remorse for what you have done to your only child. I'm sure your lack of conscience has allowed you to do whatever it takes to become the highest caste in the hybrid clans. Why would I want to inherit a kingdom built upon such a foundation?"

"Pshaw! Begone! You do nothing but irritate me. You have never cared for the struggle of your people, and you put their future at risk by running around playing super, away from those who need you the most." The lion spoke with finality and threw himself down onto his throne, clutching the armrests as if he was trying to crush them.

Prime turned around and spoke to Tempest. "I'm sorry, I tried." She lowered her head and walked toward the shimmering curtain.

Gus gasped as he saw Prime's face for the first time. Unlike her parents, who looked like anthropomorphic animals, Prime appeared human, except for her pink irises and perky ears high atop her head. Her hair also seemed to have a slight pink tint to it amid mostly white, like cotton candy.

Tempest nodded grimly and followed her as they left.

No, this can't be it. We've come so far and done so much. Gus thought desperately. Lagging behind as the others shuffled to leave, he thought of something.

"What if I can give you Dr. Flak's research on insectoid

integration? Wouldn't that be of value to your clan?" He didn't know if this was a total stab in the dark, but he hadn't seen anything besides mammalian and avian hybrids, well, ever. Which amounted to mostly the last fifteen minutes.

If the Quorian had something he could barter with, it might be worth something. When he saw the royals' eyes widen and the furtive glance they exchanged, he knew he had been correct. Gaining confidence, Gus looked at the others. Prime had turned around, mouth pursed in a thin line. Her eyes seemed to scream for Gus to stop talking but he was on a roll. It would work.

"How do you even know that name, youngling? Dr. Flak was before his time, and definitely before yours. I am intrigued you know something about the rumors of his research, but everyone knows that it was all lost when he disappeared right before the fighting began in that unfortunate misunderstanding all those years ago—" Prime's mother began before being rudely cut off.

"Do not toy with us, little man. And do not promise something you can't deliver. You try my patience by your mere presence. Don't think you can tease the court without dire punishment," the lion snarled in warning, his large face contorted in rage and contempt.

No guts no glory, Gus.

"I can get you that information, as long as we get what we're looking for as well…"

"Speak your terms, but know this: You will not leave until you have given us what you know regardless."

"Before you get any big ideas, I am pretty sure that only I can access the information, so killing me will do nothing. I also have to be in a pretty focused mental state, so I wouldn't try torturing me, or stressing me out by harming my companions. We can make this a win-win."

"Out with it!" the impatient king demanded.

"I don't have it on me, but I can access it quickly. What *we* need is to find somebody. We were told she was taken here, but we have no leads."

"That's incredibly vague, little man," the cheetah chided, her voice playful yet retaining some patronizing undertones.

"If you can't help us, then—"

"I never said that!" she said sharply, honeyed words turning icy for just a moment as she relaxed her pinched features as quickly as they had appeared. "We have someone we use for such... jobs. But we would need much more information. There's no guarantee that even he could help you, but if anyone could, it would be him."

"Then I will volunteer to stay until Gus provides you the information, as a show of our good faith," Prime offered resolutely. "You will allow them to check on your lead, and if it is of dubious validity then I am under no obligation to stay."

"Done!" the two royals said in unison, eyes afire.

Gus' heart felt like it had been hit with a large mallet. He wasn't even sure if he could deliver what he had promised, and now Prime had put herself in a position she obviously wanted no part in just to secure the deal. He tried to keep the horror out of his eyes as he saw a Cheshire grin spread over Prime's parents' leonine faces.

CHAPTER THIRTY-SEVEN

In My Head

Prime glanced over and her eyes narrowed slightly as she saw Gus' hesitation.

"Gu~u~u~s... what does that expression mean? Do you have the information to trade or not?" Prime whispered out the side of her mouth.

"Well, sort of..."

"What?! You can't back down from a promise to the High Court!" she hissed, catching herself and speaking with forced calm. "They will torture you. Play with you for their pleasure! Don't forget their cat aspect—it influences how they deal with their prey. Even worse, they can bring you to the edge of death and back, thanks to being able to access and read your remaining health."

"But they're not supers, they don't have a display—"

"There are some supers in Hinansho. They just have made certain pledges to be able to stay here. Some of the more devious ones aligned themselves with the clans and especially the High Court. You know what an inquisitor is, don't you?"

"No, but it doesn't sound good."

"It isn't! Do whatever you can, but you have to get that information," Prime pleaded with Gus, horror in her eyes evident with her huge pupils that would have been at home in an exaggerated anime reaction.

Crap. Why can't I just keep my big mouth shut? I thought I'd have more time to play around with the cube, but when are things easy and convenient?

Gus turned to Aurora and whispered, "Can you watch over me while I delve? I don't know how long this will take. If they pressure you—say that it's heavily encrypted and I need time to decode it properly, or the data will be destroyed. That may buy us some time."

"Be safe in there…"

The words faded away as Gus focused on the cube. He turned it to the yellow side. After unlocking the directory, he knew this was the appropriate plane to access the insectoid research. He had never delved this side, which didn't bode well. It could be anything in there. He could feel the skin on his face tighten as he fell into the plane.

Hot wind and a burning sun beat down on him from above. Shielding his eyes from the glare and sand whipping around, he found himself atop a small dune. A sandstone path led forward to a large temple of some sort. It sat like a squat trapezoid, pillars, statues, and obelisks stood aside a wedge-shaped opening in the middle.

Gus stumbled down to the path and hurried along it to get out of the merciless heat. As he walked along the path, he could swear he saw something in his peripheral vision. Crawling under the sand, burrowing there, but it was hard to tell with the sand whipping around. Anytime he turned to look, all he saw was the sand carried by the wind over the dunes.

As he approached the temple, gold scroll-work traced around the entrance. Hieroglyphic characters were arranged vertically down both sides of the angular doorway. The shade inside must have dropped the ambient temperature by at least ten degrees. Gus rubbed his eyes, already raw with squinting amid the scouring sand.

Brushing it away as best he could, he felt the cool stone walls. They were pristine, not like the old timeworn Egyptian structures in the real world. These looked like they were finished yesterday, blocks still having sharp edges. Others were smooth and seamless, though he could see differently arranged bricks.

Bright frescoes lined the central corridor, disappearing into the darkness as the corridor extended away from the doorway. An earthen clay bowl filled with a pungent liquid sat just inside the doorway. Next to it was a gravy-boat-looking dish with a small wick made out of some twisted fibers. Gus touched the liquid and rubbed it through his fingers; it was slippery like oil, and it smelled waxy, like crayons. Gus dipped the vessel and scooped up some of the oil, holding on to the wick so it wouldn't fall out.

Unfortunately, he couldn't find anything available to light the wick, so he was back at square one. He remembered how fortunate he was when he first got powers that fire was never a challenge thanks to his early abilities. He would probably never have made it without them. Gus racked his brain on how he could light the wick and wondered if he could find some glass that he could focus like a magnifying glass or lens. The sun was certainly bright and hot enough that it wouldn't take much to focus.

Gus checked and realized for the first time that he wasn't wearing his normal clothes, that this was a virtual environment and he was wearing a tawny flax tunic that hung on him like a shapeless bag. He had no pockets to search. A cursory search both in the entryway and outside the temple revealed nothing but sand.

He sat in the shade with his feet sunning outside the doorway and exhaled in a burst.

Hells bells, now what? If only I had my abilities here.

Gus checked to see if he could bring up his internal stats.

Maybe his perception would allow him to see in the tomblike temple.

With a thought, he found he actually could bring up his stats, though the normal display he saw around the periphery of his vision was absent. With a more concentrated focus than usual, he could temporarily bring up some information, but it faded like an afterimage if his attention wavered. His stats were the same as they had been outside of the cube.

Gus got to his feet and walked down the long hallway, waiting for his enhanced senses to kick in as the light waned the further down the tunnel he progressed. Unlike reality, he didn't have any form of night-vision, at all—which seemed like an odd paradox, since this resembled a VR game.

Do I have any abilities? he thought distractedly as he cracked his knuckles.

Some brief words flashed in front of him before disappearing:

Inherent abilities available in yellow zone.

"What's an inherent ability?" Gus asked no one in particular. Having an internal personality like Nick made it so talking to himself all the time didn't seem so strange, as his rhetorical questions would usually get answered. Here in the cube, Nick couldn't be accessed.

Gus wondered if it could be a type of ability and tried to think of what best fit the description of 'inherent.' It was one of those words that he was sure he knew, but when he had to define it, he had no clear idea.

Screw it. Let's just do this with trial and error. Gus stomped back to the entryway, reed sandals slapping noisily on the flat stones. He picked up the lamp he had laid there and racked his brain to remember his abilities without the aid of his display as a crutch.

Might as well start at the beginning. He picked up the wick between two fingers and tried to recall the sensation when he used **Wreck-It-Gus** to create fire. He fully expected it not to work, but he could feel the flow of MP and the wick quickly began to glow.

He had to push much harder to get the effect, but *it worked*. The dry wick fizzled and smoked as he gave his ability a rest. Using his fingers, he plunged the whole wick under the oil and wrung it out before trying again.

This time the wick produced a familiar, steady flame. The scent was unappealing, but it was light.

As he descended the decline, more frescos became visible in the flickering light of the lamp. Gus turned to look at them as he heard a clicking by his ear. Raising the lamp, he saw a large beetle the size of his fist crawling towards him along the wall. The light of the small flame caused the immense bug to back up and flee as if it were poison. Somehow the bug squeezed into an almost indistinguishable slot at the junction of the ceiling and wall.

More scuttling in the dark, directly behind Gus, made him turn with a start.

A small splash of oil fell out of the lamp as he twisted and the wick rocked back and forth, almost being washed out with the oil.

The ground was covered completely with hordes of the large bugs, crawling over each other. Like their brother, they retreated with reckless abandon when exposed to the light. Centering the lamp in the corridor, Gus saw that the ceiling was also covered with the bugs, the scraping and clacking of their carapaces sending a chill down his spine.

They also had a distinctive odor that stood out among the stale peanut smell of the rancid oil. Something definitely unpleasant on a visceral level, at times so pungent that Gus had to cough and fight dry-heaving. The action caused his loose oil to rock the little wick again and Gus forced himself to get it under control.

Blinking away a tear and clearing his throat, Gus' eyes fell upon one of the frescos. This one depicted two of the typical sideways-posed Egyptian figures. One in the lead held a lamp similar to Gus', and the same beetles were fleeing the beams of the lamp. In the picture, Gus recognized them as scarabs. A lagging figure had an extinguished lamp and was being beset by the insects. There was a section missing in his arm, and white bone showed through the opening.

Gus swallowed, trying to get some moisture down his raw throat. The message was clear: No light equals bugs eating you alive.

Gus picked up the pace, trying to evaluate how fast the small lamp was using the oil and where the halfway mark was, so he would know when he would need to turn back. A quick glance over his shoulder showed the tiny white opening of the temple, further away than expected. Scarabs had repopulated the walls and ceiling behind him and Gus got back to descending.

The fragile nature of the lamp required him to walk slower than he would have liked, to both avoid spilling oil and also to keep the tiny flame from extinguishing. Gus knew he could light it again, but he was unsure how quick these bugs would be in the time it took to relight the wick, and how he would focus on the wick without being able to see it.

As he descended, the quantity and size of the bugs appeared to increase more and more. He tried to keep looking straight ahead, keeping a steady pace. Shadows in the far periphery of the small sphere of light around the flame hinted at what lurked there. Along with the number of bugs, the crackling, crawling noise they made was unsettling in its own right.

How long is this damn tunnel! Gus thought as he wiped sweat off his hands onto the tunic, taking care not to rock the small lamp. The oil was definitely getting lower now.

Was it past halfway? It definitely looked like it was burning more quickly as the oil got lower in the rounded base of the little gravy-boat lamp. The only consolation was that he could move more quickly as the oil dropped lower into the lamp.

Imagining he must look ridiculous, like one of those speed walkers, he pressed on.

Please let there be another vat of oil at the end of this passage! A trickle of sweat fell into his eye and stung, but he blinked it away, not wanting to remove his hands, both of which were stabilizing the little lamp. He wanted to wipe it away with his upper arm but didn't dare. Shaking his head didn't do anything to divert any perspiration from falling.

As his heartbeat increased, Gus wondered if he could pull out of the delve if he saw he was getting close to losing his light. He had a fear that if he did so, he would lose his lamp and wick and he would not be able to go back into the tunnel. The large vat would be heavy to carry, and its narrow, rounded top probably would not allow the light to spread out enough to keep the scarabs at bay. He growled at the futility of the situation.

After what seemed like an eternity, the passageway flattened for a small stretch and then opened into a wider chamber.

Finally! The small room was relatively small and, to Gus' chagrin, there was no other vessel with oil in the room. No sconces or other items along the walls. Gus checked the lamp and saw just a small splash of oil in the bottom of the lamp. His eyes darted around but aside from the carved hieroglyphics on the walls of the circular chamber, there was nothing.

Scarabs began to pile in the doorway in droves, choking the opening so that Gus couldn't exit even if he wanted to, they were so thick. From there they spread out, crawling along the walls until he was totally encircled. Backing away as much as he could, he ended up in the center of the room, and the bugs kept coming. They were so thick that the space around Gus was actually shrinking with the layers and layers of the gross bugs crawling endlessly in a roiling mass.

Instinctively, Gus began to crouch as the bugs crawled on the ceiling, dropping like rain when they hit the outer edge of the light and getting briefly stunned. He looked into the small lamp and saw the thin film of oil. The wick began to spark and smoke as the flame began to gutter out. Gus tried to exit the delve. Whether he could get back was immaterial, there was nothing here for him.

And nothing happened.

Gus struggled to pull out of the cube but met resistance, as if he were under countless blankets pressing him down.

No, no, no!

CHAPTER THIRTY-EIGHT

Dust in the Wind

Gus lifted the flame up as high as he could, trying to give himself as much light as the poor lamp could muster. The arm holding the lamp was trembling in anticipation of his demise and he put his other hand down to stabilize himself. There was a small grating noise as his fingertips brushed against something depressible on the floor.

Squinting, Gus couldn't make out below him, but his fingers frantically probed for something, anything. His fingernail caught the end of a flat ring, flush with the ground, and he pried it up in desperation. The lamp flames were dipping lower and the masses of bugs swelled in response to the shrinking light.

Gus pulled up hard on the ring, twisting and turning it. Anything to move it or cause it to react. There was a loud bang, followed by a series of other noises overlapping. The white noise of falling sand, the squelch and crunch of bugs being crushed. Plumes of sand filled the chamber and Gus buried his mouth and nose in his shoulder to avoid inhaling the mess. A pungent scent as whatever ichor inside of the smashed bugs wafted out in the musty, sand filled air.

After a tense second, blinding beams of sunlight flooded into the chamber, highlighting Gus like a spotlight. The wave of scarabs was almost upon him, and they struggled to flee from the bright light as it burned down into the chamber. Smoke began emanating off the carapace of the slower insects, knocked aside by the flight of the others. Others flailed about, having fallen on their backs. They tried in vain to rock onto their feet as their hairy legs writhed in the burning sunlight. More sand began draining away, and the swath of light increased dramatically. Motes of dust and sand shone blindingly in the room and Gus pressed his eyelids tightly shut to give them time to acclimate.

The sound of scrabbling scarabs receded to a dull, distant murmur that faded to silence. Gus opened his eyes to see the bugs were gone, no evidence of their presence besides tracks in the sand extending from his position to the exit. Pulling the collar of the tunic to cover his nose and mouth, Gus rose to his feet and looked at the chamber, which looked totally different when illuminated by the noon-day sun. The sand and dust quickly settled, and Gus saw that four large stones had fallen near the edges of the room, exposing windows to the outside.

Though he had felt like he had descended a great deal, the opening above appeared to only be twenty to thirty feet above him. The weight of the stones had also lowered the entire floor of the chamber, revealing grates into which the residual sand fell, making a faint *shush* as it sifted into the darkness below. Gus shivered again, glad the openings were small enough that a scarab couldn't crawl through. The whole ordeal had made his skin crawl and twitch, even though he knew the bugs wouldn't brave the light.

A cramp in his hand made him look at his hand. He still clung onto the ring with a death-grip. He finally let go of the ring, letting it *clank* as it fell. Gus' pull had lifted a foot-high cylinder out of the floor. Shaking and rubbing blood back into his hand, Gus saw that the center of the stone cylinder was hollow. He crouched down to look into the opening and saw something nestled in the shadowy recess.

Looking around, he found the discarded lamp buried slightly in the sand where he had dropped it and used it to probe into the opening. A large yellow gem the size of a lemon began to glisten as the hot desert sun played across its facets. As Gus picked up the gem from the sand a prompt filled his display:

Welcome Dr. Flak!

Followed by another menu with *Journal Entries, Trials, Results, Protocols*, and other tabs with techno-speak so complicated Gus could only guess what they contained. Gus checked the Journal first, perusing the first entries.

I believe that I have found the ideal storage medium for my further work. With the breaches in security that allowed the unscrupulous to profit from my work on mammalian integrations, I will be much more careful as I progress in this new direction. The medium of Quorian cubes is one that has always fascinated me, and more so now that their creator has passed. The knowledge of their creation, unfortunately, has passed with him, but I was able to glean much on their function and programmability before his demise. I was able to find three other cubes, all inferior ones with only a couple of sides active and functional. One was specialized to the point that it has lost all plasticity and could not be altered.

Still it provided a structure and blueprint that I have been able to extrapolate to practice and learn how to modify the cubes.

This cube, where I will store my life's work, will be the epitome of all I learn. My most precious knowledge, hidden away from those who would attempt to take it again. My first goal would be to lock access to each facet under each successive side. Inability to unlock the environments sequentially will provide additional security. I know the cubes cannot be hacked in the traditional sense, but as experience tells me, often your worst enemies are those closest to you.

To wit, I've locked the first layer of information with a test that only I should be able to navigate. Supers will find that their abilities will not function in this virtual environment unless they are one of the few who possess an inherent ability. Even then, it would need to be one that allows one to manipulate light or energy. I have designed this temple as a gauntlet that will trap anyone who attempts to steal this information, super or not. Once past the initial chamber, one will be committed to finishing the trial and will not be able to leave the simulation.

Failure will result in acute neurogenic shock leading to physical death within a short period after the event. I believe that this will deter further attempts to access my work once these consequences become known.

I plan on layering each facet with similar protections to safeguard the information contained in this cube.

Gus closed the window and swallowed. For a minute, he just stared at the shifting dust motes as he tried to absorb the bullet he had dodged. If he had failed, he would have died! Like permadeath, died! And left Prime and his team screwed back in the real world. And it sounded like the other sides of the cube were just as dangerous, and he had been fairly cavalier about exploring them without a lot of protection or even knowledge of what he was dealing with. A chill washed over him despite the hot sun at how his team would have suffered if he had not been able to complete the trial he didn't even know he was undergoing.

He had to close his eyes and take several deep breaths to calm himself of the panic that threatened to overtake him. Actions had consequences. As if his grandfather was lecturing his recent folly, the words returned to him again, almost accusingly.

...There is always responsibility, regardless of whether there is great power or not.

Gus sat reeling, glad no one could see him sitting there in the virtual sand.

What the hell am I doing? One of these times I won't get lucky and other people are going to pay for it.

Being a super was no joke and he couldn't just keep making things up as he went. It would only work for so long. How close had he come to dooming Prime to a life of possible slavery, all because she trusted him to be competent enough to get the job done? What would happen to her daughter when Mom mysteriously disappeared? What other things did the Crew keep to themselves that made the frivolous risks Gus was taking much bigger gambles than even he knew?

He needed to get to know the others better. Despite how uncomfortable that made him feel, it was his duty and they deserved it. They had earned the right to have him know the stakes which depending on him required. Gus looked down at the gem he was clutching in his hand. His hand gripped it tightly, the strain of his guilt manifesting in his clenched fist.

I will do better. I have to do better. I need to make some plans and find some direction for a change.

CHAPTER THIRTY-NINE

Under Pressure

Gus opened his eyes and looked at Prime just inches away. Blinking, he wondered how long he was under for this time.

"Well, what are you waiting for? Get in there and get the information," Prime said through grit teeth, pulled ostensibly in a forced smile for those watching them.

"How long was I gone?"

"Gone? You didn't go anywhere." The light pink fur bunched on her furrowed forehead, and Gus could tell she was having some doubts in putting her faith in him.

Totally justified doubts, Gus thought.

"I mean, how long have I zoned out for? It felt like I was in for a couple of hours."

"Are you joking? You just asked Aurora to watch over you, and then I said 'be safe in there,' and then you closed your eyes and opened them. That's it. You're telling me you got it? That quickly?"

"I... I guess so. Time in these cubes is trippy and weird—"

"You're totally certain? Do you need to check? I don't want to tell them we have it if we really don't..."

"Let me double check," Gus pulled up his display, noting

with comfort that everything was back to normal. Living without a display was unsettling. It was such a part of his life now that he felt incomplete without it.

"Nick, a little help, please," Gus asked mentally and Nick highlighted the tabs and settings to open. Sure enough there was a yellow file and a directory he could tell was the Quorian cube, just like a remote drive.

"I got it, Prime. Confirmed."

She nodded and turned away from him to face the court.

"We have the information agreed upon. I will stay while my companions follow up on your proposed lead. Upon their return, we will exchange the information and our transaction will be done."

"Fine," Prime's father growled through pursed lips. With a nod, the gorilla steward proceeded forward and handed something to Gus, bowing and then returning to his place.

Prime's mother leaned forward, as if she were about to pounce, eyes widening as she unconsciously licked her lips. "Do not trifle with us, manchild. We expect you back within a day, or I will send my hunters after you." She sniffed the air while staring directly at Gus. "I have your scent. It has been too long since we have had a hunt, and my hunters would thirst for prey of your 'variety.' If you are not back, my daughter stays with us and I will have your head on my wall as a trophy. Have no doubt of that, little rabbit."

Gus locked eyes with the cheetah woman, determined not to lose the stare down, but Aurora gently grabbed his arm and coaxed him to leave. Unwillingly, he turned and let her lead him out.

———

The rusty door slammed shut behind them, Sir Rhino taking more confidence now that Prime was no longer with them. He definitely was using more force than was necessary to close the door in as obnoxious a way as possible. The three stood there staring at the empty alcove where their ship had been, totally vacant. Attempts to raise anyone on comms were met with silence.

"Well that's just great," Aurora blurted, stomping her feet and clutching her fists beside her.

"*I know!* It's been one of those days," Gus added.

"Okay, everyone stay calm. It's probably nothing. Let's not assume the worst. They could be circling around, having to make way for some other delivery or something similar."

"No, it is bad as you expect," a voice whispered into Gus' ear.

"Gaaa!" Gus swat reflexively at the disembodied voice as Grimdark phased into view. The ghostly voice elicited a squeak from Aurora at his sudden appearance which quickly transformed into anger.

"You do that on purpose, you creep! You know everyone hates it!" Aurora fumed.

Grimdark just smiled sardonically and shrugged.

"Transport had to leave. Competitors found us and were very mad. They arrive and offer disappeared, being marked fulfilled. Since Crew parked right outside the doorstep, you see. I vanish while they fled, leading others away. Almost one hour ago and no communication since."

"Damn you, Leto! This whole job sucks. We can't win for losing!" Aurora griped.

"Do not kill messenger," Grimdark remarked, shrugging again.

"Well, what do we do? Fly on our own?" Gus suggested, stepping between Aurora and Grimdark.

Grimdark raised a finger. "I slow you down, so will stay here."

"Anyone have any better ideas?"

"Waiting isn't really a great option, as we are once again on a time limit. I'd say rent another car, but I don't know how we'd do that without Yuki's help. Or how we'd pay for it." Gus put his hands on his hips and looked up into the ever-present fog, trying to think of what to do next.

"Where are we even going, Gus?"

Gus took a closer look at the item in his hands. Gus followed the prompts and found another entry next to the Quorian cube. Opening it, he found the drive the ape steward had given him had a single file with map coordinates. He slid the nav-point to his companions. "I don't know what Kenway is, but that's the next stop on the tour."

"How do we get there though? We can't fly and maintain any kind of stealth," Aurora added.

"We walk," Tempest replied without emotion. "Look at the coordinates, we can make it from here."

Gus looked at the dark alleys ahead of them, and a rumble of thunder mirrored what he was feeling inside.

"Let's go." Tempest began walking down a gangway leading off into the gloom. Aurora looked at Gus, grimaced, and then followed. Another rumble of thunder followed by almost instantaneous rain was the cherry on top as Gus blinked and shook his head.

"Okay, I guess we're doing this," he muttered as he stepped past the others. He clicked the coordinates on his display and blue chevrons appeared along the path to indicate where to travel. The small size of the number indicating the destination further dampened his mood.

The group began traversing narrow alleyways that provided dubious support, as they were connected to the adjoining walls with rusty plates. Every once in a while, Gus would peek between the gap between the ground and the buildings and see a glimpse of something zipping by below, illuminating the mists as whatever it was sped by. The gap was a good six inches, maybe not enough to fall through, but one could easily lose something if they were careless.

Despite the aged and weathered walls, there was no rubbish to be found littering the alleyways. Either it was washed away by the ever-present rains or there were stiff penalties for dropping trash into the void, as it could hit someone or something. *Maybe they have their own version of the beachcomber robots.*

Besides there being no trash in the alleys and passageways they snaked through on the way to their destination, they were relatively abandoned. Perhaps they were at a high enough level in Hinansho that the powers that be had "managed" the homeless population, forcing them to a more suitable level where they would be out of sight and out of mind.

With the amount of rain that was constantly falling on their path, he doubted anyone would stay in this particular stretch of alleyways for long unless they had an established shelter. As if in response to his thoughts, the rain began to fall harder, rattling off the sheet metal roofs like a sustained paradiddle.

The trip soon became monotonous, tall buildings blocking anything but the narrow path ahead, then splitting and continuing. Occasionally, they would be moving upwards, other times they were making a series of labyrinthine turns, trusting the directions to lead them to their destination. While the rain let up on occasion, at times a drain emptied in the center of the path, and it was impossible to avoid as the drainage water from above hit the path and splashed everything in a large radius. One just had to embrace the fact that they were going to be wet and miserable as long as they traveled these alleys and walkways.

Gus rubbed his tongue along his front teeth, wishing he could at least use some shielding to keep the rain from constantly falling and pulling his hair into his eyes. Whether it was the foul weather or the cold, his headache returned. It started at the base of his skull and began to creep up over his head, turning the driving rain into a unique variation of Chinese water torture. As it progressed, he began to feel crushing pressure from his temples.

He shook his head to flick off some rainwater and the pain flared, driving deeper into his head.

"Gus, your neurotransmitters are taking a huge dip," Nick advised.

"Of all times." Gus sighed as he swiped water off his face, wary of moving his head too much.

"Evaluating the feedback from the Mandrite core event, I have been trying to determine what alleviates and what exacerbates the effects. Using the **Telepathy** skill provided the most significant benefits. Perhaps this allows your brain to sync to a normal baseline somehow and reset, to an extent. Thus allowing you a reprieve from the psychic stress of the excess abilities pushing for assimilation."

"Probably not the best option with everyone wide awake, Nick," Gus thought in reply.

"After this, **Ether Crafting** offers a benefit, followed by your use of **Electric Mind** in conjunction with the Quorian cube. But these are an order of magnitude less than **Telepathy**."

"Anything to make this go away," Gus pinched his eyes shut and had to lean over and take some deep breaths when a nasty surge of nausea-inducing pain blurred his vision.

Aurora turned, pulling a large swath of wet hair behind her ear. Seeing Gus bracing himself on his knees about fifty feet back, she signaled for Tempest to stop.

"Gus, are you okay?" she asked, jogging over to him. He only lifted a finger, unable to respond with his eyes screwed shut. After a minute, he gasped as whatever was bothering him ebbed.

"What is going on? Gus, talk to me!"

"I... I don't know," Gus lied. "Stress headache, I think. The rain isn't helping, either."

"It's been a stressful mission; it can be very overwhelming," Tempest confirmed. "We're getting close, do you need us to help you walk?"

"Nah, it is fading a bit more now. I think I can make it. Let's just go before it comes back." Gus groaned, forcing himself to stand.

Tempest nodded, giving Gus a pat on the back. "You let me know if it starts again. We can't help you if you don't talk to us.

Got it? We'll get BoJack to take a look at you as soon as we all meet up. I'm hoping we get the information and we can all get the hell out of here. I've had enough of Hinansho to last me a lifetime." Tempest waved Gus forward and they continued on their slog.

He knew they were watching him, keeping an eye on him in case he stumbled or showed any signs of relapse. At first it was irritating, but as time progressed, he began to doubt if he wouldn't pass out at an inopportune moment.

As Gus checked the distance to destination, Tempest was right, they were much closer now. Gus picked up his speed, eager to be finished. The alley finally spilled out into a wider courtyard area. Repurposed bits of technology and materials were used to great effect, and the group began to see more individuals stirring about.

The presence of augments and hybrids, even disheveled and dirty, lifted Gus' spirits a bit, making him feel more secure they were on the right path, despite the display's mapping trail being ever-present. The lack of locals in the alleys set him on edge for some reason in such a big, bustling city. Even this group in the courtyard seemed to cluster together, as they opened their tiny stores and workshops which appeared to double as their homes in the off hours.

Following the blue chevrons, this area of Hinansho became more and more developed, giving way to actual storefronts and more foot traffic. At the end of a large intersection, they realized they were at their destination. A large transport resembling a pirate ship was embedded into the nearby shops. With the overgrowth of shops and walkways that stretched overhead to different buildings, the ship's traveling days were long past, but it was an impressive sight by its sheer size.

A large gangplank led up to the second story opening. A garish holographic sign lit up letter by letter, announcing they had arrived.

CHAPTER FORTY

Jack Sparrow

Walking off the gangway, they stepped onto the creaky wooden floor and took in the ambiance of Kenway's place.

The esthetic was decidedly nautical—to the extreme. Though it would have no place on an actual transport, there was a large wooden mast in the center of the room, and upon the bow an individual that could only be Kenway sat in a large throne. He was obviously an augment, and he pet a large tiger at his side as he watched his men work.

Different hybrids were rushing to and fro, stacking items into different piles as they assembled orders. Crates were loaded and checked, wrapped with a dark cellophane, then transferred to levitating pallets.

"Aaah, I get it now," Gus hit his head, nodding. "I wondered why Kenway sounded familiar." as he took in the decor.

"Does he have a gun instead of a peg-leg?" Aurora whispered, squinting as she looked up at the figure.

"It's an RPD, and my scan shows that it works," Tempest confirmed.

"I haven't seen someone who screams 'I'm overcompensating for something' like this in quite a while," Aurora said while shaking her head.

Tempest elbowed her. "Not the time…"

"Sorry," she whispered, eyes looking back at Kenway, trying to detect if he had heard her with some augmented senses, despite being over two hundred feet away.

Curled up by the side of the throne was a large tiger. Gus noticed it also equipped a similar, albeit electronic, eyepatch. The large animal raised its head and peered at them with hungry eyes. Well, one hungry eye and the other emanated a ruby colored beam, with servos enlarging and constricting around the synthetic eye.

Seeing them enter, Kenway motioned them forward with a mechanical hand. Gus could see different attachments folded along Kenway's forearm, among them a blade, a hydraulic clamp, and other attachments he couldn't make out from this vantage.

As the group approached, it was more evident that the throne was the head of some large robot, the lower jaw jutting forward to form the base of the seat. Kenway leaned forward and spread his arms wide.

"What can I do for you today, my esteemed guests?"

"We are looking for someone; we were told she was in Hinansho." Tempest said, stepping forward.

"Well then you have come to the right place!" Kenway said as he sprang to his feet. Or foot, in his particular case. "That is what I do. I find things, often very difficult things, and match them with those who want them." He held a finger out as if lecturing a naughty child. "One thing I must ask though, who referred you to me? It determines your rate. My services are not exactly *inexpensive*…"

"The Aslan clan sent us." Aurora admitted, her eyes betraying her distrust of the man.

A stormy expression darkened the cyborg's features for the briefest of seconds, then warmed back to his used-car salesman grin.

"I… owe them some favors. I assume they gave you something to find me?" He held out his multi-tool hand; the articulated human hand folded back and an extension with a USB port and other connectors folded out in its place.

Gus fished out the drive and stepped up to plug it in.

"Aah, yes. There it is. Ooh. You must have done something substantial; this is a valuable marker. This pays off a sizable portion of what I owe, so consider me your humble servant. I do believe I can help you. If this person you seek is in Hinansho, I can tell you where they are. I am probably one of the few people who could do this, so the clan was wise to send you to me. Come, let us discuss the details and I will get started."

Tempest stepped forward and Kenway motioned him to follow. The large throne, which was obviously a death's head now that it was unoccupied, was a large helm with wooden spokes extending around. With an adjustment, the wheel rotated horizontally to form a table. The center irised open to reveal a large circular screen.

Kenway asked questions and added the information as the trio responded, just by holding his multi-tool hand over the screen. Panels and windows opened and closed as Tempest explained everything he knew about his wife's absence.

After about thirty minutes of discussion and questioning, Kenway's face looked concerned with the incoherent results on the crowded screen.

"Oh, dear," the pirate said, rubbing his human hand over his polished bald head. "Ooh. That is not good." His face puckered as if he had just tasted something extremely sour. "Not good indeed. For you, that is…"

"What is it?" Tempest pressed, hungry for any answers.

"Well, it seems that Mengele has her, you see…"

Gus shook his head, not recognizing the reference but gave a start when he saw the color drain out of Tempest and Aurora's faces.

"Who is he? Dad, Aurora, snap out of it. Who is Mengele?"

When his companions couldn't respond, Kenway explained. "Mengele has a... reputation for experimenting on his subjects. His specialty is exploring the limits of human capabilities. His methods are—well, extreme is too delicate a word. He is totally detached and amoral about how others feel. This allows him to pursue some lines of study which most would find, how would you say... unsavory?"

"He's a damn butcher," Tempest said, eyes staring ahead vacantly.

"True, true. That is an apt description. I am sorry, but you did ask. I can give you the coordinates to his last known where-abouts. This 'Gwen' was transported here on a research visa only a short time ago, and this coincides with my data on where Mengele should be. Are you still interested?"

Tempest reached a hand forward woodenly, still in shock.

Kenway slid a virtual file to Tempest and did an about-face. With a flick of his hand, the helm-screen went dark. "And that concludes our business. I trust that you can find your way out?"

Tempest nodded in a daze as he reviewed the contents of the folder, turning to leave. Aurora and Gus followed, and Gus kept looking back and forth between his shell-shocked father and Kenway, who had sat again in his massive throne and crossed his legs. He waved his fingers in an effeminate gesture of goodbye or dismissal, then leaned back, clasping his wrists and looking upwards in thought.

The supers left Kenway's ship in silence and stood in the now crowded intersection as an assortment of people rushed by. The day was in full swing and more shops were open along the entire street as it had been transformed into some sort of outdoor market. Smells of various foods wafted in from different directions, as well as music and the shouts of people hawking their wares.

"Will someone tell me what this all means?" Gus demanded, looking to the dazed supers.

"It means that your mother may already be gone. Even if

she is alive, she may never be the same," Tempest croaked, almost breaking into a sob.

Gus looked at Aurora, who just nodded grimly.

CHAPTER FORTY-ONE

We're Not Gonna Take It

"Now what?" Gus asked, at a loss.

"Not much we can do until we meet up with the Crew. Coordinates are on the border of Hinansho. We can't travel there by ourselves," Tempest said, appearing to slowly come out of his stupor.

"I hate to ask, but if we're going to be here for a while, do you mind if I do a little shopping?" Aurora asked. "I think there are some components I could really use to help find Gwen here."

Tempest waved her off with a distracted wave. "We're stuck here until the Crew finds us, go ahead."

As Aurora threaded through the crowd, Gus' eyes pinched a bit. When she was out of earshot, Gus turned on his father.

"What the hell, Dad? We just got this bombshell dropped on us, and her priority is shopping? You're just going to let her go?"

Tempest came over and laid a hand on Gus' shoulder. "We all deal with stress differently," he said, voice still detached and aloof.

"Uncool. We have better things to do right now—"

"Do we? We may already be too late. If the stories I have heard about Mengele are even partially true… well, we need to think realistically."

"Why aren't you angrier? You're acting like you're a zombie. Doesn't any of this make you upset?!"

"Of course it does! I'm still processing it, but what good would getting angry do? Gus, in my duties with Purple Faction, I have always had to keep a level head when others were losing theirs. In my experience, worry or bombast do little to resolve big problems. This, though…" He looked up at Gus with steel blue eyes, uncertainty there for the first time Gus could remember.

"Do you realize how I've hung all my hopes on finding her again? I never doubted that we would be together again. It's what has kept me going all these years. We are linked, Gus; I can see her icon on my display every day, and it is a constant reminder that she is still alive. Very few super couples reach that synchronicity—ever. I just never questioned exactly what state she would be in when I finally found her. What will I find waiting for me if—and that's a big if—we can even get past Mengele and rescue her?"

"Is he really that bad?"

"Oh, he's all that and more. And he's never been caught. All that's been found are the macabre results of his evil work. Things that are worse than any sane mind could conceive. The fact that she's here in Hinansho where people experiment and alter their bodies without any oversight doesn't help my mind from spiraling out of control with the horrific possibilities. It's no wonder Mengele has a base of operations here. I suppose I should be grateful that Gwen was recently moved here, although that's cold comfort. He has her, and nothing will be right again if we can't get her away from him."

"Everything will work out," Gus tried to console his father, but the words sounded hollow even to his own ears.

"Tempest, Gus, Aurora—do you read?" Seneschal's voice crackled over their internal comms.

"We're here," Tempest said, his voice brightening. Gus was impressed how his father could project an aura of confidence and control while his face was still pinched and furrowed with worry. He had no doubt his father would erase those physical signs when back in front of the Crew. "It's good to hear your voice again, Seneschal. Is everyone alright?"

"Nothing I couldn't handle, but those bastards were tenacious. I would have been here sooner, but I wanted to make sure we lost them for good before meeting up again. How are things on your end?"

"We finally know where she is, after all we've been through."

"I see…" Seneschal replied, almost forlorn.

"It's not all good news, however. Mengele has her…"

"Mengele's here? We need to hurry, then. Who knows what he has planned? Or how long she will last?"

Tempest winced as if slapped. He took a second to regain his composure before he spoke. "Agreed. Send me coordinates, and we'll meet up with you when you find a place to land. We have a lot to plan."

"Will do." Seneschal clicked off the comm.

"Let's find Aurora and get the hell out of here," Tempest growled, his voice affectation gone, revealing his frayed nerves.

Gus followed as Tempest marched into the crowd, hitting shoulders and barreling through people as they made their way through the press of the busy marketplace. Gus shrugged apologetically to those who bore the brunt of his father's lack of patience as they scowled back at the pair.

Tempest made a beeline to Aurora, who was finalizing a purchase at a stall with trays and multiple bin organizers with tiny drawers for even smaller components.

"I'm sure you've heard. Are you about finished here?"

"Yes, they had more than I expected! I'm excited to try some new designs." Her excited tone became somber as she turned and saw Tempest's expression.

"Great, follow me. Seneschal just sent me rendezvous coordinates. The sooner we get underway, the sooner we can put this all behind us." Tempest turned quickly and began plowing through the crowd again.

"Sure, sure." Aurora cast a quick glance at Gus who grimaced.

She mouthed, "What happened?" to which Gus only shrugged. Grabbing her purchases distractedly, she followed Tempest to a crowded landing zone surrounded by food vendors. Gus' stomach growled as the tasty scents of food hung in the air, but he knew Tempest was on a mission and would not wait.

"Mmm, rations it is, I suppose," Gus muttered to himself as he looked longingly at another market-goer eating a skewer of grilled meat. The transport lifted off almost as soon as they were aboard. Tempest had sent the coordinates ahead to Seneschal, and she was wasting no time in heading to their final destination.

Grimdark met them, glad that they had reunited with the Crew safely. He went into an animated retelling of what had happened to the Crew. Gus was sure he took some creative liberties, but it was an entertaining tale of how Seneschal had pushed the rickety transport to its limits and managed to lose their pursuers, who were in a Mach Corvair.

"How did we ever beat someone here if they had a Mach Corvair? I hope we didn't make any enemies. Our competition has some deep pockets if they were using a Corvair for courier work," Aurora said, eyes wide.

"Custom weapons package as well. Everything top of line. We speed off when they pick me up. Seneschal very, very good pilot," Grimdark explained, showing the most emotion Gus had ever seen him display.

"Everyone to the common room. We need to plan en route. We're getting my wife out of there!" Tempest barked over the ship's comms.

"I've never seen his edge-lord side," Anastasia replied.

"He's using it to mask his worry, don't take it personally,"

Harmony replied as she walked by, her hand trailing along Grimdark's shoulders, noting his change in demeanor with Tempest's command.

Does she flirt with absolutely anyone and everyone? Gus thought, just as Harmony looked directly at him and winked.

Gus followed the Crew as they entered the main central area of the transport and awaited Tempest. He appeared in the doorway leading to the cockpit, and held onto an overhead pipe in the exposed ductwork as he surveyed the Crew.

"Is everyone here?" he asked severely, eyes searching and mentally cataloging the team. "Where the hell is Darik?"

"Oi, right here!" The Keeper replied, pulling his head out of a panel, headlight flashing in the group's eyes. "Just tweakin' things; they got a little misaligned during our romp through Hinansho." Seeing Tempest's expression, he ripped off his headlight and fell into place with the group, dusting himself off.

"I'm sure you have heard by now—but Mengele is here, and he has my wife. Who knows what other supers are in his little house of horrors. As much as I would like to bring everyone out of there, that may not be possible. Gwen is top priority, but if we can bring anyone out with us without compromising her extraction, then I say we do it. Because this is Mengele, I do not want to go head to head with him. I would prefer we sneak in and sneak out, completely undetected if possible.

"To that end, we need to pick up Prime, as she will have the most experience with this type of mission. The Aslan HQ is in the opposite direction, so we need to hurry. I don't trust Kenway, and I wouldn't be surprised if he's in league with Mengele. He knew where Gwen was a little too easily for my tastes. I may be wrong, but we need to be prepared for anything."

"Let's make the bastard pay!" Darik cheered.

"As much as I want to do that very thing, I'm afraid we're outclassed. We have no knowledge of what he has been doing here, who is working for him, and how he has evolved in the past decade he has fallen off of everyone's radar. There's just too many unknowns and we don't have the time to investigate them thoroughly. I do *not* want Gwen to get transferred anywhere else or... worse."

Tempest cleared his throat before continuing. "For now, the plan is to check out these coordinates without being detected, determine when the best time to extract Gwen is, and then be in and out as quickly as we can. I want to kick some ass, but we have to save that fight for another day. Let's get Prime and get going. How are we in terms of our shrouds?"

"Shrouds are running low on power; we will probably only have another 8 hours," Aurora reported, checking the suits.

"Power them down until we absolutely need them. Seneschal will let us know when we are close. Let's finish this and get the hell out of here."

CHAPTER FORTY-TWO

Hellcat

"Since our new friends know about the Aslan clan's HQ, I'm going to be dropping you off nearby, then circling back. I don't want to have to shake them again and waste any time," Seneschal told the small group as they crammed into the small cockpit. "I'll sync this timer so you can meet me at the drop off coordinates. Be there or it will reset and I'll have to make another circuit and come back around. Do *not* make me do that, if at all possible." A timer with twenty minutes popped into life in the lower left of Gus' display.

With the plan set, they headed for the cargo bay, ready to jump out as Seneschal made the brief stop near the Aslan's alcove.

"Are you okay, Gus?" Aurora asked.

He self-consciously stopped massaging the base of his skull. "I would be if these headaches would go away." He stretched his neck back and forth, forward and backward, trying to relieve the tension and pain. "BoJack couldn't find anything wrong."

"You think it's from, you know, the crystal? Didn't you say that's when the headaches started?"

Gus nodded as he fell in step with Aurora. "I thought they

were going away for a while, but they've recently started getting worse. Some things help but then the rebound seems even worse."

"Still not sleeping?"

"I don't dare to, that's when **Leech** kicks in and assimilates any absorbed abilities. I just know there's too much in the buffer that I can't risk it. At least until we get Mom. She needs me until then, so I'll tough it out."

"Don't try to be too strong on your own for too long. That won't serve anyone. You have to communicate when you're on a team; we need to know if you're on the edge. I still think you should tell the group about everything."

"Noted. But let's wait until we finish this op. We don't need any distractions—we're almost in the end zone. Don't worry about me, I won't let you or the Crew down."

"It's not about disappointing us. We can't help you if you aren't honest about your status."

"I can pull my weight. Don't worry about me. I'll get the job done. I'm just looking forward to some downtime when all of this is over."

Aurora gave Gus a sidelong glance. "Alright…" she said, letting the issue drop.

"Are you guys in position for the drop and dash?" Seneschal asked as the ship began to slow and rotate.

"We're good," Tempest confirmed as the gangway began to open, its noisy hydraulics whirring as the roar of engines and whipping wind intruded on the relative peace of the cargo bay. As the gangway yawned open, buildings were revealed as they zipped by in the mists. They were still moving at quite a clip, and a chill wind circulated into the room through the open hatchway. Tempest made a motion for the others to activate their shrouds.

"*Get ready to go in three… two… one,*" he indicated with hand motions.

The ship did an abrupt spin and the bottom of the gang-plank oriented a couple of feet above a familiar alcove.

Everyone slid down the gangplank and the ship shot off again as soon as Gus' feet were clear, even before he had touched down on the alcove. They rushed to the doorway as the ship disappeared into the darkness and the countdown timer began ticking down.

Sir Rhino reluctantly let them in, muttering under his breath as they were led back to the throne room.

The throne room was darker than before and the primal, animal scent was more evident. The thrones were backlit by an orange glow, and they were allowed to wait there while someone conversed with the hybrid sovereigns in the shadows. With a gesture, the figure left, opening a doorway to the side of the thrones, leaving it open. Light spilled in through the door as the beaded curtain in front of it rattled to rest.

"I must admit, I did not expect to see you back so soon." The lights brightened to allow the trio to view the leaders again, as well as a larger group of muscular hybrids accompanying them on their dais.

The queen purred, one claw scratching her whiskers. "I had almost hoped you would have left our daughter and gone on your way, but perhaps this is for the best. She is here in body only, and her time among the supers has only made her more defiant and uncooperative." Another gesture and two servants held the curtain apart so the princess could exit onto the dais.

Prime stepped through the doorway into the throne room wearing a flowing dress with large slits that showed her legs up past the hips. Thick laces held parts of the dress in a provocative cut that emphasized her femininity much more than the biker's outfit she usually wore.

As far as Gus could tell, just her head and tail had catlike fur. The swath of skin that arced from her shoulder across her chest was as human as they came. Prime's fluffy pink tail flicked in agitation as she stood by her parents, her arms tightly folded, accentuating her modest cleavage. Her ears were pressed firmly down atop her head as she glared at her parents.

"We will be taking the cube now, please leave it with our

steward," the queen commanded, and on cue, a small hedgehog hybrid with bifocals scuttled forward with a tray, bowing his head as he approached Gus.

"*No!*" Prime roared. "That was not the agreement, and you know it!"

"Daughter dear, if you ever want to leave here, you will realize that you are not in a position to bargain. We are the Aslan clan and we will take what we are due," her father said dismissively, holding a large paw out, indicating there was to be no interference from her, princess or not.

"So this is the honor of the Aslan clan? If your word is so cheap, I don't know how you hope the other clans will respect you. Once honor is lost, it is not easy to regain. If you are not worthy—"

"We will honor the agreement, child," her mother interrupted, the last word spat in distaste. Her leonine mate threw her a scathing look at being overruled.

A little hedgehog man approached, and took a small box from another small servant that resembled a meerkat. Gus slid Dr. Flak's file over toward the box. To his surprise, the entire file was transferred, not merely a copy.

"You didn't think we would let you keep the information, did you, pet?" the queen asked, noticing Gus' shock. "This information's value lies mostly in its exclusivity. And that is well within our rights. Do you have a problem with this, daughter?" The cheetah sneered at Prime who petulantly agreed. "I'm sooo glad you approve," her voice purred, dripping with sarcasm. "I assume you will want to be leaving with them?"

"As soon as possible."

Her mother waved her away, as if she was something offensive and smelly. The gesture was the epitome of 'take it away, it displeases me.'

Prime stormed down the steps, pointing at the meerkat steward. "You. My gear. Now."

He scrambled off on all fours as Prime came and rejoined her group.

Aurora looked her up and down, nodding in appreciation. "Why were you keeping this all wrapped up?"

Gus tried to keep his eyes from roving. Prime was much more attractive than he would have ever given her credit for when she was all done up, and she had relaxed any pretenses of hiding her gender. She now strutted like she was a model as she stopped to answer Aurora.

"I don't plan to anymore." Prime reached her hand out as the steward came scuttling out with her duffel. The shape of her helmet visibly bulging in the canvas bag

"We're leaving," Prime announced in an imperious tone.

"Do you want to change before we go?" Tempest asked.

"No, I just want to get out of here as soon as possible."

"But the others—" Aurora gasped.

"It's about time they knew. I'm tired of hiding. I'll be okay with whatever happens here on out, I have almost nothing left to lose."

"Just know that if you leave again, you will be renouncing your claim to the throne," Prime's father bellowed across the throne room.

"I never wanted it in the first place," Prime said over her shoulder.

The medallion she had used to get them in the door was clutched in his hand and crumpled as he clenched his paw into a fist.

"I never wanted any of it." Her tail flicked in agitation.

"So be it," he growled. The queen patted his arm placatingly as she looked at the contents of the drive the steward had delivered to her.

"We have gained so much more. With this, the Aslan clan will be the undisputed ruler of the hybrids, with or without her," the cheetah soothed. She slid a file over to him and his face went slack as he saw the contents. The pair both began to laugh with glee.

"What have I done?" Gus wondered as he turned to follow Prime and the others out of the headquarters.

CHAPTER FORTY-THREE

Hot on the Trail

"Aw, hell *no!*" Harmony yelled as Prime came into the common room. Hints of a Texas drawl apparent from her usually squeaky, bubbly, Betty Boop voice. She kept looking at the trio as they boarded, sputtering.

"Are you all okay with this? Bringing a mutant on board?" She looked at the star-struck Crew.

"I am Prime." She dropped the canvas bag and knelt, unzipping it to reveal the characteristic helmet inside. "Or Sanura, if you prefer."

"You… you *lied* to us! And your helmet, *that's* why I couldn't read you," Harmony said to herself in realization. "Who in the Faction knows about this? We have to report her. There could be others. I knew things seemed off, but this explains so much. We've been infiltrated by mutants!" Her voice became more shrill as she jumped from conclusion to conclusion.

"Calm down and shut the hell up!" Tempest roared.

Harmony abruptly stopped her tirade, but she quickly regained her composure, eyes pinching ferociously at the rebuke.

"You should know what it's like, Rockland——" she said defiantly, although her tone was more restrained as she saw how livid Tempest was.

"And Gwen was there to pick up the pieces, remember? That's who we're going to get *right now*. Pull yourself together. She's the reason you volunteered to come in the first place, was she not? *You volunteered.* I didn't force anyone to come, but while you're here, you damn well better listen and follow the chain of command. I'm not asking you to come along or even work with Prime, but I *need* her on this last part of the mission. If you refuse to help, then stay the hell out of the damn way. Do whatever you want when you get home, if it makes you feel better." Tempest hid none of his anger as he let loose.

"My father lost his powers at Rockland! The Faction threw him away, and they've been harboring her? She's one of them! Did you know about it? Someone had to know."

"As a matter of fact, I didn't. And I don't care. Prime has a spotless record and has never betrayed any super on a team of hers or the Faction in all her years of service. Rockland happened decades ago, and I'd like to think that we've all matured somewhat in the intervening years. No one here was a part of it." Tempest waved at the entire Crew. "Hell, *even I* wasn't a part of it. So don't be offended if no one rushes to embrace your prejudices. I put a lot more faith in actions than words, and Prime has earned respect in my book."

He cleared his throat and continued. "I'm sorry about your father," he said in a calmer voice, edge not totally gone. "I didn't know him, but I've heard stories. You should know from what happened to me that I am all too familiar with being 'discarded' by the Faction, despite years of service. So don't preach to me about what's fair."

Harmony glared at the rest of the Crew, still in disbelief that none of them had backed her up.

"No one? Some team!" she whined and shook her head. "I... I can't deal with this right now." She stormed off, her heels popping on the floor as she left the common room.

Members of the Crew blinked and the hum of the ship was pronounced in the resounding silence that followed.

Gus watched as the Crew alternated either staring at Prime, the empty doorway where Harmony had left, or conspicuously ignoring both.

Tempest keyed his comms. "Seneschal, you know where we're headed, let us know when we get close. Aurora, Yuki, you'll be with me as we try to gain access to the facility. Yuki, I want you to get us access and find out what his schedule is like. I need to know when he leaves."

"On it," Yuki said, flipping open her laptop.

"Gus, you'll be with Prime as a lookout and communicating with us when we're clear to breach. We'll need to stake this place out for a bit to determine the best time to grab Gwen. First, we need to confirm she's still inside, then come up with a plan to retrieve her. I want to know exactly where she is, so we can be in and out quickly."

Tempest looked up and saw the rest of the Crew staring at them as they planned. "I'm sure you guys can find something to keep yourselves busy. Trust me, you *don't* want me to assign you something right now…"

With those words, everyone sprang into action, suddenly remembering something vital that they needed to take care of at that very moment.

———

They finalized their plans, a large portion of which would be a waiting game and then settled in as the transport passed fewer and fewer buildings as they traveled to the outskirts. The outside faded to obscurity as holograms and lights ceased to illuminate the gloom, and only an occasional lightning crash would highlight the rain-spattered windows.

"This place is in the middle of nowhere. Is it even part of Hinansho? I'm surprised we're still even in the storm radius,"

Gus said as he looked out the window for some hint they were approaching their destination.

"I'll bet he has to keep it separated so no one knows the crap he's doing there," Yuki replied, shuddering a bit and pulling her sweater tighter around her. "Normally a hospital is in a central location."

"Or it keeps the riff-raff away by being where only the elite can access it." Darik poked his head out and growled before disappearing back into the guts of the ship.

"You would be surprised how casually many of those in Hinansho view human life. It's partially why I had to get out of here. Even though I was higher up in the caste system, it always bothered me how little value and effort was dedicated to maintaining basic rights. Everyone thought I was odd for not just enjoying my station. I knew Hinansho would always be part of my ruin, someday. I just didn't know it would happen so soon," Prime whispered. The melancholy was so thick in her voice that it made Gus' heart hurt. Knowing more about Prime's past than he should have made it that much more difficult.

The image of Prime's daughter popped into his mind, and he knew that this was part of the despair she was feeling. He focused on her in his mind's eye, looking at the girl and noticing that the edge to his headache started to recede. Encouraged, he chased after the memory as he stood next to Prime in silence.

What was her name again? Madge? Madeline? Maddy? Something like that. He longed to help her somehow, but he was no expert at family relations. Plus, bringing it up unbidden would tip her off that he knew things she would most likely want to keep personal and secret. Even if he had the communication skills, his hands were tied. Par for the course. Yet again, Gus was no good to anyone but himself.

Despite all her struggles though, Prime looked... strong, somehow. Like those lighthouses on small rocks in the ocean that are beat upon mercilessly by the waves, yet still resist the tide, day after day. Gus had thought he had felt alone at times, but his own struggles seemed to pale in comparison. It made him feel even more immature and weak that he couldn't manage his own feelings and that he was so prone to magnifying how difficult his own situation was when there were people going through so much more. And they bore it with grace and determination.

Gus would never have guessed at the things that haunted both BoJack and Prime from looking at them, whether it was Prime's stoic calm or BoJack's easy smile and the good-natured camaraderie he showed everyone in the Crew. He hoped that he could wrestle with his own demons and keep them in line so he could do what he must. If they could, he should at least try.

"We're here," Seneschal's voice crackled over the comm.

Gus pressed his face to the window and saw a large building, alone in the mists. High intensity lights burned back the darkness and illuminated every section of the large cross-shaped building. The central tower stood three floors higher than the rest of the wings. In each quadrant surrounding the building, there were areas to park.

One quadrant held all types of ambulances and other medical transports, another appeared to be for employees. Built up along one side of the property was a large hill festooned with all types of plants and a path that one could take to walk around outside while convalescing.

Had Gus seen the facility without any other info, it looked like a clean, well-kept hospital that took care of its patients. And perhaps it did for the most part, with the shady underbelly only applying to some of those within. There was enough traffic in and out of the parking area that they didn't need to approach surreptitiously at all. Seneschal dropped them off and the two teams separated.

Tempest, Yuki, and Aurora circled towards the loading bays, and Gus and Prime headed up to get a better overwatch in the garden area above. There were cubbies near the path entry with umbrellas and Gus got one for himself and Prime and they began walking up the path. He was surprised to see others walking in the rain. The path they were on was lit up by numerous ornate lamps. The drizzle of rain highlighted as it passed into and out of the cone of illumination.

They continued walking in silence, the only noise the crunch of their steps on the gravel path amid the rain spatter. Along the path, there were covered benches that faced the hospital down below, while others were situated facing inwards, at the main fountain and carefully cultivated arrangements of flowers and trees. They sat and stared at the hospital down below.

"Gus, I have something to ask you..." Prime began, her voice hesitant.

CHAPTER FORTY-FOUR

Demon Kitty Rag

"Do you have any reservations being stuck on a mission with me?" Prime asked while looking at the facility below through some binoculars.

"Not really, no. I'm a little curious because I've never met any hybrids until recently. I've always lived in one of the capital cities for Purple Faction, so my life has been pretty sheltered. I did wonder how you fit in with the Faction, being different and all. Was that hard? I still feel like a fifth wheel among everyone else."

"Really? You honestly have no opinion?" She lowered the binoculars and looked at Gus, her cat-slit pupils widening as she assessed him.

"No, what's the big deal? Everyone's been walking on eggshells, but we're probably more alike than different."

"Oh? And how are we similar?" she asked, propping her chin up with the back of her hand, a wry smile on her face.

"We both have family issues, obviously." Gus waved towards the hospital. "Apparently, my dad is a lot different when at Purple Faction, so you all probably saw a different side of him. Things seem to be changing, but that's only since I got powers."

"It could be that he realized some hard truths after his demotion too. Have you considered that?"

"I've been rethinking a lot of things lately. Things that I'd always assumed were true and how recently I'm seeing how limited my world-view was."

"You're right about one thing, Gus. Family is tough. They can hurt you more than anyone else without even trying, it seems." She broke eye contact and looked down at the hospital. "Sometimes I wonder if some people are destined to be alone. I thought I had escaped all the drama surrounding my parents when I left Hinansho. Only to have my personal life spiral out of control as well." She pulled her knees up to the bench and hugged them tightly.

"I have felt alone in a crowd more times than I can count. I never got the suspicion that you had anything going on. Hell, all of the Crew seem to have it so together, it makes me self-conscious. I don't really know what the hell I'm doing half the time, just flying by the seat of my pants."

"I'll let you in on a little secret. We all do that more than we'd like to admit. We hide it well, but a large portion of Academy training is on controlling your physical reactions." She relaxed her legs and extended them in front of her, letting the rain patter on her feet. "Can't have the regs losing faith in us, that could result in chaos!" Prime said in a deep drill-sergeant voice, curling her arms like a bulldog and puffing her chest out.

"Whatever the reason, you guys have learned it well. I never sense that any of you are out of control or worried. Someday I'll get there, right?"

"You're funny, Gus."

"Yeah, but looks aren't everything," Gus said, picking at some grass at his feet. "What do you think you're going to do when you head back?" Gus dared asking, surprising even himself as the words spilled out.

"I don't think I *am* going back. The cat's literally out of the bag. You saw how Harmony reacted, and she wasn't even directly affected by the whole Rockland mess. I guess that's not totally fair. She probably got an earful from her father as she grew up, so that's understandable. I don't begrudge her of her opinion. I resent my own parents for their part in that fiasco and dragging me into it. I'm going to be dealing with the fallout the rest of my life. She comes from a certain point of view, and that's how she's seen the world for her whole life. I was much the same at one point."

"Wow, I wouldn't be making excuses for her if I were in your position," Gus replied.

"It reminds me of the time I was blinded during a mission. I was too near a massive photon flare from some supers from Green Faction that we were battling. They were to my right and my right eye bore the brunt of the damage. With healing, it took me three weeks before they even dared attempt a surgery. And that was only for the less-affected left eye. Once it was done, I had to wait to see if the right eye would improve enough to be restored, or if it would be permanently altered. Plus we had to do it on the sly, so no one would know I was a hybrid."

Gus turned and peered closer at Prime's jade colored eyes. "So are they…?"

She just laughed and shook her head. "There are many things in my life that I've taken for granted. I didn't realize how much losing one eye would change everything I do. It made me realize how much a tiny shift in perspective, a mere inch or two, could provide enough information to provide the depth and distance. It forced me to be aware of what I was missing without this different perspective. While I could see with only one eye, I was incomplete. I knew that there was something missing."

"Like what?" Gus asked, extending his own feet and watching the rain drip on his boots.

"It made me contemplate what else I was missing by staying in one fixed perspective. To confront the things I was ignoring by refusing to consider another point of view. I can tell you're trying to work out what to do and seeking out advice, but I'm afraid that I can't really help you.

"My advice is based on my experiences and what works for me may not work for you. Trust me, don't put too much faith in the answers other supers give you. They're just as human as you. Full of faults, biases, and weaknesses. Don't accept anything someone else tells you just because you think they have it all figured out. Do your due diligence, and realize what got them there most likely won't get you where you want to go."

"That's not super reassuring. It's basically saying, 'figure it out yourself.'"

"There will be lots of voices telling you what to do. I'm sure you're probably afraid that you'll listen to the wrong one. Or you could be afraid that if you listen to what your gut tells you and you're wrong, you are in the same place of failure; especially if you've made big mistakes before.

"When I was younger, I thought I would eventually stop making dumb mistakes. But here I am, still making them on a regular basis. I think that's why I keep to myself. I've been burned too many times. Listened to others more than myself. Usually, my gut is right and the more I've trusted it—the less complications life seems to have.

"The problem with relying on the advice of others is that you can become dependent on it and avoid making those choices yourself. Either that or their advice does not fit your circumstances and you will blame them for the consequences. Neither are positions of power. You have to find your own way. I know that's not what you want to hear, but it's true. There are no shortcuts to figuring out this super business."

"How do you keep going, though? How can you stay strong through the challenges and trials when everything appears to be beating you down? I feel like I'm losing a war of attrition and eventually I won't have anything left to give." Gus was careful choosing his words; he didn't want to reveal anything that would clue Prime that he had been digging around in her thoughts.

"Sounds like you gotta find your 'why.' There's different reasons why some of the Crew do what they do. I think everyone does the best with the cards they've been dealt, and try with all their might to make everyone think they're sitting on a royal flush when they only have a pair. There is some truth in 'faking it 'til you make it,' though. Which is why it's a standard for Academy training."

"I feel like a fake." Gus tossed the bits of grass he had been meticulously shredding into tiny bits onto the ground.

"When I was first learning how to use my powers, they made you do these drills in the Academy. They never really worked for me, because I process things differently and access my powers in a relatively uncommon way. Ways to visualize connecting to your abilities or how to power them with MP. I can't tell you how frustrated I was in the beginning, with how easily the others progressed and improved. I struggled just to keep up. It wasn't until I let go and relaxed that things began to flow."

"Do you remember any of those? Maybe they could work for me?"

"Whoo. That was such a long time ago. Since none of them worked for me, I'm probably the wrong person to ask. The other cadets would get mad at me as they tried to help me and their suggestions didn't work. As if I wasn't listening or giving their technique an honest try. I eventually figured it out, but I think that's where I started keeping to myself. My suit and helmet already made it harder to connect with people, and that just complicated things. I couldn't reveal I was a hybrid, so it was what it was.

"I have always been an outcast, hiding what I am from everyone. My parents gave me no choice in whether I wanted to be a hybrid. Who knows what damage has been done with all the tampering they've done with my DNA? I'd be lucky if I didn't get cancer from the hodgepodge of genes they've inserted, deleted, and spliced.

"From somewhere in that tangled mess though, I must have gained some affinity that led to my powers. But if I could do it all over, I think I would still choose a normal life. No powers, just plain vanilla reg. And that would be enough."

"You would give up your powers?"

"In a heartbeat. I've chased the lure of acceptance almost my whole life. By revealing that I am a hybrid, things will change for me in the Faction if I choose to go back. I would see less and less active missions and be given more administrative duties, until things become so miserable or boring that I get forced out or quit. A lot of people resent hybrids after the Rockland conflict.

"A few supers died, but regs don't know how many hybrids were killed or hurt in the protests, but it was *much more* than any supers that were hurt. Still, I can't blame the supers for trying to stop the abuses that were taking place. Experimentation had run amok, people harming themselves and others with no regulation or safeguards. It was a mess. It still is in sanctuary cities, it's just gone underground."

"Is that what Harmony was talking about, when she was talking about 'down there?'"

"You don't even want to know what has happened to those failed experiments with hybridization. People that were more beast than man, stripped of enough humanity and then abandoned to the lower levels of Hinansho. Confused and feral, fighting to survive. It's horrible."

"Yikes..." Gus shuddered.

"All most people wanted was a place to live their lives without excessive regulation. There was fault on both sides but no one hears the hybrids' side of the story."

"Then tell me. We're going to probably be here for a while."

"You asked for it, Gus..."

CHAPTER FORTY-FIVE

Kitty

"I grew up in the Outskirts. Kind of the suburbs of the suburbs, where Faction influence is less intense. This was about ten years before the Rockland conflict came to a head. There were some hybrids in my hometown, but we were still a fringe group. Some people looked down on us, but it was nothing like it is now.

"I was painfully shy and when someone noticed me at school, it was a whole new experience for me. I always felt awkward with my ears and tail. Girls can be pretty cruel in high school. Hell, my track record has been abysmal regardless of age. I was always an easy target, but when one of the jocks noticed me, that's when things really became better *and* worse. The pranks and mean-spirited comments and bullying escalated from there. But it was worth it.

"Harlan was amazing. I couldn't wait to get a message from him or the brief time we had together. He was a year older, so we shared none of the same classes, and even our lunch periods were different. My parents didn't like him because he wasn't a hybrid, and I could tell *his* mother was hoping it was just a passing phase. A curiosity in Harlan's life that he just needed to get out of his system. Her disdain emanated from her despite her phony smiles and polite conversation.

"Long story short, I got pregnant right after graduation and we got married soon afterwards. From there, my mother-in-law's facade fell away. Shannon's criticisms escalated, and there was always some advice I needed to know in order to take care of her precious son as he deserved. If we weren't so damn poor that we had to live with his parents, we might have been better off, but that's just how things worked out.

"But I loved him, so I put up with the insults and demeaning questions. Have you ever had anyone ask if you knew how to do something as menial as washing clothes, or making a simple meal? It was degrading, but I had been demure my whole life. So I accepted it as my fate. I was lucky to have Harlan, and that was just the price I was required to pay.

"When Madeleine came, I can't tell you how glad I was to see she had no obvious hybrid tendencies. I didn't want her to have to deal with any of those challenges. It was also a benefit that Shannon took to her so well. While I was still unredeemable in her eyes, this was her granddaughter and they showered her with all the praise and love they could. It was enough for me.

"I was happy for a time, until Harlan began to cool towards me. Either Shannon finally got to him, or the dynamic changed when Maddy came, but he became crueler and more dismissive. Eventually he asked for a divorce, and I relented as Shannon's influence became more and more intolerable, and there was no reason to try to make things work if the relationship was over.

"At first things were equitable and we shared time equally with Maddy. Things were civil between us for a couple of years, then life took another turn, as it always seems to do. Harlan met another woman, a reg named Elaine.

"I was happy that he found someone else to be happy with, but I was as naive as ever. If I ever thought Shannon was horrible to me, then Elaine was on another level. She hated me instantly. I didn't even recognize her, but she was among the group of girls that had picked on me mercilessly. She was a cheerleader but wasn't that cute, in my opinion. Some people don't age well. She obviously didn't let that affect her over-inflated sense of her own importance though.

"The hell that woman has put me through the last six years has been almost intolerable. I think if Harlan was left to his own devices, he would share custody of Maddy, and I would be much more a part of her life. I know she hates hybrids, and she is always threatening to take away custody of Maddy for some trumped-up reason or another. I try to stay out of her life but she keeps finding ways to drag me into her drama."

Prime's knuckles cracked her fists clenched as the feelings became more intense. She then spread out her fingers, forcing herself to continue with calm.

"She *should* be happy. Elaine's family is rich, and owns numerous businesses. Harlan managed to get an easy job with one of them, and they make a lot of money and live in a nice house. Still, she has the gall to press me for child support. When I was accepted into Purple Faction, she pressed me to revise my contributions so they could get more out of me.

"I think she suspects that she can reveal that I'm a hybrid and she uses that to threaten me with all types of things she will reveal to the Faction. Nothing direct, but her tactless insinuations leave no doubt. The problem is I'm not entirely sure she's not right. If it wasn't for her greed, I doubt she would have kept it under wraps for so long.

"As it is now, I only get to see my daughter sporadically throughout the year. The itinerant nature of missions for the Faction is another factor that she uses to manipulate me and to try to limit any claim for custody. So I'm torn. But now that may not be an issue. Perhaps my reveal was long overdue. I just don't know where I fit in anymore, though. The Faction is the only true home I've ever felt at least partially accepted. It still is cold comfort that Elaine can't lord that over me anymore.

"I just don't get why she is so spiteful and vindictive. I have never done anything to her, but there must be something inside of her that makes her that way. If Maddy wasn't involved, this would be so much easier, but the thought of that woman poisoning her with her vitriol and all the things she must say about me, it makes me almost physically ill. Maddy is young and I don't think it is as damaging now, but it kills me that one day my own daughter will despise me because of her influence."

"Doesn't Harlan step in?"

"That gutless wonder? No. He kowtows to anything that shrew says to him. She has a way of flying into a screaming rage and is used to getting what she wants. I secretly think that she's a lot like Shannon and Harlan responds to that. Subconsciously or not, I think he responds to it like she's his surrogate mother, running his life for him."

"I think I would have found it very hard not to arrange some convenient accidents to make her life miserable for a change!" Gus said shaking his head. "Doesn't she know who she's messing with? That's kind of ballsy to get on a super's bad side."

"Oh, believe me. The dark things I've imagined. Sometimes I even worry about how far I'll go. I think secretly she wants me to try something. That way she can point to that act of retribution and show Maddy I'm really as horrible as Elaine says that I am. That little girl is going to have a hard time growing up with that woman, and sometimes being a beacon to her is all that gets me through the tough days."

"Wow," Gus said, not knowing how to respond.

"I did warn you," Prime said, laughing. "That actually feels good getting that all out. Probably not what you were expecting. Did you get some of your mother's empath skills and draw that out of me?"

"Hmm? No. I don't think I got any powers that my family has. At least not yet. I don't know how it all works genetics-wise."

"You mean you aren't a legacy?" Sanura arched an eyebrow.

"You mean getting powers from my parents? Not that I know of, but I got sick in my tweens and there's been a lot of memory loss. Some of it has come back, but still there are some blank stretches. So I guess it's a possibility, but I haven't seen anything specific in my abilities."

"I never talk about my past. Too much darkness and pain there. Thanks for listening, that was actually very cathartic. I probably should have done that a long time ago. Sorry for making you my emotional dumping ground."

"No, no. Actually, that's kind of reassuring in a weird way. I feel more comfortable just knowing that I'm not the only one struggling. I have felt incapable for so long. I know things haven't been ideal here for you in Hinansho. But if you aren't going back to the Faction, you can spend some more time with Maddy. I think you'll like that," Gus encouraged.

"You're right. I imagine after this mission I'll have a lot of time on my hands. I'll make plans to pay Maddy a visit. It's been so long since I've seen her in person. Even longer that I've seen her without the helmet, I wonder if she even remembers what I look like. That's something I have to fix. Plus seeing the look on Elaine's face will be priceless."

CHAPTER FORTY-SIX

Let's Dance, Boys!

"Are you good to go, Yuki?" Tempest asked.

"I think so. Hospitals have pretty heavy encryption, so make sure I don't get interrupted. That snapback disconnection is super bad, maybe not kill me outright, but I'd be a veg for sure."

"You can count on us," Aurora said, giving her arm a firm squeeze before they headed out of the small communications room, closing the door behind them.

Yuki was surprised they had found the equipment shed on the outside of the hospital, but when she saw the signal amplifier, the reason was clear. They needed some way to punch through the constant cover the weather provided and something this powerful would have disturbed the sensitive medical equipment inside.

She folded her arms and looked up at the wall of switches, ports, and modules. She had a couple of false starts before she finally cracked her knuckles in frustration.

You wanted to be a field agent, so buck up! And with that she threw her hands forward and activated ***Slice***.

———

A bitter cold wind slapped Yuki in the face. She coughed as she took in a surprised intake of the freezing air, her lungs tightening in protest. She quickly swapped her outfit, and a warm white parka formed around her and blocked the wind like a wall of warmth. Occasionally, bosses would have accompanying suits that offered protection in their native environments, and Yuki was lucky she had obtained this Arctic Fox set years ago. She adjusted her goggles and with a start, began to turn in a complete circle as deja vu set in.

She had been here before. Or at least in the same AI construct. She squinted at the horizon and found a city there, standing as a bastion against the cold and the wind. Chuckling to herself, she knew that the city was a decoy. Anyone who attempted to reach it would find that it always stayed out of reach, like a mirage in the desert. Wasting the hacker's energy fighting the elements until they had to drop out of the slice.

She swept her thigh-high boots back and forth, pushing aside snow drifts that shouldn't be there in the wild windstorm that blew constantly across the ice field. As expected, a hairline seam was visible. She removed a glove, and with a lacquered fingernail lifted the handle from the smooth ice beneath her.

Bracing herself, she heaved on the handle and a large block lifted out, as if it were oiled on the edges. She swung to the side and dropped it, making a hollow *thunk* as it hit and scraped along the ice like a curling stone. Yuki stared into the depths below and could see dark cobalt water rushing by quickly. Its urgent *shush* as the underground river sped by in the depths.

This could be a trap. When things are too easy... What if I get trapped down there underwater?

No, she had to trust herself. Before she could overthink, she pinched her nose and pencil dove into the cerulean waters below.

There was a brief sensation of falling, then her boots crunched on some dry leaves in darkness.

Ha! I knew it.

Crickets chirped and a chorus of frogs sang in the darkness. Yuki could see an enormous moon hanging overhead, much too big to be natural, illuminating a nondescript forest. Reverting her suit to her default, she climbed a nearby tree to see where she was.

About a mile away, she could see a large compound complete with numerous watchtowers and spotlights scanning the empty space surrounding it, occasionally illuminating the treetops of the forest. A large wall topped with razor-wire encircled the compound, and she could see figures moving about atop the watchtowers, backlit by the moonlight as they occasionally changed positions on their rounds.

She tried using **Data-mine**, but the distance was just too far. Marking the nearest tower on her minimap, she opened up her bestiary. This job would take some infiltration skills, and she needed to be a ghost instead of rampaging in. There were at least twelve towers that she could see, and they were fairly close together. That could get dicey if she went in guns blazing. She climbed down into the canopy after she had narrowed down the possibilities to three and then made her final choice. **Summon!**

Gia "Cerise" Valleta

Raised by V'omarr monks since childhood, she is skilled in over twenty-one disciplines of death. Over a thousand kills are accredited to her, although no trace has been found of her presence in the vast majority. Some suppose that the number is actually much higher. The fact remains that no one is safe from her when she has been tasked to eliminate them.

Silk Stalkings: *Sentient silk ribbons that respond to the user's will. Have a reach of over one hundred feet and can be utilized as a weapon as well.*

*Note: If any of the runes woven upon the ribbons are disrupted or damaged, control and utility of skill is drastically compromised.

Sheer Shear: *Stealth kill up to two enemies using coordinated attacks with Silk Stalkings. Gia must be undetected by targets for ability to activate.*

Shadowstep: *Flit from one area of concealment to the next, avoiding detection in the intervening space.*
Silhouette: *Disappear into the environment by holding perfectly still. Active for one minute before a five minute recharge.*

It had been a while since Yuki had used this avatar, but within a few steps she felt the feedback iron out. She felt agile and did a couple of deep stretches, moving with fluid ease. She admired the skintight black suit, emblazoned with gold highlights and mystic icons. The ribbons hung from her arms, connected from the wrist to elbow. They undulated in the air, suspended and waving as if they were underwater.

She thrust one arm forward and the ribbon shot out and severed a nearby branch, quickly catching it before it could drop to the ground. She lowered it to the forest floor and then oriented herself with her minimap. Then she began to navigate the branches. The silk ribbons maintained their tone, holding her aloft as they pulled her from tree to tree at almost whiplash speeds, dodging and shifting so that she didn't catch on anything or get hit by an errant branch.

Reaching the edge of the forest, she could see the towers in much more detail. ***Data-mine*** worked this time as she spied the figures atop the watchtowers, their red eyes visible glowing in the dark.

Soul Scavengers
Guardians of the Gulag, who rapidly swarm anyone invading their territory and drain them dry.
Carry-on and On: *These soldiers are exact duplicates of each other and can activate an ability to communicate with a hive mind, making them ideal for warning others when they are alarmed.*
Soul Tear: *With focus, can rip MP and HP away from a target. Amount drawn increases with additional Soul Scavengers attacking the same target.*

With the information, she could also see red cones illuminating her display, where the sentries were scanning the area around them, adding red spotlights intermingled with the bright white ones. Yuki jumped down and caught herself with the ribbons, lowering herself soundlessly to the ground.

Timing the pattern of the spotlights, she darted across the empty space until she was at the compound's wall. She was out of the path of detection this close to the wall, so she began to climb with the ribbons and barely stopped short as a spotlight from an adjacent tower crossed in front of her path.

Activating **Data-mine** again, she was shocked to see the number of red circles populating the side of the tower. Scanning the tower on the other side, she observed the chaotic path of lights. While it appeared erratic at first, there was a pattern there, and after a couple cycles, her predictive algorithms kicked in and she felt confident scaling the tower.

Again, the herky-jerky tugs of the ribbons moved her up the side of the tower. Occasionally, she had to stop to let her senses settle but she scaled the tower and hovered with her eyes just peering over the edge of the roost. Two guards were there, one watching the forest and the other keeping an eye on the neighboring tower.

Seizing the opportunity, Yuki vaulted into the middle of the turret and flung her arms out sideways while mid-flip. The two Soul Scavengers were beheaded such that the heads did not even separate from the bodies. The two sashes grabbed them before they could fall and slowly lowered the two guards and Yuki to the floor below the parapet wall. Thankfully, these digital constructs had no blood or gore to contend with.

Yuki waited to see if any alarm would be raised, and after a tense five minutes, she dared peek above the parapet wall. The patterns had not changed, so their hive mind ability must need to be consciously activated. A critical failure in design. Looking inward at the compound, there were multiple small bungalows arranged in concentric rows. In the center, there was a squat structure, and all roads lead to it like spokes from a wheel.

The majority of security appeared to be focused outward;

there was little that she could see patrolling the inner confines. Her inner paranoia porcupine prickled at the whole process being too easy. It was possible that they didn't expect anyone to pass the first illusioned gateway, but usually breaching an AI fortress was a constant battle from start to finish. Something felt off. Unable to assess exactly what was bothering her though, she could only press forward.

Updating her nav-point, Yuki grasped a nearby zipline and slid down amid the bungalows.

CHAPTER FORTY-SEVEN

Something for your M.I.N.D

Yuki stared at the large building in front of her, an unpleasant stench becoming cloying as she got closer to the mushroom-colored building. There was also a rhythmic hum that reminded her of the breathing of someone asleep. The ground vibrated on the 'exhale,' tickling her feet and sending shivers dancing along her spine and back.

Bright light spilled out of the building—so much that it was impossible to see inside. She attempted different angles but kept having to blink her eyes as she looked into the multiple door-ways that surrounded the building. It was like staring at some high-beams, and it killed her night vision.

The area appeared deserted though, at least on the streets. Yuki kept her guard up; she could sense something stirring in the small bungalows and it was uncertain if they held prisoners or foes. The space around the building was empty, and there appeared to be no doorways on the ground level. A flat plat-form encircled the structure and light blared out of the windows on this level.

With stealth out of the question, Yuki ran for the building, leaving long shadows bouncing after her in the light, unnerving her with the feeling of exposure. When she was close, she used her ribbons to vault her up to the second-story platform and crouched down to see if there was anyone following her.

Nope. Nothing. The lack of a normal boss or even resistance was making her more paranoid than if there had been constant attacks. It made her feel like she was missing something vital that she would regret when everything began to hit the fan. She growled as she strained her perception and came up with nothing.

Yuki peered into the second story window. Inside was deeper gray, with brown accents, further reinforcing the fungal look. The smell though. It wasn't like mushrooms, it was... something else. It was on the tip of her tongue but she couldn't quite place it, but deep down some part of her must have known because of the trepidation she felt. The closest thing that kept coming to her mind was beef broth. She just hoped that whomever had done the security on this AI had cut some corners, since it was unlikely for anyone to complete a double-layer slice.

She leaned forward to brace herself as she looked inside but pulled her hand away. It was warm! And soft, like flesh. Revulsion made her gag slightly. Gross. She pulled her hand away as if the wall was hot and shook it, trying to fling off the unpleasantness that made her skin crawl. Strands of something sticky and syrupy trailed from her fingers as she pulled her hand away, but there was nothing to wipe them on to clean them.

Something was in this place and she had hacked enough AIs to know that this looked like a boss lair. And it probably wouldn't show itself until she was irrevocably committed.

So be it.

She gripped the sides of the window by activating **Silk Stalkings** and she used them to launch herself into the room. She sailed through, swan diving and executing a flip. She caught herself with the two ribbons, absorbing the impact of the fall and keeping her just shy of touching the floor.

Nothing happened.

Easing herself to the ground, she scratched her head and looked around, groaning as the leftover syrup on her hands came away on her hair. This room was just a big hollow chamber, brownish white, and stinky as hell. The only thing different was a small raised circle in the center of the room. Taking a tentative step forward, the ground wobbled like a trampoline, rebounding slightly with each step. As she got closer, she could see a small opening in the rubbery floor.

A pulsating mound of pink trembled in the center of the large room, its top barely visible from the gray membrane that surrounded it. As Yuki stared at it in disgust, there was a flatulent release and the pink material began to extrude from the opening. The membrane became taut as it stretched, and the mound began to widen, revealing its wrinkled and shriveled surface.

Yuki retreated back as the floor began to flutter and the pink kept forcing its way out of the ever-widening opening. The more that was visible, the more it had the appearance of a... brain?

Yuki activated **Data-mine** on it and got very little information.

M.I.N.D.
HP: ??
Weaknesses: ??
Abilities: ??
Good luck!

Yuki scowled. *Dammit to hell!* She began to pace like a cat, backing ever closer to the wall as the M.I.N.D. continued to spill forth. *How big* is *this thing?*

Sluggishly, it began to raise in the air, its veiny purple red and pink color contrasting with the bone-like background as it squeezed its way out of the opening. Phlegm-like gobbets of syrupy slime dripped off of its corrugated surface, hitting the floor in large splatters.

The miasma intensified as its source was revealed. Yuki had to cough to keep her gorge down as a wall of stench hit her in the face. An acrid, sour taste still reached her tongue despite her best efforts.

Along the seam of the two lobes, thorny teeth could be seen as it emerged, folded almost parallel to the groove.

The brain hung up and trembled for a bit, struggling to push through, then the raised metal rims of two shutters embedded in the front lobes made it past the lip of the opening. Shutters irised open and closed within the brass rings where the eyes should be, each moving independently until they saw Yuki standing there, mouth agape. They centered on her and the rings spun, telescoping out of the brain to get her in better focus.

Yuki thrust her hands forward in a forceful clap, the ribbons shooting forward. She intended to plunge them deep into the giant brain before it could fully emerge. There was a loud *clang* as if a gong had been struck, and two diamond-shaped shields were floating in front of her sentient sashes. She tried to dart them around but they reacted too quickly to circumvent, easily parrying any of her probing attacks or feints.

To make matters worse, she could see more of the rhombus-shaped shields detaching from the inner walls of the chamber and begin to circle the brain as it continued to extrude from the floor. By the time the stalk of the brain stem was visible, there were three rows of the shields rotating around the brain, surrounding it on all sides. Their mother-of-pearl shimmer was mildly hypnotic and Yuki had to force herself to stop staring at their rhythmic motion.

She tried launching the ribbons with more force, winding up like a baseball pitcher to see if she could power *through* one of the shields, but it only resulted in a louder gong sound that reverberated a little longer. The shields seemed to pick up speed as she exerted more energy towards them. She charged towards the brain, hoping to throw it off, but a group of eight shields came together. Their sides joined together seamlessly and the whole shield wall shot forward like a piston.

Yuki was hit like a freight train and flew into the back wall. The soft, organic nature of the structure absorbed her impact for the most part, but the attack still rang her bell. She shook her head to clear it, and saw that the diamond-shaped shields had resumed their circuit around the brain.

She had the inklings of a plan. With one ribbon, she lunged forward and with the other attempted to grab the shield that moved to block it. Success! She got a grip on two of the edges and held the shield in place. It quivered violently, trying to break free, and Yuki shot her free sash out and scored a glancing strike on the soft brain.

There was a bellow of pain and another shield dashed in, point first, and sliced through the center of the ribbon holding the shield, which sped off as the end of the ribbon fell limp. With the runes destroyed, everything from the cut to the end of the ribbon was limp and just hung there. Sagging down like a child's arm in their parent's jacket.

She could whip it around but it would not move of its own accord. The dead weight made the ribbon much slower as well, and another shield crashed into the ground like a dart, its point driving through the end of the sash and firmly fastening it to the ground.

More shields shot like arrows, pulling down more of the ribbon despite Yuki's efforts to wobble it or flip it sideways. When it was securely fastened and Yuki's movement was restricted, the shields attacked. One swept her feet from behind, and she was airborne for a second before four more fused shields hit her midair and pushed her to the ground.

Once on the ground, the other sash was secured in a similar manner, sharp shield tips piercing the delicate gold writing and destroying **Silk Stalkings'** effectiveness.

With her held down, the brain settled to the ground with a heavy crash. Puddles of sludge and goop were thrown upward and she had to turn her head so none would splash in her mouth. She shook her head to flick away some of the ooze that began to slide down her hair onto her forehead.

Another heavy *thump* and Yuki looked up. Over the edge of the shield on her chest she could see the brain, lurching forward ponderously like a slug. It stretched forward then let its bulk fall with a crash. The seam between the lobes opened more, and rows of teeth were visible, sharp and pointed like a lamprey, curling inward, waiting to gather her up and pull her inside.

The shutters whirred as the servos inside dilated and closed in anticipation. The shields atop her pressed down harder as well. She tried to wiggle out but she was pinned in place like a prize butterfly. The teeth made a clicking noise as they occasionally hit each other in their excitement. They extended further out of the maw, as if each one yearned to gain the first taste of her, competing with the others.

Well, this sucks! How are you going to get your ass out of this fine mess, Yuki?

CHAPTER FORTY-EIGHT

Problems

Yuki groaned as the shields pressed down harder on her. She felt herself getting smushed into the soft floor, and her flailing intensified as the reality of being totally smothered became all too real. Kicking her feet, she could only manage tiny, impotent little hits against the shield wall. She felt her foot getting caught, but could not see what had grabbed her. With a quick shake she managed to free herself, hearing a ratcheting click.

Yuki's back began to get damp as the pressure caused a dingy brown liquid to be expressed from the floor as the shields kept pressing down on her. It became hard to focus on anything as the inability to move became more and more claustrophobic. What could she do? None of Gia's abilities would work. Should she revert back and shed her avatar?

The shields would still have her trapped. There would not likely be time to roll out of the way; even though her natural form was smaller than her avatar, it wasn't *that* much smaller. She would have access to her other abilities though. Summon would be on cooldown, so she would lose that advantage. By keeping the avatar she effectively had double the HP, since when Gia's HP ran out it would be the avatar that dissipated, leaving her natural form intact. *Think, Yuki!*

Her left foot caught something again, frustrating her. *What the hell! Is the floor trying to grab me and eat me too?*

Another click sounded from the other foot, but this one seemed to echo in her mind and time seemed to slow down, just as if she had activated **Overclock**.

One aspect of this avatar came into razor-sharp focus. Her heels happened to be stylized high-heel guns. She had never used them, and had forgotten that they even existed, but directing her focus there, she found that her kicking had cocked the hammer back on both revolvers. With a guttural yell, she pointed her toes upward and aimed at the M.I.N.D.

*Blam*Blam*Blam*Blam*...

The shots boomed much louder than she ever expected, shattering teeth and ripping large burrows into the brain. Soft tissue was shredded as she emptied both chambers into the fragile, fleshy enemy. With the sound of shattering glass, the shields fell apart and clanged on the ground. Yuki rolled quickly and activated **Silhouette** while the brain was shuddering in the center of the room. Its HP bar was taken down about 30%, and it looked stunned.

Yuki looked at herself and saw that most of her ribbons had been ruined, and she could only use a few meters of the ribbon before they fell limp. Her own form shimmered and was visible in her display, emphasizing her stealthy nature.

She began to see some of the shields trembling as the M.I.N.D. began to recover from its stunned status, and Yuki realized she wasn't going to have a lot of time before it was back at full capacity. She ran towards the large boss, and noticed that the prismatic outer surface of the shield was not present on the reverse side of the fallen shields.

If you're going to dress like a dominatrix, might as well act like one.

Yuki targeted the back of a shield and, using the **Silk Stalkings** like a flail, she whipped a fallen shield on its dull matte back. To her delight, it shattered, throwing bits of shrapnel all around. Taking care not to damage the ribbons, she began taking out as many as she could. *Crack*! *Crack*! *Cra-cra-cra-CK*! She sped up as some of the shields began to slowly rise from the ground. The random nature of her hits allowed her to stay undetected as she whirled and spun.

The shields that had managed to get airborne were still not under full control, and a well-placed whip shattered more of them, their shards embedding in the soft surface of the boss with meaty *thunks*.

But when Yuki grabbed an entire shield and flung it at the creature, its sharp point managed to penetrate more than halfway into the brain. The tooth-filled maw between the lobes roared in protest, only to be filled with more broken bits as the dagger-like remains clinked off shuddering teeth and sank into the soft tissues behind them.

Another deflected shield hit the corner of one of the glass oculars, causing a spiderweb of cracks to snake across its entirety. Servos whirred in protest and the brain began to buck on its brain-stem like an enraged bull in its agony, jumping and dropping amid broken bits, further impaling itself.

With fewer shields to focus on, the M.I.N.D. managed to lift some of the few remaining shields and they began to fling blindly about in a mad attempt to hit Yuki by chance. Only by using **Shadowstep** was she able to dodge three shields coming from different directions. Two of the shields collided midair, but only spun off wildly, regaining their trajectory after a wobbly interruption. Hitting on their 'strong' sides wouldn't damage them, unfortunately.

Yuki tried to reach out and grab another shield, but it was moving too fast and she worried about having her ribbon totally cut off, leaving her with only one weapon.

They began to bob as they spun madly around the brain, angry hornets protecting their disturbed hive. Despite all the damage that had been dealt, Yuki had only managed to bring it down to 60% of its max health. The damage from the shards was not going to cut it. A quick check showed her heel-guns were empty as well.

The shields were flying so quickly and erratically that any attempt to whip the M.I.N.D. itself was quickly dashed. After severing a foot-long length of her more intact ribbon, she retreated back to look at her options. The shields only spun faster and faster, compensating for their number being cut in half. The enormous organ swung around, unable to keep itself aloft for more than thirty seconds or so before crashing down, causing a multitude of shards to bounce up into the air. After impaling itself, it would jump up again, swaying like a top-heavy cobra before crashing down again in a different spot.

Yuki could see that the key to ending this was the relatively narrow brain-stem. But how to get to it? She doubted she could even approach amid the shields that jetted by so quickly they were beginning to blur together.

If only those damn shields were out of the way!

It wouldn't solve everything; she would still be at the mercy of the bucking brain and getting flattened as it slammed to the ground. But the brain did cast a large oval shadow beneath it... Before Yuki had too much time to think, she saw the boss rotate slightly as it began its fall. But it was going to fall on top of the shield that stuck out of it! Like a cat ready to pounce, she pumped her legs. A bone rattling moan resonated through the chamber as the M.I.N.D. landed on its own shield, sinking it deeper into the lobe and temporarily the shields flew off like shuriken, lodging in the walls and floor. Before it could totally settle to the ground, Yuki took her chance and activated **Shadowstep.**

"Does she always twitch like that? How do we know if something's wrong?"

"I honestly don't know, Aurora. She hasn't been in the field long enough to really get a feel for her capabilities."

"Well, I hope she——" Aurora paused, looking up from Yuki's prone form as if she had heard something suspicious.

"You see it on your minimap too?" Tempest asked, voice turning severe.

"Unfortunately, yes. You think she'll be okay?"

"Do we have a choice?"

Tempest keyed on his comms. "Gus, follow our location nav-point and meet us, we've got company. Prime, Yuki is at this nav-point, stay in stealth and make sure no one harms her while she finishes her slice."

"Okay," Gus confirmed.

"Copy. I'll be there in five minutes, Prime out."

"They're at the hospital's mass transit exit, let's go," Tempest urged Aurora as they tore out of the small equipment shed.

"I'm only seeing two..." Aurora gasped as she ran up the covered walkway.

"For now. Let's hope it stays that way."

"I hate running. I hope whoever is behind those red dots on my minimap is ready for an ass kicking, because they've put me in a very bad mood. Who even knows we're here?"

"Isn't it obvious?" He spat before shouting, "Don't do this, Kenway, we had an agreement."

Rounding the corner they found the bald man affecting a golf clap.

"Aye, and I've honored that agreement. You have the information you wanted. Now that our business is completed, I have just found another offer. Seems someone is interested in anyone poking around in their affairs, and is willing to pay good money if I can deliver the meddlers to the interested parties."

Gus turned and slid down an embankment, slipping on loose moss and sludge to join the others, neon lights illuminating the alley with blues and reds in the undulating mist.

"Liar!" Gus yelled, catching his breath and swiping his hair out of his eyes.

"I am a dishonest man," Kenway said with pride. "And you can always trust a dishonest man to be dishonest—"

"You think you and your cat can handle all three of us? I take it your cronies didn't want any part of this?" Aurora challenged the pirate as she saw the odds had tipped in their favor.

Kenway shrugged. "Why split the bounty?"

"I know you better than that, pirate. The only one you could compel to go with you is your tiger, isn't it?" Tempest remarked sardonically.

Gus recognized the tone and found it affected Kenway in much the same way it had him—reckless anger.

Kenway opened and closed one fist, the hiss of pistons echoing in the alleyway. A sharp crackle sounded as a taser attachment sparked to life on his multi-tool arm.

"This has grown tiresome. Let us be done with it!" Kenway roared as he launched his attack.

Gus saw a red dot appear on his chest and looked up to see the tiger leaping toward him, some of the neon light glinting off the metal fangs rapidly approaching.

"Aww, crap…"

CHAPTER FORTY-NINE

Eye of the Tiger

Gus tried to dodge out of the way but the tiger was so massive it still bore him down. He was carried backward with the momentum and his head hit the ground with enough force to make his vision blur. Nausea swept over him as his headache returned in full force. His hybrid armor had shielded him somewhat, protecting his head enough so that it didn't crack like a watermelon. He felt shaken, but not winded from the impact.

A high-pitched squeal emanated from his shoulders as the tiger flexed its claws, only to find them scraping harmlessly on the gunmetal gray of hybrid-Nth concentrated there. Gus could feel a low rumble through the legs of the tiger as it turned toward him and began to growl.

Gus felt a hot and humid breath on his neck as the tiger bit down, trying to clamp down as Gus' hybrid armor moved to resist the killing force. The tiger tried to reposition its jaws but was thwarted at each attempt. Then it targeted his neck. Despite his armor's best efforts, each time the tiger clamped down, the force of its jaws closed his airway as the pressure encircled his entire neck. If the tiger had only closed down consistently, Gus would have been choked out in no time.

His hands flew up, his right arm finding only short bristly fur. He punched at the creature but it did no damage from his prone position. His left hand slapped against the metal housing on the tiger's chest and side, ripping and grabbing madly for something to gain some advantage, but the metal casing remained intact, protecting the delicate components inside.

Gus saw that his shroud only had 5% battery life left. They would be exposed and detectable as supers regardless, so might as well use his powers. He activated *Xyzzy* for the first time in what felt like forever. As expected, both he and the tiger teleported, but Gus used a push from **Advanced Flight** to spin them so the tiger was underneath. While he hovered there, the tiger fell away from him.

Instinct took over and the large cat tried to twist to land on its feet, but the distance was too short and the large beast landed right on its shoulder, mid-turn. There was a crunch followed by sparking and a scraping sound as the tiger's right foreleg collapsed.

Suddenly, the tiger turned and a beam shot out of its eye. The red blast bore straight into Aurora's back and quickly tunneled through her to shoot out the other side. She dropped and her electrical attack at Kenway pop-fizzed into nothing. She fell hard to her knees, gouts of blood starting to pour out of the wound in her abdomen. Gus tried to fly over to help, but another angry red beam sliced through the air, bringing his attention back to the animal.

How did it have enough intelligence to do that? Was this a hybrid gone too far, rather than a cyborg tiger?

Before he could think too much, the tiger spun and began to charge, much more quickly than expected with its damaged leg. It leapt into the air and before Gus could review his abilities, he activated **Zeno Effect**. He had only used this once before, but it froze the tiger midair, and it was easy to sidestep its trajectory.

The eyes of the tiger rotated to watch him as Gus cycled through his abilities. When this was all over, he really needed to focus on using every one of his abilities and training them to be used more intuitively. Finding one he liked, he activated *Ice Shard*. Two daggers of ice appeared, clearing the air of a good portion of its ambient fog. Gus plunged them into the tiger's side and sliced.

One broke off at the hilt, hitting a rib that appeared to be reinforced with some metal as well. The other sunk home and the tiger erupted in a closed-mouth roar, still unable to move. He sawed it back and forth, trying to do as much internal damage as possible, but his overzealousness caused the blade to break off within the tiger.

Damn it! This would be a different story if Jet was here.

He held a hand out and activated *Krackle*. Balls of energy formed in his hand and Gus scrambled up to aim them at the tiger as his body went rigid and the ability fizzled out. Gus collapsed onto the ground, face falling into a puddle as his body continued to buck and tremble. He could see Kenway pointing finger guns at him, the ends sparking with blue electric energy, before turning to face off against Tempest again.

His display showed a stunned debuff and a counter with fifty-seven seconds remaining. Gus looked up at the tiger suspended above. It was watching him with anticipation as it hung in the air. It could have been his imagination, but he thought he saw the tiger smile.

Another wave of pain stabbed into Gus' brain as he lay there in the dirty rainwater. The exertion and use of his powers flared his headaches to life like a beast awoken. With the pain, Gus found that he couldn't focus on his abilities at all. They felt slippery and unmanageable.

The more he reached to activate something, anything, the deeper he felt a hot poker of pain stab into his temples. Letting go for a bit, the wave of pain receded. When he tried to focus again, he couldn't even open his display. The countdown timer for his debuff appeared to go even slower. Forty-nine… forty-eight… forty-seven.

Hazarding a look, he saw that the tiger was in a different position, but as he kept his attention on it the movement slowed.

Looking at the tiger's debuff, he was reminded of what *Zeno Effect's* conditions were:

Zeno Effect: Focusing on the quantum state of an object or target will freeze its passage through time, preventing physical movement or skill activation while observed.

Gus locked his eyes on the tiger, and it looked back.
They waited to see who would be first to break free.

––––––

-Blink-

Yuki reappeared under the massive brain as it began to descend again. Falling to her knees, she crossed her arms and slid on the slippery slime that was smeared about. As she approached the brain-stem and right before hitting it, she brought her arms apart, severing it at the root. The edges sheared effortlessly through the soft tissue, and with a heave, Yuki used her last reserves of strength to slingshot herself from underneath the large brain as it toppled and crashed into the floor a final time.

The floor rippled and shook as a yellowish-brown fluid sprayed up from the cut brainstem like a geyser. Deprived of its connection, the brain twitched like a fish out of water, all mobility lost besides its death rattle.

Yuki wiped her face, flicking away a handful of slime and spitting in disgust. Sitting back with a loud sigh, she saw that her knees and shins were studded with tiny bits of shield embedded in the leather. She winced as she pulled out some of the larger pieces which had pierced her outfit, tiredly throwing them to the side. With a prolonged exhale, she tried to slow her breathing, looking at the spectacle before her. She groaned and hung her head.

At long last a message appeared:

*Congratulations, you have defeated the **M.I.N.D.***
AI added to Summon bestiary.
42,000 XP awarded.
You have reached level 41.
You have reached level 42.
Root access allowed. Do you wish to exit? (Y/N)

Yuki shuddered as the ecstasy of leveling caused her to momentarily forget the weariness she felt.

Whooo! Yuki sighed as she exhaled deeply. When she opened her eyes again, the awful smell and carnage were beginning to fade, and the remains digitized and fell upwards like rain in reverse, disappearing after hitting the roof above.

Yuki accessed the root and began searching. Alarms were going off all over the system as she opened the interface. She was worried she had set something off until she noticed the alarm codes.

What the hell are you guys doing out there?

CHAPTER FIFTY

Only Human

Gus watched in horror as the tiger began to become unstuck in time and finish its arc to the ground. It took only seconds but the tiger touched down on the ground with a light splash and slowly turned towards him. It seemed to know that he was helpless and walked around him, batting him with a paw as it circled.

Thirty-seven seconds... what are you going to do when you finally can move? If it's not too late...

He tried to open his abilities again, and his brain exploded with pain. He crushed his eyelids shut as the mother of all brain-freezes stopped his panicked mental scrambling.

The tiger roared right next to Gus' ear, so close and so loud that it began ringing. He couldn't even flinch away. He could feel a wet nose sniff the back of his neck, giving him goose-bumps. The tiger moved on, but the effect spread to his whole body. Even the hair on his head felt like it was reacting. Though he was not moving, a feeling of dizziness overwhelmed him, and he started sweating.

It's going to end soon.

He kept his eyes shut, waiting for the inevitable mauling to start. Bracing himself for the attack. His tongue felt dry in his mouth, and he could taste something metallic. He felt pins and needles in his arms and legs. It was going to come too little, too late. His body was waking up—but even when it did, his powers would not be available.

A stillness set over him as he stopped struggling. There was nothing he could do now. He could hear Aurora's groans now. The thunder rumbling above. The soft *pat* *pat* as the tiger walked around him. The smell of chlorine that tickled his nose.

The counter was at twenty-two when it happened. It was different than he had expected; deafening noise and burning heat. He felt his body flip and then nothing. His body was still numb, yet the countdown timer was still counting down. *Odd.* He tried to assess his situation but everything was dark. Much different than he expected. *Why do I still have this headache?*

A gentle hand gripped his shoulder and flipped him over. He saw his father kneeling over him, brushing wet hair out of his face. The last seconds of the countdown timer elapsed and Gus could speak again.

"Are we dead?" Gus gasped.

"Far from it. You were close to the blast but I don't see that you were hit. Blasted lightning takes such a long time to charge, and even longer to target. It helped that these two were covered in metal."

Gus lifted his head and saw Kenway lying on his back down the promenade. Looking the other direction, the tiger had been flung the other way, only then noticing the pock marks in the paved sidewalk and smell of burned hair and ozone.

"A-a-aurora…" Gus struggled to sit up, but had to lie back down as he felt lightheaded.

"She's fine. Just relax, Gus. I gave her some gels and she's got some wound clot on the area. Her bleeding has already stopped, and her Nth are stitching her back together.

"Yuki just sent me a message; she's turned off the alarms so we can use our powers freely now. But we have to hurry and meet her. She's already inside. Let's go get your mother."

Gus nodded and let his father help him to his feet, which were still a little shaky.

Aurora was already standing up, wiping blood off of her outfit, but he could see the swath of skin underneath was smooth and intact.

"You about ready, Aurora?" Tempest asked.

In response, her mouth fell open and she just pointed. The circular glass roof that covered the promenade had three figures standing on it, staring down at them.

"What now?" Gus sighed. The ceiling exploded, and glass rained down as the three figures dropped through onto the promenade.

The leader shook his duster, flicking off broken chips of glass and revealing a blunderbuss fastened to his hip. Its brass bell glimmered before disappearing as he settled the front of his trench coat.

Another touched a dial alongside his head and focused some bulky oculars, shifting his shoulders as he settled the large backpack he was carrying. Seeing the tiger, he shuffled over to the body and started picking at the metal parts on its face and arm.

The leader turned and saw Kenway's prone form while he lifted the pinched front of his Stetson, tilting it so the tiny bits of glass fell off and calmly placing it back on his head.

"Good, we won't have to bother paying him," the leader said in a smoky, raspy voice. Turning to the supers he cracked his neck and pointed at Tempest. "I assume you're the ones who poached our deal with the Clan?"

"That's going to cost you!" a wiry one in the back piped in. "They were going to give us one cubic unit of Endurium. Do you know how long it took us to track that down?! You've ruined seven months of hard wor—"

A stern scowl from the leader cut off the reprisal mid-sentence.

"He's not wrong. I can tell from our scans that you have a fair amount of Endurium on you, so you can hand it over, or there will be... trouble."

Gus laughed. "Was… was that on purpose?"

"We don't have time for this," Tempest growled. "And I've had it up to here with all of these interruptions and distractions. I guess these things are worthless now." He dropped the burnt-out shroud. "I don't know who you are, but you picked the wrong day to get on my bad side. I'm sorry you didn't get what you wanted but I'm warning you, you don't want to cross me. Not today. Let's just go on our ways and I won't give you the ass whipping you so clearly need," Tempest said savagely.

"Is that so?" the leader said, running his thumb and index finger across his mustache, straightening it. "Well, let's get to it then, boys."

Before he could even react, the leader had drawn a gun in each hand and shot at Tempest and Aurora.

Gus saw the wiry one in the back roll forward and aim his fist at him. With a whistle-tweet, two darts stuck into the wall inches from Gus' face. Gus activated **Wreckognize** and dodged, hearing a loud shriek and another flare of pain as he used an ability on instinct.

Black Lotus: ?
Associations: Luddites. Little is known about the Luddites except their predilection for steampunk or gaslight modifications on modern technologies. They rally around a female leader known as the "Prophetess," who appears to be working for another unknown entity.
Powers: No Nth detected. Subject is in the database as a suspect for espionage. At least twelve assassinations are attributed to him, due to their questionable manner of death. Possibly many more have gone undetected. Kills always mimic natural causes or progression of medical complications. Specializes in poisons, entheogens, and pharmaceuticals.

Before he could line up another shot, he was covered in a glittering shower of energy as Aurora hit him with **Ion Storm**. His father was surrounded by a whirlwind, and none of the shots from the guy dressed like a sheriff were penetrating to hit Tempest.

The hook-nosed man in the back dropped his pack and pulled out a drone which took flight as soon as he threw it in the air. "You idiots ruined it!" He pointed at the tiger. "Nothing to salvage, everything's a melted mass of slag!"

Gus saw the drone approach, making a beeline toward him. The gadgeteer looked at a display, then looked up with a wide grin, exposing gray, worn teeth behind his thin lips. He pointed at Gus with a bony finger.

"There! He's got the Endurium!"

All three of the attackers turned toward Gus and charged.

———

Yuki's eyes fluttered open.

"Well that was a mess," she said as she got up from the ground.

"What was?" Prime asked, materializing atop some machinery in the corner as she dropped out of stealth.

Yuki scuttled back and fell on her butt again.

"Holy hell. Don't do that!" Yuki held her chest as she took a moment to catch her breath. "I had to turn off all of the sensors nearby, and I can tell you that there is *much more* security here than would be warranted at a normal hospital. The others set off all kinds of alarms. I was able to shut off most of them, but I don't know if they alerted anyone before I disabled them."

"Let's go join the team, I haven't heard anything for too long."

"Prime, wait. We need to get inside—*now*. It's only a matter of time before my backdoor gets discovered and we're permanently locked out. I'm sure the others have it covered. Follow me."

Prime cast a look towards the direction of the combat, then reluctantly followed Yuki.

Arriving at a side door, Yuki extended her hand and tiny fibrils extended and briefly interacted with the keypad, which blinked green. They slid inside and found themselves in a cement-lined corridor. Pipes of different sizes and colors extended in both directions and Yuki briefly checked her internal map then turned and headed down the maze of corridors.

They slid out of the maintenance tunnel into a storage room. Another interface with a large machine and there was a rumble and whir within. A small metal window opened up and Yuki plucked out a small bundle. The machine chugged along, and another window opened. Yuki grabbed this bundle and tossed it to Prime.

Unfolding it, she found it to be a scrub top and bottoms. They both donned the outfits over their own clothes and Yuki found some puffy blue bouffant caps that covered most of Prime's pink downy hair that was obviously less than human. Kneeling, Yuki opened a zipper on her belt and extracted a small box. Punching a few buttons, the small box spat out a rectangular ID with Prime's picture and credentials on them.

"Kate Mandu? Really, Yuki?" Prime said, putting a hand on her hip. Yuki printed some more of the IDs for the rest of the team and retrieved more scrubs, hiding them in a corner, as she tried not to look Prime in the eyes.

"No one reads these anyways. Besides, I didn't think you'd look. It is a fully functioning ID though, and we have full access with these." Her arm disappeared to the elbow as she once again fished around inside the zipper portal. She came up with two clips and tossed one to Prime. Sliding it through the ID, she clipped it to her pocket.

"What does yours say?" Prime pressed.

"It doesn't matter," was Yuki's curt reply.

"Let me see," Prime slid by gracefully, plucking the ID with a practiced motion that would make any pickpocket envious. "Oh, ho ho!"

"Give that back, we've got to go. Stop goofing around."

"I'm so sorry... *Doctor* Kasa, head of neurology." She held the ID out in a deferential bow.

Yuki rolled her eyes and hissed, "Let's go, already!" She

snatched her ID out of Prime's hand and exited the storage room like she owned the place.

Prime followed, smiling to herself.

"What do you think you're doing?" a loud voice boomed.

As Prime stepped into the hallway, Yuki was backing away from a large gorilla of a man staring down his brows. A flustered Yuki sputtered and stammered as she looked back at the angry individual she had barreled into inadvertently. In desperation, she looked back at Prime. Her expression said it all.

I blew it!

CHAPTER FIFTY-ONE

Doctor! Doctor!

"You damn doctors think you can treat us orderlies like crap! Now you're raiding our scrubs, just because you can? Typical. And watch where you're going!" He gently pushed Yuki to the side with a beefy hand and continued on his way down the corridor.

As Prime watched him leave, she saw that he definitely was a hybrid—simian, most likely. She could see silver hair on the nape of his neck going down his back, visible on the scrubs' low neck-line.

Yuki scooped up Prime's arm with a big grin and she giggled at the release of tension.

"Hoo! I thought that was it for us. Well, you can rest at ease, there's hybrids working here. Makes sense in Hinansho. This is the main floor; it functions as any regular hospital. What we want is found in the M wing. We'll wait for the others there."

Yuki nodded at another doctor passing in the hallway. Her face became serious and stern. "Doctor."

"Doctor," he replied, nodding in turn.

"I've always wanted to do that!" Prime just rolled her eyes. "My dad always wanted me to be a doctor. Now he can't say that I was a disappointment. C'mon, it's this way," Yuki urged, pulling Prime along with her.

————

The whirlwind that was around Tempest only increased in size. Within the storm, Gus could see hailstones and chunks of ice.

Grabbing Aurora's hand he pulled her down an embankment and behind a tree.

"I've only heard of him doing this, but we need to take cover!"

An unholy whistling began to sound. There were shouts but nothing could be understood as the cacophony increased.

"Cover your ears!" Gus screamed and then pantomimed when he found he couldn't even hear his own voice. They both felt a huge pressure wave extend overhead, pushing them down into the soil around the tree. There were loud cracks and icy shrapnel spread outward. Alarms sounded as vehicles in the parking lot hundreds of feet away had their windows smashed as they were pelted with the debris. The silence afterward was eerie.

Aurora followed as Gus scrambled up to the promenade and saw his father down on all fours, shaking his head. The others were blown back in different directions, unconscious but alive.

"It's been a long time since I've nearly bottomed out my MP," he said, coughing and massaging his temples.

A whirring brought their attention to the drone, as a panel on its center opened and the propellers spun one final time. Bright glittery dust flew out, covering the supers. Gus spit and puffed out a big breath, catching the full brunt of the blast.

"That's annoying as hell. I'll be combing this out of my hair for weeks," Aurora said, holding up some strands of hair trying to remove some of the particles. Tempest raised a wind that blew away a majority of the obnoxious particles. Aurora kicked Black Lotus, and turned on the other Luddite who had released the drone in retaliation and was calculating her next angle for maximum bruising.

"Leave them, Aurora, Yuki needs us," Tempest gasped, his voice raw like he had been screaming too much.

She gave them one last scowl and growled as she followed Tempest. "Glitter? How stupid can you get!"

They followed the nav-point, finding the door propped open and made their way to the stockroom and found Yuki's stash.

Gus held up his ID. "Ah yeah, Yuki knows me. Dr. Angus M. Young—Cardiologist at your service! What's yours say?"

"Paul N. Storm. Hmm. I don't get it." Tempest shrugged as he slid into his scrub top.

Gus just chuckled. "You wouldn't. You're old. How about you?" He looked at Aurora.

"A. Borealis, RN. Ha-ha. Like I've *never* heard that one in the Academy. Let's just go already." Aurora headed out the door when the nav-point was refreshed to show Yuki's new position.

They followed, trying to walk quickly but had to temper their speed when they started drawing attention.

"Where are you guys, *he's here!*" Yuki whispered urgently over the comms.

"We're coming as fast as we can," Aurora responded. "People are watching us."

"I have an idea," Gus said, grabbing a stretcher alongside a hall. "Aurora, jump up and lay down."

"Wha—"

"Just do it!" Gus pressed.

Aurora rolled her eyes and crawled onto the stretcher. He threw a sheet over her lower legs and motioned for his father to grab an IV stand. He handed one end of the line to Aurora. "Hold this under the sheet. Okay, let's run!"

As they ran down the corridor, people opened doors for them and hugged the walls to allow them to pass. They were able to make it to the entry for the M wing, which had two security guards who waved them to stop. After scanning their ID cards and getting a green light, the guards motioned them through and returned to their posts.

The hallways beyond were practically empty compared to the rest of the hospital. Nurses stations stood empty as they wheeled Aurora down the halls.

"Guys, what's taking so long? I just received a notice that Mengele's personal transport is being prepped for launch. We have to go now if we're going to catch him!"

Tempest motioned for them to stop. "Aurora, I want you and Prime to go after Mengele's ship—we can't risk losing him again. If possible, keep him from leaving. If not, follow and we'll catch up. Gus and I will meet with Yuki and find Gwen. Go. Go!"

Aurora sped off down another hallway and Gus and his father took off another direction. They were close now, only two hundred feet ahead.

They burst through the swinging doors and a man on the second story turned to face them. Gus saw Yuki hiding under a workstation nearby.

The man on the balcony looked at his watch.

"You sure took your time. I was wondering when you would arrive." He began slow clapping with a sardonic grin on his face. Gus froze, he had seen that face before. He *knew* Mengele!

Gus' mind flashed back to his dreams. The ones with the alchemist and the shadowy steward. The face was the same. Angular jaw, circular wire-rim glasses, and small gap between his front teeth as he grinned. Time froze for Gus.

He heard his father's gasp come from beside him. "Doctor Weft? You're Mengele? By the Nth, what have I done?"

Mengele viewed them both, bowed politely then spun on his heels, walking through a doorway that irised shut behind him.

Gus shook himself out of his stupor and ran for the stairs, staggering to a stop when his father just stood there.

"It's my fault. I let her do this. I didn't know..." Tempest stared at his hands in disgust as if they were covered in blood.

Gus hurried back and grabbed his father by the hand. "He's

getting away, we have to go!" He tried pulling his father forward, but Tempest only stumbled and fell to his knees.

"I did this. She was always headstrong, but I could have done more. I killed her."

Gus shook his father, trying to snap him out of his torpor. "It isn't your fault! But I need your help. Tell me, is Mom's icon still there?"

Tempest could only manage a nod.

"Then there's still hope. Pull yourself together; she needs us. Who knows what Mengele will do to her if he gets to her before us!"

Those words brought Tempest back. He shook like he had been hit with a bucket of ice cold water and turned with more awareness to Gus and nodded as he regained his feet. They ran up the stairs after Mengele.

A sturdy metal door stood blocking their passage, but Gus saw his father's desperate eyes as he clenched his fists by his sides, slowly cocking them back. He felt his ears pop as a pressure gradient began to build up between his father and the door. It became so uncomfortable that Gus had to stand back. *Time-sight* activated and Gus felt the need to distance himself from what was about to happen.

A glance over his shoulder showed his father clenching his teeth with effort. Veins bulged on the sides of his head and he was soon covered with beads of perspiration. He thrust his hands forward, releasing the built up pressure towards the door. Air blew past Gus as ambient air flew into the void created by the pressure differential. When the wind died down, he saw his father calmly stepping through the doorway. Gus followed, staring in awe at the blades that overlapped to close the door blasted back like a metallic bloom.

Everything in the room beyond was shoved to the far wall, piled up in a heap like driven snow. They cleared the doorway and Tempest turned to Gus. The strong smell of antiseptic was insufficient to cover the smell of urine that hung in the air. Hallways spread out in different directions. This looked like some sort of hospital or convalescent home.

"I can feel her! We're close." He stopped and closed his eyes. "This way, Gus, she's this way!" Tempest ran off to the left with renewed vigor. Some of the doors were open in the facility and from within Gus could see sunken, withered forms connected to a myriad of wires and tubes. Muscles atrophied away until the residents were little more than flesh-covered skeletons. A sensation like a cold bony hand stole around his heart as he contemplated if his mother was in the same state.

"Please, no..." Gus wished with desperation as Tempest skidded to a stop at another intersection then took off down another hallway.

"Mengele has boarded his ship! Are you guys coming?" Yuki said in a panic.

Tempest ignored the comment as he ran like he was crazed. He paused outside a room with the doorway cracked.

"I... I don't know if I can go in, Gus," Tempest said, voice devoid of emotion.

"I'll go," Gus said quietly and he pushed the door open.

CHAPTER FIFTY-TWO

Bittersweet Symphony

As Gus stepped inside, the rhythmic beat of the heart monitor showed his mother's pulse and oxygen levels. A respirator noisily inflated and deflated. He looked at the woman before him, who almost looked like a different person than the one he knew in his memories. There was gray in her hair now, and a tangle of electrodes were attached to multiple areas around her head. Though a respirator mask covered her face almost completely, it was unmistakably her.

"Mom?" Gus asked, stepping closer to the bedside. As he gripped her hand, careful not to disturb the IV ports taped there, her eyes came open. They were glassy and vacant. Looking forward but not seeing anything.

"Mom, it's me, Gus." He looked her in the eyes but no recognition passed there. Who knew what medicines she was on? She was probably so zonked she didn't know her own name.

"Dad, get in here!"

Tempest burst in and, seeing his wife, he ran to the other side of the bed.

His mouth quavered open in horror as he tried to form the

words. "What have they done to you? What have I let them do?" he finally managed through a tight throat.

"She's alive, Dad, she's alive. That's what matters."

"Tempest, he got away. I don't know how he got aboard—he must've used another entry—but he's gone. I'm sorry," Prime reported over comms.

Gus saw that his father didn't even register the news as he slowly approached.

Gus dropped into a seat by the bedside, putting thoughts of Mengele out of his mind. He looked at his mother. She was gaunt, and just looked *frail*. He wondered if it was even safe to transport her in this condition with how much medical paraphernalia that she was connected to. Would the shock be too much for her?

He looked at Tempest whose emotions were having a battle across his face. Regret, worry, and anger all fought for dominance. Gus was surprised to see that worry overtook the others.

Yuki poked her head into the room. "Anything I can do?"

"Get BoJack down here. We need to get her out of here. Now," Tempest quietly ordered in a detached voice.

Yuki nodded and began to murmur on her comms as she left, leaving the family alone again. This was not the reunion that Gus had always hoped for in his dreams. Mom was supposed to make everything better. Bridge the gaps between him and his father, and help them connect at last. He wasn't sure what, if any, of his mother was left.

Time became drawn out. At some point, BoJack arrived, and they managed to disconnect Gwen from the multitude of monitors and equipment. Only by BoJack using his ability was he able to sustain Gwen as they made their way back to the transport. Gus barely registered the sheer number of rooms they passed with people in identical situations as his mother, wired to the gills.

Gus registered some of the other Crew but they were not impeded on their way by any of the staff as they made their way out of the hospital.

They passed another ward that was full of what looked like fetuses floating in jars, bubbles percolating in amber liquid as they were fed through a synthetic umbilicus.

Gus held the door as they slowly moved his mother through a control room filled with monitors. He stared at the screens showing all sorts of hybridization attempts, some more successful than others. Whatever Mengele was doing here, he was pushing the envelope of what had been tried before. None of it shocked Gus. He was already numb from finding his mother in basically a vegetative state, her future uncertain.

Eventually, they all were back on the ship and headed out of Hinansho at long last. If he never saw this place again it would be too soon. The medical suite on the transport was small, so Gus stayed outside while BoJack and his father tended to his mother. He stared out the window as they finally broke through the barrier and back into the sunlight. Gus took no pleasure in its simple warmth. It didn't touch the chill that had spread to his core.

He closed his eyes and let the light shine in on his face. He could feel tears welling up and threatening to fall, and so he kept his eyes closed, willing them to go away. He had longed to feel the warmth of the light again in that dismal place, but it did little to raise his spirits or kindle his hope. Mengele was gone. Escaped scot-free to who knew where. Probably to some other hidden place where he worked his horrors on others.

There were other sanctuary cities, all of them wary of supers. He probably had bases at every one of them, working away happily, free from any interference from supers or anyone who would stop him.

A hand on his shoulder made him cough. He tried to surreptitiously wipe at the corner of an eye to wick away the extra moisture there.

"How are you doing?" Aurora asked softly.

Gus looked up at her and bit his lip. He just shook his head. If he spoke now, his voice would betray him.

"There's still hope. I know Mengele got away, but I

managed to put a tracker on his ship. It should ping any moment now to the satellite network. And it's all because of you, Gus. If you hadn't gifted me that crafting ability, I wouldn't have been able to make that tracker. We can find him. I just wanted you to know. I know it looks dark right now, but don't give up." She turned and gave him some privacy.

Gus forced a smile and nodded.

"Thanks," he managed to croak, voice almost breaking as he coughed and cleared his throat again to cover.

"Sure," she said. Normally her voice was so curt and almost abrasive, but he had felt her genuine concern. Taking a series of deep breaths, he felt the emotions subside to a manageable level. The sun glistened off the ocean below as they began to bank.

Seneschal came over the comms. "Gus, can you come to the bridge? Your father wanted me to talk to you; he won't leave your mom's side—"

"I'll be right there," Gus took one last look at the expanse of blue and made his way to the cockpit.

———

"We have to head back, Gus. We missed some crucial communications while we were incommunicado in Hinansho and it raised some red flags. There won't be time to drop you off at the manor, unfortunately. I think things will be okay with the Crew if we spin our story a bit. I'm sure that bringing Gwen back will be the main focus, and not what we were doing to bring her back. Plus the intel on Mengele should be useful; we have so little to work on for the more elusive villains. The public expects us to deal with them because they are beyond any reg's abilities to manage."

"I get it, you guys have responsibilities. I'm just glad we got Mom back."

"Your father says we need to get her back to the Faction so they can look at her. I can only imagine what she's been through. Hopefully, someone can ease the psychological stress she's undergone and coax her back out as we nurse her body back to full health."

"Did you know her, Seneschal?"

"Yes. We were… at odds at times. But there isn't anything I wouldn't do for your father. We're all on the same team."

"I'll let him know. Thanks for telling me."

"I'll make a general announcement soon, I just thought I'd let you know why."

Gus headed back to the medical bay and poked his head in, giving his father the news.

"She's stable," BoJack said, weariness evident in his voice. "She should be fine until we get her back to the Faction, anyways."

"Thank you, BoJack. It is going to be a major undertaking taking care of her, so it is probably for the best that I am out of leadership. I can focus on helping her heal, and not worry about neglecting any duties at the Faction. A priority I should have rearranged a long time ago." Tempest reached out and gripped Gus' shoulder.

"Gus, I know you want to come along, but I kind of need you for a bit. You're not an official member of Purple Faction and it would take a while to get vetted anyways. Then you would have to go through the Academy before you'd be official and could join us on missions. I don't want you tied up like that. Excuse me if that's selfish, but I still need you to be available."

Aurora poked her head in and pointed to Tempest and Gus, signaling them to follow.

BoJack waved a hand. "I'll watch her, don't worry."

"I'll be back in a minute," Tempest promised, taking one last look at Gwen before closing the door softly.

"Seneschal just made an announcement that we're heading back to HQ. They want me to make a full report since I was captured. One problem, though. You know that tracker I put on Mengele's ship? Well, its signal is very weak and intermittent. If you could sync it with the manor's scanning network protocols, I think you could boost the signal. If he gets too far out of range, we may lose him. It's only a level one tracker, so it has limited access to the network. By connecting it to the full power of the manor, we could keep track of him in real-time. When the Crew has finished up with Faction business, we could come back and deal with him together."

"That's good thinking. Thank you so much for not letting him get away."

"It's the least I could do. I owe you."

"You don't owe me anything, Aurora. I'm grateful you helped me keep the manor from Manticorps, and gave me my first lessons on being in a team. I'm horrible at 'thank yous,' but I really am grateful for all that you have done. I wouldn't be here without you, I'm pretty sure."

"I don't know about that either. You're pretty savvy. But thanks. Mengele has made a refueling stop in Spain, so he should be there for a while, at least a day. We need to get you back to the manor within a day."

"I'll authorize a portal," Tempest offered.

"I guess that's settled. It'll be weird to be home again, after all that's happened. I just wish it were under better circumstances."

"We all do," Aurora said. "ETA is less than an hour, so I'm going to gather my things. You guys good?"

They both nodded and Tempest went back into the medical bay. BoJack came out soon afterward and put an arm around Gus.

"Hey, your dad says that you've been having headaches again. Let me check you out again."

"Aren't you tired?"

"That's the life of a medic, Gus. Utter boredom, stop-your-heart stress, or bone weariness. It's part of the job description. Your dad said he saw you struggling in that battle at the hospital. What's going on?"

"Headaches again, much more intense. Any time I try to access my abilities," Gus admitted.

"Is that it?"

Gus sighed. "Well, to be honest, I've really been doubting myself again. I still feel like I don't deserve to be with you guys. I'm worried I'm going to mess up and compromise the team. I was a liability at the hospital."

"It happens to the best of us, Gus."

"I suppose. But, on top of it all, I just feel weary. The stress of all these responsibilities is crushing me, but I can't let everyone down. I can't let *myself* down. All those promises I made about what I would do differently if I only had the chance. I don't want to let myself get cynical and justify why I am not being true to what I think is right deep down just because I am painfully aware of my weaknesses. I realize that I made a lot of those choices in ignorance and naivete, but I still feel that I was onto something when I made those commitments."

BoJack smiled ruefully. "I would like to tell you that it goes away, but that's not really true. That feeling will be with you as long as you try to be a super, unfortunately. You just learn how to manage how much it affects you to a certain extent."

"But how do you choose what is the best thing to do? My mind is full of conflicts and I feel paralyzed by making a crucial failure. Mixed in with that is a weird type of malaise that is sapping my motivation. No one really knows me as a super. But in a weird way, I feel like I represent regs too, and I don't want to turn my back on them and treat them like second-class citizens now that I have these powers."

"Which is probably a good thing," BoJack said and Gus pressed on, encouraged.

"I keep thinking: '*Why me?*' Of all the people who could have gotten powers, I happened to get them. At times I feel guilty, almost like I cheated to gain my powers instead of being worthy of them somehow. I haven't really told the others, but I have an ability that lets me take powers from other supers. Stealing them. Benefitting from the work and effort it took to hone and develop those skills from level one."

BoJack's eyes widened, but he nodded as Gus talked through his worries.

"Gus, my life has been pretty tough. Still is, I guess. No one really knows a lot about my past, but there's a lot of pain there. I've also gotten to the point where I've been at rock bottom. I just kept asking myself: 'What do I need to be happy again?' I thought about it for ages. At first, I thought I just wanted to be free of all the negative influences in my life, but then I recalled my brother. After our parents were killed, he never really recovered. To avoid the whole situation, he sought to escape more and more, divorcing himself from this reality to spend more and more time in virtual games, where he could live an alternative fantasy life of his choosing. Eventually, he chose to check himself into a game hospice."

"A game hospice?" Gus questioned.

"It is an option for those with severe depression that are classified as suicide risks. Basic body functions are supported while the individual stays wholly immersed in the game, only pausing to sleep. They blend the transition using sedatives and in-game prompts so the game becomes their whole reality.

"The trade-off is that even with the nanobots, their lifespan is shortened considerably. Humans weren't designed to lay there prone for long periods of time. The body stagnates and they eventually pass as it just stops functioning. The euphemism they use is 'failure to thrive.' But Bobby failed to thrive a long time before he ever went to the hospice. Twenty-two years old and that was his choice."

Gus didn't know what to say as BoJack paused, allowing the silence to stretch as he gathered his thoughts. His own issues seemed so small and insignificant compared with how this guy had dealt with multiple issues that would have broken Gus if even one of them had impacted his life. And he showed none of it to the world. He didn't parade his struggles in front of others for sympathy or special treatment. On top of that, he had even found a way to be happy.

"Do you feel guilty? Like you could have done more? I'm

not saying that I think you didn't help him or anything, but looking at myself, I think I always wonder if there is something I should have done that would have made a difference."

"At first I did, yeah. Every damn day." BoJack nodded. "Especially since I have a healing ability. Kept trying to see if this was just a problem with his brain chemistry that I could tweak and then he would be better. Some super-serotonin modification that would snap him out of his funk. I tried to be there and be supportive, but he just became more and more detached."

"That must have been hard."

"It was. I was a reminder of his old, painful life so, as he transitioned, he became less responsive. You can receive messages and even calls in-game, but he stopped accepting them more and more until he wouldn't answer them at all. Whenever I would visit in person, he would be in his pod. I would stock the fridge and even make some food at times, leaving it for him to reheat. Near the end, I visited a week later and found that none of the food had been touched. I ran to his pod and banged on the lid. I pulled him out of the gel and removed the leads, laying him on the spongy mat outside. His pallid skin hung on his gaunt frame. He was wasting away in every conceivable way. The pod had sustained his base nutritional needs and the gel and nanobots managed waste removal and circulation so that he didn't get bed sores but he looked like death boiled over."

"Wow," Gus whispered.

"After that, he signed some simple forms at the hospital and was moved directly to the game hospice. Apparently, it's much cheaper for the government to do that than support them, provide training or counseling." He sighed.

"So how do you do it? How did you find a way to be happy? I struggle with all these emotions and doubts almost constantly. Do you just push them down, or just stay so busy that they aren't as pressing on your mind? I'm always worrying about the 'what ifs.' What if I don't do this? What if I don't make the right choice that would be obvious to someone with more experience?"

"I stopped comparing myself to others a long time ago. It was one of the things that was bringing me down. Asking myself, 'Why did this happen to me?' was something that always brought me down. It made me feel powerless. When something else happened, it felt like life was just piling on the misfortune. I went down that road, trying to see if I was bringing this misfortune on myself by some negative karma I had somehow gained. Envious of other people's lives who seemed to sail through without a care, and how often those people were dishonest or at least extremely unethical. And no repercussions happened to them; in fact, they seemed to be thriving."

"Exactly! It's so discouraging," Gus agreed. *He gets how it feels.*

"I had to let all of that go. It's toxic. It either makes you feel superior and loathe those who you deem to be beneath you, or you loathe yourself for being so broken, incomplete and unworthy. Sometimes horrible things happen and it isn't anyone's fault. Or it is and you can't change it.

"I don't want you to think this all happened overnight, either. I'm just lucky I had the time I did with my parents, Bobby, and my wife."

"What happened with your wife?" Gus blurted before he could restrain himself.

"That's probably a story for another time. Another tragedy, unfortunately. The real question you have to ask yourself is, 'Do you want to be free from anything bad ever happening to you, or do you really want to be capable of handling any challenge that comes your way?' Avoiding struggle involves no growth.

"I have gone through many painful experiences, but even if I could go back and change them, I doubt I would now. There were times when I obsessed on finding a super with a power that would allow me to go back, but with the years I have a new perspective. I know who I am better because of how I reacted to all of those challenges. The choices I made, the bonds that became deeper, the habits I formed. I was forced into the situation, but I chose how those affected me. I think too many people give their power away. Don't do that, Gus. I would rather fail a thousand times than fail to try once."

"I wish I was okay with my failures."

"There are no failures. That's good data on what doesn't work. Accepting that, I was a lot happier, along with letting go of the notion that things should be fair. I now expect things to be hard. It changed something fundamental in my mindset. Then I was able to change how I felt. There were days when I just wanted to sleep all day, looking for the escape of dreams. If not for my brother, I may have stayed in that state for too long. When I finally confronted those insurmountable challenges, I began the process of overcoming them."

"That really resonates with me, man. Thanks for sharing that. It gives me a lot to think about."

BoJack turned and looked out the window, watching the rain hit the window outside the transport. "Anytime. I hope it helps, and you don't take as long as I did to sort things out. I'm beat, so forgive me if I nod off for a bit."

Gus nodded and turned to his own thoughts. He tried to discover what would make him happy. Really, what were his expectations before he could feel happy? He closed his eyes and tried to relax. He could feel the pressure slowly draining, like a pinhole in a beachball, but he would take any relief. After a time, he noticed that the draining stopped and he opened his eyes. BoJack sat there slumped in the seat, fast asleep.

Snapback pain hit him like a bat between the eyes.

I need to do something. This is going to kill me.

"You are correct," Nick said. "Your brain is failing to make necessary neurotransmitters and there is no biological reason for this to be happening. I have stimulated the appropriate receptors and signal cascades, and your body is not responding. You need to do something, and soon."

"Hey, there he is. How was the vacation, Nick?"

"It was you who was ignoring me, so here we are."

"Sometimes you are a real pain in the ass..." Gus grumbled.

"That is only because it is the quickest way to your brain," Nick quipped. "I would suggest *Telepathy*, as it has exhibited the biggest reduction in symptoms."

"Here goes nothing. Sorry, BoJack."

Gus activated *Telepathy*.

CHAPTER FIFTY-THREE

No Mercy

It was difficult to get anything at first, the experience a cross between balancing something slippery and fine-tuning a weak signal that jumped around a bit. First, he got feelings, which were all over the board. Anger, fear, adoration, worry, loss, pride, each emotion bursting into focus then warping into the next.

What is he dreaming about?

Gus felt like a ghost as a modest apartment came into view. From his point of view, he was hovering in front of a much younger BoJack, wearing plaid pajama bottoms and a T-shirt. He was kneeling in front of a sobbing young woman with auburn hair thrown up into a messy bun. Her face was in her hands and her hair had fallen forward, masking her appearance. He intuitively recognized her as BoJack's wife.

"It's always something. If we have any luck, it's bad luck," she spat amid the sobs. "First the miscarriage, now the lawsuit. I can't win; it's like I'm cursed."

BoJack reached forward and held her forearms as she trembled and cried.

"We'll make it through this, babe, we've been through worse," he said softly.

"I'm just so tired. All I've done is try to help people, and they turn around and do this! Why is the insurance not covering this?"

"I don't know, everything happened when the policies were renewing. They said something about the overlap of when everything occurred. We'll fight it, don't worry—"

"I'm already frayed to the breaking point; this couldn't have happened at a worse time. It should be illegal what they're doing. They have to cover us! We can't handle the cost of a lawsuit all on our own. And that lawyer that said it would be almost a quarter of a million to defend against a case like this, even though I did nothing wrong!"

"I know it's infuriating, but there are worse things that could have happened. We have each other, and we're healthy. Things may be tough, but it's nothing we can't overcome." BoJack looked up at her imploringly but the woman's sobs turned to shouts. She appeared to not even have heard any of his attempts to console her.

"And telling us that we should just settle? And let them win?! It all seems so wrong. The system is broken if it lets people take advantage of others like that. Where is our protection? Am I just guilty until proven innocent? She's lying! We should get a Magistrate, then counter-sue for libel or perjury or whatever."

"It's not a criminal trial, so there won't be a Magistrate to read and evaluate everyone's thoughts. Even if it was, this lady might be convinced you were in the wrong and we would be in the same position. They can only discern intention and emotion—"

"Then what should we do?" she wailed up at the ceiling, a grimace upon her face as if in pain.

"I don't know, but we didn't work this hard to lose everything. I'll fight, if you want us to fight. We can settle if you just want to be done with it all and move on. I'm totally on your side whatever you choose," he soothed.

"I can't deal with this right now," she choked out, wrenching her arms out of his caress, and ran to the bedroom, slamming the door. He sat there kneeling, looking over his shoulder at the closed door, chewing the inside of his cheek as he thought. She needed space when she was overwhelmed. He wanted to go to her, but knew now was not the time. A tear slid down his face now that she was gone, he had to stay strong for the both of them. He had to—

Gus was pulled backward out of the memory. He instantly felt guilty and self-conscious for viewing such a personal, private moment as the sensation reversed and he came out of vision and his own sight began to resolve. He didn't know how Magistrates read thoughts for a living, especially with all the dark things they must see and deal with reading the minds of criminals. He could feel the emotions and thoughts as if they were his own. Gus had a new respect for BoJack. How did this guy stay so positive? He never would have guessed he had been through—

"Gus… *Gus!*"

When he had fully dropped out of the ***Telepathy*** transition, Gus found himself facing an angry BoJack. He was so close he could see the whiskers on his face and the heat of his breath.

"Whoa, give me some space. You're in my bubble—" Gus tried to back away.

"I'm in your bubble?! That's rich, cuz. You were delving me right now, weren't you?"

"Delving you?" Gus asked, cocking his head.

"Reading my thoughts. And probably have been for a while. I thought it was weird when my migraines were coming back, but now I think it was you poking around in there." BoJack poked Gus in the chest accusingly, twisting his finger like a drill. "Am I wrong?"

Gus' sheepish look told BoJack what he already expected.

"Unbelievable. I open up a little bit and this is what I get. What made you think that was an okay thing to do?"

"Sorry, I was just trying to level my **Telepathy** skill, I'm almost to level twenty…" Gus' explanation died on his lips as he saw BoJack's expression turn even angrier.

"I trusted you, mate. I would have told you anything you wanted to know. And this is how you do me? More is expected of us since we have these abilities. If we aren't going to police ourselves, who are we expecting to do it? Just because a super *can* do something doesn't mean that they should."

"Whoa, whoa. Why are you so mad? I didn't see the harm. In fact, I think I know you a lot better now."

"No harm? You've just basically committed the mental equivalent of rape and it's no big deal to you. Just trying to get some XP, that's all, BoJack. Is that where your head's at?" He sneered in disgust and looked away from Gus.

"I'm sorry. I didn't know it would affect you so negatively, really."

BoJack looked back at Gus as if he were a grotesque, yet fascinating bug.

"I think I really misjudged you. I know you're new and all, but this goes beyond. Way beyond. It should be a common sense type of thing. Does anyone need to specifically tell you that you shouldn't use elevated strength to destroy property, or get in a fight with a reg and potentially maim them or kill them? Does it not seem wrong to go rifling through someone's personal journal or pictures? In what universe is it okay to do that in their minds? Private things are private for a reason."

"But Magisters do it as a job," the words spilled out unbidden and Gus cringed as BoJack's tone became even icier.

"Magisters are appointed and they see criminal cases. The only time they delve people who haven't committed a crime is when two parties are trying to reach an agreement through mediation and compromise. Two willing and aware parties. It disturbs me that you are even trying to justify this in your mind at all."

BoJack turned and grabbed Gus' suit by the collar, pulling him close.

"There are too many takers in this world, Gus. And they have no business being supers as well. And I don't give a damn who anyone is, I will fight that type of selfishness down to my dying breath." He let go of Gus with a slight shove, as if the contact made him dirty.

"You think I'm overreacting, don't you?" He eyed Gus up and down.

Gus' jaw opened and closed as he tried to formulate something to say.

"I won't do it again, seriously. I didn't mean to pry—"

"Damn straight, you won't do it again. Let's just keep our distance for a while. We can still work together, but some redrawing of boundaries is definitely in order. Just… later." BoJack looked flustered and just put up his palms, shaking his head before turning to leave. He stood there a second and without turning around growled one last thing to Gus. "I told you about a lot of things in confidence. Things I expect you to keep to yourself. There could be a lot of blow-back on me if it got out that I've told you what I have. And I would be *very* put out if that happened. Do you understand me?"

"Yeah," Gus said, his throat suddenly feeling dry and parched.

There was a grunt of acknowledgement and BoJack stormed away.

Gus looked around the common room and was relieved that, for the time being, no one was there to witness the spectacle.

So stupid! You knew how guilty that made you feel when you did it, that should have told you it was wrong! Gus mentally berated himself.

The decision was cringe-worthy when he looked at it in retrospect. He battled with himself to justify how he needed to level to be a part of the team, and get to a point where he could actually contribute and not be a liability, but they all sounded hollow, even to himself. The shame made him want to avoid BoJack, but he knew he couldn't do that. He was never good at apologizing and had lost friendships before by avoiding confrontation, just wanting to escape how uncomfortable the conversation would be.

Was he a "taker" like BoJack had said? The words stung, but they hurt all the more because as Gus reviewed his decisions, he found most were driven by selfish motives. All with the guise of getting to the place where he someday could help others.

But the headaches! Gus noted that his symptoms had disappeared. Blessed relief, but was it worth it? He wasn't sure if he had learned or gained whatever "key" the Oracle implied Gus needed to get from BoJack, but a fundamental difference between them stood out in stark contrast. BoJack put others' welfare before his own, and his focus was a mutual win for all parties involved.

And what about Prime? What was he supposed to learn from her? They both seemed like deep rivers that showed none of the turbulence underneath a calm exterior. Gus felt his own life was reckless flailing on an inner tube in the rapids, just trying to stay afloat. And now he probably just blew a chance to gain those skills he would have learned in the Academy. A willing mentor whom he just pissed off, probably for good.

Gus felt sick to his stomach. *Yet another good thing I've screwed up...*

CHAPTER FIFTY-FOUR

Home Sweet Home

Seneschal dropped Gus off at a transit station near his home before the rest of the Crew made their way back to Faction headquarters. He was familiar with the neighborhood, but everything seemed... *smaller*, somehow. As if he had lived here as a child and then grew up and the dimensions were not as he remembered them.

He began walking to his apartment, becoming aware of the looks people were giving him. Usually he was in what he called "stealth mode" before he had abilities. No one noticed him, or ever paid him any mind in the past. Granted, his suit was torn a bit and a little ragged and smudged. The huge black polearm he was carrying was less than subtle as well.

Getting some new clothes wouldn't be a bad idea.

He stopped at a nearby bank kiosk and pressed his finger on the screen and waited as his eye was scanned.

Biometrics evaluated... confirmed!

Welcome, Gus Vannett.

How may I help you today?

Gus checked his balance and was surprised to see the amount of money in his account. Without any expenses, he had accrued nine paychecks directly into his account as if he were still working on Graviton's station. The process was most likely automated and with no one to change the system, it would continue in perpetuity. Whatever the reason, Gus was flush for the first time in a while. He withdrew some money and tried on some clothes in a nearby shop.

It took a while to find something in his size. He couldn't get a thigh down the pants leg of a pair of jeans whose size was loose on him before everything had happened. After a couple tries, he found something that fit his new frame. He picked up a couple sweatpants and shirts, shoes and socks. Even his shoe size had increased from a 10.5 to a 12.

So weird!

He hadn't thought about his physical changes in any real way, and was lost in thought as he walked back to his apartment, not realizing that he didn't have a key until he was entering the parking lot. He stopped in to see the landlord.

At first, she was upset that he had disappeared without a trace, and that she should have sold his things. Her attitude was mollified as Gus paid his rent to current and an extra $50 on top of back rent to get another key. Pretty steep, considering she had a whole stack of them already made in that drawer, but Gus could care less.

He opened the door to his old apartment. A hot, stale smell like a thrift store hit him as he stepped inside. A layer of dust coated everything. He had lost everything he had owned of major value on the station, and the small room that greeted him was more spartan than he remembered. He looked at one wall and saw the empty wall mount where he had hung his favorite guitar. He walked around the tiny room; it seemed like forever ago that he had lived here.

He hit the air conditioning as he entered the small kitchen, which rattled noisily to life. He then pulled apart the yellowing curtains to open some windows in an attempt to freshen up things. The A/C always took a while to ramp up and get cold. He knew there was nothing perishable in the fridge, but he cracked it open anyways. Some condiments, a jar of pickles in the far back and a single soda. He grabbed it and opened it as he toured his old home, feeling like a stranger.

If he knocked all of the walls out, the whole thing was probably around the same size as the master suite back at the manor. He walked into his bedroom, seeing the small twin bed there. His old computer was set up in the corner on a card table with a folding chair. *How long did I live like this?*

He flicked on the computer, thinking maybe he could check his emails. The sheer amount of junk there discouraged him from really searching. He was about to turn it off when Nick spoke up.

"I can sort that for you," Nick grumbled. "What do you want?"

"Just if there's anything from my friends; Dave, Chuck, or Jim."

"Here you go." Two messages were highlighted. Both from Dave.

"You can delete the rest," Gus said as he opened the first one.

Gus,

How's life on the station? Can you even get emails up there? Well, life sucks for the rest of the gang. That other job we got didn't pan out so we're back looking for gainful employment. It's been a dry spell, work-wise.

Jim's been in an accident and he's still in the hospital. He's in intensive care and they won't let anyone in to see him that's not family. Chuck has just disappeared, emails get returned and his phone comes back disconnected. It's lonely out here bud. I hope you're doing well. Anyways, if you get this drop me a line sometime.

Your bro,

Dave

Looking at the date he saw that was before he had called Dave from the island. Gus saw that the next email was fairly recent.

Gus,

Hey, where are you man? Well, I've got some bad news. My sentencing was today and I'm going away. It may not be that bad. Here's to hoping, right? Anyways, I wanted to catch you before I had to go, but no such luck. I don't know when I'll be back, they haven't really given me a lot of details about the process. My counsel said to plan on a year, maybe more, so I'm letting my place go. I hope to see you on the other side of this. Look me up in a year or so. I'll keep this email around and check it when I get back. So, yeah. I'm glad you're okay, man. And cool thing with the powers. I wish we could have met up, but it is what it is. Good luck with everything and don't forget the little people!

Later brotha-man,

Dave

Gus flushed a bit. He was somewhere in Hinansho when Dave had sent this, doing his own thing. A stab of disappointment made his heart ache that he hadn't been there for one of his few friends. *Par for the course, Gus.*

With nothing else to do, he decided to look up Jim and Chuck to see if he could touch base with either of them. Doing a quick search, he quickly found that Dave was right. Chuck wasn't even listed. He looked up the address of the hospital and jotted it down. No time like the present.

A twenty-minute ride later, he stood in front of the hospital where Jim was supposed to be. A feeling of revulsion hit his stomach as he looked at the hospital.

Too soon.

He braced himself and walked inside.

Calm down, Gus, not every hospital has nefarious things going on behind the scenes.

He had to wait in a long line at the harried intake desk. They were obviously understaffed and overworked. Tensions were high from both sides. One who had to deal with brazen rudeness and the others who had to waste valuable time in an inefficient system. Gus observed everything from his new perspective.

How would anyone fix this? This was the kind of problem that the everyman has to deal with on a daily basis. While supers go about their business, he couldn't recall anything done along these lines. He tried to think of possibilities, but came up with very few constructive ideas. Even with BoJack's level of healing ability, one person would barely put a dent in helping the sheer amount of people here.

He wondered if hospitals were like this in districts controlled by the Green or Orange Factions. Were less resources allocated here because of Purple's credo of Might Makes Right? Were the chronically sick viewed as non-contributors to society, so they merited less attention? He honestly didn't know, and felt a little shame at being so oblivious to something that was clearly a big problem.

"May I help you?"

Gus realized the receptionist was talking to him.

"Oh, sorry. Yes. I have a good friend that was checked in here. I wanted to see if I could possibly visit him? I just got back from an extended tour of duty." He had planned what he would say, and thought phrasing it as if he were a veteran would get him some more leniency to visit.

"Name and birthdate," she asked in a bored voice.

"Jim Roark, July 24th, 2018."

The woman tapped on some keys, then wrinkled her nose. She tapped more keys, hitting them harder, then turned to Gus.

"I'm showing that he was admitted a couple months ago, but I have no information on where he is located or his visitor status. Are you sure he didn't get discharged?"

"I don't think so? I mean, I have a squad mate who told me he was here before he got... deployed again, but I didn't get to talk to him before he left."

"Uh-huh..." she said distractedly as she hit the keys a bit more. "I don't know what to tell you. This system was outdated ten years ago. It's possible that someone didn't process his paperwork correctly, or that he was moved somewhere and they didn't enter that information correctly. As you can see, we are very busy today." She grabbed a business card and slid it over to Gus. "I recommend you contact this number; they could possibly help you better. I'm very sorry I can't do more, sir...

next!" She waved at the next person in line and Gus distractedly looked at the card.

Patient Relations
Sarah Turner

He absently slid the card into his pocket. Walking out, the doors slid open silently and he left. He stood there with his hands on his hips, staring at the fountain in front of the hospital. This homecoming was nothing like he had envisioned. All of his friends were gone. The Crew was going to be occupied in the Faction for who knew how long.

Rather than taking a ride back to his apartment, Gus just began walking. He didn't even need to put any thought into it, as his display showed him a pale blue path needed to get back home without even needing to ask.

Passing a pawn shop along the way, Gus stepped in and checked out the guitars. He lost himself in playing and trying out the different ones, and settled on an amp and guitar. At first, he was worried he would get exhausted carrying it. By the time he rounded the corner of his apartment, his muscles weren't even cramping or tired. He practiced until dark, losing track of time and escaping into his music. At least *this* felt like home.

CHAPTER FIFTY-FIVE

Alone

Tempest contacted Gus early in the morning. Gus set down his guitar and noted it was already past two in the morning.

"Hey Gus, I didn't think I'd catch you awake."

"I don't sleep well these days."

"Well, your mom isn't doing well, and I'm going to be staying here for a while. I hate to impose, but Aurora's champing at the bit to get the tracker linked with the manor. It's dropped off her tracking a couple of times and fortunately the network caught the signal. We have an unsettled score, so I agree that we need to keep tabs on that monster. I can send a courier to deliver it to you, and then give you a ride to the portal station. I hate to rush you, but—"

"You can send it now, if you want," Gus broke in.

"Really? I thought that would be a harder sell."

"There's not much left for me here anymore. My friends are gone, and I want to get Mengele as bad as you. Is Mom really bad? Be straight with me, do you think she'll recover?"

"She's stable for now."

"That's not what I asked. Will she ever be the same? Like we remembered?"

There was a long silence. Gus checked his display to see if they were still connected.

At last Tempest replied, "I honestly don't know. But I'm going to do everything I can to get her what she needs. She's a fighter, Gus. If there's a way, we'll all find it together."

"Yeah, I know. Send the courier, you know my address?"

"Of course."

"Can I see her one more time before I leave?" Gus asked.

"I'll send you some of my feeds. The Faction won't let outsiders come in, especially unvetted supers. I'm sorry, Gus."

"I get it. Well, whenever you're ready."

"Should be there in about an hour."

———

Gus stepped through the portal and made his way to the control center on autopilot. He just felt numb as he connected the tracker, referring to the notes Aurora had left. As promised, Mengele's ship populated the display. After making some adjustments, the computers extrapolated Mengele's likely destination, somewhere in South Africa if he didn't change direction. Now it was a waiting game, sitting here being useless until everyone could come back. Gus leaned back in his chair, the silence he had missed when the Crew was ever-present now felt unwelcome. Isolating and alone. But perhaps that was how things should be.

How did everything get so screwed up? This was not how things were supposed to work out. Jumping through all of these hoops only to find that it could be for nothing?

Then screwing things up with BoJack, who had been nothing but helpful. *What is wrong with you, Gus?*

He was surprised how his mind sought out someone else to blame. Like a dirt trail with deep ruts he was disturbed how, even after recognizing this, his brain tried to come up with even more justifications on why the blame wasn't totally his. How Basileus was partially to blame because if he hadn't messed with the Mandrite core, Gus wouldn't be having the headaches. Or if he could just level like normal, or sleep, or any number of things *then* things would have turned out better.

Once he had seen it though, he couldn't unsee it. This was his fault, and he couldn't shift any of the blame. Or at least he was tired of hiding behind those excuses. Tired of always having things act upon him and him just scrambling to react. Most of all, he was tired of waiting until everything was perfect before he felt comfortable doing anything.

It was time to grow up. It was long past, actually. A super shouldn't always be using others as a crutch. That must be what the Oracle wanted him to figure out from Prime and BoJack. They both looked at the world differently than he did. And they didn't let all the crap hold them back or stop them from acting. As much as they seemed to have it all together, they still struggled.

He had always entertained the notion that eventually there would be a time of transition, just like in a video game. When you've finally got everything upgraded, and collected enough resources or have them generating passively that you don't have to manage them constantly.

Life would never be like that. There would always be something. What had BoJack said? *Life levels up in difficulty with your skills?* The idea felt foreign, different from what he had always fantasized about his future. That someday things would be ideal. That day would never come.

A chime startled Gus out of his musings. He skimmed past some other battle stats and XP drops from different steps on their trip to the hospital and battle with Kenway and the three strangers.

You have leveled up the skill: **True Sight** *to* **Level 2!**
XP awarded: 500.
FP awarded: 1000.
1440 XP to level 21.
You have leveled up the skill: **True Sight** *to* **Level 3!**

XP awarded: 750.
FP awarded: 1500.
690 XP to level 21.

Well crap. There it was. No room for argument. After the level up, the foreign-ness of the idea seemed less intangible and easier to accept. As if he had believed that way for a long time. With the clarity, other things became much more evident and his naivete made him burn with shame.

He buried his face in his hands, rubbing hard as he thought. *Why can't I get my act together? Am I ever going to have a place where I actually deserve to fit in? Or should I just accept my lot as a screw up and keep walking my lonely road? Am I unable to rely on others because deep down I know that* I am unreliable *and I'm subconsciously sabotaging myself?*

If there was an opposite of the Midas touch, I think that would be my true ability. My first powers are all centered around the word "wreck," and that can't be a coincidence. Perhaps I'm just geared to take things down and ruin them, and I'm just causing myself a lot of frustration and pain by trying to swim upstream against my nature. All this struggle with nothing to show for it. If I'm destined to just ruin things for myself and others, I should distance myself and not drag anyone down with me.

I'm not sure what the Oracle wanted me to see, but for the most part, I just see how small I really am. That the problems I've built up in my mind are really insignificant in comparison to the real tragedies that people are going through on a daily basis. You would never know those struggles because they keep them to themselves and don't wear it on their sleeves, yearning for sympathy and support. They deal with it stoically and don't make it everyone else's problem.

Supposedly I'm an adult, but I can't stop relying on people for every little thing. Then selfishly grabbing any advantage for my own benefit, and somehow, I convinced myself it was so that I would have the ability to help others at some point. Trying to numb the realization that I may not be wired to be a super. That I lack that kernel of goodness deep down in my core that will make my motivations pure and selfless.

All my life I've been searching to fit in, to finally find my place. I've changed how I acted to be a part of the group. And even that was a selfish motive. I convinced myself that if the Crew thought I was part of the team, then all of these doubts that constantly resurface could finally be dismissed once and for all.

Gus sucked in a breath as a sudden spasm of pain started at the base of his skull and began creeping up his head.

"Oh damn, not again," he groaned. He dug his index fingers into the area but the pain refused to subside. *Perhaps Karma is real. And this is some kind of consequence for my past.*

As if in reply, his father's expression at the hospital haunted him, vividly remembered behind his closed eyes as he tried to dissipate the effects of the sudden headache. He had seen how his father had been almost broken when they found his mother in the state she was in. And that look.

His chest tightened as the wraith of guilt clenched around his heart. That look bored into Gus' heart as he remembered it. *You did this. She's like this because of you.* Though nothing was stated, Gus knew this was true without any words being spoken.

The brightness of the sunlight pouring in the room was intensifying his headache, so he staggered to the hallway. He leaned back against the wall and slid down to the ground. At some point the pain began to ebb and he opened his eyes and looked up at the ceiling, which shimmered with the reflected afternoon light.

He saw it play across the faint texturizing they had done on the ceilings, and it looked like waves. No, more like the swirling mists of Hinansho, but with fog so thick it swallowed those who ventured in, never to be found again.

A lost soul in a city of lost souls. The dismal miasma mirrored how he felt on the inside perfectly. Roiling darkness of equal parts rage at himself for his weakness, contaminated with depression for poisoning everything he seemed to touch.

They competed for dominance within him, one urging him to give up and go far away where he wouldn't hurt anyone else. The other to get vengeance, to burn himself up in the attempt and rid the world of the taint of his negative influence. Perhaps he could do both and do the world a favor, and make things right again—at least for everyone else.

As he grabbed a hold of this thread, his resolve firmed, and the despair gave way to decision. This felt right; he could make up for all the damage he had caused. As long as he succeeded, it wouldn't matter what happened to him afterward. The price seemed acceptable, and he wasn't going to drag anyone else into his fights anymore.

The Crew only came here because they felt like they owed his father a debt, but he had done nothing to expect them to help him. They had retrieved his mother. The job was done. Everything left was up to him. They said they would eventually return, but what if Mengele disappeared while Gus waited and did nothing?

The void he felt inside worried him. Was something fundamentally wrong with him? He knew he should feel gratitude for all that the others had sacrificed, staying with him and his father as they risked their lives on the ridiculous adventure. He should feel gratitude, but there was nothing there.

He had always felt different than his peers, but the sensation of this lack of emotion seemed something that would align more with a sociopath than a super. Could it be that his path led him to a darker destination? If it did, why waste time fighting against it if he was going to be equally miserable either way?

Congratulations! You have chosen your second Guiding Principle.
Guiding principles offer many benefits as long as you hold them in solemn regard and do not break them, offering stat boosts and enhancements as long as you remain true to the tenets of the principle.
You have chosen: Sacrifice.
When you are working in a team aligned with your values and views, you receive a +5 increase in all basic stats and a 10% increase to XP gain while the status is maintained. Be true to yourself, and you will continue to grow and develop!
Access to a unique team ability based on team dynamics available:

Conditions: You must have worked with a team a minimum of three months for this perk to become effective.

The prompt stood there for a minute until Gus finally dismissed it. For whatever reason, this appeared to be his destiny. It was nothing like he had hoped that it would be. He compared his options: what he had dreamed in blissful ignorance, and what would do the best good.

All those times he had imagined what he would do differently if only he was a super. How he would show everyone the things he could do, if he only had the chance. It had just magnified his own selfish scrabbling to prove himself to others. That he had some worth that they just didn't see. That the whole thing was just a misunderstanding, and now that they could see the *real Gus,* everything would be clear and everyone would be happy.

But he had failed. Again. For the millionth time, and he didn't know how long he could keep fooling himself. The universe kept batting him down as he tried to rise past his station into something else that was incompatible with his nature. It would be better to burn up in a blaze of glory than to allow himself to go down the dark path that beckoned. Or die of a brain aneurysm or something with these headaches. He had to do something. *Now.*

Gus clicked accept on his second Guiding Principle.

There were some preparations to make first.

CHAPTER FIFTY-SIX

Stutter

Aurora burst into the motor pool and saw Rory lying down. He was reading on the worn couch in the corner, his feet up on the opposite armrest.

"Rory!"

The large man looked up in startled surprise, and tossed his book to the couch as he jumped up to embrace Aurora, swinging her around and squeezing her tight.

"I knew you were going to be alright! You've always been a smart one." His bristly beard tickled her neck and she pulled away to take a look at her old mentor.

"I've missed you so much! So how have you been?"

A dark shadow passed over Rory's face before he could turn away. "I can't really talk about it." He started to fidget with his fingers in a way she had never seen him do.

"Rory, what's wrong?" Aurora pressed.

"S-Something is rotten in the s-s-state of D-D-Denmark," he managed to stammer.

"What?"

"S-S-Strange things are afoot at the C-C-Circle-K," Rory,

was turning red, trying to get the words out, as if he had a life-long severe stutter.

"What is wrong with you?"

Rory braced himself on his knees, panting. Little by little, he pulled in ragged breaths as his airways began to open again.

"Are you okay?"

"That's a negative, Ghost Rider," Rory said with a little less struggle.

"Okay, weird. But I'll play along."

"I write the songs that make the young girls cry..." Rory sang, the stuttering becoming less pronounced.

"What?" Aurora looked at Rory in confusion as the burly man began to twitch his head like he was listening to a Haddaway song. His head bob was towards a messy desk. Invoices with oil stains on the edges littered the top of the desk.

Rifling through the papers, she saw no rhyme or reason. A small shelf with chipped blue paint drew her attention. Paper-back books with the spines cracked from multiple read-throughs were lined up there. Only one book was hardcover. A thin one, practically pristine, with a leather cover.

Sliding it out, she quickly found that it was a journal. As she opened it, Rory let out a relieved sigh, tension draining out of him like a deflating hot air balloon as he sagged back into his sofa.

She thought it odd that he wouldn't be concerned with someone reading his most private thoughts, but she skimmed to the last entry:

Things aren't right here. And it isn't just here. I was talking this morning with some of my buddies in my old squad. One is in Eurasia, and another in Australia. It's the same story there. Something is wrong with the leadership. What happened to Tempest has been happening all over the place. And we've all been too divided and distracted to do anything about it. Someone is behind the scenes, moving us all like pieces on a game board. Those who didn't step down voluntarily like Tempest have met with mysterious 'accidents,' if you get my drift. We've been led to have this constant rivalry with Orange and Green

Factions as if they were our real enemies. Bickering back and forth, while we ignored who is pulling the strings just off stage. I fear it may be too late. They are making everyone go through some reassessment. Mine is tomorrow. I don't know what kind of brainwashing is going on, but things are getting weird. Even the most vocal in their criticisms have suddenly turned taciturn and distant. It's so out of character.

I don't know what I am going to do. Travel has been restricted. There's been no transports to repair, and I'm going stir crazy with being cooped up in the shop. You never realize how much you get wanderlust until they say you can't go out. I've always been a homebody, but now I have this foreboding that I just need to get out.

There was another dated entry, but after that there were just scrawls and scribbles, as if a small child was trying to draw.

Aurora looked up at Rory. "Did they do something to you?"

Rory nodded woodenly, even that small gesture taking obvious effort.

"And now you can't talk about it…" She stopped to think. "Do we really need to get out? If so, how?"

"Roads? Where we're going, we don't need roads," he said in a grim voice.

"A transport, then. I thought they were limiting travel. You can get one? Of course you can get one. I need to get the others before they go through this processing." Aurora accessed a terminal nearby, looking through the directory. "Let's see where the rest of the Crew is… Yuki and Darik are in the C wing, Pulse and Anastasia are in the same area on the second floor. I can't tell where any of the others are, maybe they've already been processed? At least having most of the Crew in close together should make our job a little bit easier. I'm not seeing Seneschal or Pulse."

She widened the search and found Harmony and Grimdark in Admin, probably doing their debriefings.

I have to get to Tempest and let him know what's happening. Too many thoughts raced through her mind as she tried to come up with a plan on getting everyone out safely.

"You're my only hope," he said, laying one of his mammoth hands gently on her shoulder.

"Don't get your hopes up, we're not out of the fire yet."

———

"This is the part I hate the worst about being a super. Debriefing. Takes so long and it always feels like an interrogation," Harmony griped to Grimdark as they sat outside the soundproof office. Grimdark sat stiffly upright, his arms folded and eyes closed.

"We could have to write up our own reports, trust me—is worse." he replied matter-of-factly, keeping his eyes closed.

"At least this time I actually have something to report, and they make us wait out here like kids outside the principal's office. They need to know about hybrids in the Faction."

"So you will tattle?" He cracked an eye and peered at her.

"You mean you're not?!" Harmony folded her arms with a harumph. "Why is everyone protecting her? She's a hybrid, they need to know—"

"Unless we are reporting to someone who is a hidden hybrid? Neh?"

"Well… Wait, what? You think it goes that far?" Harmony bit her fingernail as she contemplated the implications.

"I joke. Partially. Something here is… *off*. Isolation… That is new. We have done nothing treasonous, so their motives confuse me."

"I've noticed that too, people have been keeping to themselves. It's creepy. What do you think is going on, if it's not hybrid infiltration?"

"I believe it is infiltration. Just not hybrids. Something even worse has—"

The door swung open and a burly man with slicked back hair looked out. His face marred by a perpetual scowl.

"Grimdark, you're up," he barked with a sharp motioning of his head to get in the office.

Grimdark calmly rose and stepped into the room, hearing the *hiss* and *click* as the door sealed behind him. Mr. Burly jabbed a thumb at the open doorway beyond and returned to his seat and picked up a newspaper he was reading.

Grimdark straightened his waistcoat, cracked his neck, and entered the office. Once again there was a *hiss* and *click* as the slender man behind the desk pushed a button and the door sealed behind him. He stared at Grimdark for a few seconds, assessing him, then waving towards one of the chairs in front of the desk. He steepled his fingers while continuing to evaluate Grimdark.

Grimdark stared back. These types never intimidated him, despite how they tried. He kept his expression impassive, waiting for the supervisor to speak first. With irritation, the man pushed up his wire frame glasses and cleared his throat.

"From what I hear from the other supers, your group has stumbled upon what appears to be an abandoned base?" He licked a fingertip and looked through some papers arranged in neatly staggered overlapping piles and slid one out of the ream. "Yes, this is it. From an old file, but still it would make a valuable addition to Purple Faction's resources."

"That is not correct."

The man's eyebrows lowered. "It is not valuable? I would have to disagree…"

"It is not abandoned. It has been claimed, and DNA-keyed to new owner."

"Yes. I had assumed as much." He set the paper down in front of him and laced his fingers together, resting them atop the report. "This is the main reason I have called you in today. I have enough from the other reports that I believe we have a good idea of what has happened in your absence, and we need to get all of our agents on the same page. You have missed the ceremony in your absence, I presume?" He pulled another report from a pile on the other side of his desk. "Yes. You're on the list. We'll need to take care of that before you go."

"Before I go where?"

"Why, back to the base to claim it for the Faction instead of whomever has taken it."

"But it already *belongs* to someone, who has—"

The interviewer blinked and shook his head sharply as he interrupted. "I would strongly urge you to reconsider."

"My answer is firm. The base is not ours to take."

"I would remind you that you are a member of Purple Faction, and that Faction interests take precedence over any personal friendships or alliances." The assessor shook his head with exaggerated disappointment.

"I will not do it. What do you want the manor for?"

"That is not your concern. But I can see that your lack of cooperation will require us to do this in a less *savory* way. Because of the insolence of supers like you, who want to make their personal agendas supersede the goals of the Faction, there have been some changes implemented. You will go through the ceremony and bind yourself to Purple Faction before you will be allowed to go out on any more missions. Your older brother has already gone through this process. It allows those in authority to impose certain… *sanctions* on those in their steward-ship. As long as they are compliant, they will have full use of their powers, but we need to tighten the reins. Too many supers have been running at cross-purposes to Faction interests, like this 'mission' Tempest dragged you all out on without Faction approval."

"Did he not request time—"

"Yes, yes," the man said abruptly, waving the comment away. "But this was a personal issue, and he used Faction resources to deal with it. My superiors and I are willing to let it slide this once, because it has provided the opportunity for the Faction to gain from the debacle, but that is the only thing preventing you and the others who accompanied you from censure and reprimand."

"That is not my concern. I have no obligation to help you."

"On the contrary. You no doubt have worked with whomever is in charge of the asset. Exploit this trust, and gain control of that facility. Then hand over those controls to me. Is that understood?"

"And if I refuse?"

"First, your brother will suffer. He will lose all access to his powers. Then you will undergo the ceremony, willingly or other-wise. Then your abilities will be restricted. If you persist in being obstinate, you will lose access to them altogether, among other punishments."

"Wait. You are taking our abilities?"

"No. We are ensuring that only those who are loyal to Purple Faction have use of their abilities. If you doubt your loyalty then, by all means, leave Purple and become Factionless. You will be considered an active threat against us, however. Not the wisest decision, given your current circumstances. Mmm? We can make life most *unpleasant* for your brother, and he cannot leave without our permission." A sickly smile spread upon his face as he gestured to the room.

"And if I do this, my brother—" Grimdark said through teeth he was starting to grind.

"…will be taken care of. Everything will be business as usual. You will see, this will be a good thing. It will increase the security we have within the Faction and the unity we all should express and enjoy. If we are all in agreement, then you can head to processing now."

The man pushed another button and a side door opened, and two orderlies stepped into the room and took positions on either side of the door. Their stature seemed more suited for a bouncer than a guide, but Grimdark followed them out of the room.

When the door finally clicked shut, the assessor made a couple of annotations and straightened the piles on his desk. When he was ready, he pressed another button, indicating he was ready to see the next super.

———

Harmony bit her nail to the quick as the man sprang the door open again as if he were attempting a jump scare.

"He's ready for ya," the man barked before retreating back into the room.

Harmony had been thinking about what she would say, and determined that if she felt any kind of deception from her commanding officer that she would wait until she could make an appointment with someone with more authority.

By the time she had the nerve to step inside, Mr. "Jump Scare" Burly was already reading his newspaper. She felt out to read him, but the only sensation she got from him was boredom, mingled with the aftereffects of a hangover.

Her ability had not spilled over into reading outright thoughts, but sensations, impressions, and physical statuses were readily apparent to her. The more she pressed, the more defined and distinct they became, and she could often tell what the root causes were that triggered the emotions. But it came at a cost—the target became much more aware of the surveillance. Finding nothing of note, she stepped into the office as the door opened.

"Please be seated," the lanky man said, not even looking at her as he read a memo.

Opening herself up, she noted that this was all affectation. The man was not reading the paper at all, but going through a well-choreographed routine he had done thousands of times. Not exactly the type of deception she was worried about, so she felt her nerves relax.

"You went with 'The Crew' on this mission to find Tempest's estranged wife, yes?" he asked with disinterest. This was also genuine, he seemed to have little real interest in what she had to say or report, which mildly offended her.

"I wouldn't say she was estranged, but she's been in a hospital—"

"Yes, yes. And now she is in *our* facility, taxing *our* resources. I'll have to see to that. I see that you haven't been on any missions for quite a while, with your limited skill set of... oh. I see." He turned and looked Harmony in the eyes. "Are you reading me, Miss Stettler?"

Harmony froze as his piercing glare fixed upon her, and she felt his mental defenses rise. Just before she was cut off, she felt a strong flash of a devious insincerity before his emotions melted away and she could detect no more.

"I take that as a yes?"

"No. I mean, not specifically, I kind of always have it on to detect threats," Harmony lied.

"And am I a threat?" His gaze intensified, causing her to squirm a little bit in her chair.

"N-no. I don't think so…" she hedged.

"Good." He broke eye contact and reviewed another paper, as if nothing had happened. "I see you still need to go through orientation, these men will accompany you there." He pushed a button and waved to his left as two enormous men stepped in, wearing white scrubs.

"Don't you want to hear my report?"

"Do you have anything vital you need to report?" Again with the hard stare.

"Not if you already have heard what the others have shared."

"As I expected. Carry on," he shooed her away like an annoying fly as he turned back to his work.

Harmony bit her lip as she walked toward the men. Grim-dark was right. *Something is* definitely *off.*

"Allow me, miss," the larger of the orderlies said as he gripped her upper arm with ice-cold hands. She could tell he thought he was being gallant, but his creep factor was off the charts, and she didn't need her abilities to tell her that.

Why do I need orientation? It's not like I'm a new recruit… she wondered as she was directed out the door, dread sinking into her core.

CHAPTER FIFTY-SEVEN

Zero Day

"What the *hell* are you going on about?" Tempest roared.

"Gwen Vannett is no longer a member of Purple Faction," Rampage said placidly, the sparkle in his eyes revealing his repressed mirth.

"Like hell she isn't! She never quit. She has gone through who knows what kinds of horrors in the time she's been gone."

"A leave of absence which, as I see here in my records, was *voluntary*. It has been fourteen years. I'm sure you can realize that Purple Faction cannot be responsible for everyone who has ever been a member if they chose to move on and do something else. From everything I can see in the file, the split was amicable, so we've been tolerant with allowing Ms. Vannett to stay in our hospital. She obviously requires more assistance than we are capable of managing here, would you agree with that?" The corpulent man leaned back in his chair and laced his fingers.

"She may just need some time to stabilize. I'm not sure what shock even moving her here could have done."

"That may be, but that is not our responsibility. I can give you referrals to nearby hospitals more suitable for your wife's care. I trust that two days would be sufficient to make arrangements?" He turned to shuffle through some papers on his desk.

"I can't believe what I'm hearing. You are telling me that someone who has served Purple Faction for over two decades is just going to be thrown out like last week's trash?"

"We are not throwing anyone out. If you still held your original position, then perhaps there could be some concessions made, but as things are…" He upturned his palms as if the decision was out of his hands.

Tempest brightened. "Well, that's easy then. My son has taken my place. I'm sure that he would be amenable to approving her continued stay—"

"Actually, he is why this is moving as quickly as it is. He agrees with the assessment that she needs to be moved somewhere else."

"That spoiled little… Where is he?"

"Mr. Cyclone is on assignment, and will not be available until he returns."

"How convenient. I'm assuming he will be gone for longer than two days?"

"That is correct."

Tempest clenched his fists so hard the nails bit into his palms, almost drawing blood despite his gloves. Using control honed over years of management, he finally extended his hand.

"Give me the damn list."

Rampage found the paper and slid the list across the desk, leaving it there for Tempest to pick up on his own and he turned back to his work, implying the matter was resolved. A passive-aggressive move that just made Tempest almost growl. He slapped the desk hard with his hand, startling the man's calm, and slowly slid it off the desk.

"Thank you," Tempest said with murder in his voice.

"You're quite welcome," came the reply. Not even using any effort to hide the smugness.

Tempest attempted to slam the door, but it had a hydraulic automatic door mechanism and the momentum was absorbed as the door closed soundlessly. This only irritated him all the more.

Probably had it put in since he has that effect on everyone.

Rampage had always been an arrogant ass who thought he was more indispensable than he really was. Now that the tables had turned, he was rubbing Tempest's nose in it. And putting Gwen's life in the balance for his pride! His jaw muscles rippled as he clenched in fury. There would be no bargaining with him, Tempest knew that.

Where would he take her? What if Mengele was involved behind the scenes of a hospital near him? No. He couldn't let that happen. Not ever. It couldn't be a place where he couldn't be by her side. Liberty General. It wasn't strictly for supers, so that boded well, as they probably relied on patient satisfaction rather than Faction subsidy. They would be more amenable to special considerations. On the bright side, Gus could finally visit his mother. So perhaps this sow's ear could be turned into a silk purse.

He would have to talk to BoJack. He shook his head wearily. It felt like all he did lately was ask for favors.

——————

Yuki dropped onto her bed and stared back at the door.

What was the big rush? We have to head back to headquarters like a bat out of hell and then just stay in our rooms? Stupid!

"Go back to your room and await instructions…" she said in a mocking high-pitched voice, mimicking her supervisor. They didn't even schedule her for a debrief.

They just think of me as IT, not as a real super. Yuki balled her fists.

Calm down. Clear your head. She took a deep breath and moved to her desk in the small room she stayed in at Purple Faction. Her rig took up most of the space and she checked her messages.

Don't do it… she told herself as she opened the first message from her father. As expected, it was a combination of passive-aggressive expressions of disappointment, mingled with invitations to come back and help the family. Same as always. Her father always had a way of wording things that made her almost question her own decisions.

How long was she going to stay here as a second-tier super, good for only getting someone's terminal to work? That was not why she had joined up with Purple Faction. After having experienced more in the past couple of weeks than in her previous years as a super, she knew she wouldn't be satisfied with going back to a 'desk job.' If only she could get some more experience and if someone would just give her a chance, she could show them what she could do.

Checking her terminal, she saw some of the typical commands she was able to use grayed out. *That's irritating.* A few minutes of rerouting later, she had reestablished her customary access. But someone had put blocks on the system, limiting access to certain searches and restricting what could be accessed across the board.

She couldn't tell where it originated, but it was high enough up to be put in place across all supers. A few more minutes of modifications ensured that her station would report to the powers that be that she was still on "limited access."

Now this was interesting. Was this from something internal, or an external source? Either way, it was a mystery to solve.

CHAPTER FIFTY-EIGHT

Alone Again (Naturally)

Was it stupid to go after Mengele alone? You betcha. But instead of feeling a burning desire for vengeance, he just felt like this guy had to be stopped. He had stopped moving and he was indeed in South Africa.

Hopefully his mother would recover, but from what he had seen in Hinansho, there was no way this should be allowed to go on. If he could take this guy out, then at least other families wouldn't be affected by this predator.

Following Aurora's tracker, he could pursue Mengele to whatever hole he was hiding in, up until he disappeared without a trace again. If Mengele made it to another sanctuary city, he knew the tracker wouldn't penetrate and he would be lost.

Gus figured that when he got there, he should be able to impersonate someone with his *Mimic* ability to get close to Mengele and end him. The whole plan sounded ludicrous, even to him. It was basically suicide. Throwing his life away for very little reward other than ridding the world of an evil mind.

But maybe that would be enough. He would finally have left a mark that would leave the world a better place than he had found it. If he could do that, then the powers he had been given weren't wasted. He just hoped he had time before he couldn't function and had a total mental breakdown.

Checking his FP, Gus found a small flying transport called a skip-jump and paid the FP price to unlock their use, upgrading its power supply to include solar converters. It was basically an enclosed one-man craft, and it would take almost seventeen hours to reach Mengele.

Gus stopped by the cafeteria to restock his gels with the intent of loading his dimensional pockets to the brim. Reaching into his pocket, he pulled out the ring he had taken from the super he had inadvertently killed just a little while ago. He had already forgotten about that incident, and that fact bothered him. *What am I becoming?*

Shaking his head and sighing, he took a closer look at the ring's details. It was fashioned to look like a skull, with rubies in the eye sockets. A little gruesome, but it captured his morbid curiosity as he turned it back and forth in his hands. *Why not?* It would be a good reminder of what could happen if he wasn't careful. He couldn't let himself forget so casually that actions have consequences.

Gus slid the ring on his finger and looked at it from different angles. The rubies caught a glint of light and pulsed for a moment. The ring felt perfectly sized. There was a brief pinch and a message popped up on his display.

XXX's Ring of Regeneration
By donning this artifact, you have bonded to it. This ring cannot be removed until your death.
Effects: Doubled health regeneration rate, bonded artifact.

Testing if he could remove it, Gus gave the ring a tug and yelped in pain. Taking a closer look, hairlike fibers extended from the inside of the band, embedding into his skin. Pulling harder, he felt them split the skin like tiny strips of razor-wire tugging on the bones underneath that they were anchored to.

Not just bones in his hand, but he even felt the strain in his forearm.

How far do these little root-like threads extend? Does it matter? He didn't intend on removing it, and faster health regeneration was always a good thing. With a little shame, Gus realized he had already forgotten the super's name. This would be a good indicator to center himself on what he was really trying to accomplish, and what he needed to avoid.

He changed into another uniform, leaving his regular clothes in his room. He checked his abilities and noted **Wreckord.**

Wreckord (Level 3): *Everyone marches to the beat of their own drum, but you use this to your advantage! When you songify your life in apropos ways, you will get a bonus to stats. Bonus depends on the aptness of your choice and stats relevant to the situation. Rock on!*
Note: Each song can only be used once for effect. Unlike most abilities, as you increase in your personal level, this ability loses its potency. Use this ability wisely.
For levels 20-30:
Multiplier Progression: Additive.
Cooldown: 24 hours.

Dang. That ability had really taken a drop in its boosting power. After he hit level 30, it was doubtful that it would even do much of anything. Gus created a playlist, including any song that he had ever liked that he hadn't used yet.

Go big or go home, right?

When he had finished, he couldn't think of any other excuses for waiting, so he climbed into the skip-jump, finding a way to position Jet to fit in the small space.

"Mponpeng Mine, here I come," Gus murmured as he engaged the autopilot. The ship lifted off the landing site almost silently, slowly rotating, then it shot off in a straight line. The panel to Gus' left polarized on its own to reduce the glare of the sun and Gus started his playlist. This time he hadn't really organized them into any rational order, just put everything in and hit shuffle.

You have created a song chain! Success with activities related to musical themes increased by factorial multiplier based on quantity of songs in series. Song chains have a cooldown of 24 hrs through host levels 20-30.
Crystalize by Lindsay Stirling. Song Chain Anchor.

Dubstep. No—*violin dubstep!* Always good to get him in a good mood, even though his friends razzed him about it. Time to kick some ass! As he sped off, the island faded to a blip on the horizon.

————

Prime stood outside the impressive house, looking up at the long walk to the front door. She wasn't going back to the Faction. Whether she wanted to or not, that aspect of her life was changed. But it took away the biggest obstacle to seeing her daughter again. With nothing to threaten her, they couldn't do anything to her anymore. She could begin to rebuild a normal connection with her daughter.

She rang the doorbell and it was answered shortly by an elderly gentleman, his lips permanently held in a frowning expression of disdain. "Oh, it's you…"

"Eldon, get Harlan or Elaine. I need to speak with them."

"Do you have an app—"

"GET. THEM. NOW," Prime said in a tone that brooked no argument. His eyes flashed wide and he scuttled back inside the house. She could hear a heated exchange occur inside, then Elaine's irritated voice:

"Fine! I'll deal with it. Like I always have to…"

Elaine threw the door open, obviously just waking up even though it was well past 10 AM.

Prime had never seen her without makeup before, and the woman definitely needed it. Her eyebrows were practically non-existent and her skin looked plastic and paper thin. Hair extensions were clearly visible in her thin, unkempt hair. Her eyes appeared excessively tiny and sunken as well, though they glared in irritation at seeing her nemesis there. Eldon must not have told her *who* was at the door, or she probably wouldn't have answered.

"According to our court-ordered agreement, I am here to exercise my parental visitation rights," Prime stated resolutely.

Elaine just opened her mouth like a fish out of water, exasperated until her shrill voice finally found its footing. "You think you can just come in here and take Madeline? No! You have to make arrangements. This is all highly irregular, and we can't disturb her schedule. You will have to come back another day when she is prepared—"

"Elaine, just stop." Prime raised her hand, her curved nails extending as she flexed her forearm. "You and I both know that you and Harlan have not kept your end of the bargain as it pertains to visitation rights."

"Maybe I need to make a phone call then, hmm?" Elaine said offhandedly, fishing out her Flik phone from her baggy pink robe. She fumbled to find it, then peered back at Prime in challenge.

That tactic had worked in the past, but no more. She was free! This woman couldn't hurt her anymore. She saw the crow's feet on the woman's face, and took in the wrinkles that appeared on her forehead as the threat fell flat.

"Don't think I won't call," she faltered, as Prime just waited and stared.

"Please do."

"You think I'm bluffing, don't you? Well, this is out of my hands now." She put the phone to her ear. "Yes, I'd like to speak with someone in management. I have to report something about someone working for you."

Prime just stood there, totally calm.

"Yes, the super working for you named Prime has been harboring a secret. She's really a hybrid and hides her identity."

Elaine stared back, pursing her lips. Eyes accusing Prime, *you made me do this!*

Still Prime stood there, unflappable.

"You really don't know anyone at Purple Faction, do you?" she said softly to Elaine who held out a finger, demanding she not be interrupted.

"Yes, I'll tell her," a smug smile plastered on her ugly face as she slid the phone back into her pocket.

"They're sending someone to detain you, so you had better get out of here—"

"Just stop."

"If you want to be taken into custody, that's your business," she turned and tried to retreat inside the door. Prime's hand shot out and kept the door open.

"One thing you may not know. See these cute pink ears? They have enhanced hearing, Elaine. I *know* you just pretended to make that call. You weren't talking to anyone. And to think all this time you were talking out of your ass." Prime shook her head in disbelief. "How much wasted time…"

"When Harlan hears about this…"

"That coward?" Prime's voice turned predatory. "Let him try. When I report how you two have obstructed me from having regular visits with my daughter, I'm sure they might rearrange the current arrangements to be more in my favor. Be my guest. I welcome any chance to sort out this… situation that you've both created."

"B-b-but you have virtual visitation rights anytime," she said weakly.

"Which you and Harlan limit or outright lie about when you say she's not available." Prime tapped an ear. "Remember, enhanced hearing. You think I couldn't hear Maddy asking in the background, 'Who's on the vid?' Any mother knows the sound of her child. Even in a crowd. Especially a mother who is being kept away from them." Prime leaned in close with feral intensity in her eyes. "And that stops now. From here on out, expect to see a lot more of me." She reached out a finger to push Elaine's chest but stopped just short, seeing the glint of her razor-sharp nail fully extended.

Elaine looked down her bulbous nose at the tip of her finger, eyes wide in alarm then squinting. "You think you can come to *my* house and threaten me?" Elaine leaned forward until the claws tip pushed into her skin, dimpling the over-freckled flesh there.

"Oh, it's not a threat. It's a promise. And if you doubt anything I can do, just ask Harlan, he'll let you know what I'm capable of. I'm not with Purple Faction anymore, so the choke collar is off, and you don't want to know what happens when you try to grab a tiger by the tail." She punctuated her last statement with a guttural growl that sounded fiercer than even she expected. The smile that stole across her face like a Cheshire Cat had its intended effect as the color drained from Elaine's face.

A sudden realization made Elaine's face gain a semblance of control. "You have to have an established residence. Can't have custody of a child without one. I don't know why you're not with Purple Faction anymore, but if you're not staying there, then I can't in good conscience let Maddy roam the streets. I'm sure you understand." She folded her arms, as if the argument was done.

"Oh, don't worry about my accommodations. I have a place better than this... hovel. Now if you will fetch Maddy, and tell her to pack her things, I will have her back to you in two weeks, *as per the agreement.*"

"That's not going to happen, *Prime*," Elaine retorted, spitting the words as if they were a foul-tasting poison.

Prime raised an eyebrow. "Then you are in breach. Expect to hear from my lawyers. Good day."

Gravel crunched underfoot as Prime did an about face and walked down the drive. Claws fully flexed as she tried to swallow down the pure rage she was feeling and keep it under control.

"And it's Sanura now, Prime is dead!" she called over her shoulder, not looking back.

Elaine began sputtering curses and threats behind her back but they couldn't touch her. She was finally free of this woman's influence. She had been lying about having a place, but maybe Gus would let her use the manor as a place of residence. They had bonded a little bit at the hospital, right?

He was a good kid, a little young and inexperienced, but he had a good heart. She hoped he would; Elaine was right, not having a suitable residence might throw her plans to reconnect with Maddy. She needed to talk to Gus. And a lawyer.

Gus hovered over the coordinates and slowly set down. This was definitely the place. He could see miners milling about on the ground.

The Oracle's voice echoed back to him. Seek earth, or something along those lines. He had done some research along the way and found out a bit about why Mengele might have chosen this spot. It turned out that this mine was deep. Deep enough to evade detection from satellite scans or probes with abilities. This mine generated a lot of things, but gold was its primary export. The enormous hole looked like a gigantic screw had been removed from the earth, a threadlike shelf spiraling inward.

Giant trucks were exiting the mine, carrying large loads of dirt probably meant for processing.

Gus saw workers finishing up for the day as twilight began to darken the sky.

He didn't know if they worked in shifts or just during the day, but there was a lull in the traffic as stars began to speckle the sky. The tracker led Gus to a nearby hanger installation and Mengele's ship was inside, with the door open and no apparent security. Beside it was a lift requiring a password to access. He activated **Electric Mind** and he found the password after sifting through some data.

While he began to feel more comfortable climate-wise, he

was punished with a couple turns of the vice as his headache leveled up into pre-migraine pain levels. He summoned the lift and there was the squeaky whine of chains as the machinery came to life.

After a long wait, the lift finally emerged. It was basically an open platform, loosely caged in. And it was immense inside. The bucket could have held four Humvees, and Gus's feet echoed on the metal floor as he walked in. He activated the lift and began the descent. The temperature began to increase as he descended, and he had to activate ***Energy Absorption*** as the temperature began to get hot enough to make him sweat. *How do people work in this heat?*

He would be glad when he could finally be free from pain. Not that fighting Mengele would make his headaches go away, but he figured that this would be more of a kamikaze run.

Getting the job done. One way or another.

CHAPTER FIFTY-NINE

Locked Up

"Thank you, BoJack," Tempest said as they loaded Gwen onto a gurney. BoJack looked haggard, obviously wrung out from using his powers so much to transfer Gwen to the Faction in the first place, only to have to do it once again. Tempest knew it took some of his own vitality to help others, but BoJack never complained. Still, he was more sullen than his usual chipper self, despite the weariness.

BoJack grunted in reply, turning to focus on Gwen. Liberty General was only thirty minutes away and Tempest had arranged transport. The hardest points were transitions. Beads of sweat sprang up on BoJack's forehead as Gwen was taken off machine assistance and he had to compensate, pouring MP into his abilities maintaining her vitals.

"Let's... go," BoJack choked out, obviously under severe strain, trying not to bite on the blue gels he had chipmunked in his cheeks until he needed them.

They had opted for a medical transport, but the skyways were unusually congested today. Wasn't that *always* how it was? Whenever you had to be somewhere in a hurry, that was when traffic was unreasonable, or you had someone in their 120's traveling at ten miles below the prescribed speed. Even when the vehicles flew their damn selves, some idiots still manually set the speed to slower than normal. It was maddening.

Tempest looked back at BoJack, who was beginning to struggle. Maintaining Gwen had probably taken more out of him than he had let on initially. Was this too big of an ask, too soon?

Come on! Just go, lady! Tempest raged as the transport in front of him hesitated to turn until the flow changed to cross traffic. He tapped his fingers in agitation on the steering yoke. He did not like this feeling that pervaded everything he did lately. Powerlessness. In such a short time frame, he had gone from successfully managing his entire life to everything spiraling out of control.

Hell. Who was he fooling? Things hadn't been in control since Gwen went away. His relationship with his sons, getting lost in work, and for what? They threw him out like trash, as well as manipulated his son against him. Things were still indeterminate with Gus. He thought they were getting better, but did he expect things to improve overnight?

He was torn. He needed to be there for Gwen, but Gus also needed his time. *Damn that Mengele!* Tempest wanted to make him pay, but that meant keeping Gus at the manor, away from his mother. And from him as well. Gus really had surprised him, and he wished he could take more credit for the man he was growing into. *Why had he trusted Mengele?* The thoughts and blame invaded Tempest's thoughts like an impatient child. *Well, obviously I didn't know who he was.* How could he?

He began to doubt everything Mengele had told him when he knew him as 'Dr. Weft.' As he reflected on that dark time, he could see the inconsistencies that he had failed to notice due to the pressure and urgency of the situation. There was no time to evaluate and plan before acting, something that was unlike anything in his typical life.

Were all those warnings about endorphins and keeping Gus from getting too many surges of positive emotions a load of garbage? His gut told him yes. He could see Mengele laughing to himself at all the suffering he had indirectly caused his family. Why? What possible benefit for making him suffer? It made no sense.

"How far are we? I'm slipping!" BoJack yelled from the back. Tempest put the transport on autopilot and entered the back of the ambulance-sized ship. BoJack's back was drenched with a deep V of sweat, his hair a ragged mop on his head, dripping to the transport floor. Tempest looked at his stats and saw he was dangerously close to bottoming out his MP.

Fumbling with his cloak, he opened a small compartment and reached inside. Three blue gels were inside, covered in a dusting of lint. He hated coconut, but maybe that was a good thing. He fed one to BoJack, his eyes calming somewhat at seeing the gel. Both his gnarled, twisted hands relaxed as the MP took a jump to around 30% full. They spread out, flexing as he held one onto Gwen's forehead and over her heart.

"Hoo. Thanks, man, we would have both been in bad shape with rebound effects if I don't keep this up."

Tempest tried his best to dust off another, but BoJack just shook his head, opening wide. BoJack chomped the remaining gels, swallowing the rubbery jacket without even chewing. He closed his eyes and inhaled with relief.

"Thanks, cuz, appreciate it." He took a few deep breaths to center himself, then opened his eyes and gave Tempest an appreciative look. "I think I've got it now."

Tempest nodded and walked back to the driver's seat and engaged manual piloting again. Seeing an opening, he passed a vehicle and narrowly made it through the next skyway before the flows changed. At last, things were starting to move.

———

Grimdark was pushed into a chair sitting in the middle of the room. A single light shined down, obscuring his ability to see outside the cone of light; it reminded him of being on stage. He could tell there were people seated in the shadows watching the process, murmuring quietly to themselves. One of the orderlies kept a heavy hand on his shoulder, a tacit reminder to stay put.

Did these fools have no idea of what he could do to them if he wanted?

"We have assembled here to oversee Grimdark's orientation. He has seen the benefits of the geas and has agreed to confirm his fealty to Purple Faction," an overly-theatrical voice intoned over the speaker.

Grimdark looked around but could only see the orderlies in his small circle of light.

"As his brother before him, he will submit willingly to the geas to add to our strength. Focusing our wills and intentions to become that much more powerful."

"The strong, the pure..." those hidden in the shadows chanted in response.

A large man with wine colored robes, a dark cowl hiding his face, stepped into the light and began to speak. He recited some words that sounded like some kind of liturgy and a prompt came up on Grimdark's display.

Do you accept? (Yes/No)

He almost chose 'No' but he saw his older brother, just at the edge of the light. Only his nose was lit by the cone, but it illuminated his features well enough. Pleading eyes begged Grimdark to do something. He had never seen his brother, the only man he looked up to, seem so... defeated. He had a couple days' facial hair and he looked more gaunt. His hollow eyes widened as they contemplated what Grimdark would do.

Comply or resist? What did his brother want?

He then saw the orderlies that were holding his brother up by the upper arms on both sides, his legs dangling, and he wasn't supporting himself at all.

"Choose," the large man croaked, the command amplified on speakers all around.

Grimdark made his choice.

CHAPTER SIXTY

Guys Like Me

"This is foolishness! If you know yourself but not the enemy, for every victory gained you will also suffer a defeat," Nick pleaded as Gus opened the door at the bottom of the lift, surprised to find it unlocked.

"I have to."

"Why, Gus, why?" Nick asked relentlessly.

Gus clenched his teeth in response. His mind was set. "Because, Nick. I have to do this—"

"As penance for making a mistake?"

"Make mistakes of ambition and not mistakes of sloth. Develop the strength to do bold things, not the strength to suffer."

Nick growled in frustration. "Think of what you're throwing away."

"See? Not so fun when someone else throws quotes in your face, is it? Besides, what am I throwing away? Besides myself. The manor? My opportunity? Things keep escalating, and they're spinning out of control. And that's the last place someone like me should be, out of control. It says it in my first ability. **Wreckless**. I wreck everything I come in contact with and I'm reckless. The worst of two possible worlds. Both destructive. I don't know what I would eventually turn into, but I can imagine if I continue on this path it could only get worse."

"You don't know that for sure. There are a lot of suppositions in that argument."

Gus ignored Nick and pressed on. "I don't think humans were supposed to get powers in the way I did. Without training and a real mentorship, slowly leveling as skills developed. I'm too lopsided and top-heavy. My powers are too strong to manage at this stage for someone with my maturity and skill. And so many of them bumping around that I haven't even mastered the rudiments of a fraction of them."

"So take a break and master them!"

"There's no time, Nick. You heard how elusive this guy is. If I can end him, think of what that'll do. I'm sure it will end more suffering by him being gone than anything I could ever accomplish if I worked the rest of my life. I don't even trust that I can stay in control anymore. I haven't really been doing a bang-up job so far since I've become a super. I haven't really done anything that's made the world a better place."

"You stopped those Dark Nth."

"I could have let the volcano take care of them. I think it was my greed in keeping the manor and my need to impress my father and friends that underlay all of those efforts."

"It doesn't change the fact that you did it, at great personal sacrifice. You realize that I can see those changes happening on the inside, don't you? You can lie to yourself, but you can't lie to me. You're afraid and embarrassed. But you don't have to be."

"I know you're trying to be encouraging, but I don't need a cheerleader now. The time for that is gone. I'll tell you what. If I survive this and beat Mengele, then I'll make whatever changes you suggest."

"No. You already agreed to that, remember? Why would I trust you now if you didn't keep that promise? You go off on others not keeping promises, and you do the same to yourself, which is why you doubt your decisions all of the time."

"You know what? You're absolutely right. And it proves my point. I'm unreliable. I don't deserve being on a team or in a family, because I'm a screw-up. I mess things up no matter how hard I try. I can't help it. And I'm so tired. It's so demoralizing to always be trudging uphill, fighting each step and having everything pull me down. I can't keep this up forever.

"I know myself. I quit too easily. At one time, I thought that I could hold out and keep working if one day things would pan out, but sometimes it is what it is. No matter how well I can imagine a Pollyanna future, life never turns out that way. Especially for guys like me."

"You managed to defeat Manticorps, and prevent that psycho from taking all those abilities and using them for who knows what nefarious purposes. He could have formed a super army and sowed discord and attacked the Factions and districts. Who knows what havoc the world would be facing now?"

"It's all the same. I used that situation to grab powers and abilities, thinking if I was just more powerful, then I could make a difference. I know better now. Power doesn't mean influence. There's a reason why some people can persuade others to do what they need to, and why I will always be someone who engenders doubt and has no one follow me. Because that's the way it *should* be.

"Think about it. What real benefit do people have in following me? I don't know what the hell I'm doing with just myself. I don't know why my hybrid-Nth have managed to stay with me throughout all the mistakes I've made. Probably holding on 'til they're close enough to move to another host. Either way, they're better off without me. So is my family, the Factions, and everyone else. I'm toxic."

"Giving up again. I'm disappointed."

"It's the opposite of giving up, Nick! It's going out with a bang and not a whimper. You even said so yourself, my mental situation is not improving, I probably don't have much time anyways. Am I right?"

Nick didn't reply, just grumbled.

"So it's settled. Now please don't distract me from making this last plan work, at least give me that."

"As you wish."

———

Gus opened the door at the bottom of the lift, surprised to find it unlocked.

Doesn't seem like a top secret villain lair... he thought as he activated **Phase Shift** and slipped inside. There was a camera pointed at the door, and while he wasn't visible, the movement of the door could have triggered something. He got into cover and switched over to **Camouflage,** taking in the surroundings.

Unlike the elevator, which appeared weathered and caked with dirt, this area was pristine, and resembled an upscale doctor's waiting room. The walls had vertical recesses with large lights that shone down, either on a plant, a sculpture, or some water feature. Besides the soothing trickle of water spilling nearby over a tiny rock wall, the place was silent.

Unsure of what to do next, Gus cycled through all of his perception filters, but nothing out of the ordinary was to be seen. That made him more edgy than an outright attack, but a glance at the slow but constant drain on his MP urged him to move along. He would transfer to **Phase Shift**, **Dash** to another place of cover, then switch over to **Camouflage** and wait for his MP to rebound. After encountering no resistance for half an hour, Gus was almost ready to relax when a voice came over the intercom:

"I tire of this. Meet me in conference room D when you are ready. And yes, I can see you clearly. No need to try to keep up your pathetic attempts at stealth." Gus froze and didn't move. "This isn't some ploy to flush you out, I see you crouched by that fern right there. To your right is a small modern sculpture next to the wall."

Gus looked and saw that he was accurate but still kept still. There was a weary sigh and the light immediately next to him began to turn on and off. A quick glance showed that it was the only one doing that.

Gus stood up in resignation as the lights began to flicker, indicating which direction he should go. He went through his plan again, and activated **Intermediate Shielding** to protect himself. Mengele could probably see everything he was doing, but he wouldn't make it easy for him. If he could detect him with **Camouflage** and **Phase Shift**, did he have some ability that revealed Nth to him? Would he know that Jet was more than just a weapon?

That voice. It really *was* the man from his dreams. Or memories? It was hard to distinguish which were real memories and what were vivid dreams his brain had made to process the situation. Thoughts kept intruding on his plans, half of them worrying about what he had gotten himself into, the other half trying to revise his attack strategy based on Mengele's abilities.

He had been counting on the element of surprise, but that was now blown out of the water. He was committed now though. He doubted that Mengele would just let him go. Better to face it head on. He had to resist massaging his temples as his head began to throb. *Can't show any weakness.*

With the tip of Jet's blade, he pushed in the door. At the head of a large conference table surrounded by chairs was Mengele, who was wearing a white Nehru jacket with gold trim. He tossed a tablet to the side and leaned back and looked at Gus.

"You know, I had to make sure that it was just you coming. I've come to expect all kinds of attacks from my enemies and those who disagree with my methods, but I will admit I am surprised you decided to come alone. I see leaving the crude transmitter you placed on my ship was the right choice. Not a wise choice for you, considering what has happened to your predecessors who attempted entry here. However, I tried to dissuade them—but they were persistent.

"You, on the other hand, provide a rare treat. You were one of my first projects, and I would very much like to see the results of my handiwork. Mostly to evaluate how robust the weave was, but also to see how I have improved in the interim. This, however, will not be pleasant for you, and I am sure you will resist, so let's get the formalities out of the way." Mengele stood and with a press of a button on his tablet, the chairs retreated to the walls while the table revolved into the floor, providing a large empty room. He set the tablet on the chair behind him and clasped his hands patiently in front of him.

"Anytime you are ready."

CHAPTER SIXTY-ONE

Rock Me Tonite

Here goes nothing!

Gus activated **Dash** and **Sweep the Leg**, trying to catch Mengele by surprise. With a barely perceptible twitch of a finger, Mengele's skin turned a speckled black, like polished basalt. His eyes shifted too, the color of molten gold. Jet sparked upon contact and Gus felt his attack rebound away, sending shock waves up his arm, making his hand tingle.

Mengele looked down at a slice in the leg of his pants and cocked his head as if to say, "Really?" Yet he did not move. He just stood there placidly, inviting Gus to take his best shot.

Gus launched into a flurry of attacks with Jet assisting. Each thrust and swing were countered almost lazily by Mengele. Often with only one hand, directing the blade away time and time again, barely using any body movement or effort. His transformation had made him immune to any type of slashing damage. On one rotation, the tip of his blade skated across the bridge of Mengele's nose. This elicited a slight wince. *A weakness?*

Before he could follow up with another attack, a casual

backhand crumbled Gus' shield and still retained enough force to launch him into the air. Jet flew out of his hand as Gus hurtled sideways too fast to stop his momentum with his own flight abilities. High-back chairs along the walls exploded, sending splinters of wood flying on impact. Despite his shield, the blow had taken over 30% of his total health.

He crouched and stared daggers back at Mengele.

Unperturbed, he pulled on his sleeves and returned to standing there with arms clasped loosely in front of him.

Gus let loose as large of a **Chi Pulse** as he could muster. Shimmering waves sped away from him, distorting the light as they collided with Mengele. There was a slight resonance, but it just washed over him like waves crashing on a rocky shore. Still, he stood there maddeningly calm.

Gus tried **Amber**, hoping it would slow him down. The only effect was that the resinous material adhered to his clothing. Mengele dug his fingers into the goop and with a tearing noise pulled off his clothes. It did not stick to him *at all*, and Mengele used the wadded-up ball of material to blot away any residual amber that remained. Thankfully, in this state, Mengele's nether bits were absent, more akin to a mannequin.

Panting, Gus looked at his situation in despair. This was not going even remotely like he had expected. His skin was just too tough. An idea came to mind. A quick glance at his remaining MP showed he would barely have enough. He activated **Hyper** and doubled his agility stat, then hit **Dash.**

Even with the increase in speed, Mengele's arm came in contact with Gus' hand as he blocked Gus' attack. There was not a lot of force behind this thrust though. As soon as they touched, Gus activated **Meld** and chose to match whatever substance Mengele's skin had become.

From the point of contact, inky blackness spread up Gus' arm to the shoulder. His arm immediately felt heavy, as if it were made of solid stone. Biting down, he punctured the two gels he had stored in his mouth, boosting his strength by ten points. Another quick jab and he caught Mengele in his eye with his fingertips, and they sunk into the golden orb.

Mengele caught Gus by the neck, raising him off the ground, just as it converted into stone as well. Holding Gus there two feet off the ground, he dabbed at his ruined eye, tasting the gold material there on a fingertip.

"That... was a mistake." Mengele went to the door, thrusting Gus into it, ripping it from the hinges. He stepped out into the hallway, still carrying Gus aloft. The transformation had stolen over Gus' whole body now. Unfortunately, while changed he still was using the last bits of his MP. He didn't need to breathe either, which was a plus as he was sure Mengele would have choked him out in no time. Gus' hands made scraping noises as they clawed against the arm holding it, unable to budge even a finger.

"It has been some time since someone has been able to harm me, even a little. But this ends now." Gus watched in horror as the golden splatter that was the remains of Mengele's eye began to pill up like mercury and then flow back to the socket. In less than a minute, the eye was whole again.

"You are surprised that I have healing abilities? I probably know more about human, super, and hybrid biology than the world's top ten experts' collective experience, knowledge, and skill. I am willing to go further than my colleagues and as a result, my research is in a totally different league. You know the adage cracking a few eggs and all, yes? Well, you will get a front row seat to my methods. And I will make a special effort to repay you in kind."

Two automatic doors slid open as Mengele neared them, revealing a large operating suite. The area was huge, and had large trays of instruments hermetically sealed in some kind of table. Violet light shined down, bathing the instruments in an eerie glow. They neared a metal wall and Mengele held Gus there, waiting.

The reason became apparent when Gus ran out of MP and reverted back to normal. While he did not tighten his grip on

Gus, his own body weight forced him to hold on tightly to prevent the pressure on his jaw. If it was not broken from that backhand, it was definitely fractured. Mengele punched some buttons on the wall, and a panel slid back, revealing crossed golden weapons, a sickle-like one and the other with what looked like a whip or cat-of-nine-tails.

Mengele reverently removed the sickle and turned it in his hands, rotating the tip of the curved blade scant millimeters from Gus' eyes. With lightning quick movements, he hooked Gus' outfit with the top of his scepter and sliced downward. With four deft strokes, he repeated the process on all of his limbs, leaving Gus naked and exposed. Kicking the remnants off to the corner, Mengele pressed Gus against a wall, securing him there as restraints grasped his arms, legs and chest.

Initially, Gus struggled against the bonds but found them as unyielding as Mengele's grip. The wall rotated, forming an operating table that hovered in the air. Cold metal was chill against his back and legs, and Mengele fastened a band around Gus' forehead, locking him down onto the slab.

Gus heard the hiss of the panel closing, unable to see what was happening around him. When Mengele reappeared, the sickle-thing was nowhere to be seen, thankfully.

"One thing that has always amused me is how they say how interrogation and torture never work. That the information is not reliable since people will say anything just to get out of pain. That may be true for regs, but for supers there are so many other avenues to explore. Among my other talents is an ability called **True Sight**. For a researcher, it is invaluable. I imagine that it has saved me decades of chasing after false hypotheses and faulty logic."

Gus tried to glare but it was difficult to keep the fear out of his eyes. He couldn't move his head at all! Just the harsh overhead lights and Mengele's looming dark figure over him. The back of his head began to ache with the tension of the headband pushing him into the hard metal, causing his headache to rise in intensity. He had a feeling these headaches were going to seem like minor irritations compared to what was coming.

"One side effect that I discovered, quite by accident though, was that I could also detect the truth when questioning my subjects. Even truths that they were hiding from themselves! You would be surprised how effectively this cuts through the Rashomon effect. Even supers are notoriously short-sighted, basing entirely too much of reality on feeble interpretations of the data. That's why everyone is wrong such a large majority of the time. From their limited perspective, they think they have the whole truth. Blind men each feeling a different part of the elephant."

Mengele took out a scalpel, examining its blade, cocking his head to one side before placing it back on the tray and continuing.

"I will admit it was frustrating at times having such a wide vision and being unable to share that with anyone else. So much explanation, trying to dumb things down so it could be understood. Then being greeted with constant doubt and uncertainty. That is why I prefer to work alone. My research has progressed much more quickly without wasting the time to train inferior minds. The freedom it gave made me wonder why I hadn't embraced independence much earlier."

Mengele turned and, with a deft movement, Gus felt something stab him in the forearm. The bore of the needle looked like a pencil lead—it was so big. Mengele folded over two more restraints that immobilized his arm even more as he connected the tubing to a milky white fluid-filled bag.

Gus saw it drip into a small chamber, then descended down the thin tube into his arm. At first, he thought it was some kind of anesthetic, as he felt an odd numbness as the cold liquid flowed into his veins.

"I suspect you share this type of independence, Gus, although in your case I would hazard to say it's very misguided. But it led to this collaboration. I realize it's not consensual on your part, but when hasn't humankind had to be dragged kicking and screaming into new eras? Everyone resists change so vehemently. Shameful."

Mengele walked toward the central light, and the table followed him, following some unseen command, positioning itself next to one of the illuminated trays.

Mengele fussed with arranging his instruments just so on the tray beside Gus, straightening them with a few light pushes and tweaks until they were perfectly aligned.

"There. I think we can begin now. Two things. I do not mind if you struggle, most people need to at first. There will be a fair amount of pain, and you will not be able to control your initial reactions. We have all the time in the world, so I will be patient with you. You see that IV? Your arm is secured enough that you will not be able to dislodge or disconnect it. Alarms would instantly notify me even if you did manage it somehow, directly to my display," Mengele tapped his temple. "And I am never far away. I love what I do, you see, so why distract myself with any other activities, especially as singular a one as you provide." Mengele picked up a large scalpel as a large grin spread on his face.

Gus thought he had learned what fear was from many of the things he had suffered on his path of becoming a super. He was about to learn that he had only seen the tip of the iceberg.

"Have you ever thought of what is happening to fuel your abilities? What do you call it, mana? MP? Psionic energy? They all are wrong. I find it interesting that practically no supers wonder what this mysterious material *is* and how it is used. They just accept it without question, like a door turning on its hinges. Giving no thought as to *why* it functions as it does.

"Not me. It is a matter of great interest to me and part of the reason you are not able to access your abilities right now. Without access to this mysterious MP, you are like an unloaded gun. Less even, because a gun could be used to bludgeon some-one. You are equal to a reg now."

Gus tried to bring up his display and found that he could

not. This struck him with more panic than being restrained. A wide grin stole over Mengele's stony features.

"How does that feel? To be powerless again? Back to square one. All that XP and those levels you fought for and nothing to show for it. Do you understand my interest now? Knowledge is power, and it gives me a superiority over any super who does not understand what it is and where it comes from. You are docile as a little lamb. Not that you were a match for me even when you had powers, but I think you understand the hopelessness of your current situation."

"What is happening to me? What happened to my display? Where is my MP?" Gus asked drunkenly, feeling cotton-mouthed and disoriented. He tried to struggle weakly against his bonds and even that was losing intensity as he slowly began to feel paralyzed.

"Oh no. I'm not going to reveal that information. It was hard-won and I'm not going to just tell you how it works. But just knowing the answer exists is like turning the screw, is it not? It makes the whole experience that much more delicious. For me, at least. I like to dangle it there, just out of reach, like a treat for a dog, or a key to an inmate's cell. So tantalizing and yet so elusive. I hope to finalize my findings with your help and then I can move on to the third component. It's poetic, your mother gave me the first key, and now you offer up the second on a silver platter! Once I understand and master that, I will not need my employer's help anymore, and I will truly ascend. The Nth want us to evolve, and I will be the first!

"I can tell you are getting fatigued, let me correct that," Mengele grabbed a syringe off the rack and poked it into the IV bag, emptying the contents.

Gus felt his heartbeat increase as the medicine entered his system. His eyes flitted back and forth as he began to sweat; his heart felt like an over-revved engine and felt like it would burst. *Thrum-ta-dum-thrum-ta-dum*!

"Oh, do calm down. It's just a little epinephrine, you're not having a panic attack. Or maybe you are? I just can't have you falling asleep. No, no. I've had subjects fall into comas and I could not rouse them once they were out. It's much easier for me if you stay awake. Plus a little sleep deprivation makes a subject so much more pliant for my needs. Are you ready to begin?"

CHAPTER SIXTY-TWO

Hertz Donut

Mengele was a lot of things, but a liar was not one of them.

He was meticulous in his studies, and his lab—though white and pristine—managed to be outfitted with modern-day equivalents to medieval torture devices. Gus was stretched like he was on the rack, feeling his bones pull out of their sockets. One time Mengele crushed his hand in his godlike grip, then leaned close to watch the restorative process, making notes on a virtual keyboard reminiscent of Yuki's. Upon comparing it to Gus' other hand, he noted the ring.

"And where did you get this little trophy?" Mengele stopped as he must have analyzed it, then slowly looked at a ring on his own stone finger. He looked up at the ceiling and muttered, "You will pay for that one, gamesman."

Mengele continued with his work, with even more severity, if that was possible. Long incisions were made and Gus heard the *pat-pat* of his blood pumping out and dripping onto the metal table. It collected in grooves and was collected in samples vials.

With all he did, Mengele had a sixth-sense of just how much psychological strain Gus could take before passing out. He would skirt the edge of it, and then pull back at the last second when Gus had almost succumbed to oblivion.

Then the injections. All colors of materials with huge needles that looked more like the types used to inflate basketballs than the thin, smaller ones for giving immunizations. While some of these carried some kind of healing infusion, they were almost the worst of all.

The infusion stimulated his Nth into a supercharged state, and they snapped into action to repair torn cartilage and re-affix muscle ripped off his bones. He saw bruises form on his naked body, then shift in unpleasant colors as they went from reds, to dark purples, turning a sickly green before fading into yellows and browns as if he were watching a time-lapse video.

The Nth must have been so busy repairing the extensive damage that they had no resources to mollify the pain, because wave after wave of the excruciating process repeated in different areas as the damage was managed.

In the brief moments when the intensity began to wane and Gus' breathing began to slow, Mengele would reappear and put Gus through a new battery of tests. Mengele seemed unaffected by Gus' screams and went about his work methodically and systematically. Each horror was worse than the next.

Mengele extracted tissue samples, first by cutting a large section from Gus' quadriceps muscles. And then he removed a wedge of bone afterward, with some tool that resembled a small jackhammer. Then there was the needle that extracted some of the fluid from his eye. He even winked with the eye Gus had temporarily damaged right before the needle went in.

Gus' desperate thoughts hoped for someone in the Crew to come in and rescue him, but after what felt like days, that brief hope guttered and went out. It was clear Mengele would keep him here as long as he served to satisfy his curiosity, although the grin on his face showed he enjoyed inflicting pain for its own sake.

When the tests began to take brain biopsies, Gus was on the verge of breaking mentally. A cranial drill removed small sections of his skull and samples were taken like core samples from the earth. The smell of burning hair and probably bone was sickening. The noise was deafening, amplified a thousand times as the drill buzzed against his skull.

After every injury, again came the injections and the Nth knit Gus back together again. Mercilessly healing their host according to their directives, despite their facilitation in the endless torture.

To cope, Gus reached out for Nick, but found the communication blocked and staticky. Something in those damn syringes created a disconnect between him and his powers as well as with his NIC. He wasn't sure which was occurring; he could sense them but not access them. Shapes behind an opaque glass, dimly seen. They obviously were working, since his body was being healed, but perhaps Mengele knew how to tax them to their fullest so they had no capacity for anything else besides keeping him alive.

Left to himself, Gus tried with limited success to erect walls to shield himself from the pain. He began to accept that he was all alone and that this was his new reality. The walls were the only thing that seemed to help to a limited degree.

Burrowing down into himself, he could escape a portion of the pain. It was by no means perfect, and often Mengele found ways to pluck him from his mental lair and drag him out into the searing sunlight of agony. But he scrabbled back in as soon as he was able, and the pain was less acute.

At some point, Mengele tried to ask some questions, but Gus was either too deep in his mental fortress or too exhausted to think straight. Mengele simply shrugged and continued his work, whistling distractedly. He never became perturbed with Gus' lack of response, flailing about when in pain, or any reaction Gus had to the tests. At times he just stood back and observed until Gus expended his energy, at which point he would approach again and continue.

Time became an unknown concept. Gus couldn't tell how long he had been here in the lab as each cycle seemed interminable. There were no windows or clocks, and nothing to indicate the passage of time.

Mengele did not seem to ever need to eat or sleep, he would just move out of sight until Gus had recovered and he would be there again. If he did rest or eat in those windows, Gus never knew or saw. He felt like he was always nearby though. There never was a gap between restoration and experimentation.

Gus longed to pass out, hoping that the loss of consciousness would trigger his *Leech* ability to overload and shock his system into death with all those latent absorbed powers. Why he had fought so long to avoid death had become a blurry concept at this stage. Death would be welcome. It would be rest. An end to struggle, an end to suffering.

Mengele was too good, though. He knew how far to push and when to let up, so there was no reprieve for the captive.

———

For a time, Gus huddled far in the corner of his prison of pain, his mind doing its best to shield him from what was happening. It gave him brief opportunities to think despite the pain. Not for long, as the intensity waxed and waned, interrupting his ability to focus on any one thing.

In those snatches of clarity he would have brief flashes of the life before. He perceived his life as that of a stranger, in a detached and impartial manner. Before he could get too involved, Mengele would do something that would pull him out of his refuge, immersing him in white-hot pain of yet another unexpected source, until he could retreat back to his mental cell, where he would look back at this life that seemed less his the more he observed it.

In parallel to his current existence, he saw that he had always been one who fled from pain. It almost seemed ridiculous as he observed the types of things that caused old Gus to flee to other types of cells of his own design in the past. Cells of different types, but all created and maintained by his old self.

From this vantage, he saw how ineffective they really were, and how he had chosen this isolation. Part of him felt he deserved his present self-incarceration for reacting in this way so often. Another part saw it as the natural consequence of not treating a disease; it festered and spread.

Yet another musing revealed most of his life was a manifestation of his failure to make anything of himself, and the need to hide from the shame he felt. Everyone could probably see the corruption deep within him as he could from outside of himself, whether they could articulate it or not, and avoided him.

This could be why he had always been underestimated, ignored, and written off. That he had been weighed and measured and found wanting. He expected this realization to be painful but in this small detached space, it just was. He had lived a small life by and large, almost always choosing the path of least resistance.

He didn't see himself always chasing pleasure, but he avoided pain like the plague, and it didn't take much of a threat to activate his flight response when he looked at his life as a whole. This realization did not come all at once, but interspersed over many cycles of suffering and reprieve. Somehow, though, it was an anchor. Something he could focus on to help him withstand when amid the bedlam and symphony of pain.

At some point in the cycles, Gus' mind fell to BoJack and Prime. The Oracle had said that he needed something from them. He was sure that he had missed the opportunity to take advantage of whatever keys they had to offer. But it was still something to focus on. A puzzle to unravel. A reason to withstand the void and not succumb to the darkness. Not quite a struggle or a resistance, but letting go of the reins he had so tightly grasped to steer away from every danger, perceived or real.

Both Prime and BoJack had been through suffering, of the type that far exceeded anything Gus had ever had to endure during his life before. Yet they were able to persist. He would have had no idea if he hadn't breached their privacy and looked within them with ***Telepathy***. As his mind brushed against this thought, there was a twinge deep within his core. This. This was important. He couldn't fully grasp why it was so, but he knew it and shifted his floating awareness on this concept.

Again, the tide of torture dragged him away and he had to come back, grabbing glances at this idea whenever he could before he was taken again.

An indeterminate time later, he had enough clarity to return to his line of thought. *How did they do that? How did they deal with their pain and suffering without wearing it on their sleeves, inviting the sympathy and consolation of others?* He found that he could access their memories as if they were his own, at least the ones he had already viewed. He felt the despair and heartbreak.

How had he not noticed that before? Gus could not remember feeling the emotions on his first viewing of the scene. But they were there. They felt everything, but managed to stay stoic. His first inclination was to believe they were just stronger and he was weak, but as he revisited their memories again and again, he saw that this was definitely not so. Doubt, insecurity, and uncertainty were all there, in equal or greater measures to his own. Yet they overcame. How?

After a particularly brutal cycle where Mengele had burned Gus' skin just to the edge of destroying the nerve endings, leaving them barely able to transmit pain signals—but only just —Gus retreated to his mind vault with more desperation than usual. This time he experienced a memory of BoJack where he helped the small girl. He hadn't realized this memory was in there, but recalled BoJack mentioning it while they were in the forest together after the crash.

Despair and darkness flowed through BoJack during this time of tragedy in his life, and helping the small child was almost an afterthought. An action taken on autopilot due to his training. But it made a difference.

For once in the bleak wasteland of fate, something had happened that defied the ever-present entropy of pain and breakdown. Like a light in an engulfing darkness, BoJack had found something to change his perspective. He was still encircled by darkness, but he could see a step in front of him.

With that awareness came a hope, an expectation that he could find his way out of the labyrinth. Step. As he continued to hold the light aloft, he could barely see the path ahead. He had no idea if he was going in the right direction, but it was movement. Towards... something.

What if the light could be bigger? How would that change things? From there, the memory faded, but it struck Gus. He had always been so focused on improving himself. Attempting to make himself worthy of the company of others. That his need for isolation was to dampen the insecurity he felt from bringing others down by his presence.

Deep down though, the rationale was always a bit selfish. To protect himself. BoJack had not found his light until he had put himself out there for another. Not for a reward or recognition, but for someone who could do nothing to repay him in any way, shape, or form.

He had made the world better than he found it. Because it was the right thing to do, and that act withstood the insurmountable forces that just seemed to grind everything to dust and drain the energy out of every particle until there was just a great sea of nothingness.

In some insane way, Gus felt a similar fire start to kindle within himself. He almost immediately dismissed it, having long ago accepted that nothing he could do would allow him to escape Mengele's control. Still, there was something that ignited his own hope. Irrational and strange, but undeniable all the same.

Thinking of both Prime and BoJack, he became bolder in his resolution. As the idea coalesced in his mind, his awareness expanded, almost imperceptibly. What if he could help them both, somehow, after this was over? Help Prime resolve her troubles and reunite with her daughter. The darkness seemed to roil around Gus, attempting to discourage the foolish thought, but Gus held onto it as the storm whipped him like a banner in a tempest.

Tempest. Thoughts crashed back into his awareness of his family. The haunted, broken look of his father after they had found his mother. The change that had happened with Cyclone. No, Alan. Wow, when was the last time he called his brother by his real name? He had found that he had subconsciously switched after he had gotten his powers. That with the change, he was no longer his brother; he was so much more. And the unspoken attitude that Gus wasn't worthy to warrant his attention anymore. Not to mention figuring out a way to help his mother.

As he looked at everyone who needed help, he realized that this couldn't be the end. Not if he could help it. For the longest time, he had seen the demands of others on his time as a constant drain. As if he were a bank account and everyone kept making withdrawals without putting anything back in to replenish what they had taken. It made him feel used and taken advantage of, and angry at the imposition.

Now, he saw it with a different perspective. That it was really Gus himself that had been taking from others his entire life and hoarding everything. Doling out his time and commitment sparingly, keeping the best for himself. Choosing not to see the sacrifices and contributions of others in the same light as his own. Overvaluing his portions and diminishing theirs because it wasn't what he had expected or wanted. A transactional way of looking at every interaction, and that he was getting a bad deal.

He knew full well the fruits of cultivating this viewpoint, and how it played a huge part in his own sense of self-value and worth. Plans and commitments began to solidify in his mind, only to be shattered by another session with Mengele. Each time they solidified a bit more. Promises and dreams remembered. Refined. Stripping away those things that were more for his benefit than others.

And somehow it helped.

That there was some very small chance that somehow

things would work out. Absurd as it was, an odd sense of peace sat like a speck of sand inside an oyster. He clustered his awareness around this hope, and it warmed him when he would return from the blizzard of pain that Mengele would inflict, hour after hour.

CHAPTER SIXTY-THREE

You'll Miss Me When I'm Not Around

Sanura let the holo-vid ring three times before answering.

"You have recordings, don't you?" the man said in a blur.

"Well, good morning to you too, Harlan. And if you must know, yes, I do." Sanura calmly rolled some tops into bundles and tucked them in a duffel, feigning disinterest.

"See? I told you, dammit!" she heard him hiss offscreen.

"Hit mute, you idiot, she can hear!" Elaine hissed back out of sight of the holo-vid.

Sanura smiled; it didn't matter if they hit mute or not. But it would be entertaining to see what they would say when they thought they weren't being monitored.

"I didn't think she had a place here," Elaine said in exasperation.

"She has hidey holes all over. It's debatable if they would pass a home inspection if things came down to it, but I'm sure she could arrange something quick if she needed to. Remember what we discussed, okay?" He leaned back into the frame.

Such amateurs. Why wouldn't they discuss their plan before contacting me? Sanura just shook her head as she packed some more clothes in a bag. She had oriented her holo-vid to just show her bed and the wall. It wouldn't reveal exactly how spartan and small the space was. These two idiots didn't need to know that. While she did maintain a variety of safe-houses, she didn't have any in this city. Until an hour ago. She knew this call would come, so she got situated and set the stage.

"I just talked with my lawyers, and I think they brought up some good points," Harlan began, voice tentative.

"Oh?"

"Erm, yes. He mentioned that you would be unlikely to seek legal action given the climate here for hybrids. It's different from the last time we went to court. He doesn't think you'd take that risk."

"I'm willing to take my chances." It was hard to repress the smile. Harlan and Elaine hadn't contacted anyone. She had accosted him when he arrived home and shared in hysterical details about a visit from "your crazy ex" and how she "feared for her life." They had brainstormed for a bit then finally called after Elaine's insistent urging.

A sideways peek showed Harlan looking to the side for direction, his hands and shrug telegraphing his confusion at whatever Elaine was pantomiming off screen. Sanura let him hang there for a minute before driving in another nail. She began rolling socks together, sliding them into shoes which also went into the duffel.

"Harlan, after this call I want you to take a good look at your neck. If you look closely, you will see eight tiny scars that just happen to be along your jugular. You probably thought you got them while you were shaving. But I want you to look closely at how parallel and close together they are spaced. Do you know how difficult it is to cut someone's skin just deep enough to not make it bleed? Just deep enough that when you put some pressure on it to shave, it would tear through, giving you the impression it was just a shaving accident?

"That's one of the benefits of a monomolecular blade in the hands of someone with exceptional skill. I have shown remarkable restraint up to this point. But this is a message. Like a foolish cat, you have used up eight of your lives. Only one is left. How will you use it? Making the best of it, or by further provoking me?" She put a slender finger by her cheek as she looked upward as if pondering the universe. Then she turned and gazed directly at the camera, leaning in close.

"I have nothing left to lose. You already keep Maddy away from me, so if I don't get to see her as I should, then what is keeping me from making that ninth cut just *a bit deeper*, I wonder?" Sanura looked at her nails distractedly. "I would guess that there's nothing at all…"

"We've got her!" Elaine's voice exulted. "I told you we should record everything. See? Two can play that game."

Sanura just smiled. And waited.

"I don't think we can agree to that, Sanura," Harlan said officiously.

"Oh, is that so?"

"Yes, Elaine and I have been discussing it, and I don't think that it is really safe for Maddy to be with you, seeing as you've threatened us. We've got it all recorded. So I think that a Magistrate would side with us restricting your access as you've demonstrated murderous intent. Wouldn't you agree?"

"No, I would not."

"Well, too bad! You lost!" Elaine's disembodied head popped in from the side. "We have evidence of you threatening us and I can see those tiny scars, so that's proof we can use against you."

"Is it, now?"

Elaine furrowed her eyebrows, catching on that if Sanura wasn't upset that something else was happening.

"What aren't you telling me…?"

"Do you really think that someone who could infiltrate your house and do what I've done to you would only do that? Do you realize the restraint I have had to use to not use my considerable skills to make you both disappear and make it look like an accident? I came close so many times. Eight in fact. Be thankful that I have as much control over my temper as I do over a blade."

The pair turned and looked at each other; Harlan's Adam's apple bobbed as he gulped. He absently touched his neck in a daze.

"Has it been so long that you really remember that little about me? Or did you never take the time to learn it in the first place? Did I ever forget a detail? A date, anniversary, or birthday? Never. I may be a lot of things, but sloppy isn't one of them. The thought that I wouldn't have put things in place so that my daughter would be safe is almost insulting. I couldn't very well leave her in your incompetent hands.

"For someone with a 'smart house,' you aren't so smart. Why don't you try to access your recordings? Let's see what they've captured over the last couple of years…"

Harlan's face fell open in horror as Sanura pushed a button and on their computer a video began to play.

"Who is *that woman*, Harlan?!" she heard Elaine screech.

"I can tell that you two have some things to discuss. I will be picking up Maddy next week, on Monday. That gives you three days to get things arranged. We can see how things turn out. Cooperation or mutually-assured destruction. I look forward to seeing what you choose. But if you think that video is good, I've got some real zingers. You know what I mean, *right, Elaine*?"

Her tirade cut off as she turned her vitriol on Sanura.

"Oh, you bitch—"

"Ah ah ah." Sanura waved a reproving finger. "Bitches are dogs; *I* am a Grimalkin, or at least a Molly."

Sanura cut the connection before Elaine could reply. She did think she would save the screenshot of her expression though. Priceless. Now just a few more preparations and she could take Maddy and start being the mother she always wanted to be.

She received an alert to her comms on display and was shocked to see a message from Gus. Perfect. That was exactly who she needed to talk to next. She opened the time-dated delivery and saw it was carbon-copied to the rest of the Crew.

To The Crew and whom it may concern,

If you're reading this, then it probably doesn't bode well for me. I realize that most of you have been tolerating me because of my father, and I appreciate that. Thank you all for coming to help find my mother and bring her back to our family.

A lot of things have become clear to me in the past weeks, and I have realized some hard truths that I need to deal with on my own. I don't want to drag anyone else into my drama anymore, so I'm going after Mengele. I know a lot of you, if not all, think that this is the stupidest thing that I could do. And you're probably right. But there are some things going on with me that may make it so that I don't have that much time to live anyways, so I might as well do something productive—or at least try.

I know you guys wanted me to wait for you, but in the time I was back at 'home,' it was apparent that everyone had their own lives apart from my problems. It would haunt me forever if I were to let Mengele get away and not even make an attempt to stop him. At least I can slow him down or put a dent in his operation.

If you put this code into the manor control panel, it should give all of the Crew access to and shared rights at the manor. Since Aurora has been there the longest, I'm giving her the highest access and she will be the 'Master of the Manor' while I'm gone. I would have given that role to my father, but I don't know what condition he is in. I think seeing Mom like that broke something fundamental in him, and I'm not sure if he'll recover without her. I doubt he would want to leave her side, either. If you're reading this, take care of yourself, Dad, and Mom too.

So possibly this is my final goodbye. I want to say that I'm sorry to anyone I've offended. Especially you, BoJack. I shouldn't have been so obsessed with getting more powerful and losing sight of how powers should really be used. Look on this trip as my penance. You always said that true happiness comes from doing things for others, so this is my offering. I feel like all I do is be a burden or hurt people, so it's time to change that.

I have your tracker, Aurora, and I've set it to broadcast upon my death. That way you'll know that I'm finally gone. Do not try to come save me. That's why I've made this change to the tracker. If I'm dead, there's no reason to mount a foolish rescue mission and possibly get someone else hurt. I'm done having other people bend over backward to pull my fat from the fire. Be safe. Have a good life, and enjoy the manor. I love you guys!

Gus

Sanura buried her face in her hands.

Dammit, Gus, what have you done?

CHAPTER SIXTY-FOUR

Experiment on Me

Mengele Research Results:
Subject: Gus Vannett.
Classification: O-9999
Age: 27 years old.

It is good to get back to my old routine of uninterrupted research. Returning to the regimen of polyphasic sleep has invigorated my mind and made me feel much more like myself again, in addition to allowing more productivity in the process.

Initial Findings
Subject is quite resilient, withstanding many tests that would kill a human without Nth. I have progressively increased the intensity, and subject has shown remarkable adaptability in healing and recovery. Typically, I have to allow extensive periods for healing, but with this one, my calculations show healing at 47% above average baseline rates among supers. I attribute this to his mysterious procurement of my brother's ring. That artifact came at great price and I know that it was not an accident that it found its way into the subject's hands. I

will have to speak with other members of the pantheon and determine who is to blame, though I'm confident I already know.

Gel electrophoresis has revealed unusual elevations of DNA synthesis. Subject has significantly elevated RNA and DNA; 52% above an actively leveling super's standard reference ranges. It is indeterminate whether this is a result of rapid leveling or due to an unfolding event. More analysis is needed. Prostaglandins are excessively elevated, even before the subject was stressed from various procedures. Only trace amounts of serotonin and dopamine detected. Multiple neurotransmitter receptors are bound irreversibly with altered proteins, reducing signaling efficiency. Warrants further study.

Fractal Effects
Inspecting my previous work, I have been impressed at the persistence of the folds, despite a lack of maintenance. Checking my previous notes, there were ten iterations that had to be inverted upon themselves. Currently, the subject appears to have activated the first two of these without incident. I wish I had control data to see the changes in total mass and tissue types and volumes as he transitions from one iteration to the next. I am eager to investigate the effects of folding but this subject has provided an opportunity at an ideal time to finish a project that my employer has been pressing me to finish.

The suppression device appears to be functional and I have accessed and downloaded data. It will take at least two days for it to be unpacked and processed. I had to write a new protocol to format data to the newest update. This should provide additional information on all stat changes and skill sets, and transmit remotely. Removal of suppression will still result in catastrophic cellular untangling. Still uncertain if I wish to examine this phenomenon or if the subject would be better retained to evaluate long term effects of fractal folding on macromolecular signaling as well as tissue stability after a prolonged folding event.

If it were not for the information he dangles in front of me like the proverbial carrot, I would break from my employer now. I hate being subservient to any man. Ah, the curse of curiosity. It is the only set of fetters that I think will work on me at this stage. Were I not so close to multiple breakthroughs, I doubt I could remain the subservient pet. But what acolyte would I be if I could not eventually surpass the master? All in time.

Suppression Drugs

The suppression drugs are working as formulated. Inhibition of Ka ensures that there is nothing to power abilities and breaking communication between Nth and host further aids in separating access to any form of retaliation though abilities. I have found that a suspension of Brooksian particles exhibits enough of a resonance that, when interspersed in the blood, it breaks host-to-Nth communication. The only caveat being that the body filters these particles out quite quickly, with a half-life of only 28 minutes. Constant replenishment via intravenous feed is required at this stage to maintain the effect. More work is needed to improve substantivity to sustain results.

Overall, I am quite proud of my formulation, and its efficacy has exceeded my initial forecasts. Currently, optimal results are available only through intravenous introduction of the drugs into the test subject. It is my hope that further development will allow for a more passive absorption protocol. While still in its initial phases, plans to create an aerosol form would be useful in phase 3.

Samples and Nth Isolation

I have been able to take samples and catalog all major organ systems for further evaluation. It is possible there is something in the subject's genome that makes him more resilient or easier to sync with the Nth. Unlike other supers, I have not been able to isolate individual Nth. Typically, when removing a sample of significant size, there will be Nth embedded in the sample. Removal and isolation from the host will stimulate the Nth to revert to a pluripotent stage. These can then be manipulated and used for other purposes, while still maintaining their current "generation." This process has not been improved upon since my father developed the technique.

Another complication arises in this subject: the existing Nth abandon the sample and revert to the host. They repopulate the replacement granulation tissue and eventually resume their normal operation and function when the wound site heals. Attempts to amputate limbs are met with significant resistance. Nth build up on the surface of the affected tissue and form a lattice that actively resists and retaliates, dulling and removing teeth on saw blades. It is an effect I have never observed until now. Attempts to amputate multiple limbs were similarly unsuccessful, with subsequent attempts losing more efficacy as the Nth fought back with increased skill and vigor. Very curious.

Currently, I have not been able to isolate one single Nth for study. I will have to temper my curiosity until I reap the full benefits of examining the subject. But this behavior warrants considerable study and follow up.

Meridians

Foundation node is entirely occluded, no circulation detected. I suspect Mandrite poisoning. Remaining centers are stagnant as well; they show up as dark and necrotic. I have not seen this level of corruption or even that it could occur to this extent. Even those ignorant of the intricacies of Ka have a passive flow that correlates to Intelligence stat levels. After initial tests and tissue collection, I will attempt to extract this and see if a portion of this Mandrite essence can be refined and recalibrated for transfer.

Subject has revealed no knowledge of managing flows after interrogation, which was to be expected.

Studying the physical effects of this stenosis and how it manifests in the body is a matter of interest. How does one affect the other? Can one suffer a Ka stroke with insufficient flows? All of it is new territory. This subject alone may be insufficient to understand the phenomenon, so I will have to get creative with some of the samples I have procured to this point.

Timeline
I expect to be finished with preliminary research results in approximately two more days. Then I will allow myself two days to investigate the issue with meridians in more depth. Depending on what I am able to discover and what samples reveal, I will determine if a complete unravelling event would be warranted to isolate these unique Nth as the body degrades. I hesitate because these unique effects possibly will not be reproduced in a cloned sample. Much too many possible variables at this time.

CHAPTER SIXTY-FIVE

Sugar, We're Goin Down

Yuki had to relax and wiggle her jaw. She had been taking out her frustration on a couple pieces of gum and the effort had made it start to cramp. She looked up at the room and noticed that it was dark. She could barely see that it was almost 3 AM on her Otaku clock on the wall in the blue glow emanating from her monitor.

Despite many different approaches, she was prevented from accessing certain logs and administrative communications. Like most corporations, Purple Faction employed artificial intelligence to protect its core data. Unlike most, it was a Tier IV, the highest ranked class of protection. Knowing her father, he had probably designed this particular one to be impressive. His ego would allow nothing less. Especially since he would feel the need to compensate for any weaknesses that Yuki could possibly demonstrate.

Damn, though. Yuki could not get what she needed without an outright confrontation against the AI and she had never battled a Tier IV, even in simulation; those had come out after she had joined Purple. If her father held to tradition, which he most assuredly did, Tier IV was an order of magnitude more powerful than anything she had ever fought in Tier III.

On top of that fact was that if she failed, the feedback would incapacitate her, and she would be at the mercy of whatever weirdness was going on here. She had been out for three days when she had lost a battle while still working simulations for her father's company. Even an attempt would almost certainly get her kicked out of Purple Faction for treason, as well as blacklisting her from joining either Green or Orange.

She leaned back in her chair and stretched her arms wide. Satisfying yet disturbing bone popping sounds as her back extended.

"Posture, Yuki, a young woman should have *poise*," her mother's words echoed back to her. Whatever happened, she couldn't go back. The constant correction and pruning like she was a bonsai tree, just to keep her small and in their prescribed form. She doubted they would ever see her as an independent person, and not one of their crafted creations. Every action orchestrated for maximum influence and public perception.

She rubbed her bloodshot, dry eyes and sighed deeply. Her head fell forward as she tried to resolve what she needed to do. She had always played it safe in the past. And what had that gotten her? Nothing that she wanted. It was probably why no one noticed her. She was content to stay in the background. Being the good girl, never making waves. Compliant. *Poised*. Demure.

That wasn't what she wanted, nor how she saw herself. While Purple Faction was a good step in the right direction of regaining her independence and sense of self, would it be enough to get her where she ultimately wanted to go? She had been here six years, and had not been promoted or even groomed for any type of advancement. Something had to change. But perhaps her natural invisibility to notice could be used to her advantage.

Ideas began to bloom as she planned.

———

Harmony felt the wave of conflicted negative emotions wash out from even this distance. Grimdark was in trouble. She looked up at the two slabs of man-meat that stood on either side of her, their folded arms accentuating their impressive physiques. She had to compose herself, make her face sweet and impassive despite the emotional equivalent of a nails-on-a-chalkboard constant mental screech that made her want to wince.

"They rushed me in here before I could freshen up. I need to use the bathroom—"

"Sit tight. It won't be long," the other orderly growled, still looking straight ahead, as if the door would open faster if he didn't stop staring at it.

"No, you don't understand. I had a *lot* of coffee this morning, and it's not going to be pretty. I would have said something earlier…"

"Just go." Thing One pointed a finger accusingly at an unmarked door.

"Thanks," she said as she tiptoed over and sealed herself inside. She had never been to this section of the building and the layout was totally foreign. She had hoped for an outside window or some other exit she could use, but no such luck. This was your basic single-toilet and sink bathroom. It apparently didn't get much use, or was only used by higher-ups, because it looked exceptionally clean and unused. Another mental shriek that reached a deafening peak and then sudden silence.

She realized she had fallen to her knees as she shook her head to clear it. There was a residual ringing that had nothing to do with physical sound. And Grimdark was… gone. Like he had submerged underwater, masked from her connection and familiarity.

When she worked with someone, she could tune in to their mental "flavor." Everyone had a distinct imprint that suggested a color tone, smell, or taste and shape. Grimdark's was all hard angles and points, in a deep wine-colored purple. But now, she could not distinguish him. She could tell he was still there, but there was a sea of distortion hiding him under the surface.

Bam *bam*! "Hey, you wrapping it up in there?" a gruff voice barked as he hit the door.

She actually saw the door rattle in the frame from the force of the knock. Irritation radiated like waves of heat from behind the door. She knew her usual feminine wiles would do nothing to influence either of these guys.

"Can I get some privacy?!" she yelled back, frustrated at the lack of options. Time was running out. She looked around frantically, but there was nothing. There was a small fan in the ceiling, but the air vent behind appeared too small for her hips. There was a smoke detector, but she had nothing to make any type of fire. None of her abilities had physical effects either, so she couldn't generate anything with a skill.

"They're ready for you! Pinch it off and get out here! You can finish your business later." Now the other guy had joined the first and they kept banging on the door insistently, making it hard to think.

"That's not helping! Banging won't make this go any faster!"

They stopped hitting the door and she heard some grumbling as they complained to each other. These weren't paragons of patience, and in no time, they were going to break the door down and drag her out.

———

"All internal comms are blocked. We'll have to contact everyone individually. Probably for the best; I imagine they'd be monitoring anyone on the system anyway. Rory, do you have any restrictions on things you can do with whatever they did to you?"

"Get busy living, or get busy dying," he replied with a shrug.

"Okay. Let's try this. Can you act like you're escorting me to processing or orientation?"

He grabbed her arm. "Let's go," he said with a pent up breath.

Whatever compulsion was upon him would not allow him to work against the Faction, at least not directly. Not even something negative could be uttered. Could they get creative and use that to their advantage? Use a misdirect or half-truth to circumvent its effect, and Rory would be trusted implicitly because of his agreement with the Faction?

They went over certain dialogues, finding out what worked and what didn't. When they had their routine down, they proceeded out to C wing to get the others.

The facility appeared abandoned, the usual traffic of supers moving from building to building conspicuously absent. It didn't take long for a super to trot up to them. "Hey, where do you two think you're going? Aren't you supposed to be inside awaiting processing, or at the ceremony?"

CHAPTER SIXTY-SIX

What a Letdown

"We are heading to wing C to gather some recently returned individuals and take them to the ceremony—" Rory started to say.

"Wing C? They're on lockdown, no one in or out." The super's eyes narrowed and his hand slid down the trigger of his suppression rifle. Aurora gulped and looked up to Rory. Those were new technology that were like tasers on steroids. They could incapacitate any super for a short time, but only had five charges. Still enough to deal with the both of them easily.

"I get that you're following your orders. That's all I was doing as well. General Parabellum wants this one and the others that just returned to be processed as soon as possible. I don't know who you get your orders from..." Rory paused for effect, sweeping his eyes around the abandoned compound. "But you don't look like you have that much to do. It's all the same to me, as long as it gets done." He pushed Aurora towards the super and she stumbled into his arms and he fumbled to catch her.

"I'll let him know that you're handling things from here on out. You should check in with him." Rory turned back to the maintenance bay and waved over his shoulder. "Thanks, buddy."

"Now wait just one minute! You're not pawning this off on me. I have enough of my own duties to take care of." Regaining possession of himself, he reoriented his rifle and prodded Aurora back toward Rory with the barrel. "Go on your way, but be quick about it."

"Aw, come on, man. I was just relaxing on the couch before she showed up."

"That's not my problem. Be on your way and be quick about it. You've distracted me enough from my rounds."

"Fine, fine. It was worth a shot." Rory grabbed Aurora's arms and jerked her after him. "Come on, you," he grumbled as they moved on toward C wing.

"I think Nelson is at the door there. Just tell him Wallace said to let you through. If he gives you any trouble, tell him 'alpha-tango-three.' He shouldn't give you any problems," the guard recommended.

"Yeah, yeah…" Rory grumbled, playing up the put-upon worker who would rather be doing anything but what he was.

"That… that was good," Aurora mumbled.

"General Parabellum did say that in a general assembly after we had all been through the orientation. It helps if I just tell the truth; there's no restriction. And I really would prefer *not* to be doing this, after all."

"Got it, nothing subversive. Keep it up, that worked like a charm." As they approached the outside of C-wing, Aurora wasted no time.

"No time to talk. Wallace told us to tell you alpha-tango-three and let us pass."

"Uh, err, well, I suppose…"

Aurora pushed by him and tried to open the door but it was locked. She threw an exasperated scowl at the guard, who quickly waved a keycard on a lanyard over a panel and there was a buzz as the electromagnetic lock disengaged. Aurora pushed inside. Rory cocked his head as the awkward guard stared after Aurora, still a bit in disbelief.

"Get an eyeful?" Rory asked the distracted guard, who flushed bright red.

"Sorry, sir. Won't happen again," he said, snapping back to attention and allowing Rory to pass. Before the door clicked shut, he could have sworn he could hear the guard grumbling something about "stupid spandex suits…"

Aurora stood inside looking at a directory. "You think you're up to splitting up? I get the ones upstairs and you get the ones down?"

Rory nodded in agreement, glancing quickly to see who was where.

When Aurora got to Anastasia's room, she noted that there was a large blocky contraption around the door, securing to the jamb and totally encircling the knob.

"What in the…?" She ran her fingers along the box, noting only the three green lights on the top. She twisted her head to look underneath it and saw nothing there. She focused on the box, wishing she could look inside to see what was happening.

You have unlocked a new subskill under the ability **Tinker, Tailor, Soldier, Spy: Assess.**
Assess *(subskill of* **Spy***): Evaluate traps and restraints to find their key weaknesses and how to best exploit them.*

On her display, Aurora could see through the outer shell of the black box, now appearing a light translucent gray. Looking at all the sides, she could easily see a panel that would slide if moved in this direction while that opposite side was pressed in two locations, releasing some holding pins from engaging.

She removed the cover and two red circles highlighted areas of the circuit board within. Extracting two forceps she used while crafting from another pocket, she played around with the wires, and one green light winked out. Additional red circles manifested and she disconnected one of the solder points with a snap. Another green light down. Then a blue dotted line appeared between two sections.

She was at a loss for what to do until she backed up and looked at the contraption as a whole. It then became clear she needed to complete the circuit, so she sifted through her crafting components until she found a wire and clipped it to a suitable size. With a fingertip and a little focused *Ion Storm* she welded the tips of the wire to the appropriate spots.

The box unwound, almost falling off as one surface expanded, rattling loose on the knob. The arm clamping down on the jamb relaxed, and Aurora could slide it off of the door. Deciding to keep the box for later, she found a large enough zipper on the crafting containment bag she had weaved to hold all her different components and tools. This box could probably yield a couple of new blueprints if she took it apart and examined it closely.

She opened the door and stepped inside. The *whoosh* of boot to the face whipped in her peripheral vision. Aurora bent back, barely catching herself as her flight ability activated before she could hit the ground. Anastasia bounced in a fighting stance and ready to attack again as Aurora tried to stand from her limbo stance.

"Anastasia, it's me!" Aurora hissed as she righted herself. Anastasia still eyed her warily, flicking her head to move some of the white knee-length hair out of her face. "We need to get out of here, something's wrong at the Faction. Please tell me they haven't processed you, or put you through orientation or whatever." Aurora gripped Anastasia by the arms, worried eyes peering at her desperately.

"No, they locked me in here like a prisoner. No explanations." Her stance relaxed, but she was still on guard. Aurora thought that must have been the most words she had heard the super string together in, well, as long as she had known her. Her thick Russian accent indicated that English wasn't her first language.

"Rory is with me. You probably don't know him, but he

works on transports. They have some ceremony that has done *something* to him, and they plan on doing it to us. We need to get out of here before we can't."

Anastasia just nodded and beckoned to the door.

Finding Pulse's room, Aurora made quick work of the box-lock and squirreled it away like the first. Heavy footfalls sounded on the steps, but it turned out to only be Rory, Yuki, and Darik hustling to keep up. Aurora opened the door, and found Pulse's exceptionally organized room. His boots were neatly positioned at the foot of his bunk and he sat there calmly reading a journal of some sort.

"C'mon, Pulse, we need to go, I'll explain on the way."

"I don't think I will, actually." Not taking his eyes away from his reading.

"What do you mean? We've got to get out of here," Aurora urged.

The others came into the doorway, to see how their teammate was faring.

"They told us to stay in our quarters until they had further directions, and that's what I intend to do," Pulse replied calmly.

"This is for your own good! We need to get out of here and reassess the situation. Something has definitely changed here; you can't say you don't notice it. *They locked you inside!*"

He closed the magazine he was reading and stood up. "I wouldn't know, I haven't tried to leave. But you're completely right. I'm seeing a big change. People are acting with discipline now. I don't see a ton of lambs running around giggling and talking with their friends. Wasting time."

"They're still human, even though they have powers, Pulse. This isn't a military compound."

"It's inefficient. They could all be through the Academy in three years and on to active duty, but we take four on account of the constant breaks and coddling. Just like this whole escapade we wasted almost a month doing. I didn't even do anything worthwhile the whole time. I got shot at and then just sat on the ship in Hinansho while you and a couple others ran around. Do you realize what I could have accomplished in that time?"

"You're complaining that you got a little break?"

"Tempest wasted his marker with me by requesting that I come along. If I wasn't a man of my word, I would have sat this one out. Especially with what I know now. But with his fall from grace, he probably felt he had to cash in before he totally fell out of favor and had to leave the Faction. But what's done is done, and all accounts are settled." His eyes turned cold as he peered at Aurora.

"Besides, it's not as easy for *some of us* to be as loose and free with the rules as you are."

"What does *that* mean?" she replied indignantly.

"Where is your loyalty? After the Faction dragged you out of the gutter like a piece of trash and turned you into what you are now. Now you're ready to abandon them because you 'feel a little weird' or that 'things have changed'?"

Aurora wanted to break his little air-quoting fingers. "Loyalty is why I'm here, you insufferable prick! Come or don't come, I don't care, but right now you have a choice—that will probably change. Rory is not himself; they've done something to him. To one of our own. He's been here a lot longer than any one of us, so what makes you think they'll treat us any differently?"

"I don't know that grease monkey," Pulse said with a shrug, plopping down on his bunk and reached for his magazine again. "Do what you want, I'm not being a part of it."

The others in the Crew looked back and forth between the two, now uncertain what to do.

Rory shrugged and pointed to his watch.

CHAPTER SIXTY-SEVEN

Sucker Punch

"Oh, I see you're back with us, Gus. I thought you had broken long ago. Now I am *really* impressed. I love the challenge of pushing someone to the utter limits, and it is very unfulfilling when people give up too soon. The younger generations lack the… *resilience* of their ancestors. They were made of stronger stuff. Tempered by suffering, they were refined into something durable. I did not expect that of you, however. I thought you had broken days ago. You've been fairly unresponsive since shortly after we began."

"What now?" Gus slurred through dry, cracked lips.

"This opens up so many new possibilities though. I don't want to get your hopes up, however. Everyone breaks eventually. But take solace in the fact that you have withstood more than many in your same situation.

"You know, I've been thinking. Maybe we're more alike than I initially gave you credit for. You decided to come alone. *I like* to be alone. I'll bet you thought you would do some unsavory things to me, and didn't want your friends to see you that way. Either that or you prefer solitude. No one to limit you, or hold you back. Believe me, I *do know* what that is like.

"So many people want to be your conscience and dictate what is right and what is wrong, as if those concepts even really exist. There is no need to ascribe value to a behavior, is there? It all seems like an artificial construct we humans have erected, for some reason. Does the behavior accomplish its intended purpose in the most efficient way possible? That is what needs to be sought.

"Is that not the basis for natural selection? The strongest survive? If I were weak, do I deserve to be preserved to perpetuate that weakness? No! Those must be culled out from among us. The Nth give us an excellent opportunity to advance humankind, and we refuse to take it. That is another thing that my employer and I see eye to eye upon. No more pandering to the masses—we must elevate. This trend towards making everything easier is folly. It goes against natural law! The weak are supposed to die off. They are supposed to get sick. They are supposed to be the prey that falls to the predator. It weakens the whole to artificially preserve these among us.

"I have always been fascinated by pain. What people will do to avoid even the threat of it is astounding. If you could quantify the amount of worry that exists from just the possibility of pain, I'm sure it would be staggering.

"And the amazing thing is that this perceived threat does not even need to be real. It can be manufactured or implied, and the mind will take that and amplify it into so much more. Do you realize how easy it is to influence and control others with some well calculated suggestions?

"The things people will do to avoid pain. It is so much more potent than the carrot. People will run from the stick, but they will do relatively little for the carrot if it isn't easily obtainable. I see that as part of my duty. If humankind is to evolve, we must get past this hurdle. We must learn to love pain. Through it is the only way to true change and ascendance!

"Since most will not willingly submit themselves to any form of prolonged stress, I have made it one of my pet projects to see how far we can go. And it is so much further than even I ever expected. Almost infinite potential, wasted by almost everyone. The tendency to give up is too ingrained. But not for much longer. I will blaze the trail that will lead us to the next iteration of what humankind can become.

"You, though, you provide an interesting specimen. I would not have suspected you to be one of the elite, yet here you are! Not everyone can undergo the transformation, but if you are any evidence at all, there could be more possibilities than I expected in raising those weaker among us to our level. I am not against progression, you see. If the weak can be elevated without wasting too many resources, then so be it. But the cost would need to be calculated. It's entirely possible that you are an anomaly and the trade-off is not viable. We shall see.

"I have been musing about your case as I have worked upon you. I recall when they contacted me about your situation. They told me they would hand me the situation all wrapped up tidy like a bow, and I'll admit I did not believe them. The thing was, they were right. It is mainly the reason I work for my employer, you see.

"Precision. In my work, it is not a luxury, but an absolute necessity. Take your case, for example. Do you know how difficult it is to fold the cells of a living creature so that you don't break a single strand of DNA? It's no mean feat. That's one of the disadvantages of genius. You will forever be alone. No one can understand or appreciate all that it takes to reach that pinnacle. But you learn to not need that recognition. How ingratiating is it to be adored by fools?

"I must admit, I feel a certain kinship to you. You have been touched by my hand and changed. By my grace, you have survived to this moment where you can finally serve purposes I need. Isn't it fascinating how the universe rewards natural law? You sow the seed and do the cultivation and then years later the fruit is there to be plucked. I had not expected it would be you who came at this time, but I knew eventually we would meet again. Your mother served her purpose, much more than I ever anticipated. Maybe there is just something about your family, a combination of genetics and nurture that combine in the perfect storm of probability that is ideal for my purposes.

"One thing I think I would like to see is how you unravel when I undo all of the work that I did to stabilize you. What will happen? The anticipation is killing me. And you too, now that I think of it, albeit in a different manner. However, I still have many tests to run. I appreciate that you have held on so I could collect as many samples as I have.

"You see, I rarely get the opportunity to compare the physiology of someone before and after they make the change. It does gall me that I knew so little those years ago about the less *material* aspects of our species when I first worked on you, but the science just wasn't there yet.

"I have already made some connections that have been eluding me for quite some time. Discoveries that will allow me to improve myself. And that, my young subject, was worth all the time I put in crafting your 'cure.' Stagnation is really the worst of curses, and when you are at my level, it is so difficult to eke out any sort of advancement or growth. To be so close to godhood, but have it dance tantalizingly out of your grasp.

"I think with time, these revelations will push me past those barriers that have kept me stymied for so long. So for that I thank you. Once again, I do feel compelled to remind you that this will not give you any clemency in my research, unfortunately. Ultimately, you are but a tool, used in the master's hand. You shouldn't think you deserve anything for that, wouldn't you agree?"

Gus flinched as Mengele brought out a scalpel and began to cut into the skin on his chest, using forceps in the other hand to keep it secure as he sliced delicately, teasing the skin from the muscle underneath. For some reason, though, the pain was less intense than usual.

It was unnerving to see the swath of skin being separated from his torso with such cavalier aplomb, but Mengele had not detected this change in Gus' perception. Gus did not understand it himself, but any absence of pain was such a foreign feeling after an eternity of torment.

"You are getting better at your control; you didn't move much on that one. I will have to try harder." Mengele nodded to himself as he worked. "You know, I could bend the nerves near where I work and prevent your body's pain signals from ever reaching the brain. Nerves are funny though, sometimes they don't like being manipulated. I've seen them stay numb in perpetuity, and that just won't do. Damaging the subject beyond repair is not what a craftsman does.

"An artist knows how far he can go, how much color to add, how much marble to chip away, or how deep to cut. Every opportunity is a chance to hone the craft and skill." Mengele leaned close, as if in a stage whisper. "And I do love my work. I have been practicing for so long now. Find something you love and you'll never work another day, isn't that how the phrasing goes?"

Gus wanted to respond, but his jaw felt like lead. Any attempts at speech were thwarted as his muscles refused to obey.

"I'm sure you will forgive me for not treating you like a child. My subjects learn how they are able to withstand so much more than they ever thought possible. The Nth really do offer a unique opportunity that I have found unparalleled with regs. Truly, I feel like I am getting a glimpse of the future. Of what mankind would be thousands of years in the future, after evolution has gone through countless iterations. The Nth merely accelerate this process and allow the body to reset.

"A researcher couldn't ask for a better boon if he tried. The inherent differences in various subjects alone is enough to corrupt the data. But a single subject that can regenerate, even act as their own control, it's more than I ever thought possible. You see, I've been doing this," Mengele waved his scalpel and forceps in circles to indicate his lab, "since before the Nth ever came."

"If you ask me, they chose me to be one of the first generation because, out of my peers, I was more developed and disciplined. Somehow they can assess that before integration. Capacity. That is the key." He jabbed the scalpel close to Gus' eye to emphasize his point.

"Do you know your capacity? I am having the best time exploring it with you, I must say. The time I've given you to assimilate all those changes has got to be part of your resilience. It's truly fascinating. When my employer revealed to me how he had orchestrated everything, even I was impressed. It was so... elegant. It accomplished so many things with such a succinct style.

"You know, I've always been the smartest individual in the room for almost the entirety of my life, and it wasn't until I met my employer that I realized that someone could surpass me." His eyes turned steely and manic. "That won't always be the case, mind you." He stared at Gus, daring him to confirm that Mengele would not rise above his master. He relaxed his jittery eyes when they didn't find the implied flaw he suspected Gus might be thinking.

"I've let myself get too distracted. Another of my few flaws that I need to overcome. Focus, Gus. Focus is key. You cannot overcome or accomplish anything without it. Remember that."

Mengele chuckled and turned back to his work, and things became worse from there. Gus retreated inward to escape the pain that ensued.

CHAPTER SIXTY-EIGHT

Escapade

"There has to be a reason for all of this, Aurora, and I am staying right here. You can see yourself out, and if you return whatever you did to the door back to the way you found it, I would appreciate it. I don't want to be a part of your little escapade. I already know how it will end."

Aurora worked her jaw soundlessly, trying to come up with a response. Finally, she just put her hands up in resignation.

"Sure, Pulse. If that's what you really want." She looked at the other members of the group. "Anyone else? I know I can be bossy, but if anyone isn't feeling this, don't let me pressure you into coming along." She looked at everyone, and only saw the other members of the Crew looking back with resolve.

Anastasia just looked pissed as she cast a scowl at Pulse. "Let's go then," she whispered before turning on her heel and leaving. They closed the door behind them and Aurora removed the lockbox from her storage.

"I can't believe I'm doing this…" she muttered to herself as she reattached and engaged the lock.

"I did some digging and I know someplace we can go to make a plan to get the others. They can track us most places, if they aren't already. Aurora, I think you can help us with that. Darik, can you make a portal for us to wastewater management?" Yuki asked.

"You want us to go to the sewers?" He scrunched up his nose.

"No, we just need to get some concrete between us and that signal tower. It has to be underground and I need to find a control room, some place I can access the network. So not inside the sewer pipes themselves. Is it harder to pass through different materials?"

"That's not how it works, lass. But let me see. It's much easier if it's a shorter distance and I've been there before. D'you know if we can get there from the underground tunnels?"

"There are tunnels?" Anastasia asked in disbelief.

Yuki pulled up a map and began pulling and swiping the air in front of her. Seeing Anastasia's confused look, Yuki swiped a copy over to the other members of the group. "Here are the Faction's schematics… and yes! There, if we go this way we can get there." She tapped on the destination, marking the desired nav-point.

Darik squinted as he looked at his own display before stabbing a chubby finger midair. "Here. I've been here before." He marked another point that populated the others' displays. "I'm going to do this in a series of four jumps, I think that'll throw them off. Each jump will get closer to one edge of the facility, and hopefully they'll think we just left. They can't track my jumps outside of the walls. But instead of going ahead, we'll be going down. I really hope none of you had too big a breakfast, because I can pretty much guarantee one of you will throw up with that many jumps in a row."

The group looked at each other. Yuki turned to Darik. "I don't think any of us have eaten today. They act like they've forgotten about us, and didn't bring anything up for breakfast."

"That's probably for the best. Everyone link elbows and face outwards. Yep, like that. Everyone ready?" Before anyone could respond, Darik opened a portal underneath them, which they fell into. They shot out of another portal vertically aligned, but in midair. "Hold tight!" he warned as they raced toward the ground and another portal opened.

Once again, the ring of supers was jolted in a different direction as the portal spilled them out. There was a loud *horrrk* and elbows tightened as another portal appeared. This one lobbed them slightly into the air before disappearing. The maneuver was calculated to bleed off their momentum and they were able to catch themselves as they lightly fell back to the ground, the mutual support keeping anyone from falling flat.

Artificial lights buzzed noisily in the large room. Elbows relaxed and there were assorted grunts and moans as everyone tried to stabilize themselves.

"Now I know why Grimdark hates those…" Yuki wailed as she wiped the corner of her mouth. Anastasia was whiter than her normal pale complexion.

"Thank you, I think you meant to say," Darik griped. "It's not like I can control how your stomachs respond to spatial translocation." He scowled at the others as they tried to settle their stomachs, some spitting a lot, others coughing exaggeratedly, while the rest tried deep breathing.

"You did it, Darik, we're underground. Thanks. Next time give us a little warning though, yeah?" Yuki asked, fishing a piece of gum out of her pocket. She waved the pack in offering, which most gladly accepted.

"It doesn't help. It's like ripping off a Band-Aid, lass, you just have to do it. The less time your brain has to process everything, the easier it is, trust me."

The Crew followed the blue chevrons, climbing down two ladders until they reached a rusted door. Yuki pulled on it but could not budge it.

Rory tapped her gently on the shoulder and she stepped aside. A large pull and the knob crumbled in his hands. He then dug his fingertips into the metal by the frame and they sunk in as if it were soft clay. After a little digging, he reached in and pulled the door free from its corroded door frame. He did a courtly bow. "Ladies first..."

As they entered the room, the bite of ozone and the smell of hot electronics hit them like a wave. Despite the worn outer surface, the inside of the room must have been under negative pressure. There was no dust or cobwebs, but it was apparent this area was dated.

"Just what I need! This place will allow me to access the network, but it's so flipping old no one will be monitoring this workstation. Look—half of these are analog! Can you believe it?" At getting no response from the others, she hurried on, trying out various adapters she had in a small case. Finding a blocky one that resembled a foreign outlet current converter, she slid it into a wide slit. Other contraptions, gizmos, and a laptop materialized from her zippered roll and she deftly connected them in a complicated series and began typing away.

"Just a minute, this will take a bit to connect... aaaand done. That's going to take a bit to compile so let's talk.

"I need to fill you in on what I've found. There are a lot of things, so it's hard to know where to begin." She puffed out a huge sigh. "Okay, first things first. Aurora, we're going to need you to craft us some kind of jammers so that they can't track us up on the surface. At first, I was surprised that they even could keep tabs on us. Then I worried we all were chipped without our knowledge. It's nothing like that. The system uses certain biometric scans, like the way we walk, recognizing voice pitch and it gets collated in a computer processor in HQ somewhere. Is that too complicated a system to fool?"

Aurora thought for a bit, then replied, "I should be able to come up with something."

"Good. I've checked records for the other members of the Crew. Prime and BoJack aren't here with us on Faction property. I imagine BoJack is at the hospital with Gwen and Tempest, and I haven't heard anything from Prime after Seneschal dropped her off. I imagine she's going to go visit her daughter, and we do have a single address for an emergency contact."

"Now that you mention it, where is Seneschal?" Darik asked.

"Get this—she's been sacked! No more augments are allowed in the Faction anymore. They have already turned her out with an unimpressive severance package. Thanks, but no thanks. I tried to contact her but all messages are being rerouted through HQ as well. So don't send anything through your comms! Everything is probably being read, and I doubt it's making it to where you want it to go. Not to mention possible messages that *haven't reached us*."

"Any other good news?" Aurora asked, folding her arms.

"What else? Oh yeah, the orderlies. There are new enforcers now within the Faction. They look like simple strength-based supers, but they are armed with gloves that contain some kind of power-negating technology. I didn't get the gist of how they work, but for those who resisted orientation, they can force you into it. They refer to them as compliance officers in the memos and—"

"That's what they did to Rory! It does something so you can't speak against the Faction. I'm not sure what else it does, but Rory freaked out trying to let me know what was up," Aurora piped in.

Everyone looked to Rory, who had become stiff again, his mouth pursed like he had been sucking on a lemon.

"Relax, Rory, don't try to speak." She patted his back and turned back to the others. "See? We might even have to carry him out of here when we're ready to leave. If he reacts that strongly to merely speaking against the Faction, he might totally lock up if we try to move him out of the Faction."

"He's big as a barn, Aurora! How do you suggest we do tha—"

"We'll add it to the list, Darik," Yuki broke in. "They are processing Grimdark and Harmony, *right now*, so we have to come up with a plan to save them, get the hell out of here, and hopefully find the others when we get out."

"Do we even know where they are?" Anastasia asked.

"The coliseum…"

"They're goners for sure, then. I'm sorry, Yuki," Darik said grimly.

"I don't accept that."

"That has to be the most secure part of the facility. And if everyone is there, willing to fight against us, those aren't odds I want to take, lass. It might be wise to make a tactical retreat."

"No way. It may come to that, but we should at least try. We would do it for you, Darik. We'll need all the help we can get on the outside."

"Aye."

"If we could get enough outside, I could distract them for a bit while we get the others," Aurora offered.

"I could try setting off some perimeter alarms to pull some away…"

The lights dimmed and clicked off for a second before returning to normal.

"What was that?" Anastasia asked.

"Let me check." Yuki extended some filaments from her right hand and her eyes rolled back in her head. She blinked back to normal after a brief pause. "Fire detector went off in the coliseum," she reported.

"Isn't that where Grimdark and Harmony are?" Anastasia perked up.

"Let's use the distraction to pull them out."

"Are we ready?" Darik sighed.

"Are we ever?" Yuki shot back.

CHAPTER SIXTY-NINE

Closing Time

"This had better work," Harmony said as she flicked the powder off the makeup brush and fanned it up to the alarm. She cringed a bit at wasting the high-end makeup, already having emptied half the tray. She tried fanning it upward but was not having much success. She remembered that just last month they had to reinstall a lot of detectors because they were getting set off by fawns vaping in the bathrooms. An angry memo went out that any particulate was not recommended in the restrooms until they replaced the dated detectors with new ones.

The problem was that the ceiling was just too damn far away. She threw the compact at the alarm and finally got a satisfying poof of dust, but it didn't seem to activate the sensor. She had to duck as it fell and shattered on the ground.

"We're coming in, decent or not," one of the men yelled through the door.

Harmony opened her mouth and screamed, but she couldn't hear her own voice. At that moment, a piercing wail echoed against the tile, making her ears ring.

The frame near the door bucked and then the door

exploded into splinters. One of the orderlies stuck his head in the doorway, his bald pate bright red and the veins prominent and throbbing. He was shouting, but Harmony couldn't make out anything over the din. He stomped over toward her and she stepped backward and slipped on one of the chunks of broken door, falling unceremoniously on her butt. She crab-walked backward, retreating from his approach.

He balled his fists and an eldritch green energy arced between the metal disks on the knuckles of his black gloves. She tried to retreat more but felt the cold tile press against her back. There was mayhem outside as people rushed to get out but this man was not to be deterred. Spittle flew from his mouth as he continued to yell, but it was caught up in the piercing alarm. She tried to flinch inward, scrunching up like a turtle and closed her eyes tight. After five seconds of nothing, she cracked an eye open. Eyes growing wide at what she saw.

The janitor dragged the mop across the already spotless floor. As he had done for years now. He looked into the display case of the trophy section of the coliseum and saw it lying there. The fools didn't even know what they had taken so long ago. They had no idea of the potential of the item, it was merely a memento of a victory that most had never taken part in.

Once it had belonged to him. In a past life, where he actually had been on a trajectory for greatness. It was only one of the three, but it had called to him. He somehow knew that if he could regain possession of it, that it would lead him to the others. But attempting to steal it would no doubt set off some alarms and then he would lose his only chance.

He tried to convince himself that merely being near the object was enough. It wasn't. But he had no plan for how he could possibly get it out of the heart of Purple Faction. Even worse, he feared that if he failed, it would bring attention to the object and they would learn of its true power, and guard it much more securely.

He got close, looking at the thin glass pane. A small wire connected to the frame that he assumed went to the alarm. *Wouldn't it be ridiculous if it was merely a false wire, leading nowhere?* Keeping him at bay for over a decade while he pined and cleaned. Waiting for something to change.

Who am I kidding? I don't have the balls. I'm nothing without them. I never was—

A deafening screech filled the air. His heart froze for a moment, worried he had tripped some alarm by breathing on the glass, or setting off some sensor. A flashing light made him twist, drawing his eye to the fire alarm. As he turned back, he saw that he had let go of the mop, and the handle was resting against the thin glass, leaving a large crack.

Was fate smiling upon him or giving him an ultimatum? Firming his resolve, he jabbed the mop handle into the glass and scraped it along the frame to clear the shards away. If any alarm was sounding, it was caught up in the existing wail. He reached in and touched it, feeling a pop like static electricity as he did.

Gently removing it from the small display stand, he unzipped the front of his coveralls and slid it inside his shirt, letting it press against his bare chest before zipping his overalls back over it.

Could it be that easy? All these years of waiting and that was all it took? A long-forgotten feeling began to swell within him, like a cherished childhood memory returning. Buried by the responsibilities and disappointments of adulthood, to the point one had forgotten that there had once been hope and dreams.

He stood for a moment, holding his hands over his chest, holding the item close, taking in the feeling. It had missed him too. That was clear. He didn't feel any need to stay here any longer. This job was only a means to an end. A chance to be close to it. In fact, he looked forward to the unfulfilling job of cleaning just because it offered him a chance. A glimpse. A breath. But now, it was his again. He did not need to be here. He dropped the mop where he stood and made his way to leave. He could see supers crowded like cattle trying to press their way out.

No need to go that way. The good thing about being a janitor was that you needed to be out of sight. Working when people were gone. Now that he thought about it, it was the weekend. That was odd that so many supers had assembled in the coliseum. Probably some succession battle, or those new ceremonies they were on about all the time. He could care less. He pushed open the door and walked outside.

Turning, he felt the pull to where he needed to go next. He reoriented and began walking.

———

Harmony blinked with recognition. It was Prime! She was flipping around this large man, hitting him with wooden rods, one in each hand. Despite the siren, she could hear the *thock* as one of her weapons connected with the man's hard head. They appeared to leave no lasting damage, as the gorilla of a man blinked away each concussive blow and tried to grab onto her. She bent backward, out of his reach, seamlessly flexing like a gymnast and flipping over.

With a roundoff, she skirted around his side. Prime swung one rod and hit him hard in a knee. Harmony winced as she saw it hyperextend backward just a bit like a Barbie leg. The man stumbled and knelt, but quickly stood again and shook his leg. He had a slight limp now, but it was almost imperceptible. Something that resembled a tiny rock in his shoe more than a wrecked joint.

He had become more reckless in his lunges, trying to swipe with his long arms and gather Prime into his bear-like grip. She slammed down on his outstretched hands with the staves like she was playing red hands. Her blows were lightning fast.

Harmony was amazed that the man's hand bones weren't pulverized as she repeatedly knocked them down and away. A metal disk was torn away from the onslaught, causing green energy to leak out, forming a longer arc, crackling and spitting energy like a Tesla coil.

He briefly looked at the gloves to assess the damage. She managed another crack across his forehead before she retreated with a series of backflips. One of his beefy veins split right at his brow line, allowing purplish blood to dribble into his eye. He swiped at his eye reflexively and there was a flare of green energy. The wound appeared to bleed even more and he quickly retracted his hands. Head-Wound Harry looked gruesome as he tried to shake his head to clear his vision. Prime circled him in a crouched stance, ready to pounce on any weakness.

A flash of movement in the doorway divided his attention just enough that she made her move. The man looked like one of those wooden kung fu dummies her brothers would practice on. *What were they called? Wang Chung? Something like that...* Elbows, head, and torso took a repeated beating, as every attempt to shield himself led to another attack at a newly exposed area.

Harmony was so entranced she jumped as her arm was grabbed. She started in terror until she saw Grimdark's haunted face. His pallid complexion was even more pale than usual, his eyes dark and brooding. He motioned his head toward the door. That damn siren continued to scream full blast, and probably would result in some kind of hearing damage.

Sure, ice-cold hands pulled her to her feet, but she still almost slipped on some of the debris on the polished floor. *How did Prime move so elegantly on this?* She felt like she was on an ice-skating rink. Hanging onto Grimdark's arm, they skirted around the dueling pair. As Prime saw the two, she nodded and somehow managed to attack with even more fury, arms and legs blurring as she pummeled the orderly from all angles.

As they made their way out of the room, there was a crowd and they were caught in it as it pushed for the exits. Harmony was perplexed to smell actual smoke as those from behind surged forward, pressing her into Grimdark and those around her.

She felt claustrophobic and struggled to maintain her feet as her arms were pressed to her sides. Supers jostled from all sides and the acrid smell of sweat and adrenaline filled her nostrils. The mass staggered drunkenly as it pushed. Those from behind cramming the others into each other. Sometimes those in front didn't or couldn't move, and it felt difficult to breathe as she was squeezed in a vice of human bodies. A super nearby activated some kind of electrical attack and those around him crumpled.

This relieved some of the pressure and the crowd rushed to fill the void, uncaring that people were being trampled in the process. Harmony hoped that they were resilient enough not to be hurt, but knew that some would be like her, talented in some ways, but not that much stronger than a reg physically.

Once powers had been used, it was like a spark in a powder keg. Different abilities triggered back and forth, creating pockets around those supers and Harmony felt herself carried along. Her feet tripped as she was dragged over someone lying prone, and it was only the tightness of the bodies around her that kept her aloft. That and Grimdark's vice-like grip on her upper arm.

He was focused and determined as he tried to gauge where the group was going to move in order to best follow and avoid fighting the flow. Harmony definitely could smell smoke now, and an orange glow was reflected along one of the walls. With a tug, he pulled her toward one of the exits. She was pushed uncomfortably into the metal door frame but then they rolled out through the doorway.

Grimdark continued to guide her towards the side, getting out of the path of the stampede. Harmony drew in gasps of blessedly fresh air. Grimdark didn't let her stop though, dragging her further and further away from the building. Looking over her shoulder, she could see black smoke curling into the air. The realization that her makeup ploy had done nothing dawned upon her, and she got a chill thinking about what would have happened to her.

She could only sense urgency and determination from Grimdark, no fear. Did the alarm disturb the process? She could feel him again, so she assumed it must have. But who had set the fire?

CHAPTER SEVENTY

Doom Crossing: Eternal Horizons

"I'll work on that crafting and provide a distraction," Aurora suggested as she turned to her mentor. "Rory, you should probably stay here, we don't know how you'll react out there."

"He can watch over me," Yuki suggested, "I'm going to try to enter the system from here and see if I can beat the Faction AI. If I can, I should be able to get some answers, as well as hopefully modding how the sensors track us."

"I'm on extraction," Darik offered, "but I need to find them first. That's going to be a little difficult in a crowd." He looked at the others questioningly.

"Don't worry. I can help with that." Anastasia raised her hand.

"Okay. We all meet back here after we find Harmony and Grimdark?" When the assent was mutual, Darik offered his arms, elbows bent and Aurora and Anastasia reluctantly locked arms, this time all facing the same direction. "We run toward that wall. Not too fast, mind you; you two are taller than me. Got it?" They trotted off, a portal opening a second before they hit the wall, swallowing them and irising shut.

Yuki turned to Rory. "Just make sure my head is supported,

I can tend to thrash about if things get dicey in there. Once I even gave myself a concussion." She took off her hoodie and balled it up under her head as she laid down. With a deep breath, she reached up to the port, extended her cables, and connected with the system.

———

There was the usual sensation of falling, but gravity didn't reinstate itself like it normally did. It was there, but much weaker than normal. Green-tinged light filtered through the canopy. Rich, earthy smells permeated the air, dust and pollen floated in the swath of a light that shone unimpeded through a tiny breach in the leaves overhead. Nearing a branch, Yuki grabbed it and propelled herself upward with a light shove.

She felt like a fairy as she sailed through the peaceful, sylvan environment. The feeling was so freeing. Aurora was lucky that flying was in her power set. It felt so relaxing. The arc of her floating path allowed her to land atop a thick branch. Some thick moss-like plant covered the bark, cushioning her light steps. At the end of the branch, a cute animal held a small purple fruit in its little paws. It cocked its head and looked at her quizzically.

So adorable! It had a long tail and a fluffy chest, with little stripe rings along its back and tail. The little paws looked like tiny hands as it turned the fruit, gauging what she would do. While she had never seen one in real life, this animal resembled a lemur. A sudden cross wind blew, and Yuki had to hold on to the trunk of the tree as its intensity increased. The mossy covering easily peeled away as she slid, and she had to struggle a bit to pull enough off to dig her fingers into the gnarled bark underneath and get a grip.

The diminished gravity made it harder to cling to the tree, as her weight wouldn't anchor her as she was accustomed. She also had to squint, because the wind filled the air with plumes of pollen and dust. As quickly as it started, the wind stopped, and Yuki saw that she was coated with a fine yellow powder.

She attempted to brush herself off, shaking her hair and coughing. She was never more glad she didn't have any allergies. As she swiped her eyes clear, she noticed the branch now had five of the small little animals, all facing her. They peered at each other with curiosity. She crouched and beckoned one to come closer.

One ventured forward, looking back at his fellows, and stopped about a foot away. Yuki stretched forward her open palm, trying to keep her movements slow and unthreatening. The lemur leaned forward and sniffed a fingertip.

"That's right, I don't want to hurt you, little—*damn it*!" she screamed as the lemur gave her finger a hard bite. Its little teeth tore furrows in her skin as she yanked it away.

"What the hell was *that* for?" she scolded. As the little animal turned back from looking at the others, it was licking its jaws. Its eyes had become bright red and the pupils were huge. The other lemurs became agitated and hopped from foot to foot. One let loose a barking screech and the trees began to rustle all around her. The one that bit her smiled widely, revealing predatory fangs more at home on a vampire than a cuddly little teddy bear of an animal.

Drawn to its call, other lemurs began appearing from the surrounding trees. They jumped and swung with their long arms, legs, and tails. Some joined the others, while a few landed on branches above and started crawling down the trunk with eager intention.

When will I ever learn?

Darik dropped them on the rooftop of a building near the coliseum. People were already streaming out the front doorways, an obvious choke point. Despite its name, the coliseum was not typically an area where many supers congregated. The sheer number of people spilling out the entrance was alarming, and they just kept coming.

"They're all in a panic. I can't use Dazzle or it'll block off the exits."

"You see that smoke? It really is a fire!" Darik gasped.

"Why is no one putting it out? We should have some supers here with water-based abilities!

"Quiet, you two, I need to concentrate." Anastasia scanned the crowds looking for any sign of Harmony or Grimdark.

Herd mentality, people are panicking. Thinking with their lizard brains.

There was a flash of motion and Anastasia barely saw someone slip inside a window. A zipline was anchored nearby to one of the tiers of the coliseum. Someone going *into* the fire?

The supers who could fly pulled above the crowd as soon as they got a little space around them. Some tried to grab them to extricate themselves from the crowd, succeeding only in pulling some supers back into the mass of people roiling out of the building. Others escaped and flew away. It was a massive free-for-all. Neither Grimdark or Harmony were flyers, so she could ignore those.

Anastasia's eyes flitted to face after face with lightning speed. In less than ten seconds, she had determined that out of the three-hundred people that had pushed out of the coliseum, Harmony and Grimdark had yet to leave. It was much easier to scan the entrances and evaluate and discount the new faces.

Why the terror, though? Supers shouldn't be afraid of something as mundane as a little fire. No. The faces showed something else was at play here.

As the crowd grew, she noted that whatever had overcome the supers was wearing off now that they were in the fresh air. A few began to turn back and try to make their way back inside, but they made little progress trying to fight the people pushing out. If anything, those leaving now were even more insistent and violent in their attempt to flee the building.

A flash of curly hair, lost in the crowd. Then again. And black hair with silver highlights. Jackpot!

"Keeper, come here." She motioned to Darik, keeping her eyes on the pair. She touched his shoulder and asked, "Can you see them?"

"Whoa, how do you do that?"

"Yes or no?!"

"Yes."

"Then go. You will only be able to track them for a short time after I break contact."

Darik ran off the edge of the building, cannonballing into a portal two stories down. Anastasia finally took her eyes off the crowd. Aurora was assembling something from a pile of components on a cloth in front of her. She nervously peeked up at the large spire that towered over them nearby and back down at the crowd before shaking her head and turning back to her frenetic work. She snapped two halves together and flipped a switch.

"Anastasia, clip this to your suit." Aurora backed up a step to survey her work. "Huh, that actually works. Ooh, and a blueprint dropped too. Nice." She knelt by her cloth and started working on the next one. "The next ones should be quicker. I just wish I'd finished one for Darik. Can you keep an eye on the doors and let me know when people stop coming out?"

"Of course," she said, keeping her eyes fixed on where she had sent Darik.

———

Darik rocketed out of the portal. He loved inverting the portal exits and screwing with gravity. He had always loved thrill-rides when he was younger and didn't get nauseated in the slightest. Plus he could move so much better when he wasn't ferrying others around. He couldn't see the pair at this height so he dropped another set of portals, this time exiting even higher. Some of those in the crowd pointed at him as he managed to spot Grimdark with Harmony in tow.

He quickly fashioned another set of portals, before he could build up too much momentum, dropping out to the side of the crowd.

"He's one of them!" a husky man shouted, pointing directly at Darik. Three other supers blinked as if coming out of a trance. "He's avoided orientation; look at his name. No purple diamond by it."

"I know this piece of trash. Time to teach you a lesson, midget," a voice taunted from behind the others.

Darik rolled his eyes. He recognized that voice.

Not now.

CHAPTER SEVENTY-ONE

The Beginning of the End

Finally things were coming into fruition. The groundwork he had meticulously laid was finally reaching the tipping point.

It had taken a lot of work, creating alliances and working with lesser minds, but he was getting closer to finally moving ahead with his plans. Not that it wasn't fascinating fun along the way, but this would open up so many new avenues. Mysteries that humanity had wrestled with would now be able to be unraveled and woven to fit the patterns of his design.

So many intricate shapes, all coalescing into a majestic mosaic on such a scale that only the gods would be able to perceive it. He would surpass the barriers imposed by mere humanity and become something greater than them all.

Mengele pulled the animal out of its glass case, admiring his handiwork. A perfect blending of his design. To all appearances, it was an adorable miniature bear, the size of a small domestic cat. In actuality, it was a triumph of his skills in spatial manipulation and recombinant DNA wizardry. He pet the coarse fur of the surly animal who struggled in his grasp but could not twist enough to bite the hand that held it. It was for the best. The animal would only hurt itself in the attempt.

Sharp claws extended but could not penetrate the dense material that formed Mengele's suit. Many mistook the material to be merely his skin, black as basalt and equally as hard. In actuality, the suit had incalculable layers of material, pressed in upon itself, creating a substance harder than diamond. Any pressure exerted on the outer surface would be absorbed by layers and folds as he bent reality back and forth upon itself. It allowed him to operate without any fear of contamination as well, saving the time needed to scrub in.

There were still many preparations to make but this phase was almost complete. He would change this reality to one of his own design, correcting that which he saw as aberrations and creating or importing what the design required. The others objected to even the smallest part of his plan that he dared to share, concerned about how everything would interact if he altered the ecosystem. There may be things that needed to be refined and perfected. But they would bend to his will. Everything did eventually, no matter how resilient.

Mengele played with a section of the Nun, folding it and shaping it in a hand. The others insisted on calling it ether, but the ancients had it right. This was the substance of creation. He had mastered its manipulation long ago, and had moved on to working and fashioning its counterparts.

His research with Mr. Sterling had yielded so many *interesting* results. While most supers could wield Nun, they knew next to nothing about Ka and how it, too, could be manipulated and moved, bent and fashioned, if one knew how. It took finesse, though. Unlike Nun, it had a strong affinity for what form it wanted to take, and would resist if crudely managed.

The Ba aspect would take over and stubbornly resist change, insisting on retaining its unique character. You couldn't force Ka into what you wanted, you had to *convince* it to adopt the form you wanted. And if there was anything he was good at, it was manipulation. In every sense of the word. Even those who he had condescended to serve would eventually be under his influence—and they would never know he had planned it all along.

He just needed the data from Thoth to finalize his calculations. Mengele had learned to be precise with his measurements. Mastery demanded it. Especially in the weighty matters of the soul, he thought, chuckling to himself. After years of planning, things were sliding into place. Each piece was carved obsessively to specification and polished. Then set aside until the right time. Now he was ready to slide another into its proper place.

Thoth was in his debt now, after he had provided consistent subjects for his own research. Especially those valuable ones that allowed him to finish his own pet projects. Thoth could have his imaginary worlds. Mengele had set his sights higher. Reality and beyond.

An alarm on his display caught his attention. He replaced the bear in its case and stepped out of the adjoining lab into the operatory. Gus had already rebounded, at an even more accelerated rate than before. He made some adjustments to the timing intervals, shortening it again. That was the *fourth* time. Just when he thought he had everything figured out, this subject kept providing more riddles to unravel.

His hands made a rasping noise as he rubbed them together. Time to begin again.

———

"Why?" Gus wheezed as Mengele readied himself, straightening instruments and raising the tray to just the right level.

"Why what? Why you?" When Gus only glared defiantly, he continued. "I am not sure why you are the way you are. It's like being able to dissect a dinosaur or something once thought extinct. You are different. Why? That will take some time to determine. In a way, your uniqueness makes you valuable to me. But it also sets you apart.

"I will admit—I continue to be impressed that you decided

to take me on alone. It was ignorant and foolish, but… refreshing. I have never understood why so many people rely on others for so much of their daily lives. To the point where they won't even do something they want without someone accompanying them.

"Have you ever been like them? Not going to something as mundane as a movie unless someone would go with you? Just so they can sit beside you in silence while you passively take it all in? That somehow that makes you less alone? I wouldn't be surprised if you had. Ultimately, we all are alone, regardless of how we fool ourselves. Yet that still doesn't stop the majority from chasing after some kind of validation through the acceptance of others.

"It wasn't until I realized my own uniqueness that I cast those pursuits off forever for the wasted energy they were. That which makes me unique also isolates me. I fought against this at first, but then realized that it was an unexpected boon. Without distraction, I could accomplish so much more than before, giving the requisite time needed to placate the insecurities of everyone else.

"I usually never speak with my subjects. But when I get the rare opportunity to see my own handiwork, I must say that sometimes I even impress myself. That folding was done over ten years ago, and it looks as flawless today as it did then. I see you've been able to invert the fractal, what is it, two, close to three times? How many layers do you surmise there are?" Gus continued to say nothing, so Mengele shrugged and went on. "Then I'll let you wonder. I know how many there are, but ignorance is its own reward.

"Maybe coming alone wasn't totally your choice. It is possible that you are just so repellent that no one wanted to join you, hmm? Ah. There it is, that's closer to the mark. I can see by your expression. Even still, a good lesson to learn early. Well, it would be if I were going to allow you to live.

"It's better this way. Most humans are so weak that they fool themselves into a false security by propping themselves up with other pieces of straw, imagining they are somehow more sturdy and secure. If they only knew how fragile they really were, even when they feel their strongest.

"I'm sure you thought I was just monologuing, correct? Just like all the one-note villains out there. So isolated that I need to reveal my plans to just one other soul to establish my brilliance?

"But I asked you a question. Let's try that again. How. Many. Layers?"

When Gus hesitated, he grasped Gus' neck and pushed him down into the table.

"Fff-five." Gus had to struggle to push the air out and guess. He didn't think it was even audible, but finally the pressure on his windpipe relaxed enough to allow breath again.

"Wrong! But it is good, you can follow orders. I have no tolerance for those disinclined to cooperate. That will help you suffer less. Or more, depending on how you look at things." Mengele threw back his head and laughed.

"These next steps will take some of your cooperation. Let's see how firm your resolve is…"

CHAPTER SEVENTY-TWO

Make Yourself Get Up

"This healer you mentioned in your ravings—BoJack was the name I think you said?—I will need some more information about him. The correlation of longevity that all healers possess cannot be a coincidence. I think that was part of the deficiency in my model. I assumed there were only three parts to the system, when there are possibly four, or more! I imagine you will resist giving me the information again, but such is the way of self-proclaimed heroes. Let's see, what worked last time?" Mengele tapped his chin. "Ah yes, I think it was the needle."

At these words, something deep within Gus cracked. Not in a way of breaking him, but in destroying a barrier he had erected himself long ago. Protecting himself from being hurt, he had erected a wall of self-interest. To hide from his own inefficacy and powerlessness, he had receded inwards, placing more bricks as he increased the distance from others. If you never let anyone in, then they couldn't hurt you. It was really the only way you could protect yourself.

For some reason, Mengele's threat struck something at his core. He had said it so off-handedly, as if asking to pass the salt at a polite dinner. That what he was asking was just a simple fact, and not a betrayal.

On some level, Gus was well aware of his faults and failings and his punishment at the hands of Mengele seemed almost justified. His due reward for his stupidity and hubris of thinking he could take on someone so powerful with no real plan or backup. But those he had come to think of as friends. While they probably didn't reciprocate those feelings, they didn't deserve to be dragged down because of him.

A kernel of resistance hardened in his resolve. Mengele could do what he wanted to him, but his friends and family were off limits. The man had already done enough to his family, and if there was anything he could do to distract Mengele for any stretch of time, it would be that much more time he would not be able to go after them.

He twisted his neck to look at Mengele. The simple action took a Herculean amount of effort and pushing through searing pain but he grit his teeth and forced himself to do it. The widening of Mengele's eyes was cold comfort when he saw the smile that followed it.

"Really, you're going to make me use the curare again? So be it."

Gus felt a pinch along the side of his face as Mengele injected something into his cheek and it fell into slackness despite his best efforts to keep his eye shut.

He could almost hear Mengele asking for Gus to 'give him his hate' as he peered closer, almost like he was looking through him. Mengele blinked, eyes growing wide as he began muttering excitedly.

At first, Gus thought he was talking to him, but he would trail off, then make a couple of quick notes into his virtual keyboard, speaking softly as he typed. As the curare spread out, his mouth also drooped, and he realized that he couldn't speak even if he wanted to. A thin dribble of spittle leaked out the corner of his mouth. Mengele resumed his work as if Gus was not present.

"It is precisely these types of situations where breakthroughs come from. When something deviates from expectations. It shows an error in the traditional logic. It challenges things I have assumed I understood. If I didn't know better, I would think the subject had managed to control more than just the Nun, but that can't be it. There must be another explanation. I doubt a neophyte could have mastered Ba control, when it has taken me over a decade to refine the process. Still, there is something there." Mengele paced as he tried to work through his reasoning, looking up as he thought, as if the answers were written on the white tile ceilings and harsh examination lights.

"If some substances can sever the connection of Nth to the Ka, it would stand to reason that something is left after the Ba is removed, otherwise the body would perish. A component of Akh? Can this also be separated? Hmm, yes, I will need to see if this can be accomplished without causing death, or if this aspect could be suffused to another, creating immortality?"

Gus tried to focus on what Mengele was rambling about, but it was difficult to follow without any context. He turned his attention to the ember that was smoldering within. He urged it to burn brighter, as if it could somehow do something to help him. He was divided. Most of him wanted to give up, to let himself crack and just cease to be. But the ember twinkled there in his core. Sparkling with promises of what could be. Of how it would burn in revenge. And though he could detect no outward signs, he knew without any popup that his *True Sight* had just confirmed that the ember was not wrong.

———

As the pain began, Gus focused on the ember. Focusing his entire attention on it, and it expanded to fill his whole vision. As if it were expanding or he was shrinking to nothing. It burned brighter and brighter, from orange to yellow, then blazing white. It encompassed his whole vision and then he felt his virtual eyelids close when he could take the brilliance no longer.

While it burned hot, it felt good. On the edge of pain like a searing jacuzzi or going outside for the first sunny day after a drawn out, rainy spring. He opened himself up to it and pushed his pain outward toward the sun-like ember, and felt it connect like a magnetic anchor.

He pushed pain out through the thin filament. Breathing in and then pushing out. Rhythmic. Inhale. Hold. Exhale and push. He leaned back and inhaled deeply, his head tilting back on the metal operating table. Was that blood he was smelling? It wasn't coppery though, this smelled almost like the sea. It was something different, among the constant suffering that was Gus' life now and his mind seized upon it like a rabid dog.

Each deep inhale filled his lungs with briny air. He could almost imagine the oranges and reds of a setting sun from his relaxing spot on the island a lifetime ago. Was that the wind? He leaned into a warm breeze as it caressed his face, ruffling his hair.

This is it, Gus. You're finally cracking. Your psyche is splitting or whatever happens after prolonged psychic strain, he told himself. He welcomed the change. He was lost either way and this just felt… good. That wasn't entirely accurate; it was another feeling. Gus let the sensations take hold of him and he could feel more and more as he allowed the memories to come to him. The soft cushion of his putty knee pad on the hard rock. The hypnotizing slosh as the waves undulated in and out in time with his deep breaths. The screech of gulls as they flew by overhead.

Though his eyes were closed, he could see the scene as if it was coming into focus. The palms and coconut trees came into focus, and their gentle whispering *shush* as their fronds were tickled in the wind. Gus saw a crab scuttling across the sand, which drew his eyes back up to the vivid sunset. He sat there captivated as the warmth of the sun's last rays melted away the despair he had accepted as his new reality.

The sun hid partially behind a strip of clouds that hovered parallel with the horizon. Gus stared at the clouds as they moved slowly in response to the wind. He let his imagination run on autopilot as the clouds tumbled over one another. At one point he thought they almost resolved into words. Gus looked away, letting his mind wander as he surveyed the other side of the beach.

The pale yellows and oranges flickered to deep reds and drew Gus' attention back to the sunset. The clouds were definitely resolving into words.

I'm finally losing it. But what the hell. Whatcha got for me, clouds?

It looked like they said 'wirehair' at one point, but the clouds kept moving, spinning and turning.

Just my imagination.

He almost turned away again when the clouds stabilized along sharp lines instead of their puffy, indefinite curves. Reading the message, Gus took a quick intake of breath.

We Are Here.

The message stayed long enough for him to realize that this was no trick of the light, though he was still unconvinced that it wasn't all just a hallucination. Maybe even a dream. Sleeping would be acceptable, because the surge rebound of his **Leech** power feedback would kill him and then he could rest at last.

The clouds dispersed again as the colors deepened to darker shades. More words resolved, and Gus stared at them until the sun set. This time the clouds did not disperse. They held their message as if they were made of stone.

You Are Not Alone.

CHAPTER SEVENTY-THREE

Golden Sunset

As he stared at the message, Gus wondered who could be sending it. Was it his father? The other supers? Maybe someone with mental or imagery powers?

But then the intensity of each of his senses increased and he realized exactly who had sent the message. It should have been obvious, looking back. Now he could place the feeling he had been experiencing at the beginning of the vision. It was not merely happiness, it was *hope*.

That combination of sensations had happened at a point in his life when he had felt a turning point. That new possibilities were now opened to him that he never believed would be a part of his life. That things were going to change for the better. That he had finally gotten a break in his depressing letdown of a life.

He wouldn't have ever thought about this moment in particular but the hybrid-Nth had known. Somehow, they were able to communicate in a way that typical Nth weren't, and had found this set of circumstances to transmit that emotion in the peculiar way they communicated.

Perhaps that was why it was so confusing to Gus when they

had tried to communicate in the past. They didn't have any context to share their messages.

As Gus was ruminating on this, an enormous moon began to rise, replacing the sun. It was much larger than a normal moon, and brighter by far. It began to rise above the horizon, its pale reflection creeping across the ocean as it continued to rise. The speed with which it rose was unnatural, and it slowed as its lower edge touched the horizon, balancing there.

The reflection flickered on the waves as it touched the shore. The light pooled together and coalesced as a figure stepped out of the water. It was humanoid in form, but it was also fluid. It glinted with a pale glow, shimmering like mercury. It stepped slowly from the waves and Gus saw the moonlight reflected across the head.

As the humanoid form approached, Gus could see that the head had no face at all—smooth and featureless like a mannequin. It stopped on the beach below and appeared to squint, the smooth surface puckering in. As the figure relaxed, the shape of the eyes remained, and lids opened, revealing blue eyes that glowed lightly in the dark.

Gus realized with a start that they were fashioned after his own eyes, at least the facial features around the eyes themselves. The iris reminded Gus of a wolf's, penetrating and wild.

Without breaking eye contact, the figure reached an arm up and swung it in an arc overhead. Time sped by as if in fast forward, and it was day again. The figure pointed at both its eyes with two fingers then pointed to Gus and then to the water. He aimed his attention there and saw a ghostlike representation of himself, as he returned from his deep dive to get the second plate.

As he left the water, the figure pointed at the plate and then to itself.

"Okay, I get it. You're the Kroutonium, or Endurium. Is there any name you'd prefer?"

The figure looked up and tapped its face where the chin would be as if in thought. It then nodded and its body went mercurial again, slowly reforming into a tower with multiple tiers as it tapered to the top. The hand re-emerged and pointed to the very top of the tower.

"Tower, tower. Top of the tower."

The hand beckoned, in an encouraging gesture.

"Um. Roland?"

A quick finger wag no.

"Just tell me. If you can't talk, write the words, like you did with the clouds—"

The brows furrowed and the figure shook its head in a violent 'no,' reminding Gus of his friend's little brother throwing a tantrum.

"Calm down, I'll keep playing charades, shhh. Shhh." He held his hands out placatingly. The being vibrated and wisps of whatever it was made of started to emanate like dry-ice vapor. With some coaxing, he finally settled the creature and within seconds the being was just staring expectantly as if nothing had happened. It then formed the tower again with its accompanying arm.

"Turret? Spire?"

A back and forth wishy-washy movement. The finger once again pointed to the very top of the tower, then motioned at the body of the tower with another finger wag no.

"So only the top. Okay. Penthouse?"

A vehement thumbs down.

"Capstone?"

A tenuous, waggling okay sign let Gus know he was close but not getting the exact meaning that was trying to be conveyed.

"So Cap for now. I like that. A little more personal than 'hey you.'"

The tower reverted to its previous humanoid figure. Holding its hand out, another figure bulged out of its hand and resolved into a small man the size of an action figure. As it became more detailed, Gus recognized it as himself, though it was a solid white with no shading for details. This was further confirmed when Cap pointed to it and then to Gus.

"I get it, that's me. Now what?"

The mini-Gus split like an unwound piece of rope, separating into three components, each with a different color. One red, one blue, and one a greenish yellow. Cap's other hand beckoned to the sky, where clouds had gathered to form a distinctive shape, reminiscent of his display. The figures leaped into the air and flew like streaks, leaving colored contrails behind them. They populated the areas on his display where he tracked his HP, MP, and Stamina.

Seeing the connection, Gus tried to confirm.

"So those three aspects are part of my nature, I guess? Health, energy, and MP. What would MP be?"

Cap waved its hands in a "slow down" gesture. The colored figures flashed back, and Cap pointed to the red one.

"That's health—"

A vehement shaking of the finger.

"Not health, then… Life?"

Big thumbs up from the figure.

"Not sure how that's different than health, though."

Next Cap pointed to the blue figure, which was analogous to MP. With its other hand, it made a cage around the blue character and pointed to Gus.

"So I can't access my MP. I *have* figured that out."

The figure shrugged then scooped its hand as if to say 'go on.'

"Why? Oh boy. To be honest, I really don't know what MP is. It's just the fuel for your powers."

Cap looked around as if looking for something, then again with the shrug.

"Where? Like where does it come from?"

A vigorous head nodding 'yes.'

"I don't know…"

The eyes looked severe and Cap jabbed at its temple.

"I'm thinking, I'm thinking, jeesh. So it's energy that fuels powers, and somehow the Nth must be able to use it to make abilities work. You showed it as a part of me. Has that always been that way, or only after I became a super?"

Cap held up two fingers. It pointed to the first and nodded, then the second and shook its head.

"I guess I should just ask yes or no questions so it's easier to respond. So if I'm understanding you, MP has always been a part of me?"

Cap nodded and gave a thumbs up.

"And other humans?" The nodding continued. "All humans, even regs?" Still nodding.

"That's something I didn't know. So we all have access to this MP energy whether we have abilities or not. The difference must come when we get Nth to actually do something with that—"

Cap pointed at Gus and was nodding like a madman. He had hit upon something. Cap waggled its fingertips forwards as if it was helping someone park a car. *Keep it coming.*

"So if everyone has it, and it must recharge, do we generate this energy ourselves?"

Cap waggled a finger no.

"So we don't make it, but we absorb it over time?"

Thumbs up.

"So it comes from the environment, then?"

The wishy-washy, sort-of gesture.

"Is there more than one type of MP?"

Cap leaned back and closed its eyes in what could only be ecstasy as it pinched its fingers and nodded with slow satisfaction. It stepped over to the blue thread and peeled it like a banana into six thinner filaments.

There was an orange one, a translucent one, an opaque white, dark black, light green, and brown. The threads sparkled as light glinted off them, reflecting on tiny hidden facets, refracting light slightly when it hit them just the right way.

"Whoa." Gus scooted closer to get a better look but the being put a gentle hand on his shoulder and gave him a warning look. It was only after backing up and blinking that he saw after images from the filaments temporarily burned into his vision. Gus rubbed his closed eyelids and still saw the afterimages of the sparkling threads. When they finally started to fade, it was back to a mere blue thread and the figure zipped them back together and the mini-Gus reformed and sublimated away.

The figure folded its arms expectantly.

Gus grimaced and rubbed his tongue over his teeth. When the figure didn't move or respond, Gus ran a hand through his hair.

"You gotta give me something more than that."

A finger stabbed out, wagging at Gus a number of times, each time a little bit higher before ending right above his head. It then did the pinching zip motion with its fingers and waved goodbye. It turned and stepped back into the water, its body dissolving into a brighter glint on the water's surface upon stepping completely in the water. Once the crest of its head dipped below a wave, it was gone.

What was all that about? And how does it possibly help me?

An errant wave sloshed over his feet, tickling them as the sand streamed by as the wave receded. Gus looked over his shoulder and saw a familiar outcrop. He navigated to the spot and watched the ocean and pondered what he needed to do as he watched the day settle into a golden sunset.

CHAPTER SEVENTY-FOUR

Want You Gone

"Razor. I've tried to be patient all these years. I thought we were past all this once we both graduated. Agree to disagree and just go our separate ways. I think you've told yourself a different story about what really happened. Enough that you have convinced yourself that things happened differently than they did. You were the bully. I don't understand how you've made yourself out to be the victim. It just pissed you off that despite all you did, I succeeded in spite of you. That's the real issue, isn't it? Short little Darik always beating you somehow."

Like I chose to be short. Out of all the Lusk men in his family, he was at least a foot shorter than his shortest brother. A trade-off for getting his powers much earlier than normal. While he had a much more intuitive control of his abilities, in his case it severely stunted his growth. He was never really self-conscious about it, regardless of how much idiots like Razor thought it was a dig.

"If the instructors weren't favoring you, none of that would have happened! I earned the top space, but they had to be all sensitive and politically correct. Let the little guy win," Razor finished in a taunting high-pitched voice.

"You just can't admit that anyone could have beaten you fair and square, can you? It just doesn't compute in that small brain of yours. You know, Razor, some people are wise enough to learn from the experience of others, but some just have to put their hand on the stove and get burned before they actually *believe* that they'll get burned. I've had enough of taking the higher road. It obviously doesn't work with you. If you start something, I'm not pulling any more punches. I won't hold back from here on out. Don't start no shite, and won't be no shite."

Razor rubbed his hands in eager anticipation. "This is going to be so much fun."

Behind Darik, one of the others crept up, having been stealthed the entire time, waiting for the signal. He cocked back an arm, ready to hit Darik in the back of the head and disorient him. With a swing, the punch connected and the sound of bone crunching was audible. Spittle flew. It was on!

If there was one thing that Darik excelled at, it was scrapping. He and his brothers loved to wrestle and often the bouts escalated to actual blows until their mother came out to lay down the law. 'Beat the hell out of each other, but don't make more work for me. Either by bloodying your clothes, or making a mess.'

Roughhousing was strictly forbidden for that reason. The large field behind their house had the ground constantly churned up by their incessant bickering. A smile of anticipation curled the side of Darik's lip.

Darik's spatial awareness had grown by leaps and bounds since he had left the Academy. As such, he was always aware of anyone or anything within a certain space around him. The super who thought he was being stealthy didn't realize that he displaced air with his movement, giving it a different density and thus changing the feel of the 'field,' as Darik liked to think about the space around him where he could move and maneuver with almost subconscious skill. The further removed the space, the more difficult it was, but up close, that was his wheelhouse.

He effortlessly calculated where the exit portal should be and when the attack came, it was easy to connect the two. The attack that was meant for his 'unprotected' head was redirected as he opened a portal behind him, allowing the punch to connect with Razor's jaw. The ferocity of the attack surprised all involved. Darik narrowed his eyes. *So they weren't pulling any punches either, eh?*

Everyone sprang into action simultaneously. The super behind Darik lunged and grabbed his arms, pinning them behind him. Another took the opportunity to punch him hard in the gut.

Darik just rolled his eyes as the punch was redirected into the kidney of his captor. Expecting the momentum to push him forward, he opened another portal right below him. It swallowed both him and the super holding him much less tightly after the unexpected hit from behind. The sensation of falling caused him to totally let go as he spun his arms to regain his balance.

Darik was used to the feeling and opened another quick portal. It winked closed as his previous captor passed through the air in its wake... landing on top of one of the others. They crumpled to the ground in a tangle of arms and legs.

He oriented the portal's exit so he would be propelled horizontally to the ground, and aimed to kick another super in the back. When he thought he should connect, he just sailed through the form and landed badly on the ground, right in the center of the group. As he scrambled to get his bearings, his shoulder and back exploded in pain. It felt like he had been hit with a cannonball. The force of the impact pushed him down and he slid face-first into the dirt, plowing a small furrow.

A well-timed kick spun him around and he curled in on himself. As he rolled onto his side, he saw Razor's eyes, wild and bloodshot. Blood dribbled down one side of his jaw and it definitely looked like it wasn't hinging correctly.

"Your mouth can't stop writing checks that your ass can't cash!" Razor taunted. A neon blue glow emanated from his knuckles and Darik tried to shy away from the blow, but was not quick enough in forming his portal. The impact forced him eight feet into the ground, his portal tunneling downward. Without the time to create an exit portal, he was forced to 'hold' the material, a process that chewed up a huge chunk of his MP as the dirt and rock below him were displaced. He strained to open a portal at the limit of his field and forced out the dirt and rock, but the damage was done.

The effort caused him to spasm, and was akin to a dry-heave from hell. Blood vessels burst in his eyes, turning them a bright red, giving him a demonic look. At last he expelled all of the material, but it had taken a lot out of him, physically and mentally. He lay panting at the bottom of the hole and one of the supers began stomping, caving in dirt that tumbled down the incline.

Darik began to paw at the dirt like a dog, trying to make it out of the hole and push the dirt aside as it tumbled inward; while he was not claustrophobic, he didn't want to be buried alive. He only had 25% of his MP left, and might not be able to force a portal if enough material surrounded him. He quickly realized that he was not going to make it.

———

Yuki turned and dove off of the branch, forgetting the physics of this world. She was coasting downward, but the lowered gravity was almost lazily pulling her towards the ground. The rabid lemurs were not hindered by this at all. They pulled them-selves along branches and tree trunks, moving in short hops. They stopped on the branch she had just vacated, with more and more populating the space. There were hundreds of them, and their savage faces looked out of place on their fluffy, skinny bodies.

Yuki tried swimming through the air, pulling in a breast-stroke that made no apparent change in her speed. She floated over the top of one of the smaller trees, its top barely slipping past her fingertips. She tried again and was able to grasp a little bit of a thin trunk and she yanked. Her hand stripped off the leaves and slid off. She was rewarded in gaining a little more downward momentum, but no trees were around her now. A loud Jurassic Park bellow from behind her made her look over her shoulder.

No, Yuki. Never look!

The rabid lemurs were gripping each other, holding tightly as their conjoined forms created a large gorillemur, for lack of a better term. The last few lemurs crawled into place on the head. Once again it threw out its chest and roared. The AI environments were thankfully free of certain biologic needs, but Yuki could have sworn she peed just a little. When she finally managed to pull her eyes away, the last thing she saw was the gorillemur leaping off of the branch.

The volume of the roars was getting louder and was like a demonic Doppler effect. Her frantic paddling stirred up dust and pollen in the still air. Paddling madly while scrolling through her display, she found the perfect avatar—if only she could get to the forest floor. Absolutely nothing was close unfortunately, and she was still over a hundred feet away from anything at all. She didn't want to use her only flier avatar, which would be difficult to use in the thick forest, and would not lend itself to fighting this creature.

With inhuman agility, the gorillemur used its monstrously long arms to swing to a perch above her on the nearest tree. It opened its large mouth, which was rows and rows of claws lined up. It looked like a shark's maw. The talons like claws flexed and extended.

No, not a shark. Its mouth looks like a Sarlacc!

And then it jumped.

CHAPTER SEVENTY-FIVE

Seeds of Destruction

The diminished gravity made the gorillemur's fall appear surreal, like bullet time. Knowing she had nowhere to flee, it had not propelled itself off the branch and fell at a similar rate to Yuki.

It reached out a long arm towards her, and she saw the gnashing animals that made up each finger cackling in anticipation of their next meal.

With as much willpower as she could muster, she stopped staring at the approaching monster and resumed paddling while mentally scrolling through her avatars, looking for alternatives. The more she did, the more she realized she needed the one she had chosen. She didn't want to transform until she was close though, as her small size would make her a more difficult target if the beast got close. It felt like trying to dive to the bottom of the pool, and she had some residual buoyancy that wanted to resist her efforts to get to the forest floor.

This was what sucked the worst about an AI hack. You never knew what to expect. She had liked the challenge when she was younger, but the field had really improved the complexity and difficulty of the bosses. It didn't help that the

AIs leveled up with each failed delve, so they became harder and harder to beat the more people tried to hack them. She didn't know why she hadn't thought about how Green was probably cutting their teeth on trying to hack into Purple's mainframe on a regular basis.

But as much as she hated the inability to plan, she loved the challenge. There was always something new. It definitely was never boring or routine. And she preferred the escape from her mundane life. If she was honest, she was an adrenaline junkie too. She wouldn't admit it, but she liked getting the shi—

A deep roar interrupted her thoughts as she worked to move, urging her to pull harder and descend faster. She dared another look and was horrified to see that it was closer than it should have been if they were both falling in the same environment.

No-no-no-no-no-NO! The creature was moving so fast!

It shouldn't be able to fall at a quicker rate than she was. Gravity didn't work like that. If this was an evaluation, that developer would definitely get points off for his physics engine. If anything, it should fall slower from more drag. The gorillemur cocked an arm back to take a swipe. It was close enough it could snatch her from this distance.

She blinked as something caught in her eye, stinging and burning. She pawed at it, wanting to be able to see in case she could somehow dodge the attack coming for her when something else got in her other eye. What was that, an eyelash?

The wind hit her like an unexpected wave on the beach. It carried her laterally through the air, and through blurry eyes she saw an enormous hand swing where she had just been, leaving contrails in the pollen. The wind picked up in earnest, carrying her out of range again but she had to shield her eyes. Either the size of the pollen or the fact that there was so much of it was wreaking havoc on her eyes like a sandstorm.

She tumbled in the current as a roar of frustration rose above the whistle of the wind. She was heading for a tree. She was hesitant to hit it, but realized this was exactly what she needed. She tried to roll with the hit as she collided with the mossy trunk and nearly lost her grasp as a large green chunk of something tore away from the tree trunk like sod. Her other hand managed to dig into some gnarled bark underneath and her momentum wrapped her around the trunk of the tree.

She rapidly side-shifted, moving to the leeward side of the tree trunk. Though she was upside down, she didn't feel light headed as she pulled herself down the trunk toward the ground. There was a thinner layer of the tree-sod on this side, but still it was there, sloughing off if she tried to move too quickly, but now she was making a much quicker descent to the ground.

The sound of splintering wood nearby prodded her to go even faster, taking more chances. She began ripping off the sod in large strips and throwing it to the side as she pulled herself down, kicking occasionally with her feet to propel her down-ward when they could snag some ridge of bark.

Only about a hundred feet. So close. A ripple of force trav-eled down the trunk. She could see a large hand made of blood-thirsty lemurs holding the tree she was on, pulling itself down toward her. She just hoped it was far enough away. Fifty feet. Another flash of movement to her left but she refused to look. Her eyes were fixed on a small patch of black soil between two roots of the large tree. That was her world. Everything shrunk down to a small foot and a half square.

Like an Olympic runner, she reached for her finish line, extending her arm to its utmost and triggered **Summon** as her middle fingertip touched the loamy dirt.

Cedarhowl Splintermaple

Born as the seventh offshoot of the seventh generation of her line, Cedarhowl was born under auspicious celestial signs as well as in a time of great fertility, granting her unique connections to two of the realms. They allow her to cross environments and she has used her abilities as both a warrior and mediator between those in her sphere, making her one of the most respected among animate and inanimate life. All who know her respect her as the most bitchin' spriggan this side of creation.

Nourish: Pull life force from the inanimate environment to grow at an accelerated rate.

Barkskin: Protect outer surface with a hardened shell of dead rhytidome which shields the user.

Compost: Pull residual life force from decomposing organic material, breaking it down to base nutrients. Does not affect living creatures.

Me So Thorny: Cover a limb with barbed, hollow, detachable thorns that cause a constant bleeding debuff until removed. Forcible removal will result in a base damage of 25 HP per thorn.

This avatar has not had its Ultimate unlocked. Hidden Conditions not met.

Yuki felt roots spring from her fingers and anchor her to the ground, quickly crawling through the dirt as easily as if it were water. She activated *Nourish* and *Barkskin* simultaneously as she pulled her other arm and feet to the ground and found areas to dig them into the dirt, anchoring them as well. A heavy scab-like mass began to form on her back, and she felt like a turtle hunched on all fours.

She pulled greedily at the ground, drinking in the energy, absorbing it, making it hers. She sipped through each limb, like a dehydrated hiker finally drinking something cool and refreshing through a straw.

It allowed her to increase in mass quickly, and she began to hear a susurrus as her need was sated. Instead of breathing through her mouth, she felt herself siphon energy that distilled down from the meager light above and from the air itself. She felt like a giant sieve, pulling in from every direction.

The murmurs got louder, and more pronounced and she began to understand some of the whispers.

That is not the way, an old voice said with disdain.

Too much. It is unseemly, a childlike voice interjected.

It will upset the balance. Balance at all costs, a stern voice reprimanded.

With a start, Yuki realized they were talking about *her,* and how she was taking in energy. She stopped sucking in and removed one hand from the ground, bracing it on one of the thick roots to the tree she had just descended.

Please child, no more, the thought resonated back from the root, whose outer bark had taken a blanched, almost peeled texture, like a croissant or a bad, peeling sunburn.

Yuki stopped taking any energy when a Kaiju-sized claw pried her off the ground and flipped her through the air.

CHAPTER SEVENTY-SIX

We Intertwined

Light flashed as Yuki flipped ass over teakettle, landing in a large clump of ferns. Slightly dazed, but not hurt, she could sense the gouges in the bark-like plate that had formed on her back. Instinctively, she sunk her hands into the ground, burrowing past the fern and the whispers became sharp, like tuning in a radio station. Though multiple minds were speaking, she could sort and understand them all simultaneously. There was a pause in the conversations as she joined in the awareness, lacking only the awkward record scratch.

One bold tiny voice spoke up. "You were meat. How can you hear us?"

Yuki's attention drifted downward to a small tree. Though its form was small, Yuki saw its inner essence, which was stocky and had its arms crossed, looking at her with an expression that demanded Yuki explain herself.

"I was being attacked, so I shifted to this form."

"The matters of meat are no concern of ours!" one of the tall trees boomed.

"Until they invade…" a female voice warned.

"You took from one of the Elders, explain yourself!" a grumpy old man voice demanded.

"I meant no harm; I was just trying to protect myself from… some other meat. I am sorry if I took too much for myself."

"Insufficient…"

"At least she knows what she did."

"She is disturbing our rest. I was ripped from my home!" a thin moss spirit whined.

"I do not mean to disturb any of you," Yuki explained. "Help me defeat this other… meat, and I will leave you."

"Your kind always takes. Take. Take. Take. Using us for your selfish ends."

"I… you are right. I have done nothing to merit your trust or assistance, but believe me that I do not want to harm any of you," Yuki admitted.

"I sense sincerity."

"Yes. Cannot be denied. I will lend you my poisons, it will stop the meat."

"And my thorns will taste its liquid iron."

"My pollen is quite irritating to most meat, here."

Yuki shuddered as small vines extended and touched her head. They slithered in like little snakes and once they had found a crack, they began to push. Then grow. While the process did not hurt, there was an audible crunching noise that was unsettling. Visions of a nutcracker crushing a walnut were the best description of how it felt as the multiple threads pushed their way inside. When sufficiently rooted, there was a surge. And Yuki just knew.

You have received new abilities:
Spore: *Release virulent spores that induce violent allergic reactions.*
Toxin: *Poison your target in multiple ways, through many different methods. [See variants.] Can be combined with other growths for added effects.*
Shred: *Create vines studded with thorns to hamper movement and damage enemies.*

"Now go. Keep your promise and restore our rest," the tall tree boomed again, petulant that Yuki had been given anything.

Time moved differently here. Though this communication had felt like a normal one, she knew the entire parlay had taken only the briefest of moments. The transfer of knowledge was another near-instantaneous sliver of time. She could not see the gorillemur. However, with the newfound connection to the others, she could tell how far away it was and shared in the discomfort the plants were feeling from being bent, uprooted, and crushed by its passing as if they were done to a distant appendage of her own body. Pressure from its steps tickled along roots underground, and provided a ping like echolocation or a radar.

She turned and rushed to meet the threat. As she began to run, nearby plants pushed nourishment into her feet, and she grew with each step. *Run, forest, run!* she thought as she passed a tree that had fallen, revealing a ball of upturned gnarled roots. She grabbed the trunk, wielding it like a cudgel as she caught the first glimpse of the gorillemur.

It had grown in size as more creatures had joined the conglomeration, and was now easily thirty feet tall and getting larger. Yuki yanked the tree free, shook off the dirt clumped in its roots, and swung the trunk, hitting the beast solidly in the side of its torso.

Lemurs exploded away, flung like LEGOs in all different directions. Yuki had left herself over-extended with the swing and a powerful backhand hit her and bent her over. Instead of flying away, her feet intertwined with the underlying root system. Rolling with the blow, she leaned back and was able to rebound to her upright posture in a way that would have made gymnasts and limbo-aficionados gasp.

Dropping the tree, she began to punch the creature, pushing more thorns out along her abnormally large fists and forearms as they broke off and embedded in the individual creatures. She found she could secrete all sorts of nasty poisons along their length, the variety overwhelming. Without time to choose, she just made a cocktail of the worst and kept attacking. Each hole she punched into the creature was quickly sealed with other animals who crawled to fill the gap underneath.

In frustration, the gorillemur bellowed again, calling to more lemurs who leapt down from the treetops, adding to the mass. With each punch, Yuki started activating **Compost** to break down the dead bodies of lemurs. They crumbled to a nasty paste. As the spatter began to hit the ground, she felt a surge of energy as the forest metabolized the nutrients and gave them back to her. With this assistance, she was able to grow in proportion with the monster, but she was still dwarfed by its size.

Unable to land any attacks, the gorillemur pulled itself up a nearby tree to regroup. Its bulk began to undulate and swell. Soon it would be large enough to overpower her if she did nothing. As Yuki pursued, she felt a massive drop in her power as her feet left the nourishing comfort of the soft soil. The fact that her growth had stopped as she lost her connection to the ground was not lost on the animals who began a taunting yipping noise as it jumped from tree to tree, retreating upward.

With a thought, she sent some vines to grab the creature to secure it. Briefly the monster was bound, but abandoning those lemurs, it melted out of the vine's grasp and was off to another limb. The further from the forest floor, the more difficult it was to manipulate the vines as they all needed to be rooted and they became ungainly the higher up they had to extend.

Seizing upon some of the gifted knowledge, she expelled a cloud of thorns like shotgun scatter, but the gorillemur was too agile. It easily dodged and twisted out of the few shots she managed.

She pulled herself after the creature, hearing the other plants cheer her efforts. They were excited, finally having an agent to actively defend them. Not wanting to let them down, Yuki pushed forward, looking down as she perched atop another thick branch. She wasn't afraid of falling from this height, but felt something probably best described as homesickness as she distanced herself from the comforting and nourishing safety of the ground.

More mocking yips baited her to follow, and she reluctantly began climbing again. Its ascent brought it in the direct path of more of the infernal creatures and they replenished those that were lost and then began building up, forming new layers upon layers. It's arms also grew, and its enhanced reach allowed it to climb even faster.

The gap between Yuki and it began to grow. As it moved from tree to tree, finding larger ones to climb as it fled, Yuki had to get creative and lash out with vines, swinging like Tarzan to keep up with the creature. It was not as easy as the holovids made it look, and she got hung up on branches as there were no clear paths as she scrambled to stay close to the beast.

There was a large crack and the gorillemur shifted to stay in the trees. Looking at the large treetop that had splintered in its paw, it threw it at Yuki. The monster was so heavy now that the trees couldn't support its weight anymore. Its demeanor changed from one of flight to fight as it began breaking off branches and limbs, throwing them recklessly in her direction without any real aim. A couple times, she almost lost her footing as the limb collided with the tree she was holding onto and the jolt of impact almost made her lose her grasp. She mentally grew her fingers longer, gaining a better grip.

Another branch distracted her and an inhumanly long arm flicked like a whip, snatching her while she was distracted. Claws dug into her bark skin and pressed in like ticks. She was slowly pried free from her perch and pulled across the clearing created by the broken trees. The gorillemur clenched tightly, but it did not have the strength of a creature that size actually would have.

Still, it was strong enough that she couldn't wiggle free, and her arms were tightly pressed to her sides. The lemurs had positioned themselves so that most of her thorns were hitting their hard claws and could not poke their soft, furry bodies. Occasionally, one would get poked and fall away but another would quickly take its place.

It brought her towards its gaping maw; the coordination of the flexing claws and tiny teeth deeper inside the creature's mouth was almost hypnotic in its pattern. She was going to be in the wood-chipper soon if she didn't think of something.

Always able to think on her feet, Yuki prepared her last gambit. She would probably need to be close for maximum effect but timing was everything. She hyperventilated, taking multiple small breaths, accelerating her breath. The creature mistook this for panic and was excited by her apparent fear, its anticipation escalating.

When she was as close as she dared, she activated *Spore* and breathed out a noxious orange cloud. She had put everything she could muster into it; pollen, spores, toxins and poisons. It belched out in a plume, directly hitting the mass of creatures full in the mouth, and enveloped its entire head. And it just kept coming, like her Uncle Tommy's post-Thanksgiving burps or a high-note held by an opera star, the ochre colored particles shot out with projectile-vomit force. The closest lemurs were most affected, trembling and losing cohesion with their brothers, falling down to the forest floor below.

The plume guttered out and ended, and Yuki could tell that the effort had cost her some of her mass; she had shrunk as the large claw compressed her now more-hollow insides to a smaller diameter. The head was entirely gone, a large section eroded away like a melted snow-cone. More lemurs began rebuilding the head from below.

While they did so, she was held still, as if without its faux head, it couldn't plan its attack. The chin and mouth formed again and the creature began to gain some of its thought capacity because it pushed Yuki away from itself, placing her in the center of the clearing where she couldn't gas it again. And if she attacked the arm holding her, there would be a long fall if she couldn't catch herself.

Angry eyebrows formed at last, and an eerie rictus spread across the gorillemur's face as the last of its head began to form, completing the monstrosity.

CHAPTER SEVENTY-SEVEN

I Want to Break Free

Yuki began to panic as options seemed to be dwindling away. The claustrophobic grip of the large hand wasn't helping her anxiety either. In desperation, she pushed out thorns and poisons, but the ones gripping her had dug in their claws and shriveled in on themselves into the fetal position. Other lemurs gripped tightly to them and her spines and oozing poison did not affect them.

She even tried forcing a couple large, two-foot spikes. That speared a couple but she found that she could only force out the longer spikes from eight areas, and the animals quickly learned to stay out of the path of the spikes. It had learned its lesson, and kept her at arm's length in the center of the clearing, which for this creature was a good hundred and fifty feet at this point.

More lemurs began crawling down the extended arm, forming a large ball around her, just far enough to be out of reach. Their musky, wet scent was unpleasant but she didn't feel the typical nausea in her current form.

As they built up around her, more and more light was blocked from her and, as it grew darker, the effect was soporific. Like the nappy feeling after a carb crash, she just wanted to rest.

Part of her mind screamed for her to do something. She had to fight her nature that just wanted to hibernate in the darkness. She could feel herself pulling inward despite her efforts to struggle.

No! She couldn't let this happen. The fear of the certain backlash feedback made her panic even more, but her avatar was acting on instinct. Curling up into a ball, her essence pulled inward against her wishes. Ever hardening layers as she retreated to a small condensed core. A tiny green core in a woody jawbreaker.

As she shrunk, her awareness also blurred at the edges. She could perceive less and less of the world around her, and after a dozen layers, the dead woody bark gave no feedback to the sharp claws of the lemurs. Her anxiety skyrocketed as she was encased with more and more layers. The helplessness of being buried alive was worse than she had ever imagined. Trapped. She wiggled as she tried to resist. She had felt this feeling too many times in her real life. Confined and bound. *No!*

She couldn't log off either, the option grayed out on her display due to being in active combat. Right when the feelings of panic had reached a crescendo, she was kicked from the system. There was the briefest moment of relief as she was finally free as everything burst into a blinding light. Then a grenade of molten pain exploded in her brain.

———

Darik covered his head as dirt began to fall. Darkness engulfed him as the exit collapsed inward. The only option was to go down. He made as small of a portal as he dared and blindly dove to the bottom of the tunnel. Searing pain burned his foot as he got the angle wrong. He rolled out onto the ground and clutched his leg. A thin wisp of smoke emanated from the severed boot. A quick peek showed the bones of his smallest two toes visible through the neat slice.

He lifted his head just in time to see Razor's interlaced fists catch him under the jaw. He was crouched low, like he was bumping a volleyball. Darik flew atop the small mound of dirt he had expelled, seeing Razor leaning back for some reason.

Which became clear when a huge hammer crashed into Darik's chest, slamming him down into the pile of loose dirt. A sickening tearing sound, accompanied with a pop and sharp pain when he gasped. Breathing became a struggle, and he saw lumps along his chest where his ribs had separated.

Gasping there like a fish out of water, Razor came and stood at his feet, hands on his hips. A wide grin spread on his face as he watched Darik suffer. As time seemed to slow, he noticed how bad his teeth were. His gums had receded and the teeth were already moving into a grotesque arrangement.

He cracked his knuckles and rubbed his hands in front of him, eager as a child eating his Halloween loot. Darik had always had a high pain tolerance, but the inability to breathe normally was making it hard to concentrate. He had to fight the urge to hyperventilate and pull in slow pained breaths. The others stood around his prone form, some with arms folded smugly in front of them others leaning forward, hands on their knees. Razor raised one leg up high, ready to stomp Darik right in the chest.

This is going to hurt...

———

Gus was floating above his naked body lying on the metal table. The pain was gone. At long last, he felt... nothing. He had heard of stories like this before people passed on.

Am I dead?

He moved around but felt a tension as he tried to move too far from his body. A series of seven tethers attached to his spine at various levels connected to his body, invisible until he began to pull on them. The harder he tried to pull away, the tighter and thicker they became. Relaxing, he observed himself lying there and focused on the anchor points.

As he relaxed more, he began to see tiny channels extending away from each of the crossroads. Occasionally, there was a slight movement, but nothing was moving. It reminded Gus of a traffic jam. The biggest congestion was around the top three centers, especially the top node. No movement was visible here, where the tiny conduits were completely clogged.

There was an intermittent surge as whatever was inside the conduits tried to bypass the blockage. Gus recognized the flare was perfectly synced with the familiar pulse rhythm of his headaches. While he could not feel them, their echoes were still all too clear, like a canyon carved into being by a persistent river over a millennium.

Gus looked at the lowest node, for lack of a better term. It was the least clogged in comparison and even though he was 'detached,' he could still create a pressure by flexing. It squished like Jell-O in a balloon. As the material in the lower channel started to move, Gus began to see individual particles, like small globules of oil, begin to roll through the pathways. There was sluggish movement as his pressure caused the gelatinous mass to move.

Four pathways that extended from the node, two per leg, and they fanned out like petals from a flower. It became a struggle to move the thick, sludge-like material. Gus squeezed like he was trying to eke out the last bit of toothpaste in a tube. He coaxed it along the path, finding that it only moved in one direction. Attempts to squish in the opposite direction caused it to bulge and ball up. Fearing the tube would burst, he massaged the material along the path. It appeared a dark black, but began to lighten as it quivered and started to move.

He could only exert the pressure for a little while before he exhausted himself and had to rest. The sensation reminded Gus of taking a large gasp after holding your breath for a long time, except that he was incorporeal and didn't have to breathe at all. When he felt relaxed again, he exerted more tension and the sludge began to flow again.

He went through multiple cycles of this. Push, rest. Push

again. With time, he began to gain a little momentum and as the material began to move, it transitioned from a thick, doughy consistency to something closer to syrup. The color faded as it began to separate, making it more apparent that the channels themselves were a red color and the contents must be blue since they gave a deep purple color as the little blobs rolled through the channels like tiny bits of wax in a lava lamp.

Once the obstructions were removed, the material clarified further, and each loop became lighter and lighter until it glowed a radiant red color. It began to burn with the radiant hue of an illuminated ruby and it was hard to pull his eyes away. Faster and faster the liquid moved along the pathway, flowing like a river.

As it picked up momentum, the tiny blobs within the channel began to melt and disappear. As it became totally liquid, it moved even quicker, occasionally sparking crimson pops as it flowed through the channels. It reminded Gus of a Van de Graaff generator he had seen in school, the motion generating some kind of a charge.

The carmine color was captivating, and it was hard to pull his attention off of it. The mesmerizing motion through the channels and the pattern it moved in tickled at the back of his memory. Something he had seen before, like a rune or magic symbol of some sort. But where? A video game, or piece of art from a tabletop RPG campaign?

He was unsure how long he stared there. Time in this ghostly existence seemed fuzzy. Suddenly, Mengele was there, standing over him. He couldn't make out the words, they sounded warbled like he was speaking underwater. He was obviously flustered as he scanned Gus from top to bottom. Was he frustrated that he had lost his prey, letting Gus die?

Mengele placed an ebony hand over Gus' chest and, with a snap, he was yanked back into his body.

CHAPTER SEVENTY-EIGHT

Red Rain

Words began to resolve from an incoherent mumble to sharp focus. Mengele was muttering to himself.

"Was this a trick all along? There's no way he could have reached this level that quickly. Two years to activate my base and this upstart manages it in one day? The master must be testing me..."

Gus' eyes flew open as he snapped back to himself and he took in a large gasp. His throat felt coated and dusty like the inside of a heating duct. A coughing spasm overtook him, and he had to spit out a tarry, thick sputum. Secured as he was, it fell back against his chin and slid like a slug down the side of his neck.

From the corner of his eye he saw the glint of a scalpel. Tensing, he braced himself, feeling a flicker of red and a surge of power. There were a couple of snaps as red arcs crackled along his back and the metal table. Instead of the split-second delay where he felt nothing before the scalpel dug deep and pain burned, all Gus heard was a tiny *tink*.

Mengele growled and grabbed something else from the table by him. By the way it rasped against his skin, he knew it to be the bone saw. Instead of taking a bite into his tissue, it skidded and bounced along the top of his arm. A thrum that Gus hadn't noticed was there in the background, revved up like an engine shifting gears. His back began to tingle a bit as the intensity of the sparks along his back and legs intensified. A ghostly mist formed at the edges of his field of vision, fading in and out of perception.

Mengele lunged for the IV and crushed a small white contraption on the tube that kept fluid falling into a small reservoir in measured drops. Milky liquid raced to his arm. Instead of the feeling of angry fire ants crawling through his veins, there was... nothing. Except the shifting of gears again as the thrum resonated at an even higher pitch.

Mengele rushed away, and Gus heard metal clanking. With desperation, his tormentor squeezed a large syringe into his IV bag, turning the white liquid a slight yellow color as it mixed and flowed.

The flicker in Gus' vision began to happen more quickly, and he finally realized it for what it was—his display! He could see it again! As it became more solid, Gus felt the agitated red energy ripple over him like tiny bubbles. Defying gravity, they flowed upward to cover him completely. The red foamy wave flowed over his face and in between the tight clamps on his legs, arms, and head. Then they began to merge, becoming more transparent as the bubbles jiggled and joined.

Seeing his display come into focus, Gus tried to access his abilities, and they were there. Well, some of them were. **Bound**, **Enhanced Strength**, **Intermediate Shielding**, **Shake**, **Shatter**, and all of his **Wreck** skills were there. He was going to activate **Intermediate Shielding**, but it was already active, passively. Where his skin touched his restraints, he could discern a difference between this metal and the one the table was made of.

As the red energy infused him, it needed an outlet. Pouring his attention into his restraints, he felt their unique signature. They appeared as a wide sine wave. Funneling energy into the wave, he intuitively created a wave that mirrored the metal. As he pushed the energy out, the amplitude of the wave increased bit by bit, but its frequency remained the same. Knowing there was an outlet, energy began to flow with more force. His body trembled as it became the equivalent of a shotgunned drink.

Mengele continued to try to do something, but nothing was working. There was a brief flash of heat, and Gus turned to see a large laser pointed at him, its beam aimed at the left side of his chest. Around its target, the bubbles smoothed and became completely transparent with a crimson tinge. Once it clarified, the beam reflected off, scoring the ceiling with a deep burn until Mengele released the activator and pushed it to the side with a heave.

The restraints began to glow lightly with the strain. One restraint on his hand split with a loud *crack*! The free ends rattled against each other like machine-gun fire. One by one, the other restraints began to break. A side of the first restraint to break snapped free and flew toward Mengele's face. He easily batted it away, but it sounded like a gong when his black arm connected with the chunk of metal. Shielding his eyes, he slowly moved forward as metal rattled and flew.

Gus' joints popped as he heaved himself over and fell face-first on the ground. He still felt numb, his body covered in an insensate prickle. The energy that Gus felt on the table exploded into his body. His arms were clutched to his chest, right under his chin, and Gus vomited. Black ooze poured out of him, giving him creepy flashbacks of Methiochos' tentacled body. His back arched as he forcefully expelled whatever toxic garbage was in his system.

Despite the traumatic nature of the experience, Gus immediately felt better. With a shriek, the operating table was pried up with a black hand and flung out of the way. Panting, Mengele picked up Gus like a naughty kitten, holding him by the back of the neck. With a sharp twist, he spun Gus to face him. There was a dimming of the power as Gus lost contact with the floor, but long, thin arcs of scarlet energy occasionally jumped to make contact with the soles of his feet.

Muscles bulged on Mengele's forearm, but they could not compress Gus' neck. Veins popped out on Mengele's neck and forehead as he tried with all his might to crush Gus' windpipe, but to no avail.

Woodenly, Gus reached up and grabbed the arm holding him. He could feel the same red energy pulsing through Mengele. The contact with Mengele gave another signature wavelength, this one much more complex. Gus directed the throbbing energy pent up in him into it.

Unlike the restraints, the energy felt like it fell down a deep well and didn't hit bottom. Mengele squinted his eyes at Gus.

"I don't know how you did it, but I didn't work this hard to share this power." He leaned back to hurl Gus.

Gus pulled energy up through Mengele and held on for dear life. He directed all of it through his hands as they clutched onto Mengele's arm. As his captor let go, Gus prepared for an impromptu flight, which never happened. He remained firmly attached like a tick. Gus squinted his own eyes as he looked back at Mengele. No matter how he flicked, Gus couldn't be pried off of his arm.

"Leave… that… alone," Mengele growled through gritted teeth as Gus pulled on the energy. It flowed more quickly, but the energy tumbled into the abyss and was gone. Still he pulled. As energy coursed through him, the tingle of numbness was washed away in the tide and Gus felt his grip tighten even more.

Tiny waxy worms squeezed out of his pores like blackheads as the energy pressed through him. Thin webs of energy formed all around him, converging on the pair like the electrode in a plasma ball. Equipment was cut neatly in two as the thin threads thickened and whipped into them. Some instruments converted to molten metal as a beam passed through them and flung the liquefied material to spatter and congeal on the walls, floor, and other tables.

The flow pounded onto Gus like a waterfall, battering

against him. He held onto Mengele who somehow managed to absorb all of it without any signs of stopping. The roar of it flowing around him began to be deafening and everything in the room began to be bathed in a ruby light, like a darkroom, which continued to darken, masking the contrast of everything except the arm in front of Gus and the glowing golden eyes of Mengele which burned through the crimson tide.

A profound sense of smallness overcame Gus. He felt like a dust mote next to the sun, engulfed in its utter immensity. He knew if he let go, he would be swept away. The energy coursed through him, burning away any dross which was lost into the pit. He expected to be consumed at any moment, to puff into a tiny plume of smoke, but after what felt like an eternity, the energy finally started to lessen. He blinked as he began to see his surroundings again. Without everything washed out he could see that the well was nearly full, in fact, as it was filling *too* fast.

Unable to slow the flow, energy hit the event horizon, and there was only red as the energy surpassed its limits.

CHAPTER SEVENTY-NINE

Less Talk, More Rokk

Darik refused to close his eyes or look away as Razor glared back at him. He wouldn't give him the satisfaction. Though he felt like a slab of concrete was lying on his chest, he tempered his expression to show the least discomfort. From his vantage, the uneven steps between his sternum and separated ribs appeared sickeningly obvious.

Razor raised his leg high, pausing for effect. He was relishing every moment of his nemesis' demise. With a swift movement, he fell completely on his butt, eyes bulging. Like a ninja, Darik saw the sunlight play across Prime's helmet as she ducked and sliced with a weapon he had never seen before. It looked like lightning on a stick and as it swiped through the legs of the supers around him, they fell to the ground.

One of them raised a huge sledge, swinging it in an arc to crack Prime in the head while her back was turned. Darik tried to yell a warning but it came out only as a weak croak. The crackling sword glided and sailed through another super's waist and he went boneless and fell on his face.

Right before the hammer crashed, Prime turned, ducked slightly, and swiped through the arm holding the weapon at the shoulder. Then she continued on, working her way through the circle as if she had choreographed the entire thing. As she left his field of vision, Darik saw the super's arm go limp, the momentum of the swing carrying the weapon directly at *him* now.

There was a loud *thud* as the sledgehammer that had crushed his chest landed inches from his head, and he was covered with a plume of dirt. Spitting and blinking, he tried to wipe his eyes, but the attempt at moving his arms made stars burst across his vision and took his breath away. He let his arms fall back to his sides as he gasped for air.

Something soft smacked his face and bounced over him. He was briefly irritated until he saw the small red gel bounce over him to land on the ground. As he gingerly turned his head, he also saw that Razor was army crawling toward him, a serrated blade in his hand. Darik could hear Prime scuffling with someone in the distance.

Darik made a pug-lip and blew hard, trying to clear some of the dirt from his face. He tried to focus on the small gel so tantalizingly close. Razor ground his teeth back and forth as he approached, looking like a feral zombie. Trying to put him out of his mind, Darik turned his attention to the gel.

His vision blurred as he tried to squint, wink, and screw up his face so that he could clear the dirt out of his eye so he could see. It felt like ground glass in there, and he needed to get this right on the first try. Razor was only about three feet from the precious health gel and was making a beeline to him. Closing his problem eye, Darik made his calculations and opened his mouth. A silver dollar sized portal formed and the gel dropped inside just as Razor's elbow passed the space.

Darik bit down on the gel as it fell into his mouth. It crunched as he also got a healthy handful of dirt mixed in, but he kept chewing anyway and swallowed the muddy paste. There was another crushing sensation as the bone and cartilage were pulled together. They knit and reattached to his sternum, but just barely. He would need more time or gels to fully recover.

Darik pushed weakly with his feet, sliding on his back in retreat as Razor stabbed with frenzy, narrowly missing his shin. He tried kicking out but Razor flipped the knife and almost stabbed his foot through the open slice in his boot tip. With a surge, he pushed back with a foot and his head cracked against concrete. Looking up, he saw one of the supports at the base of the signal tower.

Encouraged, Razor scuttled more quickly, stabbing and pulling himself with the knife. Razor let loose a triumphant yell, and Darik answered with a shout of his own. They roared at each other. Then Prime was there. She flicked her sword and turned to gauge any other threats. The knife flipped into the air from his grasp and landed in the back of his thigh. Razor briefly paused his yelling as he twisted and stared dumbly at the blade protruding out his leg, then began yelling again.

Seeing that everyone was down, groaning and rolling on the ground, Prime collapsed the sword and attached it to her forearm.

"Can you walk?"

Darik shook his head, unable to hear with Razor's screaming. A quick kick from Prime ended that nonsense.

"Can you walk?" Prime repeated.

Darik tried but he found he still couldn't put any weight on his arms. Moving them wasn't agony though. He shook his head and wiped his eyes, clearing tears of agony. Prime tossed three more red gels at him.

"As fast as you can. We need to get the others."

Darik nodded and scarfed the gels, licking his teeth to clear out the grit. A few uncomfortable moments later, he gave Prime a thumbs up.

"I lost them," he said after checking his display. He gave Razor a kick. "'Cause of this idjit."

"No worries. Follow me."

They skirted the edge of the compound, where groups were accumulating, watching the conflagration. Others still fled in panic, while a few were taking measures to control the flames.

Using tactical signals, Prime communicated when to wait, and when it was clear to proceed. They turned a corner and Grimdark was kneeling by Harmony as she rubbed one of her ankles.

"She twisted it," Grimdark said without emotion, but pointed accusingly at Harmony's high-heeled boots. Prime checked her belt and pulled out a gel.

"That's my last one. We need to meet Seneschal in the hangar. The others are already on their way there." The group followed Prime until they reached the hangar. The group was crowded around someone lying on the ground.

"What happened?"

"Something happened to Yuki while we were on the rooftop. She screamed like nothing I've ever heard and just went totally stiff. She's been like this ever since."

"Feedback backlash. She told me of it once, but it was a long time ago. It should pass, but it means she failed her hack into Purple Faction. It could be hours, maybe days before she's conscious again," Harmony explained.

"Great, so we're totally exposed. Unless you made those scramblers, Aurora?"

"Some, but not enough for all of us—not enough time."

"Does anyone have any good news?"

"I think I found our ship," Seneschal said, rounding a corner. "I'm locked out, so someone with Tier 2 will need to unlock it." Rory raised his hand and then froze like a statue. He began to tip and fall forward and the others rushed to catch him. They slowed his fall so he was gently laid on the ground, but he was a big guy, so they couldn't move him easily.

Aurora rushed to his side and Rory looked up at her, his eyes the only thing he could voluntarily control.

"Are you okay?" She caressed his stubbly face with a hand.

"Let's carry him. As top technician, Rory should have access, but we've got to get him to the scanner." They struggled to hoist him up and carry him where Seneschal directed. Grimdark whistled as they approached the ship Seneschal had chosen.

"A corsair? Are you sure? We're going to piss off a lot of people!" Harmony gasped.

"Oh, I'm sure. I've always wanted to drive one of these babies," Seneschal countered. "I like to think of it as a going away present."

Darik grumbled as someone stepped on his wounded foot in their shuffle to carry Rory. "BoJack better be coming with us."

"He is, I've already met with him. We're picking him up after we leave here. Tempest is staying with Gwen, whatever the Faction decides to do," Seneschal retorted bitterly. "We're here; lean him up to the scanner." It took some acrobatics, but they managed to get a retinal and hand scan done to unlock ship controls.

They carried Rory inside, and Seneschal ran to the cockpit.

"Strap in, this is going to be unlike other transports. Especially Rory," Seneschal ordered.

The ship lifted unexpectedly, with almost none of the vibration and noise of a typical transport, especially one of this size. Inertial dampeners quickly kicked in and the only evidence of motion was through the windows as they sailed out the hangar doors to pick up BoJack.

―――――

"I'm afraid you lost the pinky toe completely, and about half of the next one. That can't be regenerated. I doubt it will affect you that much in the long term though," BoJack explained. He put his hands on the top of Darik's foot and skin flowed over the crusty cauterized tissue. "How did you manage this, anyway?"

"I didn't have time to invert the portal edges. Mostly because I was being buried alive and vastly outnumbered!"

Harmony turned to Prime who was grooming herself after removing her helmet. "But you took care of all those guys no problem, right?"

"I didn't have no special taser sword!" Darik snapped back.

"My Fulgurant? I haven't used it in a while, but it works nicely as a non-lethal, especially on supers," Prime said off-handedly. "It temporarily disrupts nerve conduction. You can easily kill someone if you don't know what you're doing, but it is very effective in the right hands. Those supers should be back to normal in about six hours."

Darik rubbed his foot, flaking off the crispy bits, revealing healthy pink, though shorter, toes underneath.

"Thanks, BoJack. But damn, I liked those boots."

"I assume you all know about Gus?" Prime asked. When all she saw were confused looks, she scrunched her nose. "Don't any of you read your messages?"

CHAPTER EIGHTY

The Good, the Bad, and the Dirty

Prime clicked on the intercom. "Seneschal, you'll want to hear this too, so listen in." She turned to the group and removed her helmet. "Gus ran off to fight Mengele on his own. And he says he doesn't want us to follow. He gave the manor to us and put Aurora in charge."

"He what?!" Aurora blurted, while others looked shocked or gasped.

"But why?" Anastasia held her hands cupped to her face.

"I'll let you read it yourselves, but we have to help him. With the Faction being as it is, we need him, and to figure out what happened. He apologized to you, BoJack. What was that all about?" Prime asked bluntly.

"I'm still pissed off at Gus. In more ways than one, maybe even more now—"

"Yeah, what happened with that? You guys seemed pretty buddy-buddy there for a bit," Harmony piped in.

"I don't want to talk about it."

"She's right," Aurora said, color draining from her face. "The tracker is gone. We have no idea where Mengele is, or Gus either if he went after him. He could already be gone."

"He's not gone, at least not yet," BoJack mumbled so only Anastasia could hear.

"W-w-wait. What aren't you telling us, BoJack? How do you know he isn't dead? What's this all about? I thought we were a team. Now I'm hearing all these secrets coming out of nowhere. There's no way we can get along if we don't communicate." Anastasia censured giving everyone a hurt look. "I know I don't speak up most of the time, but that doesn't mean I'm not worried. You know we have to go after him, right? No one left behind."

"He did give the manor to us. Maybe we should head there and regroup?" Harmony interjected. A few withering stares from some of the others made her squeak in surprise. "Just a suggestion, guys…"

"If you must know, he delved me without my permission. And then acted like he was shocked that it was a big deal," BoJack blurted out, staring at his hands and playing with one of his fingernails. "And now he's run off after Mengele. Throwing his life away. I was angry at him before, but now I'm furious!" He clenched the hand into a fist. "There's so much he doesn't know, and he just runs off half-cocked."

"I had no idea. But is there any chance that he really didn't know how bad that is?" Harmony asked.

"It's possible. Hell, it's more likely than not. It's hard not to forget that he has practically no training. I've never had to deal with that. There're just some things that they pound into you at the Academy so long you just accept that everyone knows it. But who does that? Who throws their life away?"

"He is a clueless dumbass a lot of the time," Aurora conceded. "But he means well."

"I can still feel him, sense him at times. Late at night, when I'm just on the cusp of falling asleep, there's a twinge, and I just know—" BoJack confessed.

A scream ripped through the air, causing everyone to jump.

"What the hell?" Darik grumbled, quickly covering his reaction.

Yuki sat up suddenly and grabbed her head, moaning.

Everyone clustered around, trying to see if she was okay, all speaking at once. Yuki winced, pantomiming a 'shh' and taking short, deep breaths.

"I'm okay… I think. Oh, this is like the mother of all hang-overs. Hoo." She hung her head and used both hands to knead her neck and the base of her skull.

"What happened?" Aurora asked.

"I lost my hack and got kicked. That hasn't happened in forever. Got too cocky, I guess. Oooh." Her fingers dug deeper, rubbing harder.

"Here," BoJack gently laid a hand on hers and removed them. He placed his fingers there and rubbed slowly up and down.

"Aah, yeah. That's the stuff. I knew there was a reason we were friends, BoJack." Yuki sighed.

"Did you get anything while you were in?" BoJack asked.

"No, that's what sucks. Now if I try to go back, I'm locked into using that avatar. Not the worst choice, but I would need to plan. I almost always go in blind, and can adapt pretty quickly. I think this boss was power leveled by idiots playing around, trying to break in from other factions. I was overwhelmed with the power differential."

"We're out of Purple, so don't worry about any of that now —we have more pressing matters. Gus went after Mengele," Prime broke in.

Yuki sat up, breaking contact with BoJack's hand and imme-diately cringed. She pointed exaggeratedly at her neck again, and he resumed.

"I don't know where he is either. He was supposed to link the tracker to the manor and wait for us." Aurora shrugged as Yuki looked at her.

"BoJack, do you think you could find him with this… connection, you speak of?" Anastasia asked.

Yuki carefully turned to look over her shoulder. "What's she talking about, BoJack?"

"He's very, very far away Yuki."

"Is that one of your abilities? If so, why didn't you mention it before? We could have gone after him a while ago."

"I can't control it. At first, I doubted I was feeling anything at all. I thought it was part of a dream until it began to be consistent. I know he's that direction," BoJack pointed to one of the walls.

"But how? Comms shouldn't work over a long distance; it doesn't make sense we all wouldn't be connected," Seneschal mentioned over the comms.

BoJack leaned forward, whispering conspiratorially, "I'll tell you all, but this stays between the Crew. Agreed?"

Yuki and the others nodded, and BoJack looked around nervously.

"I bonded Gus as his mentor—"

"You did what!?!" Aurora barked.

"Hold on, let me explain…"

"You don't have training, do you? You know how crazy dangerous that is?" Grimdark spat.

"He needed to learn! It was the fastest way."

"And you told him the trade-offs, I'm sure," Aurora said, folding her arms and raising an eyebrow.

"Well, no. There wasn't really time for that…"

"And the risks of feedback?" Yuki added.

BoJack winced, baring his teeth and inhaling sharply. "Also no, but hear me out—"

"Are you kidding me? You just spent this time dressing down Gus for being irresponsible and grabbing for XP, and you've been doing the exact same thing? Hypocritical much?"

"Yuki, you don't understand—"

"Oh, I think things are becoming clear. Do as I say, not as I do. Because I know better. Am I hitting the high points? You obviously don't have kids, if you think that little gem works."

BoJack's countenance darkened considerably. "Don't you say that. Don't you ever say things like that. You think I didn't want to be a father?"

"Want, don't want. What difference does it make? You took advantage of him, and he didn't even know it. He trusted you, and you used him. Have you leveled up since then?"

"Twice."

"Nice. I hope you enjoyed those levels. Is that why you want to help? Don't want to let the golden goose escape?"

"I never said I wouldn't help, but damn, Yuki. It's a suicide mission. I wouldn't even recommend attempting it if I didn't know through this bond that Gus is still alive."

"I'm not going to give you the choice!" Yuki spat, poking BoJack in the chest. "You owe him. First as his mentor, and second for not giving him the full story before he made the choice. Don't you remember anything they taught us in those ethics classes in the Academy? Didn't you just say they pounded something into our brains so much that you couldn't fathom how someone could break those rules? I know sometimes they're annoying as hell but we can't ignore that stuff."

"That's partly what I was trying to help Gus understand. He hasn't had any of that training. I just anticipated more time; this whole situation has gone sideways." BoJack ran fingers through his hair and grabbed the back of his neck. "You think I don't know I buggered everything up?"

"I just want to know what you're going to do about it. Nowadays no one seems like they give a damn. But Gus is the first person in a while who has treated me like I actually have some kind of potential. So if he believes in me, I believe in *him*." Yuki stared defiantly at the skeptical looks of the others. "Screw all of you guys, I'm going to find him. Go and justify your actions to yourself. Good luck with that."

Yuki spun and stormed away.

BoJack jogged after and grabbed her arm. "Yuki, stop. Let's talk about this."

She turned and tried to yank her arm out of his grasp but his grip was too strong. Her face went hot and her eyes narrowed.

"Let *go* of me, BoJack." Yuki's eyes turned feral as she glared at him.

"Not until you listen to me. You *need* me to find him. And I never said I wouldn't help. We just need to be smart about it. I want to help Gus as much as you do, but I don't want to rush in without a plan."

"I'm listening," she said out the side of her mouth. The glare continued, but she stopped pulling against his grip and he let her go. She shook her arm, rotating it and rubbing her bicep as he continued.

"We need to figure out how to approach this. I don't know how much you know about Mengele, but I've been researching him since we left Hinansho. The guy is *serious bad news*, Yuki. He's first generation and everyone is scared of him. I mean, the fact he chose *that* name says volumes about him. He's equal parts Jack the Ripper and Moriarty. You saw some of those experiments going on in that facility. I keep imagining Gus in a place like that and I... it's tearing me up inside." He swallowed back emotion and continued.

"I feel like I'm being dipped in a molten vat of anger one minute, and then a liquid nitrogen bath of guilt and helplessness in the next. I want to help, but I don't know how we can beat someone who has had decades to hone his skills. Even if we had the whole Crew, I fear we would be outmatched." He held his hands out in front of him, half-pleading, half-defeated.

"Then we just don't brute force it. Not everything requires a direct attack. Come with me and let's get this thing planned." Yuki put an arm around his shoulder and looked at the others. "Huddle up, here's what I think we should do..."

CHAPTER EIGHTY-ONE

Behind Blue Eyes

As soon as he moved out of cover, he noticed movement to his left. Five balls of cracking plasma were heading toward him.

Slave, extrapolate his position by analyzing direction of attacks and audio feedback. Render a three-dimensional representation on my display. Use proximity markers for all attacks and codify threat levels.

As you command, came the robotic reply.

Mengele angled his trajectory for the open doorway. If he could make it to the Vault, then this would be over quickly, without surprises. Sending a quick burst of healing, he forced the skin on his feet to reconstruct. He was leaving bloody foot-prints which would not only show his position, but would be a liability on the smooth corridor floors beyond.

He pushed himself, but knew that he could not outpace this attack. He had never seen the need to allocate points into constitution, when his suit would make him invulnerable. There were more important abilities for someone like him. His perception allowed his display to give him an innate sense of the timing he would need. A quick feint to the left, diving, tucking and rolling, then resuming his run without losing much momentum. Two of the plasma balls collided with broken equipment and dissipated as they exploded in white flashes. The other three overshot his position and then began to reorient on him.

Tracking. He mentally filed the concept of guided Nun-Ba interactions as programmable functions into his memory to explore when he had time to ponder. Another feint misdirected another of the attacks into an upturned table. The interaction revealed that these constructs had very limited potential. They operated on the shortest trajectory. Utilizing this, he ducked to the side after breaching the doorway, then skirted the wall.

As predicted, the last of the attacks collided with the wall to the left of the doorway. All of his stat points in agility were initially placed to make him more efficient as a surgeon, as the system did not distinguish between agility and dexterity. Fortunately, raising the stat improved both. This became even more useful when later he developed his dimensional folding techniques.

The Nth were wasted on humans who just wanted to fight. There were so many opportunities that largely were wasted by becoming the world's self-proclaimed enforcers. Neanderthals with clubs had no place in the future the Nth could offer.

Gauging the approach on his minimap, Gus was much faster, and was closing the distance between them. Agility wouldn't help him in this open corridor. Brute force was not his forte. Precision and stealth. Misdirection and manipulation. Those were his keys to success here.

Mentally calculating a new route, he noted Gus' footfalls in the corridor behind him just as he entered a doorway to his right. That was unfortunate. Gus would have had to clear many more rooms if he hadn't seen his location.

Mengele weaved through the Graveyard. His affectionate term for where he stored most of his defunct equipment that had become outdated with new advances. There were enough obstructions here that any further plasma attacks would be easily avoided. This would take his pursuer on a circuitous route, but he could double back and make it to the Vault, going through labs and offices. Mengele crouched and slowed his flight as the far doors to the Graveyard were flung open.

"I know you're in here, Mengele."

Mengele slowed even more, but crept along the ground, moving purposefully towards the exit. If this ham-fisted rube wanted him to respond and give away his position, he was more outclassed than he knew.

"You know, you look like your head fell in the cheese dip back in 1957," the young man taunted.

How droll. Was this supposed to get a rise out of him? Mengele smiled wryly and continued his trek. They had thought calling him Mengele was an insult too. An offhanded insult to get him to change his ways. A crude cautionary tale. But he had owned it. While he shared no relation to the actual figure, he adopted the archetype and let their imaginations fill in the gaps. When the doorway was within reach, he knew it would give away his position.

"That is accurate," he replied before quickly darting through the door, locking it behind him. He imagined Gus being flummoxed as they all were when he responded against expectation. He knew who he was. More so than most metahumans. He had transcended even them in so many ways. He could sense that upon reviewing the data he would—

The nearby wall crashed outward, spilling shards of drywall and broken framing into the hallway in front of him. Gus was panting and shook himself. Somehow, he wasn't naked anymore, and residual insulation and powdery chalk rolled off of him like oil, landing in a plume on the ground around him.

"Enough running. We end this now," Gus rasped with a ragged voice.

He had been less predictable than most subjects, but the crazed look in his eyes made Mengele wary. While he couldn't read levels directly, he had made some inferences from his experiments, based on healing times, musculature, and nerve conduction tests. He had a general idea about his physical stats, but his abilities were unclear.

He was obviously a neophyte when it came to utilizing his powers in a unified and directed fashion. Nothing coordinated in his fighting technique, which would indicate a lack of formal training. An anomaly to be sure. But was it all an act? That was the suspicion that niggled at the back of his mind. The Master knew he would be more calculating with a powerful opponent, but with someone inexperienced, he could see he had relaxed his tendency to overcompensate and had taken less precautions with Gus.

Gus charged forward with some enhanced speed ability, but it was easily avoided with his level of agility, and he sidestepped like a matador. He caught his mental *tsk tsk* and focused even more. It was only the sharpening of his attention that allowed him to see the upstart rotate and try to sweep his legs from underneath him.

A quick hop was all that was needed to let the attack glide by without connecting, but it could have if he had remained cocksure and full of himself. He danced away, gaining some distance as Gus rounded on him and swayed back and forth like a wrestler.

Instead of charging, Gus pressed forward with controlled speed. He centered himself in the smaller hallway, and did not even flinch at his attempted feints to slip to one side or another. Reaching an intersection, Mengele walked backwards. *Yes, follow me Gus. Only one-hundred-eighty-two meters before I am at the Vault.* Automated defenses there should be enough of a distraction to allow him to slip inside. A smile crept on his lips before he could hide it.

Gus' eyebrows furrowed and he lunged and grappled with Mengele. He was glad he had not reformed the skin around his upper torso. Gus' hands slid on the congealing blood that clung to his pulsing, exposed muscles, not finding purchase. He barely managed to slide out of Gus' grip, but he could tell in his current state, Gus' strength surpassed his own.

He blocked the blows that Gus threw at him, feeling their ferocity fully now that his suit didn't absorb any of the kinetic force. He began to bleed more as capillaries burst and there was no skin to hold it in. Precious MP had to be funneled into healing to stop the bleeders.

Mengele had managed to keep his own feet clear of his own blood, while Gus himself became more coated in it, and had begun to lose his footing. Mengele retreated, feigning fear. Sometimes all it took was a little bait and supers lost all reason. Eager to press their advantage they would rush headfirst into the most obvious of traps. With another flash of his gray pseudo-skin, the blood rolled off of him and he stepped out of it onto the floor in front of him, entirely clean.

The meters ticked down, one-twenty-one, one-twenty, one-nineteen. At sixty meters, he should be close enough to trip biometrics. Gus loped after him, and the distance was being eaten up. Still, he was going to make it.

With a feeling of relief, Mengele stepped past the line visible only on his display. Scans began and Mengele stopped retreating. Gus paused as well, trying to ascertain what had changed. Just a little more prodding. His signature smug smile spread across his skinless face. He hoped it would still have the effect of goading Gus into attacking.

But maddeningly, no. He stood there contemplatively, his attention assessing the corridor. Shrugging, he turned casually and began to walk toward the Vault. Few could resist being dismissed as nothing. That should do the trick. He stopped mid-step when he heard the system announce:

Intruder detected. Scans inconclusive for authorized personnel. Evacuate this area in ten seconds, or retributive actions will be taken.

The system didn't recognize Mengele without skin on his upper torso.

Oh shit.

CHAPTER EIGHTY-TWO

Short Change Hero

"BoJack, how accurately can you pinpoint Gus?" Seneschal asked.

"I see a thin thread on my display when I turn in that direction. When I'm not looking that way, I feel an occasional tug."

"That's the first task. Let's see if we can triangulate where he is. We get a reading, I travel due east two hundred miles and we take another reading and compare, then fine tune 'til we arrive. Can you give me a heading with this thread of yours, or whatever it is you see?"

"It's just a direction. I don't even know for sure—"

"Aurora, can you design something that can fine tune his tracking? It'll make this quicker if each reading is as accurate as possible."

"I can try, I've never really done anything along those lines…" came the sheepish reply.

"It's kind of hard to believe that you're in charge of engineering, since your tracker and the scanning blocker didn't really work out, ya know?" Harmony quipped to Aurora with a shrug.

"Not as hard as believing you're the *empath* of the group, and that you're named *Harmony* on top of it. Ironic, ya know?"

"Ah, *daaamn!*" Darik whooped, slapping a knee.

"Everyone stop it!" Anastasia rushed in between Aurora and Harmony as the mood shifted. "I'm sure we can figure something out, no need to turn on each other."

Aurora spun and seated herself at one of the nearby tables and pulled components out of her kit. Her head bobbed as she looked at her display, pulling and swiping at the air in front of her.

I'll show that hussy what's what… she muttered unintelligibly as she connected a couple of components and tried arranging items in her virtual display.

"Yuki, I may need a bit of your help to interface this with BoJack; you up for a sync?"

"Show me what ya got."

"…aaaand done! Try that, Yuki. It works in the sim. Your mileage may vary." She handed a small contraption that looked like the guts of a small phone. "You can connect here." Aurora pointed to a USB port.

"Wow, old school. Weird flex, but okay. BoJack, accept my party invite. Good. Here goes." She held the compass interface in her hand and blinked. "Oh, that's actually kind of clever. Let me make a quick adjustment… that should do it. BoJack, accept that widget."

"Now wha—wow. That's pretty cool. Seneschal, I'm getting a reading of ninety-five degrees," BoJack said with wonder. "It's jumping around a bit but that's close."

"Yuki, I'm sure you can triangulate with a couple of readings? Comparing our current GPS with the next reading?"

Yuki nodded as she chomped on her gum. "Then we can extrapolate his position, I get you. Yeah, and I can check satellites as well, and that will tell us something about where we're heading and what to expect there. Hopefully, the satellite system is still as easy to hack as when I was twelve. Got current coordinates, thanks, Sen."

"How long should that take?" BoJack wondered aloud.

"Five, maybe ten minutes?"

"You're really that good?" he asked incredulously.

"You have no idea…"

———

"Got it! It's close to Johannesburg, South Africa. Target is about fifty miles southwest of there. Change your heading to these coordinates."

"Adjusting… ETA is four hours, thirty-seven minutes."

"How fast are we moving? I don't feel anything!"

"A smidge over Mach two. I *love* it. This is the smoothest ride I've ever had. The predictive algorithms for the dampers compensate for fluctuations in existing temperature, wind currents. Top shelf. Yuki, what's it look like where we're going?"

"Pretty obvious. It's a huge hole in the ground."

"A trap?"

"It looks like a mine. Hmm. The world's deepest mine, deep as ten Empire State buildings…"

Darik whistled, impressed.

"I hate confined spaces," Yuki pouted.

"This was partly your idea, Yuki…" Harmony reminded her.

"I know. But I still hate it. I can't sit on the sidelines for this one. You'll need me to hack the doors and security. I'll be fine. Just don't tease me and get me worked up. Got it?" She glared at Harmony and then at Darik. When they agreed, she went on. "I'm reviewing the last three days footage, and I don't see anything out of the ordinary. Transports are docking and leaving all the time. Mengele could have been on any of those —you can't see the call signs from above, and I'm just going on satellite feeds. A lot of these ships look the same to me. It's hard to tell without a frame of reference, this could be normal mine activity. Who knows?"

"I don't like it," Darik said.

"But what can we do? This is probably how he has remained hidden. Doing his work from shadows," Grimdark added.

"We will be fine if we just focus on our objective. All we're doing is sneaking in and getting Gus out of there. No heroics. No revenge or retribution. Get in, get out. Remember the plan. Done. Everybody on board?"

"When we get close enough, I can try to remote hack the facility. I won't be able to get much, but I'm hoping for some schematics. That'll help us finalize our entry points and tactics."

"Yuki, we're ready for another reading," Seneschal said over the comms.

"Already?" BoJack rattled off the current coordinates.

"Course correcting, thanks."

"Everyone has their projects, get to work. We only have a couple of hours."

———

The corsair was large enough that it took some time to find a place to land without obstruction.

The Crew filed out and made a beeline for the hangars. Yuki had found a single shaft descending to a section isolated from the rest of the mine. It annexed the mine at different levels, but ran parallel to the depth of the mine, though it was straight and narrow like a core sample. The mine itself was a multi-tiered circular pit.

"Hold up, guys. This area is much more sophisticated than it looks."

"It's dirty and run down."

"On the surface. That rusted metal on the hangar is mere siding. Pressure plates are there, there, and there," Yuki warned, pointing to different patches on the dirt road and forest. "Follow me."

They filed after her and she swiped the information to their displays. The hangar door was quickly hacked and they headed inside.

"That's it, alright, and the tracker's still there." Aurora pointed to Mengele's ship.

"I recognize it too. Good to know we're on the right track," Darik agreed. "So we go down this elevator, huh?

"Looks like it."

Darik squinted at the floor of the lift, and stomped once or twice then listened. "Are you guys up for a little adventure?" he asked as the rest of them joined him in the lift.

"Darik, NO!" was all Harmony got out before a large portal opened up below them and then they were all falling down the shaft below the lift.

"Don't overthink it!" he cackled with glee as they began to pick up speed. The chill air rapidly warmed as they fell, musty and earthy. Lights began to flicker, then strobe as they fell faster and faster, passing various levels. A dull orange glow grew in intensity as they fell. Harmony hugged herself tightly, while Aurora slowed her own descent with her flight skill, pulling away from the others.

When impact was imminent, the Keeper opened another portal and they shot out the exit, flying back up the shaft. Darik alternated the polarity of the portals and they quickly slowed as gravity acted like brakes. When they had slowed sufficiently, he let the group land on the cement pad among four mammoth springs on plinths.

Harmony's hair was wild and disheveled as she fumed. "Don't. Ever. Do. That. *Again!*" Everyone pressed fingers to lips and shushed her as her shrill scream echoed in the narrow shaft. She pursed her lips but continued to glare.

"Look how fast we got down here," Darik whispered and shrugged. "Sometimes you just have to jump in the pool. Don't overthink it." They climbed the nearby ladder as Darik made another portal through the heavy metal doors, and they crawled out onto the Berber carpet that was definitely out of place in a mine.

Bright lights illuminated the corridor, and even the temperature was regulated to normal levels. If one did not know better, they might suppose they were in an office building of some sort. Yuki knelt by a nearby keypad next to a door and tried to sync with the system.

After a brief pause, she shook her head. "These aren't part of the main network, unfortunately. I can tell that no one has unlocked, entered, or exited these offices for a while, so thank goodness for small favors. We'll have to find someplace else—"

A tremor rocked the floor, causing the group to stagger.

"What was that?" Anastasia gasped.

"Earthquake?" Yuki said, face draining of color.

Lights flickered and went out briefly, kicking on again after a second.

"I can feel him more strongly now. He's this way," BoJack pointed down a hallway. They began to head down the corridor when the lights went out and they were plunged into the dark.

CHAPTER EIGHTY-THREE

Sapphire Bullets of Pure Love

"Harmony, what do you got?" Darik asked, looking up at her.

"It feels empty. I can only sense two minds besides us. Even if there were someone hiding with shielding for mental protection, there still is an ambient pressure that I can feel. Unless this guy is using mechs, it should only be Gus and Mengele."

"Can you tell anything about his emotional state?" BoJack asked.

"It's kind of stormy. I'm getting a lot of reds."

"Reds?"

"Yeah, emotions have a flavor, or color. Reds are usually fight or flight responses. Anger, severe fear, pain. Those kinds of things."

"Can you tell how strong he is?" BoJack asked with bated breath.

"Sort of? The colors are really vivid, which usually is a good sign. When someone is very ill or about to pass, the colors fade to blacks, grays, and whites."

BoJack exhaled deeply.

"What about Mengele?" Grimdark added.

"The same. He has blues and a tinge of green mixed into his reds. Kind of psychedelic."

"What do blue and green represent?"

"Blue is deep thought and excitement, when you are really engaged in a fulfilling task. Green is shame."

"Shame? He can feel that? The guy's a psychopath!" Darik huffed.

"It can also be insecurity, embarrassment, or humiliation too. They're all similar and hard to distinguish exactly when the other colors taint them. Blue isn't good for Gus though. It means Mengele is enjoying what he's doing right now."

"So he could be torturing Gus as we speak! Let's get moving, we may not have much time."

Anastasia gently grabbed BoJack's shoulder as he started to head for the doorway. "Running in unprepared will do us no good," she warned.

"It's a miracle he's even alive. What are we waiting around for?"

"You know protocols, BoJack. Chill. If I can find some terminal or kiosk, I can deactivate any latent defenses, then we can proceed without being blindsided."

"Well let's get the show on the road then, Yuki. What else do we all need to do?"

"Green lights on everyone's wristbands?" Aurora asked. Everyone gave a quick check and mumbled agreement. "Remember, you only have enough for one charge. Once it kicks in, you're draining the energy cell until it's gone. So make sure you don't use it by reflex. I can't make any more," she warned.

"This schematic is wrong," Yuki said as she analyzed the corridor's layout. "While plumbing, ventilation, and electrical are largely the same, the blueprint shows a corridor going straight here, where there's only a wall."

"A secret passage?"

"Possibly. Or faulty data meant to confuse. It could just as easily be a trap."

"It's always something."

"I'll check it out, wait here," Anastasia mentioned as she walked toward the wall. Her form began to glow, and a purple outline surrounded her frame as she became more incorporeal, fading from view right as she reached it.

The Crew waited in eager anticipation and time ground to a halt. Grimdark strained to hear but only shook his head as the others stared at him.

After about five minutes, Anastasia popped back into the room with a purple flash.

"Yuki is right. There's a corridor there. The floor and walls appear identical the whole length—illuminated tile. It runs for about two-hundred-fifty feet. I didn't see any sensors or anything, but I couldn't phase through the walls there, which was a little unsettling. There's a bulwark at the far end of the corridor, also unphasable, so I don't know what's beyond," she reported.

"That's pretty close to the central hub. None of these rooms are labeled, but the fixtures would indicate nearby labs," Yuki remarked.

"If we can even trust them, that is," Darik said. "So, are we breaking it down or portaling through?"

"We don't seem to have set off any alarms so far, why don't we try to keep it that way?" Anastasia replied.

"As you wish." Darik placed his hands on the wall and spread them wider, pulling open a large portal. A warm almond-colored light glowed from the panels beyond.

The Crew stepped through and Yuki held up a fist. "Guys, this area is shielded, which is weird. No signals can go in or out. Be on your guard," she warned.

"Hold on." Aurora began to float and started moving down the passageway. She moved past panel after panel. When she was near the midpoint, she reached a tentative toe to the next panel and put some weight on it. Nothing happened. She put more and more until her full weight was on the ground. Turning back to the group she continued to walk, sliding a foot in front of her and probing for any triggers.

"I don't like this," Anastasia said, holding her hands close to her mouth, unable to bite her nails while wearing gloves.

"We've got these, she'll be fine," Darik said shaking his wristband.

Slowly Aurora crept back, as if navigating a minefield until she was back with the Crew. "That bodes well; proximity and pressure don't seem to set off anything."

"Yet..." Darik added, holding a finger up.

"You're such a troll!" Harmony griped.

"Yeah, but I'm an *alive* troll, sweetheart," he said with an exaggerated wink.

The group proceeded carefully down the corridor. If anything, the soft lighting was warm and soothing. When they reached the middle, Aurora took flight and moved forward again, this time half the distance remaining to the far bulkhead. Once again, she worked her way back, probing as she went.

"This is dumb. We're taking too long. I can feel him—we're getting so close," BoJack said impatiently.

"It does seem like this may just be a shortcut. Maybe it's shielded so people can't find out about it with scans or some such?"

"I still don't like it."

"Let's check out this bulkhead," BoJack turned and pushed past Aurora and stepped beyond into the untested areas. After three panels he turned back. "See? Nothing to worry about." He continued until he was in front of the large door. He turned back. "Well? What are you waiting for?" Everyone followed.

"I can't see a way to open it; there's no controls. At least on this side. This section of corridor looks like all the rest."

The group got to probing the walls and bulkhead, looking for some kind of mechanism or switch.

"Looks like it's portal time," Darik put his hands on the bulkhead and tried to spread them. "C'mon now, don't be difficult."

"What's happening?"

"Is it shielded too? I haven't heard of a material that's portal-proof."

"It's resisting... like it's super thick. It would have to be over twenty feet deep and that doesn't... seem... feasible," Darik strained through grit teeth. He tried harder, and finally he let his hands drop with a grunt. "Gimme a minute and I'll try again."

"Um, guys, do you see that?" Harmony asked, pointing to the far end of the corridor. Lights winked out at the opposite end of the tunnel, speeding up as they approached the Crew.

"What did you do, Keeper?" Grimdark asked.

"Hey, it wasn't me. I swear. Well, maybe it was. I need a little more time though before I try again." He wearily got to his feet and put his hands in the small of his back. "I'm getting too old for this," he groaned, punctuated with a series of pops.

"I can't see anything happening besides the light going out. Does anyone else detect anything?" Aurora asked, squinting her eyes.

"Nothing here."

"Me neither."

"Get read—"

Before Darik could get the words out, the floor became electrified. Everyone crumpled to the floor as muscles short-circuited. The soothing light winked out a second later, leaving only the occasional *snap* as energy arced. There was a hum, followed by a series of *thitt* noises, as tiny darts shot into the group, some rattling on the floor as they sprayed down. There were small flashes all around, as the darts hit their targets and rolled off.

Grimdark managed to push himself to his hands and knees, and more of the darts flared across his back as he made himself a target. A guttural growl escaped his throat as he activated his **Drain** ability and pulled the energy into himself. The pops diminished rapidly as Grimdark's eyes began to light up from within. The growl turned into a roar as his last bit of MP was finally evaporated away.

At some point, darts had begun to stick and accumulate along his back. Energy dripped out his back around the darts like blood. Some even dislodged and fell, pushed from the inside out. It was only a small fraction though, and Grimdark's eyes began to dim. He collapsed hard, hitting his chin as his arms and legs slid away from him.

"Someone deal with those blowguns!"

Anastasia waved a hand and darts rose like little spaceship fighters awaiting her command. She flung them into the barrel of the blowguns and they crammed in like ants, fighting to force their way back inside their home. She bared her teeth and there was a grinding noise followed by a loud *crack*. A hissing followed and the darts stopped coming. Anastasia dropped to the floor like a discarded marionette.

"How is everyone?" Yuki asked.

"These little bad-boys did the job, Aurora. I didn't get hit by a single dart." Darik saluted her. "Why has no one outfitted us with personal portable shields before? That could have been bad."

"It *is* bad," BoJack said as he began pulling darts out of Grimdark's back. "His shield gave out and he's got a massive dose of tranquilizers in his system. Everyone help me. Pull those by the flights and don't touch the tips."

"Flights?"

"The wings of the dart. Have you never been to a pub?" BoJack ripped the tattered shreds of Grimdark's suit off his back to expose the area. The skin was already puckering and swelling and resembled acne from hell. He put his hands on a small section of Grimdark's back clear of darts while the others frantically pinched and extracted the rest. A milky-yellow fluid began to slowly bead up on his skin.

"Hurry, his heart's stopping! Get those darts out of there!" BoJack screamed as the beads grew then began to pool together and drip down his side. BoJack moved his hands to another section, leaving pristine handprints as he touched another bumpy swollen area.

"Gels! I need MP gels. Get him to bite on a red," BoJack ordered as he continued to work, biting savagely on a gel and chewing aggressively as his hands trembled on Grimdark's back. "More!"

The others fed him gels and the material just kept coming, flowing like toxic pus.

"There. He's stabilizing. I'm not. Losing. Anyone. Else," he gasped in fitful breaths. BoJack appeared to age visibly with the effort.

Everyone cheered when Grimdark moaned and asked, "Wha' happened?" in a dazed voice.

BoJack slumped back on his heels, eyes drooping. "I'm tapped, cuz. Imma need a nap..." he slurred and his head dropped down on his chest. He almost fell forward onto a pile of extracted darts but Darik grabbed him and held him.

"That sucked," Yuki said.

"Not only that, we're still stuck here."

CHAPTER EIGHTY-FOUR

Karma

The scanners couldn't detect enough of his unique biopattern to identify him!

Mengele directed **Focused Heal** on his face. It itched like ants swarming over him but he resisted touching it. The action burned through a fifth of his total MP, a hefty price, but he knew what the defenses would do to him without his suit.

The pale light played across his head again.

Insufficient data. Scans inconclusive for authorized personnel. Evacuate this area in five seconds, or retributive actions will be taken.

Panels slid open and six turrets whirred to life as their cyclotrons began to spin as they powered up.

I definitely *have to recalibrate these in the future to accept more than just surface scans.* The healing was cannibalizing some of his own tissue for building blocks to create the skin at an accelerated pace. He hoped he wouldn't go through all of this and his outward appearance would not be changed enough to satisfy the scans.

He held as still as he could as the burning itchy feeling spread over him, burning like a butane torch as it progressed over the rest of his body. He poured everything he had into the process, mentally counting down the remaining seconds until the turrets spun to life, squinting against the scanning light playing up and down him.

Identified. Welcome Dr. Mengele. Would you like to access the Vault at this time?

"Why yes, I would." He nodded to Gus, tipping an imaginary top hat, then took one step.

And promptly collapsed to the floor.

———

Gus stood at the imaginary border where the scanners would kick in. Mengele had just taken a faceplant and was just lying there quivering. The system had recognized him at last, but the turrets were already in position and primed to fire. Angry barrels under the turrets spun, whined, and pulsed. He looked back between Mengele and the turrets. This was going to hurt.

But hasn't this always been my problem? Indecision and doubting, afraid of imagined consequences that may never happen. Fear of pain, real or imagined. And no one there to support me in the moment of choice.

Really though, when the chips are down, the only one I've really ever been able to count on is myself. Especially when the tank is empty, and I have nothing left to give. The thought came to Gus about the sad state of most humans, that most people were running on empty tanks, expecting others to fill them up when, really, it was something people often have to do for themselves.

I've held a lot of resentment at those whom I felt should have taken it upon themselves to help out, whether it be my parents, the Crew, or even Nick. Relying on others, with all their own imperfections, and wondering why I keep getting disappointed that there's no effort to meet my actual needs, and not what they think is best for me—or the least effort.

No epiphanies or even any warm fuzzies came as he stared at Mengele lying there. No one would know if he beat this monster right here, right now, and was consumed in the process. But compared to the pain he had endured in the last days, his desires of acceptance and camaraderie seemed small in scope.

I'm going to just keep on, doing the things I know I should. Constantly repeating the mantra: seek right action, not right results. I have to become someone else. Someone who is not affected by the lack of support. Someone who can be even more self-sufficient and overcome, despite all the people actively and passively trying to pull me down. And not get distracted by being disappointed or angry at those who are so caught up in their own lives that they aren't able to lend a hand.

I've made it this far. I can make it the rest of the way. I'm sure when I get there, a lot of people will come out of the woodwork, like in Henny Penny, tapping themselves on the back that they were 'so supportive.' And I'll let them believe that delusion. But I'll be all the stronger for it, having had to improve myself to get what I need. To shore up my own belief system to create something of this broken, defective shamble I call my life. To work at the diamond in the rough that everyone passes over as worthless until it shines in majesty after it is cut and shaped.

I am not content lying underground, being unnoticed and of little use. If those closest to me can't see me for who I am, I will shine brighter and brighter until I find my tribe. And nothing is going to stop me.

Gus took a step toward Mengele and the turrets shifted and targeted him. Gus activated **Intermediate Shield** and stepped forward purposefully. He grunted as multiple beams began striking the shield, causing resistance as he pressed forward. He leaned into it and pushed, watching the shield integrity sizzle down like a lit fuse.

I am just going to keep pushing myself until I feel better. Like when I get a cold, yet still have to work. Just power through the feelings of malaise and weariness. I will not lose momentum. I think this is where I hit the stumbling blocks with my goals. I get this storm of trials and then I hunker down in survival mode trying to make it through, and everything I built gets tossed around and destroyed. Habits broken, progress lost, and so on. From here on out, I am staying out in the storm. Progressing Relentlessly. Even if it takes a while to achieve my aims, I will push through.

Gus crouched and powered through the resistance, pushing with powerful legs to move the shrinking bubble of the shield closer to his enemy.

Just because I don't feel support from others, I won't let that shape my behavior in supporting them. I made that promise to myself all those years ago when I was just a reg. The world needs this guy gone. And I will get it done!

The shield imploded and Gus felt multiple spots of intense heat, burning pokers pressed against his skin. Before he had met Mengele in person and been subject to his whims, he might have flinched away. Though the sheen of hybrid-Nth covering him rallied to deflect some of the energy, he still felt the white-hot beams bleed through and burn into him.

Mengele's arm twitched and fingers crawled, pulling his arm toward the large opening door.

No you don't!

Gus heaved and took a large step. It was like trying to wade into the ocean against the pounding surf, but he timed his movement to force himself to go on. Gus tried to absorb the energy but something about these beams refused to respond to the ability.

Mengele chuckled as he pushed with a leg, looking like a drunk frog scuttling on the ground. He cast a quick glance over his shoulder at Gus.

"Those beams will overcome you regardless of what ability you use against them, my poor boy. I'm afraid you'll never reach me. I'm already regaining enough stamina to escape."

"*No!*" Gus roared. The intensity only felt like it was increasing as he moved closer to the turrets, and they adjusted subtly to remain focused on him. Gus was forced to a knee and it took a massive effort to get back to his feet. He felt the strain from his shoulders to his heels as every muscle flexed to resist the pressure.

Meanwhile, Mengele was crawling ever quicker into the room beyond and was lost from sight, the bright beams and their energy spatter hiding him from view. Doubts of how he was going to fail again, like he always did, began to crawl into the fringes of his mind. Gus pressed forward in spite of them, his resolution crushing them like a hammer. He had been through hell. He could do this.

He reached a point where he could not move forward. He was being supported at an unnatural angle as he pushed and leaned and the beams pushed back. Pain increased, but touched a memory. He had been introduced to the thirty-one flavors and types of pain on a regular basis, and this one was distinct.

When he saw it, he kicked himself that he didn't notice it sooner.

The beams are made entirely of that new energy!

At the realization, a new tab appeared on his display amid the perception filters and he could visualize the energy, connected to the turrets and extending into the walls, down to some large turbine far below. Looking to his newfound channels he saw that they were completely empty, scoured clear when he had poured it all into the suit. Some kind of entrainment had yanked every residual amount of the red energy out of him. *But what if…*

He tried to funnel some of the energy toward the empty center at the base of his spine. The pain dropped by degrees. It was surprising how slowly it was filling in comparison to the sheer intensity of the energy he had been fighting against.

He opened himself more and the beams actually began to bend, concentrating on the internal spinning disk. It began to glow and spin quicker and energy began to cycle along the four paths up and down his legs, then returned to the central disk. It felt like he had a miniature CERN inside of him, except that all the energy was traveling one way—for now.

He pushed forward as the resistance waned, stepping with more surety and speed as the energy filled him. It was nowhere near filling even the smallest section of his pathways by the time he reached the doorway. Mengele was there at a cupboard cramming gels into his mouth.

But that was not what made his jaw drop open.

CHAPTER EIGHTY-FIVE

I Won't Back Down

Accept party invite? (Y/N)

Gus numbly accepted the prompt.

"Is that Gus?" Harmony pointed. "What's he wearing? He looks like a Ken doll."

"Who cares about that? Get in there before the door closes," Darik said, herding the others inside. BoJack was still kneeling, so Darik hoisted him over his shoulders in a fireman's carry and moved him to the room beyond.

"Ah, so the cavalry did decide to come." Mengele turned to face Gus. "I'm a little disappointed in you, really. I thought you were one of those sulky lone-wolf types. I should have known better."

"Dude! Why is everyone naked?" Harmony asked, taking in the scene. "What's been going on here?"

Mengele looked down at himself and shrugged. "Hmm. Yes. You'll have to ask your friend about that, he's the one who removed my clothes."

Questioning eyes panned to Gus, who stared back in surprise. "You guys came for me? But why?" Movement at the corner of his eye broke his attention from the Crew. Mengele was slinking toward a small airlock door on his side of the room.

"Where do you think you're going?" Gus shook himself out of his stupor and began to run towards Mengele.

"You looked like you needed some private time to reconnect. I'll be on my way."

Gus lunged and barely managed to grab one of Mengele's ankles as he did a flip at the last minute. They tumbled to the floor, hitting a nearby tray and knocking over its contents. Beakers and vials shattered on the ground. Mengele quickly regained his feet and gave a disappointed glance at the destruction.

"What a waste. Why must you so-called supers generate so much collateral damage in your efforts? Have you no finesse? You get a couple of abilities and treat the world just like a small child with a new toy hammer."

"Some things need to be razed to build something better," Gus retorted, attempting another grapple.

"That won't be so easy now that I've regained my composure a bit," Mengele chided as he hit Gus in the back with the side of his hand. Plates formed right before impact, thinning the pseudo-skin of hybrid-Nth around him. The power he had felt earlier from Mengele wasn't there but it was still enough to flatten him on the ground. Mengele backed up and cocked his head to assess his work.

Gus, you can't let him hit you like that again. He's activating an ability. I can't decode exactly what the hybrid-Nth are trying to tell me, but another hit could be fatal! Nick warned.

Thanks, Nick. Long time no see.

Gus pushed himself to his knees and got up on shaky feet.

What the hell was that?

He felt his legs pulse and they quickly regained their stability as some of the red energy ebbed out into his tissues to compensate.

"Unexpected. Yet refreshing," Mengele remarked and dropped back into a martial art pose, bouncing lightly on the balls of his feet. Almost casually, he raised his left hand as a ton of shrapnel flew at him, stopping as it hit a wall of nothingness and dropping to the floor.

"How is he doing that?" Anastasia gasped.

"Don't let him touch you!" Gus warned, circling around to the others, waving them back.

"Oh, Gus. How unsportsmanlike of you. Astute, yes. But it will avail you nothing. At the risk of being pedantic, you and your fellows have no chance of defeating me. Look at this poor man, he's barely conscious and I haven't even laid a finger on him. Yet." He waved a dismissive hand at BoJack. "I would implore you all to leave, but I have dealt with too many with your saccharine sentimentality to hope that you would abandon your mawkishness. Let the lesson begin."

Another salvo of items careened across the room and a thick blue liquid revealed a dome shape surrounding Mengele that ran down the sides, leaving the barrier invisible again.

"Hiding behind shields? Not so tough without your armor, are you?"

"This? This is not a shield." He gestured at the air around him. "It's miles of folded space condensed into a single millimeter. Anything that meets the plane expends all its energy as if traveling through the intervening space. I assure you any type of attack will lose potency before it ever reaches me. It's only by my selective manipulation of that space that makes it possible that you can even hear me."

He put his hand by his mouth, in an overly-theatrical stage whisper, "But let them waste all their MP trying to get through."

Gus squinted, trying to read if Mengele was bluffing.

"Guys, give him all you got!" Gus yelled and started activating his abilities, trying to focus them on one section of the shield. Before being lost in the flashes and explosions of color as energy splashed over the egg-shaped dome.

Mengele folded his arms, calmly. His expression said it all. *I'll wait.*

When the first barrage died down and there he was, affecting a large yawn before checking a non-existent watch.

"You see that was just foolish. But 'heroes' always have to try. Right? So what have you accomplished?" He counted the items on his fingers. "One, you have revealed your abilities to me by your attacks. Those who held back are obviously support for the team. I just need to find the healer. Probably that poor fellow that's totally drained. Yes, your expression just betrayed you. You all need to get some reins on those emotions, or they will drag you broken and bloody to parts unknown."

He turned and stared at Harmony, shaking a finger and frowning. "My thoughts are my own, voyeur. A mind as weak as your own could only dream to understand anything you could manage to find."

Harmony's eyes bulged and then she swooned. Her nose began to bleed as if punched. She folded and fell to the floor, only partially caught by Aurora.

Mengele surveyed the motley rescue team. "You tried your best, and yet I remain unscathed. Now I will show you what it's like to tangle with a true master. With someone who wields the power to bend the very fabric of reality. This was entertaining for a while, but it has become tedious, and I fear you have nothing left to teach me. I have work I must finish."

Without warning, he spun in a circle, outstretching an arm. Trails of energy fanned out, targeting the supers.

Prime deftly dodged out of its way. Aurora flew quickly upward while Darik formed some portals. He reversed the attacks' trajectory back to Mengele, diverting the two heading for BoJack and Harmony. Unable to form one for his own in time, he slapped at the connection as his MP, stamina, and HP began to quickly drain, funneling back to Mengele.

Gus dashed laterally to avoid the attack aimed at him, stopping near Grimdark and pulling him out of the way.

"So tasty." Mengele licked his lips as Darik's energy transferred. The trail winked out as Darik staggered drunkenly and fell hard on his rump. He then swooned and fell onto his back, arms spread wide.

Prime crouched, pulling something from her belt. She trained the cylinder on Mengele and fired. A concentrated green beam shot out of the end, and actually hit Mengele, eliciting a small yip. As he moved quickly out of its path, Prime tried to regain the angle. Mengele waved his hand slightly and the beam refracted far to his side.

"Nice try. Most lasers have too much divergence to even cause any damage. Easily countered though with a little dimensional folding."

Prime had to quickly disengage the laser as Mengele had twisted the beam back toward her. The energy curved and slingshotted back toward her, and she barely had time to disengage the beam before it sliced through her.

While she was dodging, Mengele flung another hand, first at Prime and then at Aurora. There was a scream and Aurora crashed into a table, clutching her face, blood pouring through her fingers. She didn't reappear after falling behind it, out of Gus' view. Prime retreated into cover, her suit shredded and torn in multiple places. Multiple thin bloody lines bled on her skin and soaked areas of her pink fur crimson. After she had ducked into cover, Mengele turned back to Gus.

"So here we are again, Gus. That was the group coming to rescue you, yes? I'll bet you looked up to them. Admired them. But look at them, broken, bloodied, and weak. Once I deal with you, and clean up this... untidiness... I will have even more playthings to examine. And I will make you watch it all, Gus. Even if I have to cut off your eyelids. You will *watch it all!*"

CHAPTER EIGHTY-SIX

Sometimes the Good Guys Finish First

None of my abilities are working against him… Gus thought frantically, trying to find some weakness. Something he could do. *None of my abilities are working…* Why did that set off that familiar tingle?

Deep in Gus' brain, hybrid-Nth formed a chain, and rerouted an impulse along a new pathway, connecting axons that had never communicated with each other. Becoming a living conduit as neurons fired in a new way.

Like the damn turret!

Gus made ready to activate **Krackle**, but he took it slower now. Upon activating the ability, he saw the ether weave and dance, forming the structure of the projectiles. They looked like a cockle burr, with the spikes growing and shrinking as energy moved about the outer skin. He could sense the step when the outer shell was complete and the ether construct was to be filled. He flexed his legs and tried to let the energy in his red pathway fall into the empty construct.

The process was not easy. It started to comply, but Gus had to force it out. Pinpricks of pain began to add to the wounds Mengele had given him, but he could barely feel it through the adrenaline. It was like uprooting a large weed or pulling your own hair out at the roots. With a heave, Gus directed the energy into the spiky containers, which flared to life with a ruby light.

He launched them toward Mengele but found that once primed, the energy was coming out, and he had no way to stop the flow. So he kept activating **Krackle** and building more containers to catch the energy spilling out. He had completed three sets of the balls and was forming his fourth when the first of the ruby fireballs hit the barrier.

Gus knew that calling them fireballs was inherently wrong, but had no time for deep thought as the energy continued to overflow, and his entire attention was consumed with creating vessels for the energy. Something told him that if it were to spill out without a way to contain it that it would be bad. Like every molecule in your body exploding at the speed of light kind of bad.

The edge of the barrier began to sizzle and warp like melted plastic. It charred and smoked and then it was through, leaving a gaping hole that sagged in its wake. Gus was so consumed he missed the smug expression falling from Mengele's face into something akin to fear.

Placing his hands in front of him, he continued to form more barriers, pulling all his efforts into creating a thick wedge of a shield. The **Krackle** balls shrank and melted to nothing, but the ones behind penetrated deeper from the trail their fellows had blazed.

The two of them stood there, frenetically working. The clusters of projectiles grew thicker and more concentrated as Gus sent them off to their target. And at last it was gone. Gus braced himself and watched the attack march on like a juggernaut. The outer layers of the barrier peeled and separated like an onion until they were so damaged, they dispersed into nothingness.

Mengele was not to be discouraged; barriers formed and were pushed outward as new ones were formed below them in rapid succession. These ones resembled square plexiglass plates, each new one staggered at a slight angle to create a starlike pattern as it spiraled outward.

"Go ahead, waste all of your MP on those barriers," Gus said through cracked lips, but he doubted Mengele heard.

A message popped on the bottom of Gus' display. He read only a portion before swiping it away.

Congratulations! You have added a modality to a power. This will upgrade all martial abilities that use energy to Tier II abilities…

Not now.

Seeing a red gel nearby, Gus pulled himself along the counter, not trusting his throbbing legs, and threw the gel in his mouth.

There was a massive surge of strength and HP. His legs immediately regained their strength and he moved toward Mengele, who was tiring. The protective plates were spilling out considerably slower now. One of the energy balls made it through the fringe and detonated when it hit his shoulder, knocking him back, tearing a large chunk out of the shoulder, revealing muscle and glistening bone.

The fall was fortuitous for him, because the few remaining projectiles passed through the final barriers and traveled above him. Detonating from proximity, but without direct contact. There was definitely damage, but there would have been little left of Mengele had they hit him point blank in the chest.

Now, Gus, go now! Nick urged.

Gus waved away the fumes and smoke and grabbed Mengele. He clamped down on his throat and lifted him in the air.

"I can see why you like this. It feels good to be on this end for a change."

Mengele kicked and flailed and razor-sharp threads hit his chest and lower body. Many ricocheting off, others slicing the surface, even others boring straight though, leaving pinhole sized wounds in their wake.

Gus' knuckles cracked as he tightened his grip. Instead of fear, Mengele had a creepy manic expression on his face, as if encouraging Gus to keep going. He could only force out tiny gasps and squeaks. There was nothing to discuss. This man was poison personified. Mengele's eyes darted left and he stopped struggling. A wide smile played across his lips and there was a groan behind his shoulder.

"BoJack!" someone yelled.

Gus felt a twinge, like someone had plucked a sour note on a guitar string, and knew BoJack had indeed been hurt. That was new. But he couldn't be distracted. The others could help him. Gus locked eyes with Mengele, boring into him as he pressed harder and harder.

I never thought I would feel this way again... Gus heard in a faint whisper. It was reminiscent of using **Telepathy** with that same ethereal filter to any spoken words. Hardening his resolve, he let it go and focused on crushing the life out of Mengele. The little roach was resilient.

Roach? That's a new one.

The thought surprised Gus and he relaxed his grip for a split second, allowing Mengele to draw in a ragged breath.

You can hear me?

I can, and I can tell you that you very well may end me. But doing so will be at the cost of your friend bleeding out over there. Us roaches take a lot to kill, you know.

The statement rang with truth as his **True Sight** ability pinged. He growled internally, leaning close to Mengele.

This isn't over.

For now it is. And you've just kicked a hornet's nest. I wasn't lying when I said I was disappointed in you. When we meet again, maybe you will have learned how these others are a liability. Eventually, you'll see. Now go help your fragile friend.

Gus flung Mengele, who managed an easy flip, landing on one knee, and casually started rubbing his neck. He slapped a panel next to him and slid into the doorway. There was a vibration and rumbling. Gus turned and ran to his friend. It was bad.

The others were holding hands on his wounds, but it wasn't enough as blood burbled between hands white with pressure. Mengele had managed his cutting ability and they couldn't leave BoJack's side.

Gus slid to a stop and turned back, looking for another red gel. Anything. He opened drawers, display racks, and cupboards that lined the room. Weapons, armor pieces, electronics, tissue samples. But no damn gels.

"Hurry, Gus!" one of the women shrieked as he searched. With a fierce tug, the fifth drawer of a large rolling cart opened and there were gels inside! The weight of the extended drawers caused the cart to tumble forward, and Gus barely snatched three gels before the cart toppled.

Gus slid to a stop by BoJack's side and bit the corner off of a gel, then squished the gooey contents in his slack mouth. He looked worse than Gus had ever seen him: blanched like a drowning victim but shriveled instead of bloated. The only hint that he was alive were the sunken eyes slowly turning to Gus in recognition. With one gel in, Gus gently closed BoJack's mouth and massaged his throat, hoping that it would go down the right tube and BoJack wouldn't choke.

When nothing apparent happened, Gus ripped into another gel and force-fed it to BoJack.

He gripped Gus' hand with a weak hand and moaned, "Worth it…" in a voice that sounded like dust escaping a sealed tomb, before his head fell back.

CHAPTER EIGHTY-SEVEN

Take What You Want

Gus held his mentor, lying limp in his trembling hands. Why was he shaking? He noticed the movement coming from BoJack.

"I had you all there, didn't I?" the corpse-like man rasped, his laugh turning into a hacking cough.

Yuki gave him a light punch on the shoulder.

"You're a real bastard, you know that?!" Anastasia spat, throwing her head back and stomping off. This only made BoJack laugh all the more.

Gus fed BoJack the last gel and he was able to chew it himself. Color started to flood back into his cheeks. His hair was still sweaty and slicked back, but as everyone removed their hands, the cuts were already nothing more than red scratches that faded to pink and smoothed out before their eyes.

"Glad you're back, buddy." Gus clapped BoJack on the shoulder and then cast his eyes around the room. He flipped the cart and took out the small bin that held the gels inside. After making the rounds, everyone was out of immediate danger and BoJack saw to everyone's injuries and was able to reverse any damage utilizing the surgical instruments that were readily available. Soon everyone was back to 100% and searching the room for any loot they could find.

The Vault was a treasure trove. Aurora had found two tool benches and was organizing her kit, taking and cataloging all the parts like a kid sorting their Halloween hoard. Component after component dropped into her well organized kit composed of many zippered pockets.

"Mind if I keep a lot of this?" BoJack held up one of the handheld devices to Gus. "These would cost mega credits to buy. I doubt even large hospitals would have the budget for most of this."

"Take it all; I don't care if I ever see this place again," Gus said, looking back towards the lab where Mengele had worked on him and shuddering a bit.

"Um, about that..." Yuki tiptoed forward. "It might be a really good idea to claim this base as our own. You know, hack in and change the accesses so Mengele can't get back in here after we leave."

"You sure he wouldn't have some kind of backdoor?" Darik asked.

"You wound me, Darik. Have you been sleeping this whole time? I can do it."

"Let's clear off one of these recovery beds, so you can access the system and hack in." Gus turned to drag one from the neighboring operating rooms.

Yuki grabbed his arm to stop him. "Yeah. If I do it, I'm going to take the long way. It'll take a lot longer, but it's also safer. I've had enough excitement for just a little bit."

"Go ahead, Yuki, I like 'safe' once in a while," Gus agreed. "How long do you think it will take?"

"I won't know until I get in, but I guesstimate two hours. Give me two hours. If it's too much, I'll drop a worm in to ruin all of the computers here. Without something to manage the heat down here, I guess the whole place will break down pretty quickly, and Mengele will be hard pressed to salvage anything. Is that enough time for you?"

"The sooner we're out of here the better, as far as I'm concerned."

Sanura removed her helmet and preened her fur a bit to tame it, waiting patiently for Gus to finish. When Gus' attention was free, she addressed him. "Forgive me, I've got to get back. I have a date with my daughter. There should be something in the hangar I could use. I will join you all back at the manor when I get her. I may even bring her there to meet you."

"Why don't you take my skip-jump? I'll send you the coordinates." Gus reviewed his logs and slid over the information.

"Thank you, that will save me some time." Prime bowed slightly and ran toward the exit.

Grimdark sat near Harmony. She still had a drawn expression, staring straight ahead, mumbling as Grimdark spoke with her.

"Is she going to be okay, BoJack? Did you find anything when you checked her out?"

"No mental damage, but she said something about how Mengele turned her ability back onto her. She said it was… 'invasive,' but wouldn't go into much detail. I think she just needs some time. What about you, Gus? How are you doing?"

"I… I'm not ready to talk about what went on here. Just know that it was horrible. Give her some space too. Nothing good comes from brushing up against that man."

"That reminds me, I have something to show you that I think you'll be interested in. Follow me." BoJack gestured to a display case filled with vials.

———

There was no room to move in the small porta-potty-sized ship as it flew along its preprogrammed trajectory to Mengele's closest base. In truth, they were designed to ship specimens, not people, but it worked in a pinch.

There was little to occupy his mind, so he retreated to his memory palace and ruminated on the battle. Partitioning his mind, he reviewed different aspects. One raged with the bitterness of failure and loss of his materials. The utter waste galled him. He finally understood why others put self-destructs into their bases. Better that no one gain access to his hard-earned assets than they fall into the hands of those... unworthy ones.

Hopefully one of them would blow themselves up tinkering with one of the weapons. The thought made the side of his mouth twitch in a faint smile.

Another partition noted that he had leveled recently. It had been so long ago that he had hidden the indicator from his normal display. He had reached level 249. When he hit 250, he should have everything he needed to confront his employer and move to the next stage. He pursed his lips as the ecstasy soothed away the remaining pain. When the glow faded, he was back to his familiar numb feeling. He almost missed the pain.

A separate part of his mind evaluated his and Gus' tactics in the last battle, replaying it over and over in his mind. He could only see the barest hints of what the upstart had done, but this much Mengele knew. He had found a way to connect foundation energies to active abilities. Mengele had not been able to do that. Yet.

Not only that, but he had drained the entire well of free foundation energy in a huge radius around the epicenter of the blast. He turned his attention inward on his own meridians, still raw from the experience, and found a pleasant surprise. While the energy he had struggled to gather and refine was all gone, the channels pulsing like an aching tooth, orange light caught his attention. A large section of the second disk had been chipped or eroded away, revealing the next node.

Maybe it was all worth it.

Examining his other nodes, he saw a narrow wedge of yellow on the next meridian and the rest of them showed visible cracks, all the way to the top. *Excellent!*

There was so much to do. Revenge to plan. Designs for his new suit to mentally construct and test so he would be ready when he got to his new lab. And pondering. So much pondering to do. Each partition of his mind worked on its task, and the hours slipped by unnoticed as he worked.

One thing became clear as the time went on, Mengele felt something he hadn't in quite a while. A challenge. A new adversary to dismantle in every aspect, the same way he had with his body. He turned and looked at the small case of samples. Twenty-five pristine tissue biopsies in nutrient baths, each stimulated to keep them alive.

So many plans.

————————

"I'm in!" Yuki shouted. "With eighteen minutes to spare, too! Having that other data from the hospital really helped. I already had big sections already cracked, and he used the same security here. No AI though. That was nice."

"Were you able to change security to keep Mengele out?"

"Already done. Oh, and I interrupted some huge file transfer he was in the middle of. No doubt he got some of it, but a fair amount should be corrupted from the distortion of interrupting the feed. Unfortunately, it ruined the data on our end. But do you really want to know what he was up to?"

"Actually, I do." Gus' face turned serious. "Anything you can find as far as research goes, store it remotely and delete everything when we leave. I don't want anyone dabbling in whatever hellish experiments he has been doing down here for who knows how long. But maybe there's a clue in there about what he did to my mother. There has to be."

"I didn't think about that. I'll copy it, but don't expect me to go through it. That guy is sick."

"I won't, just get me everything. Thanks, Yuki. Hacking in was a good call."

"Just doing my job."

"Can we talk later? I need to wrap up some more things here, but I have a proposition for you." At her expression, he backpedaled. "Nothing like that, but I need your help with something." BoJack stepped up, tapped Gus' shoulder and gestured to the side of the room before moving there and waiting. "Like I said, we'll talk later."

Yuki flashed a big peace sign and winked.

As Gus came close, BoJack whispered, "So, have you made any decisions on what to do with them?"

"No, but are you sure we should keep this hidden from the others?"

"Yes. Trust me, yes. Supers kill other supers for something like this. Especially the higher tier they are. Keep it to yourself. For now."

"Still feels wrong, but I'll trust you—for now." Gus turned to the rest of the Crew. "How is everyone doing? Ready to head back?"

"All of us are registered into the system and I've armed it against anyone else. Mengele will get a rude awakening if he decides to come back," Yuki reported.

"Bah, that little rat will manage to squeak out somehow. His kind always does. I'm done here, I'll go call the elevator." Darik turned and headed down the long corridor, which had reset to its warm glow.

"Wait up, Darik, I'll join you," Gus said and trotted over to his side.

CHAPTER EIGHTY-EIGHT

Getcha Back

It was done. Mengele had escaped, but BoJack was safe, and he'd make that trade any day.

He thought he would feel more excitement at finally being free, but it hadn't caught up with him yet. None of it felt real. Except the lack of constant pain. He almost felt numb to be absent from the constant pain and stress. In the stillness, he noticed a flashing icon on the side of his display indicating pending notifications. No doubt there were a lot of messages there to peruse, but he couldn't deal with them now. A strong hand slapped him on his back as he walked in step with Darik.

"Very impressive, lad. Very impressive."

"Mengele got away, though."

"You made the right call. Some of the others might disagree, but in the end, family is all you have." They walked in silence and called the lift from the surface. He thought about the situation while waiting for the lift to descend.

They had come for him. Somehow, they had found him in the middle of nowhere with no help. But why?

He couldn't think of a reason, and he found that he didn't care. He had always felt like he was on his own, with no one reliable in his life. Had that finally changed, or had he just refused to see who was there all along? He reflected on all the things he promised himself would happen if he got powers.

He always thought he'd be fighting for the less fortunate. He had never thought that his colleagues would have as many challenges as the regs did. It was always hard to see things clearly when they were high up on a pedestal, though.

Ideas formed in Gus mind. Paths he had never considered. Possibilities. He got so lost in his thoughts that Darik had to nudge him when the lift finally arrived. They went back to the surface and Darik took him to the corsair.

"Wow."

"She's a beauty, ain't she?"

"I'll say."

"Come aboard, we'll get ready for takeoff."

The inside of the ship was nice and comfortable. It was how he had always imagined a billionaire's luxury jet. He ran his fingers across the top of one of the seats.

"Rich Corinthian leather," he muttered with a smile.

———

The ride back was uneventful, though a somber mood permeated the group.

"I know exactly what Harmony's feeling," Nick said abruptly.

"Yeah?" Gus replied, looking over at her.

She was repeating some of the same phrases. "He saw everything," and other barely intelligible mutters.

Grimdark insisted on staying by her side, but at times she barely seemed to notice his reassuring hand gripping hers as he massaged her forearm gently, trying to console her.

"When he dosed you with whatever that white poison was, I was cut off. Not only from communicating with you—but from everything. The Nth are part of a collective; you would best know it like a hive-mind. The others are always in the background, but we can't communicate directly. It's like being in the room with a sleeping person. You can sense their presence but not interact. Even when we are stripped of our interfaces after an apocalypse event and we prepare for the long trip to another planet, we lose our individuality, but we are always together."

"No, I get it. Being alone sucks."

"Down there, I was plunged into an abyss of solitude. Much like you experienced in that bottomless pit. But there was nothing. No communication, sensation, or feedback of any kind. I was cut off from the quantum server. Do you know what that's like? I have nearly instantaneous access to anything I need to know, even if I can't divulge it directly to a host. But that connection was totally severed. I feared that I would be alone forever. That may not sound so bad to you, but for an Nth, being cast out is our version of hell. Over time, I felt like I was losing pieces of myself. Drifting apart like an ice cube dissolving in that void."

Gus remembered his own experience in the pit, and shook his head. "I know what you mean. Time does weird things when you're in the dark like that."

"The worst part was that I had no idea if it would ever end. It felt like an eternity. With how quickly we process information, to suddenly have… nothing. I have never seen a host go insane, but I could see how an Nth could lose themself in such a situation. Nth never 'die' in the typical sense, we simply reincarnate as a new construct for a time. But that is the first time I have experienced the potential for oblivion."

"I guess we humans just know that death is part of the package. Still scares the hell out of us, though. The unknown."

"Fear, yes. Mine was that I would be permanently locked out of the system if I ever did get out of that awful place. Just like a hacked Nth. That might be a fate worse than oblivion. Seeing what was there but being permanently separated from it. I know I have been severe with you, Gus, but this persona drives me to be tough on you. I realize now that possibly there was a different approach that would have been more effective."

"You know, Nick, I wonder if it was what I needed all along. Things are just clearer now. The headaches were driving me crazy, and I was too busy trying to meet an impossible ideal I had created. It just took a series of extended torture to put things into perspective. All the stupid things I worried about just seem so inconsequential now. Through the pain, it brought the present into laser focus. I'm going to try staying here for a while to make some changes. I'm sure I'll make a ton of mistakes, as usual, but I'm not going to let it paralyze me like before. I'm not making any more excuses for myself."

"So you're saying that I should've just signed you up for Mengele's program from the beginning, and we could have skipped all the unpleasantness between us?"

"You do what you need to do, Nick. I've got a hard head, so it's probably the only thing that would get through. I'll be more open to suggestions. The more I learn about these powers, the more I realize I really know just about nothing."

"And that's a good thing. Believe it or not, you haven't been conditioned to fit someone's agenda. You're free to pursue your own path. With all the inherent advantages and disadvantages of that responsibility."

"I didn't used to think so, but you're probably right. I'm a living paradox when it comes to relying on others. I can't stop myself from relying on people's opinions, but I want to be independent at the same time."

"It's more common in humans than you think. Remember that."

"Hey, I just realized the headaches are gone. They got swallowed up in all of the other things going on, but they really are gone."

"Your system is clear too, hormone levels are stable, and no buildup of any toxins of any kind."

"You think I am done with those for good?" Gus perked up.

"Hard to say at this point, but most likely no. But this indicates there's a way to cleanse it out. We just need to figure out how."

"That's something, at least."

"Why don't you check your logs? I think you'll be pleasantly surprised."

Gus clicked the icon:

Through extensive cycles of physical attack and damage, you have upgraded **Resilience** *to* **Enhanced Resilience***.*

This upgrade increases against any physical damage and resets the overall ability to Level 1.

Enhanced Resilience (Level 1): [passive ability]: *Grants extraordinary resistance to physical, projectile, and explosive damage due to a passive ether shield that absorbs and deflects attacks above melee speeds, as well as focused physical damage. Increases efficiency of Nth healing, giving a 10% speed improvement, increasing an additional 1% per level. Nth also become more efficient at repairs, especially among similar or recurrent injuries.*

500 XP Awarded.

100 FP Awarded.

3,825 XP to level 21.

There was a stream of damage notices. Gus saw that he had gotten down to 10 HP at one point, but Mengele had backed off, allowing him to regenerate. He also saw health boosts amid the damage. Something must have been in the IV to counteract the abuse, helping Mengele to get back to his work faster.

Enhanced Resilience continued to level amid the endless damage notices. Ending at a whopping level 21 by the end of it. That added up to an additional 3000 XP and 750 FP when all was said and done.

Other notices were interspersed as well.

Congratulations, you've traded your wishbone for a backbone!

You have unlocked the base function of **Bound***! For good or bad, you become aware of each other regardless of distance.*

(You didn't think that "jumping" was the extent of this ability, did you? Really? Who wants a jumping superpower?)

This upgrade increases scope of its function and resets the overall ability to Level 1.

Additional effects follow:

Bound (Level 1) [20 MP]: *Jump with increased ability, energy stored upon landing, aiding height and power of successive jumps.*

Bound Base function [passive]: *Form deep connections with those whom you shared intense emotional experiences. Currently bound to three(3) entities.*

Jet

BoJack

Mengele/Dr. Weft

Gus blinked at this new information. Yes, it was true. As he paid attention, he felt a pull in different directions. One along their current heading—that must be Jet, whom he had left at the manor. The other was close and right behind him, which would be BoJack, and then another, thin as gossamer. Gus heard his knuckles crack and looked down at his clenched fists. He released them and shook out the tension.

Where the lion's share of XP was from **Wreckord**. It was actually still playing! Somehow it had been muted during the process and continued to play the entire time since he had started it at the manor. There were incredible amounts of stat boosts and one shocker was an XP multiplier when the chain was stopped. It had leveled thirty-two times and there was still eight days, fourteen hours, and change left on the playlist. Time to grind some training in the next few days, and maximize the effects of the multiplier. He had never seen that but he would definitely take advantage of it if he could.

Through extensive cycles of physical attack and damage, you have upgraded **Cleanse** *to* **Spiritual Cleanse**.

This upgrade increases against any physical damage and resets the overall ability to Level 1.

Spiritual Cleanse (Level 1) [50 MP]: *Eliminate toxins of all types from self or others who possess Nth. At higher levels, can create remote*

effects on those who do not possess Nth. When combined with fundamental energies, can be utilized to clear more entrenched toxins, on a micromolecular level.
500 XP awarded.
100 FP awarded.

More leveling notices followed, and Gus sank back in his chair with the euphoria of reaching multiple levels at once. He even received Guiding Principle bonuses for sacrificing the opportunity to kill Mengele that multiplied with a compassion bonus. This took him to level 23, and filled his progress bar to almost level 24.

"Nick, I think I know how we can get rid of these headaches for good."

Just then the corsair banked and a familiar island came into view. Pangs of homesickness hit Gus harder than he had expected it would.

He was finally home.

CHAPTER EIGHTY-NINE

Brand New Day

Shortly after landing, Gus gathered everyone together.

"We've been through a lot. I want to thank you all for coming to get me. Let's get some rest and meet up tomorrow at say, noon, and go over everything." There was nodded assent among the Crew and they dispersed to their respective rooms.

Gus caught up to Yuki. "Is this a good time?"

"Sure, I suppose."

"Yuki, I don't know any other way to say this, so I'm just going to come on out and ask. I really need someone with your skills at the manor. I realize you're Purple Faction and you probably have a better gig over there. I can't offer the same things they do, and I'm not trying to poach you away, and I'm babbling…"

Gus took a deep breath and continued as Yuki looked at him impassively.

"Even if it's only for a short time, maybe like a freelancer. I'm seeing more and more that I can't do everything myself. I need to get things set up here at the manor and optimized so I can be ready for the future. My big fear is that I invest the FP into the wrong things and limit my options in the future, so your expertise would be essential, at least in these beginning phases. Plus we have to get a plan for this place in terms of security. And that's just of the two things I've thought need attention, there's undoubtedly a lot more."

Yuki looked up as if in deep contemplation, squinting one eye. "I'll do it on one condition…"

"Anything, if it's in my power," Gus agreed, eyes imploring.

"I don't like to be tied down. If I do stay, don't be thinking I'm going to be here forever. Are you good with that?"

"Sure, sure. Anything else?"

"Well, a little birdie told me that you have a unique ability, and that you could, maybe, possibly, give me an ability I could use for offense. Something I can use while not jacked-in to the virtual world. I would *really* like to be a super who could actually take care of myself instead of just being a specialty case." She eyed Gus expectantly, trying to keep her expression demure and controlled.

"Okay, yeah, sure. But this stays between us, alright? I don't need to tell you that if people knew what I could do, I would get a pretty big target painted on my back. The only problem is that there are so many abilities it can be hard to choose one that is perfect for you. Do you have any thoughts?" he whispered conspiratorially.

"What if we went to the Oracle and I asked her? Besides, she said she wanted to see you again, right? Kill two birds with one stone."

"That's not a bad idea," Gus mused. "You're not worried what her ask will be?"

"Nah. Besides, I'm tough. And I love a good dare; it'll be fun."

"If you say so," Gus said, rolling his eyes.

"Can we take one of the skip-jumps?" Yuki suggested.

"Sure—"

"And I get to drive. But you have to give me access."

"I think I gave all of the Crew total access before I left, to… you know."

"You sure you want to leave it that way?"

"If I can't trust you guys, who can I trust? By the way, thanks for coming for me. It means a lot to me."

"For all the good we did. You probably would have beat him without us there."

Gus made the adjustments in the manor tab on his display and Yuki's eyes rolled up in her head, showing just the whites. A few seconds later, they returned to normal.

Looking her in the eye he continued. "I realized a lot of things in that pit. About how I've been doing things and my relation to others. I've wasted a lot of time worrying about the future and lamenting my past. Using old experiences to limit what I'm doing right now. I have always felt… detached. But when I saw you guys down there… well, a lot of things clarified for me."

Yuki looked up at Gus in silence.

"Okay, sorry to make it weird. Let's meet up tomorrow after the meeting."

———

At the meeting the next day, everyone caught up on what had happened, Gus' story leaving out the worst of the details.

"Well, all of you are welcome to stay here as long as you wish," Gus offered. "And if any of you need anything in the meantime, I want each of you to know that I am more than willing to help. That includes if you think there are any upgrades to the manor that will help you develop your skills; let me know and we'll get it in the queue."

Grimdark motioned like he was going to raise a finger, but thought better of it and shook his head.

"I mean it, anything. Yuki and I have an appointment to make—you guys will be okay here?"

With no other items the meeting adjourned and Gus and Yuki made their way to the lift.

"You know how to drive a skip-jump, Yuki? I thought you were the stay-at-home type."

"Oh, I've had my eye on them for some time. I already spent some time looking through the manor's capabilities before I had any access, so I have some idea of what's possible. Skip-jumps have always been a passion of mine, so they caught my eye. And for the record, I am *not* the stay at home type, as much as everyone wants to stuff me in that box." She emphasized the latter with the most severity Gus had ever seen on her usually playful expression.

"You mean you took flying lessons?" Gus asked, surprised that she had that training.

"Yeah? More like I took my father's skip-jumps out for street racing without him noticing? Flying's pretty intuitive, but racing takes skill."

"Here, let me make a couple of preliminary changes to some settings, 'til we get up top."

As they exited, a large door slid down into the mountain. The hangar door yawned open and revealed myriad ships in the large area carved out of the rock. Some were large and others small. All had a vintage look to them, bubbles and curves instead of the sleek angular shapes of modern transports. It was the first time Gus had seen most of the designs as he took a good long look.

"This way, I have one picked out." Yuki maneuvered past ships as Gus goggled. The manor had so many secrets to uncover. Finding the ship she wanted, she climbed atop it, opening a panel and checking some fuel lines. She opened the door for Gus, bowing and motioning for him to enter. He chuckled and jumped into the passenger seat. This model resembled a dragonfly, two bulbous windscreens looking like eyes.

Yuki pulled herself inside and extended a tendril from her hand directly into the front panel.

"What are you doing?"

"Upgrades," she said with a wink.

———

They set down in the glade and walked into the forest. The weather was cool, but there was less fog and the lower humidity seemed to chill them less than when they had come the first time.

"I knew you would come," a voice croaked from behind them.

The two supers started at the unexpected address. They were still a way from the Oracle's clearing and were lost in their own thoughts. Turning, they saw her perched lazily on a large branch that hung low alongside the path.

She dropped to the ground, her knees emitting a popping sound that made Gus wince. The Oracle looked unaffected as she strode up to them. She cocked her head at Yuki and smiled and nodded.

"Very good, you are wise to come to me," she said knowingly.

"Then you know what I want?" Yuki ventured.

"Yes, child. But you still must ask."

"I want to know what the best power Gus could gift me is."

"When the vampire's son is hungry with betrayal, you must be marked with his magic. Are the terms agreeable?"

Yuki screwed up her face, and looked at Gus. He shrugged, as bewildered as her.

"Speak quickly, dearie, the offer remains only for so long…"

"Okay, fine," she quickly agreed.

"Done!" the Oracle said and rubbed her hands together, the sound oddly like the rustling of autumn leaves as the deal was struck.

"The ability you seek is called Manifest. Can you see it, boy?"

Gus did the odd thing with his eyes that allowed him to sift through the abilities and found it there, lying in the depths. The ability felt odd to him, distinctly feminine and alien. Becoming aware of it had made it stand apart and put a tension on him, as though he were water and it was oil, pushing to separate from him. He stepped to Yuki and placed his hand on her temple and let the ability transfer to her. Like a cool trickle of water, the ability rushed to the surface, flowed out of him, and Yuki trembled as she took it in.

"Well, what does it do?" Gus asked, not having even checked the description before he gifted the ability.

Yuki gasped as she checked her display for the ability description, a manic smile spreading across her face. In a daze, she made a sliding motion and Gus saw the text:

Manifest
Restricted ability:
Prerequisites: Slice 30, Hack 30, Summon 30, Intelligence 50
This ability allows one skilled in summoning virtual avatars to manifest them into physical reality. This ability's description is unable to be revealed to anyone lower than required levels until unlocked. Allows one to summon previously captured intelligences, and ability is inactive without history of captured AI.

"What's a virtual avatar?"

Yuki said nothing and gave Gus a huge bear hug. She gripped him tight and he thought he heard Yuki sobbing. When she finally let him go, he saw that there were indeed tears in her eyes.

"I'll tell you on the way back." She sniffed and wiped at her eyes, laughing at her fortune. She pointed at the Oracle. "I think she still wants to talk to you."

Gus saw the Oracle waiting patiently. Her eyes looked hungry though, like a predator and a twinge of uncertainty twisted inside his heart for a moment. Yuki mouthed 'thank you' to the Oracle, and made her way back to the transport.

When Yuki was out of earshot, the Oracle came closer, invading his space as she was apt to do. "I am impressed again with you. I wondered if you would be up to the challenges, and I see I was not disappointed. If you recall, I said that you must ask for what you want when I spoke with your friend, do you recall?"

"Yes, ma'am."

Ma'am? Was that an appropriate address to the Oracle? It almost felt borderline offensive but there was no other word that sprang to mind. Her demeanor asked for respect. Demanded it. Her eyes softened a bit, sensing his discomfiture. Or enjoying it, it was hard to tell.

"And…" she drew the word out expectantly.

"And I found out a little with the answer you gave me. I don't regret my question, but I have as many as ever."

"You can still ask," she trailed off suggestively.

"But I already——"

"Oh, did you now? I recall saying some things that may have been interpreted as an answer, but there was no direct ask, if I am remembering things clearly."

Gus stopped to remember. Had he asked? Verbally, at least? He knew what he had wanted to ask but couldn't recall saying the words out loud. As if she had read his mind, and possibly he just assumed that he had said the words? He would have to ask Yuki if she remembered the question he had posed.

"Are you beginning to see why I warned you from traveling down this path? There is no leaving it until you reach the end. One way or another. You have grown much. I am happy to see that I did not err in my decision."

"So I can ask——" Gus tasted clove and a tingle on his lips as she pressed a finger to them, stopping him from speaking.

"It is better to wait. What is asked must be answered. Once asked, the door closes. It is the way. Go. Follow your path. Trust. Ignore the illusions. There will be many. And that is all that I can say." She leaned over and looked over Gus' shoulder. Her eyes widened in surprise and Gus turned to look. There was no one on the path behind him.

When he turned around, there was only a rustling of leaves as a small whirlwind died down, accompanied by a slight cackle.

I can't believe I fell for that.

"Thank you," he called out to the empty forest.

CHAPTER NINETY

Goodbyes

"Gus, I've got some bad news."

"I'm not surprised, but what is it, Nick?"

"You're building up those same byproducts in your brain again. It's trace amounts, but they are forming, and the rate is quicker than last time."

"That's about what I expected. Do you know anything about forming Mandrite crystals or even what they are? Maybe I could extract those abilities and stop this process and get back to normal. I wouldn't mind a long rest, and sleeping in."

"Hmm… I can't access that information, but it seems to exist. I am not sure that humankind has reached that level of sophistication yet? Usually if one member of a species makes a discovery, it becomes available, but usually only on an 'you must ask or it won't be divulged' basis."

"The only thing that helped was that red energy. Foundation energy, the prompts called it. I need to find some more until I get this sorted. Nick, what's the lowest part of the manor? Maybe I have to be deep underground like in the mine. I began to detect that energy when it was in high concentrations in the mine, but I haven't really seen any since."

"I wish I could tell you more, but that's also locked. It's worth a try though. Manor records show there is an empty room at the base of the manor, probably for storage. It'd be interesting to see if you can notice anything there."

"Let's go." Gus headed to the lift and was directed to select the third button from the bottom. From there they made it to another service elevator and descended some more.

"I can feel it. It is increasing in intensity, but nowhere near what it was in the mine." The elevator clanged as it opened and Gus stepped out into a large chamber. His footsteps echoed on the hard floor, the only light spilling in from the elevator. Gus stepped back as he took it in. Even cycling through his other perception modes, he found it difficult to see anything of consequence.

"Is it totally empty, Nick?"

"There's nothing on the schematics, try yelling as loud and long as you can." Gus did so as Nick switched to a new view. The sound waves looked like the tide going out as they fanned away from him. They encountered nothing but the far end of the chamber before reflecting back. The room was high, maybe three stories and oval in shape.

"Sacred guano, Batman! I've got echolocation, Nick?"

"Unfortunately, yes. I worried you would take this and run with it…" Nick replied with a deep sigh.

"You worried right! You know, past Nick would have been very happy to show me this." Gus chuckled with glee.

"It's only useful in a limited number of situations, so don't get crazy."

The elevator began to buzz from being wedged open and Gus let the door slide shut. Darkness enveloped him, but he could see faint shading denoting the far wall and ceiling. Gus could see the ripples of sound caused by his footsteps as he moved to the center of the chamber. A quick look back showed the elevator's position, but this was absolute dark. He continued to the center of the room; the effect was like being in the middle of a large arena.

"Wow, it's like a really *dark night…*"

"Go ahead, get it out of your system," Nick said, voice thick with affected boredom.

"Are you not entertained?" Gus boomed.

"No, I most definitely am not. Are you able to do anything here or are we about done?"

"Let me try." Gus sat down and tried to figure out what he needed to do. "Any ideas, Nick?"

"Sorry, this is new territory for me as well."

Gus tried to open himself to the feeling he'd had in Mengele's lab, but too many thoughts rattled around in his brain. Pain definitely had a way of narrowing his focus. With some difficulty, he dismissed the intruding thoughts that wanted to impose on him. Questions, such as what if he couldn't help his mother get better, or what if another group came and tried to take the manor arose. Unlike the past, he was able to shed the emotional weight of worry that these thoughts usually gave him.

I've worried too much about a past I can't change and a future I don't know will even exist.

It became easier to let those thoughts go. Gus turned his focus on the inner path. It was much fainter now, like an unused trail slowly being overcome by the surrounding vegetation. He mentally traced the path, traveling it. Skating down the pristine conduit, circling through each of the four extensions before returning to the nexus and then moving down the next pathway.

As he traveled, his thoughts became distant and there was only the path. Down. Up. Enter another door. Down. Up. Door. The process syncing with his breath. He exhaled more deeply than he thought possible, and it was as if he was expelling thousands of tiny spheres, their contents spent. Each inhale started to draw in one or two of the spheres, now filled partially with a red glow.

He followed the glowing spheres as they continued to travel down after passing through his lungs. Drawn down into the channels below, passing through his body as if it were a ghost. His mind chased the few spheres as they traveled in the center of the conduit, suspended there as if the walls were an opposing magnet, keeping it bobbing and balancing them equally away.

Breathe out, more spheres spilling into the surroundings, breath in, a few more of the filled ones coming back, trailing after the others like train cars. With each breath there was an inexhaustible supply of the spheres, continually pouring out. Only the filled ones came back when inhaling.

Gus began to see something. The red spheres within him began to pull on the other spheres filling from without. The process increased in speed and Gus felt the energy race along the track, reminding him of the afterimage of a sparkler as it was waved in the air.

There was a loud gong, which broke Gus' attention, and his perception of the spheres became foggy then disappeared altogether. The rosy glow he had begun to perceive from the filling spheres nearby also evaporated into total darkness once again. As he came out of his concentration, the gong softened to the mild chime of a skill leveling up.

You have leveled up the skill: **Mindfulness** *to* **Level 9!**
1800 XP awarded.
1800 FP awarded.
595 XP to level 24.

Gus sat there in the darkness, thinking about what had happened, until Nick interrupted.

"Good, you're finally back. Do you have any idea of how long you were in your little trance?"

"What trance?"

"The one you've been in for the last thirty-six hours! The others have been trying to contact you, but I didn't want to disturb your concentration. There's apparently another issue. I tried to reassure them, but they are becoming progressively agitated."

Gus got to his feet, surprised he wasn't achy and sore from remaining in one position for so long. Nth were great but they had their limits on what they could do. He felt energetic like he had when he was first on the island. Well rested and alert.

"Let's go see what's going on."

"I told them where you were, that you were not to be disturbed, but also that you were safe. There was a little grumbling, but they accepted it overall," Nick informed Gus as he hit the call button.

———

"Sorry for being gone for so long, there was something I had to check out in the manor. I had no idea it would take so long. What's going on? What's happened?"

The Crew separated and Prime sat there dejectedly. Her eyes red and swollen as she dabbed at them with one of Grimdark's pocket squares. As Gus approached, she broke down again.

"They took her, Gus! They took Maddy. When I went to pick her up, Eldon was there—"

"And who is Eldon?"

"The butler, or manservant, whatever. He was there in the center of the big house that had been hastily packed and moved. They were gone. They commanded him to stay there and give me a message. Eldon trembled but delivered it to me, he even wet himself when he was done. I think he thought I was going to kill him right then and there. But it turns out I can't even be mad at him. He's indentured and had to obey. They told him if he did this, his contract was paid."

"I don't know what all that means, but what did he say?"

"He quoted them, reciting it like an actor in a play: 'Sanura, thank you for giving us time to liquidate everything and disappear. With my connections, you will never be able to find out where we've gone. And you'll never see Madeleine again. You brought this on yourself, and only have yourself to blame.'"

Gus flushed at the audacity, and took a knee by her and grabbed her hand. "You helped me get my family back, and I'll help you get yours. No matter what."

Quest Granted: Family Ties.
Quest objectives:
1) Find out where Maddy has been taken.
2) Reunite Sanura with Maddy unharmed.
Optional) Seek suitable punishment for the offenders.
Quest rewards*: 75,000 XP.*
Time requirements*: 3 days.*
Accept (Y/N)?

Gus accepted immediately. "Everyone, get ready. We have three days. I don't know why three, but let's get this done."

CHAPTER NINETY-ONE

Master of Puppets

Gus sat in a sunny patch on the top of the manor. The mammoth corsair covered most of the landing pad. Aurora wanted an hour to try something before everyone left, and Yuki insisted on coming, eager to try out her new ability.

Everyone but Harmony was going, and she was still a little petulant when it came to Sanura. Harmony appeared to be regaining her normal mannerisms, and had rebounded from whatever Mengele had done to her.

Prime had mentioned to the team that when she wore the helmet, to refer to her as Prime, especially around others, but with it off she was just Sanura. Gus didn't really see the distinction, but for some reason it was important to her.

While waiting for the others, Gus tried to practice meditating again, but he gave Nick the message to pull him out if the others were ready to go. The wind whipped in from the sea, easing the heat of the summer sun. Gus focused on his breathing and he was able to visualize the sand-sized spheres again, spilling out with each breath, floating to the ground like soap bubbles.

With eyes closed, he could sense them accumulating around

him, when one winked yellow like the first star at twilight. As his attention focused on it, another sphere glowed a cerulean blue. Slowly the yellow and blue spheres lit up, but were unmoved when he inhaled deeply.

Nick roused him as Seneschal exited the lift and entered the ship to do her pre-flight checks. Gus got up and stretched, looking out at the waves crashing far below.

"Gus, that seems to be keeping that mental buildup from accumulating. Those levels are virtually undetectable after you go into a trance."

"Finally, some good news for a change. I didn't manage to collect anything that time, but I'm totally relaxed, like I just got out of a hot tub after a nice massage."

The lift opened again and the rest of the Crew exited in a large group. Everyone was in good spirits as they gathered together, talking animatedly.

"Gus, guess what?" Anastasia grabbed Gus's hands with excitement. "Aurora and Yuki found a way to tap into local cams and scanners to track where they took Maddy! We basically just have to go and backtrack their route. The logs are overwritten every week to save on storage so I think that's why we only have the three days. But it should be smoother than when we were be-bopping around Hinansho trying to find your mother."

"That's good news, Anastasia. I think things might finally be turning around for us all."

"I spoke with Harmony, too. I tried to convince her to come along and put past prejudices behind her, but she was stubborn. I didn't press her too hard, but this is the situation now, and we're going to all have to get along, somehow. She's still contemplating whether she wants to stay or go back home. You may have to choose if you prefer Prime or Harmony, if it comes down to it." Her voice was laced with concern.

Gus sighed. "That's disappointing, to be honest. But she has to decide what's best for her. She's welcome to stay, or we can get her a portal back home if she'd like. Maybe she just needs some time, though. We've all been through the wringer."

"She misses her family, so maybe if she could contact them, that might help…"

"I'll see if there's anything Yuki can do to improve communications when we get back. We're sitting on a lot of FP after our recent escapades, so we can get some goodies. Yuki just hasn't had time to review what we need in the security aspect, but I'm sure we can do something to stay connected."

Darik waved for them to get aboard so they could get underway.

———

Mengele landed with a thump, bringing him out of his thoughts. He had already completed two projects in his mind and was eager to implement them. As the door slid open, he looked at the receiving bay. Humid air filled his lungs, refreshing after the stale, canned air of the capsule that was poorly filtered. He could feel the energy around him throb in time with the crash of the nearby waves.

Leaving the large warehouse structure, he stepped out to a nearby railing. White foam surged as the sea pounded violently on the rocks. He breathed in the briny air and smiled. A quick check of his internal clock showed the time was later than he had expected. His handiwork should be manifesting very soon.

He massaged his neck as he remembered Gus's grip on it. Despite the angst of the moment, he had been able to keep his head on his shoulders, quite literally. Dimensional folding was an intricate process, especially when one could not breathe. But, as always, he had done it. He had worked his way in and unwound the next level of folding, breaking the fine threads that kept space contorted into the complex fractal folds.

Mengele could imagine the two split ends fizzling away like tiny fuses. When they reached a critical tipping point, Gus would literally explode if he had not managed to unlock the third iteration. And even if he did, the process would start over again until he was totally unzipped.

No matter how unique the upstart was, leveling to 100 in such a short time frame was virtually impossible. Life was good. And it was only going to get better. He just wished he could record the expression on Gus' face when it occurred.

———

Gus settled into a chair and practiced meditating again. The others were combing through data and cheering as they found various hits. He smiled to himself and began. Green was the sphere of the day as he fell into his routine, yet like the others he could not pull any of it in.

It was progressively becoming more natural to activate the ability. He had settled into the cyclical routine when he noticed some distortion. He tried to ignore it, not wanting to fall out of concentration, but the static became more distinct, though still transparent. In like manner, the white noise around the distortion clarified before buzzing back into static. Bit by bit, the interference faded.

Gus saw the back of a man who was hunched over, surveying something that he couldn't see. The lanky man stretched to his full height, muttered something, and paced for a couple of steps before massaging his chin and turning back to whatever he was inspecting. This went on for some time. Gus noticed more about the individual as he saw him in profile. He had an aquiline nose and there were tiny pince-nez glasses perched on the bridge of his nose.

He turned about face during his pondering and was startled to see Gus staring back at him.

"Oh, this is unexpected. Our paths were not supposed to cross for…" He peeked over his shoulder. "At least another three moves. Bravo. You look quite different, I must say, since I last saw you. How are you liking superpowers? Everything you bargained for?"

He paused for the briefest of seconds, then went on distract-edly as if Gus had replied. "It never is. But that would mean…" He turned and looked at what Gus could now see was some kind of table with multiple tabletop miniatures on it, reminding him of role-playing campaigns with his friends. He slid some pieces around, looking up to the left and right, confirming something to himself before turning back to Gus.

"The probabilities were low, but they are never zero! No matter how unlikely. This is the part of the game I like best. You know, it took me quite some time to arrange all the pieces just so, and then you had to be naughty and move one when I wasn't looking. That's cheating, young man." He waggled a finger in Gus' direction. "It won't do at all. Now I have to shift some resources to finish placing the other pieces. One always thinks they have time," he rambled to himself, shaking his head.

He turned and gave Gus the same searching look he must have been giving the figurines earlier, eyes appearing large in the round glasses. Grabbing one elbow, he cupped his chin with the other hand. "Well, my boy, are you ready to play?"

"I'm done playing everyone's games." He tried to make his voice menacing, but it came out barely a squeak.

The skinny man tittered. "It's funny you should say that. I'll bet you are looking for dear old mother, are you not?" He looked up at a screen only he could see. "Everything is func-tioning as it should, so I see my colleague kept his promise and kept her alive—for a change. I keep telling him not every turn is a gambit for knowledge. But he just gets more pieces, since he sacrifices so many. So gauche. But where was I? Ah yes, the game! What you think you have recovered is merely a husk, a vessel unfilled. If you want to see your mother hale and whole again, you will have to play. There is no other way, unfor-tunately."

"What are you going on about?" Gus demanded, but like before, his voice sounded like he had sucked in a gulp of helium.

"Can I tell you a little secret? I have been waiting a long

time to see how this campaign ends up. Generations of stacking and building, and now I'm almost ready to tip that first domino and watch the whole Rube Goldberg machine take off. Can I tell you another? You *will* play, whether you want to or not. The contestants always do. Now go, and don't come back until I am ready for you!" He spun on his heels with an effete sniff, and the vision crumbled into a shower of pixels.

Gus was kicked out of his meditation just as suddenly.

Who was that guy?

EPILOGUE

"It's beautiful, isn't it?" Dennis asked, arms folded as he looked out the viewport of what was once the Von Neumann orbital space station. The liminal edge of the sun's rays could be seen crawling across the Earth's surface below as another day dawned.

Voltekka tilted his head to the side, examining the sight. After a pause that bordered on awkward, he responded simply, "Quite."

Dennis smiled at his benefactor's quirky demeanor.

"I assume you have come to discuss our progress and what needs to be done?" Dennis cringed, as his habit of trying to fill the lengthening silence kicked in, unbidden. He had become more used to Voltekka's taciturn nature, but still fought the need to fill the quiet with something. Voltekka hated blather and he awaited a rebuke as the mecha turned to look directly at him.

"No, I can easily check progress remotely. I am here because —" He paused mid-sentence and held up a single mechanical finger. Dennis' eyes focused in on the finger, seeing tiny emitters studded upon them. He had never been this close, but Voltekka's seven-foot frame put them right at eye level.

An alarm began to sound, startling him out of his thoughts. It was relatively quiet, but compared to the silence that was the norm, it was jarring.

"...of that." Voltekka finished. "Let's watch, shall we?" Displays popped to life, controlled remotely as Voltekka synced with the system. Multiple monitors came to life and Voltekka even patched into their comms, and Dennis could hear them speaking to each other.

A force of five supers was entering through a breach in the side of the station. Slipping inside, one replaced the circular metal housing and spot welded it with a glowing finger. They proceeded down a corridor to where the high-grade materials and components were kept.

"It should be just down here," the lead muttered, staring at a scanner as he motioned down the end of the hallway. Only two-hundred-fifty feet or so."

"Good, let's loot this station and get out of here. This place gives me the creeps," a female super piped in, the edge evident in her voice.

The supers made their way down the hallway, looking up occasionally at the non-descript gray walls as they neared the vault at the end. One rubbed a hand along the wall, then turned to look at his fingers as he rubbed them together.

"Something ain't right. If this stuff is as valuable as the boss says, there should be some security. This feels like a trap," a gruff voice cut in.

"Don't be so paranoid, Rowland. Always something in the shadows with you," a jocular voice teased. "My father wouldn't send us anywhere that was dangerous. This is an easy score. It's a pain in the ass to get here, so that's why no one has claimed these materials. Forty or fifty years ago, this station was abandoned with the people on board. Their shipment of oxygen was en route to the station when a big battle of supers broke out. The transport was crushed as collateral damage, and forgotten during the fight."

"Damn corporations probably didn't think it was fiscally feasible."

"Either that or there wasn't enough time. Maybe they didn't care and planned on sending up more people, but that's when the Shift occurred and everything changed."

"Oh, call it what it was, an uprising," the female spat with disgust.

"Supers taking over the governments was the best thing that has happened to the world for a long time and you know it," the gruff voice broke in. "Besides, *you're* a super; you'd think you'd be glad we never had to deal with a Keene Act or Sokovia Accord situation. Seizing control was the right choice."

"Whatever," she replied dismissively.

As they spoke, Voltekka recalled the event vividly, a small window opening in the lower left of his display as the memory played again. He saw himself, Merlin ushering his crew into the spacesuits that lined the airlock. Once they were secure, he would go and get his own. There weren't enough here to fit everyone including him. Fortunately, there was one in a special bay in his office. The suits would buy them a day at best, but it could be all they needed until help arrived. If help arrived, that was.

The video jumped as Merlin began to feel the effects of oxygen deprivation. Flashes of him getting into position and having the suit clamshell down over him. Such an odd design. He must have succumbed to asphyxiation soon thereafter, as the suit took the initiative and Merlin felt a burning like liquid lava permeate his body, joining the less severe burning in his lungs as he gasped for breath.

He woke much later and found that he had recovered, and rushed to check on his crew, finding them all dead, rictuses of pain and terror frozen on their faces. The corporation hadn't bothered to send viable oxygen tanks. He shook his head in disgust, looking at the pressure gauges. He shifted as the intruders reached a key waypoint.

The group reached the vault and a member of the group

that hadn't spoken came forward. Voltekka zoomed the view in to see what the thief was doing. The figure reached out a hand with a conical glove that suctioned onto the surface of the vault. Voltekka felt a biointerface attempt to connect with the electronic lock. He smiled internally as he sent a mental command. He synthesized the same command onto the invaders' comms.

"Voltekkers: Violate!"

Each member of the group stiffened, and slowly looked around. Panels from the empty hallway began detaching, revealing the large mecha underneath, indistinguishable from their creator.

While there was red along the enamel white of their exteriors, there was much more when their job was finished.

ABOUT CARL STUBBLEFIELD

The author began his plans for world domination by first becoming a dentist. It is a well-known fact that dentists have unearthed the ancient secrets of how to crush the hearts of men and to hear the lamentations of women and children. When this was insufficient, he created worlds where he could torment the good guys before moving to the next phase of his plans. Known for nefarious accomplishments that involve crippling dad-jokes and debilitating puns.

From his secret lair hidden in the Pacific Northwest, he lives with his wife and three children. They haven't left yet, but the mountain is covered with genetically altered wolves and other creatures. I'm sure that's just a coincidence, though.

Connect with Carl:
HenchmenUnite.com
Patreon.com/Henchmen_Unite
Twitter.com/ouroboros999
Facebook.com/groups/CarlStubblefield

ABOUT MOUNTAINDALE PRESS

Dakota and Danielle Krout, a husband and wife team, strive to create as well as publish excellent fantasy and science fiction novels. Self-publishing *The Divine Dungeon: Dungeon Born* in 2016 transformed their careers from Dakota's military and programming background and Danielle's Ph.D. in pharmacology to President and CEO, respectively, of a small press. Their goal is to share their success with other authors and provide captivating fiction to readers with the purpose of solidifying Mountaindale Press as the place 'Where Fantasy Transforms Reality.'

Connect with Mountaindale Press:
MountaindalePress.com
Facebook.com/MountaindalePress
Twitter.com/_Mountaindale
Instagram.com/MountaindalePress

Henchman by Carl Stubblefield

Artorian's Archives by Dennis Vanderkerken and Dakota Krout